Our Stories, Our Truths

Tsai Chia-Ling

ISBN-13: 9781234567890
ISBN-10: 1477123456

Cover design by: Art Painter
Library of Congress Control Number: 2018675309
Printed in the United States of America

For
Mimi Friedman
and
Michael Pryce

Acknowledgement

My sincerest thanks to Chen-Hsiang (李禎祥), Siao-shen (沈聰榮), Professor Chen Shih-Meng (陳師孟), and the first readers: American mom, Carrie, Darnell, Migdalia, Mohammed, Sue, and Ted.

Without you, I won't be able to present this story with confidence.

All Start from Here:

A Little Frog Wants to Know Nothing but the Truth

Since last week, twenty-seven-year-old Mei-Ling (美玲) has watched a lot of TV. Moreover, she has been watching only political talk shows, which is very unusual, because she dislikes those shows. In her opinion, most political commentators and politicians are dishonest people. There are only a few of them who actually can be considered respectful people, who express their opinions with the moral sense of right and wrong.

Mei-Ling is not an ill-tempered person. However, so many times when she was channel surfing and passed by a political talk show, she could feel her blood pressure rising even though she just listened to those people talking for a few minutes. Several years ago, Mei-Ling read newspapers and learned that many people, especially middle-aged people and seniors, ran to the hospital to see their doctors because they had been watching too many political talk shows during election season. They had splitting headaches, high blood pressure, low appetite, anxiety, depression, and sleeping problems. Mei-Ling couldn't believe it at the time, but slowly, she came to understand that this was no joking matter.

One must ask, then: Why does she suddenly want to watch those political talk shows?

Something is bothering her. She wants to know something. She studied history at university, but she hadn't heard of the things that those political commentators have been discussing lately. Mei-Ling can't remember when she began to think that people in Taiwan are like little frogs living in a well by the government's intention and believe the sky that they see is the whole universe. Luckily, one day she jumped out of the well.

To question the government wasn't an easy thing for Mei-Ling. Since she was little, she and her schoolmates had been told by schools how great the government was and that President Chiang Kai-shek (蔣介石, 1887–1975) and his son and successor, Chiang Ching-kuo (蔣經國, 1910–1988), were the greatest leaders ever. Little Mei-Ling had believed it because she trusted her teachers. As a result, she and many people in Taiwan respected and loved the two presidents with their whole hearts. However, if what people have believed is actually a big fat lie, it will be revealed eventually. After all, there are always some righteous people out there who would fight to show the truth to people even though it would cost their freedom or lives.

To learn the truth is always a shocking moment to Mei-Ling, no matter if it is a small truth or a big truth. Moreover, she has to deal with some uncomfortable feelings, such as anger, disappointment, or sadness. However, the positive feelings always come to Mei-Ling in the end, so she has learned that truths are so much more powerful than lies. Truths can knock on one's conscience and bring up the courage to fight with the evil government.

1

A Melanoma on a Beauty's Face:
Te-tiam-a

Mei-Ling was born and grew up in the east county of Taiwan. The county is considered the most beautiful place by most people in Taiwan. Mei-Ling can't agree more with that opinion after she traveled to many places on the island. Unfortunately, there is a spot in her town that is sinful and ugly. Mei-Ling had a great fear of it when she was young. Once, she described that spot to her younger sister: "It's like a melanoma on a beauty's face." Mei-Ling still hates that spot even though the business has been dying away over the past twenty years. Moreover, whenever she passes by the spot, she feels that the despair and tears from those young girls and women seem to be still lingering there.

You might have guessed what the spot is, and you are probably right. It is a red-light district.

According to Mei-Ling's *a-bu* (阿母, "mother," in Taiwanese), about fifty years ago, in the 1950s, the red-light district in the town wasn't just in that spot. It was about ten times bigger than the spot, which occupied almost one-third of the busiest area of the town. When Mei-Ling was about six years of age, her a-bu started telling her and her younger sister, Mei-Ai (美愛), about some terrible stories of the *te-tiam-a* (茶店仔, "brothels," in Taiwanese) in order to protect them.

Protect them?

It can't be right to tell children the stories of te-tiam-a. Moreover, protect them from what?

Everyone in the town knows the ugly fact that those

te-tiam-a belong to the local gangsters. Most young girls and women in te-tiam-a are not voluntarily working as prostitutes. Some of them are minors, kidnapped and sold to the te-tiam-a. Some of them are sold to the te-tiam-a by their parents because of poverty. Some of them are the payment for their parents' debts. It is hard to believe that many parents actually signed a ten-year contract for their daughters and renewed for another ten years when the first contract expired. The gangsters lock those girls up. Each one of them has her own small room, and that is her world.

Thirty years ago, the red-light district started to become smaller, but the most bustling area of the town was still full of energy. Sometimes, maybe the gangsters were in a good mood. They would send one guy to buy some food that the girls liked as a treat. Once in a blue moon, people would see a gangster taking a girl out to a nearby restaurant to dine or buy food. Mostly, they just bought food. Probably, they did not want to draw too much attention. Even so, it must have been a precious joy for the girl. Finally, she could breathe the air that was filled with freedom and see the world that she no longer belonged to.

Mei-Ling's parents owned a small restaurant in that bustling area. Anyone who wanted to have a good time came to this part of town. There were movie theaters, video-game stores, tailor shops, boutiques, shoe-repair shops, shaved-ice and fruit-punch stores, and all different kinds of restaurants.

Those restaurants sold rice dumplings, braised pork rice, thick pork soup, wonton soup, meatball soup, sliced noodles, stir-fried rice noodles, sugarcane juice, oyster omelets, rice tube pudding, ba-wan, mutton hot pot, stir-fried mutton, stir-fried seafood, and more.

Well, the "more" was something quite scary to Mei-Ling

and Mei-Ai. There was a snake store that sold people the whole set snake meal: snake blood alcoholic drink, snake gall alcoholic drink, and snake soup. According to diet therapy in Taiwanese society, eating the snake set meal is good for health, for the skin in particular. When Mei-Ling was in high school, she had an acne problem. Some people suggested that she should try the snake soup. They said, "It's not horrible like what you think. The snake soup is light, and snake meat tastes like chicken breast and also a bit like fish. Try it. You will like it!"

"Like it? No way!"

Mei-Ling couldn't imagine herself eating a snake. Not only was she afraid of snakes, but she also believed that people had enough food to eat. She did not understand why people wanted to eat snakes and dogs. One time, at university, Mei-Ling had a discussion on this subject with two guys, and they had different opinions from her.

They asked her, "Then why do you eat cows, pigs, chickens, lambs, and fish?"

Mei-Ling didn't know how to answer the question for a few seconds, and then she said what most people would say: "Because dogs are our loyal friends."

They giggled and said, "So we eat cows, pigs, chickens, lambs, and fish because they are our enemies?"

Mei-Ling was speechless and had a sudden headache. She really couldn't fight with their ideas. Maybe they were right. Furthermore, a thought flashed across her mind. "Does that mean I will have to be a real vegetarian, no meat, no egg, no milk, and no fish if I truly care about animals' lives?"

Mei-Ling stopped thinking deeper because she loved her pork.

Well, another scary food sold in the area was dog meat.

When the Japanese ruled Taiwan (1895–1945), in order to solve the flood problem and develop the town, they built a ditch. When the ditch was done, they built two graceful small stucco finish bridges and planted willow trees on each side of them. Mei-Ling was born in 1970. Way before she was born, the willow trees by the two sides of the ditch were replaced by stores and restaurants. The restaurant that sold dog meat dishes was on the opposite side of Mei-Ling's parents' restaurant.

When Mei-Ling and her younger sister, Mei-Ai, were little, they slept in a small room at their parents' restaurant every night. Their parents would usually wake them up to take them home around 2:00 a.m. after they finished closing the restaurant. The two little sisters were always cranky when their a-bu woke them up, except for a few days in a month. In those few days, they were woken up by dogs' howling. They would open the window and look to the direction where the dog-meat restaurant was. Usually, it was about 1:30 a.m., and the whole area finally fell asleep. Without neon light, it became dark with the dim street light. Therefore, on some beautiful nights, Mei-Ling and Mei-Ai could see clearly the moon and stars in the sky. However, they usually didn't have a mood to appreciate the beautiful sky. They searched for something, an escaping dog.

Perhaps because they didn't want people to see the slaughter, the owners of the dog-meat restaurant killed dogs while everyone was sleeping. Although the dogs' howling sounded louder and scarier in such quiet time, no one but the two little sisters would get up and show concern. It was better.

Once in a while, Mei-Ling and Mei-Ai would see a dog that the restaurant owners were going to kill had escaped. The dog would be howling and swimming in the ditch, fighting for its life. The two little sisters got so nervous—and afraid too. How they wished they could shout their support for the dog, but they could only pray for the dog quietly. Therefore, they were so thrilled when the dog got away.

Naturally, Mei-Ling and Mei-Ai both disliked the dog-meat restaurant. In addition, whenever they passed by the restaurant, they had strange feelings. Perhaps the Taiwanese folk beliefs had an influence on them. Most people believed that when lives were taken away violently, their spirits would wander in the places where they were murdered. However, Mei-Ling and Mei-Ai didn't like the dog-meat restaurant for a more crucial reason.

When Mei-Ling was seven years old, a German shepherd had bitten her right on the bottom. Since then, she had been afraid of large dogs. Moreover, she had begun to watch the stray dogs in the neighborhood so that she could prevent the horrifying tragedy from happening again. As a result, Mei-Ling could recognize those stray dogs. In fact, Mei-Ai could too. That was why the two sisters knew that the owners of the dog-meat restaurant kidnapped the stray dogs.

There were two large cages in front of the restaurant, and there were two or three dogs in each cage. When people walked by the restaurant, the dogs barked.

"Sis, they're Little White and Big Black, aren't they?" Since the dogs were in the cages, the two sisters had no fear.

"Yes, they are! Oh my God. Those *bei-bei* [伯伯, *old uncles*, in Mandarin] kidnapped them!"

The owners were two old men who had come from China after 1945. Mei-Ling and Mei-Ai didn't like the two old men. Besides their kidnapping and killing of the stray dogs, there was an essential reason that the two sisters disliked those two bei-bei.

Mei-Ling and Mei-Ai had been told since they were little to keep a distance from those Chinese bei-bei who came to Taiwan after 1945.

"Don't talk to them. Don't let them touch you. Don't take their cookies, candies, or any kind of food."

"Why?"

"They might hurt you."

The two little sisters thought someone might hurt them, which not only frightened them but also made them believe that those Chinese bei-bei were not good people. Even though their a-bu also told them that not all Chinese bei-bei were bad, it was too hard for the two little girls to distinguish who was good and who was bad. Therefore, naturally, they listened to their instincts and stayed away from all those Chinese bei-bei.

Their a-bu felt sad. She wished she didn't have to tell her daughters to be careful around those Chinese bei-bei, but she had to. Well, that was not all. There was one more thing quite dangerous around her daughters, and she also needed to warn them.

Mei-Ling and Mei-Ai's parents bought a house one block away from their restaurant when Mei-Ling was six and Mei-Ai was four. In other words, Mei-Ling and Mei-Ai's home was also near the te-tiam-a. Living in the area that was so close to te-tiam-a made a mother worry. Thus, Mei-Ling and Mei-Ai's a-bu frequently warned them not to go near te-tiam-a when they played with friends.

"A-bu, what is *te-tiam-a*?"

"A bad place."

"Bad people are living in there?"

"Something like that."

"What bad thing do they do?"

"People who own those places make young girls and women do bad things."

"That's really bad, but why don't the girls run away?"

"They can't. The owners of those places lock them up."

"How come the police don't go to rescue them?"

"The owners and the police are friends."

"How can the police be friends with bad people?"

"It happens. So, you see, you two have to stay away from te-tiam-a. In fact, you shouldn't get too close to the whole area."

"Why?"

"There was some news in the paper. Some bad people kidnapped young girls and sold them to te-tiam-a. I don't know if those owners and workers of the te-tiam-a in our area kidnap girls or not, but we just need to be careful."

"That's scary! A-bu, Mei-Ai and I won't go near that area. We promise."

2

A-hue

During the summer break, Mei-Ling and Mei-Ai usually went out and played with neighbor friends in the afternoon. It was the happiest time for all of the children but the worst time for many adults. Because of the style of living, most adults would take a nap in the afternoon so they could be more energetic to work until ten or eleven o'clock at night. In fact, some of them, like Mei-Ling and Mei-Ai's parents, even worked till midnight or after. Therefore, it is easy to understand why it was so important to those adults to have an afternoon nap, and the summer break was their nightmare.

Well, a group of happy kids playing together would very easily get excited, talking, screaming, laughing, and even fighting. As a result, Mei-Ling, Mei-Ai, and their friends got yelled at in a rage quite often. In fact, a couple of times, a woman who owned a hair salon splashed a bucket of water on them. Thank goodness they were not stupid, bad kids. They never got mad but felt embarrassed about their behaviors, so they calmed themselves down by playing something else.

It was amazing that these kids would never run out of ideas and always knew what to play. They played baseball, hide-and-seek, jump rope, hopscotch, freeze tag, Chinese chess, card games, Monopoly, and more. They usually changed their game to Chinese chess, card games, or Monopoly after they got yelled at by the angry adults. Nevertheless, they were still happy like sunflowers and wouldn't stop playing until the sun went down. The reason was simple. It was their summer and school-free time, so a few scoldings or some water wouldn't discourage them from enjoying their vacation.

Including Mei-Ling and Mei-Ai, there were usually about eight or nine kids playing together. Once in a while, a few kids from different blocks would come and want to play with them. They were friendly kids and always welcomed outsiders. There was no rejection ever.

Although Mei-Ling and Mei-Ai are grown up now, they still remember a girl who played with them several times in one summer. That summer, Mei-Ling was ten years of age, and Mei-Ai was eight. Mei-Ling, Mei-Ai, and other kids never knew that girl's full name. Somehow, they called her A-hue (阿花, in Taiwanese). *Hue* means "flowers." It was very strange that A-hue just let everyone call her A-hue as if it were her real name.

Now, Mei-Ling tries to think about why they called her A-hue. Probably, it was because A-hue behaved like *a-hue*.

What?

A-hue behaved like a-hue. What does that mean?

Was she sweet, gentle, elegant, and pretty like a flower?

Oh, well, in the culture, when a girl or a young lady does not talk with manners and behaves a bit wildly, people will describe her as a-hue.

When A-hue showed up the first time, she just stood by an electric-line pole and said nothing. However, Mei-Ling could tell that she wanted to play with them, so she invited A-hue to join in their game. There was no doubt; no one rejected her, as usual. At the moment, they were playing freeze tag. This is a simple game. Even kids who have never played it before will learn how to play in a few seconds just by watching. Therefore, they didn't need to explain how to play freeze tag to A-hue. In Taiwan, freeze tag is called "a ghost catches people," and unexpectedly, A-hue volunteered to be the ghost.

Unlike most kids, Mei-Ling found that A-hue liked to be the ghost very much, because she let herself get caught all the time. Thus, she also was the kindest ghost ever. She liked to give everyone a chance to say, "Freeze." Mei-Ling also found that A-hue loved the games that involved running, such as

17

Simon Says and Red Light, Green Light. Moreover, when she ran, her smile was bigger and prettier.

There was one thing troubling Mei-Ling, though. She was unable to understand what A-hue talked about sometimes. Not only did she speak with a lisp, but she also said somethings that Mei-Ling had a bit of difficulty comprehending. In fact, Mei-Ai felt the same way as well.

For example, A-hue would say, "Bao-Yun [寶雲] Mama this and Bao-Yun Mama that." Who would call her mother like that? Don't people just say, "*My* mom?"

Or she said, "Bao-Yun Mama said she would buy me a lot of beautiful clothes if I behaved like a lady."

Well, it was very true that A-hue was very far from a lady. Look at her: she had very short hair but still had two ponytails on each side of her head, which made her look like a clown.

Mei-Ling asked her a-bu, "But we'll all eventually become ladies when we grow up. Why does she need to become a lady right now?" At the time, Mei-Ling and Mei-Ai didn't know the brutal fact behind those words.

In the beginning, the kids didn't know where A-hue lived. They thought that she probably was from another block. Surprisingly, A-hue was their neighbor. She lived in a house that was five houses away from Mei-Ling and Mei-Ai's home. It could be because they were so into their games that no one saw her come out of the house.

About the house, A-hue's home: Me-Ling and Mei-Ai both had a fear of it! Well, it was a gangster's home. Mei-Ling and Mei-Ai eventually learned that A-hue lived there, but it wasn't because they saw A-hue coming out or going back to that house. They learned it from their a-bu. Apparently, gossiping was most adults' hobby, and they had a great ability to get news. It seemed the adults had known a great deal of A-hue, but they, the kids, did not even know A-hue's full name or where she lived.

One afternoon, Mei-Ling and Mei-Ai didn't want to play card games, so they invited A-hue to play Barbie at their home. A-hue was so happy. Her eyes lit up, and she couldn't wait to go and play.

A-hue seemed to talk faster and louder when she was excited and happy. She didn't stop talking all the way to Mei-Ling and Mei-Ai's home, which made them worry that A-hue might wake up their a-bu. Luckily, their a-bu was busy that afternoon and hadn't gone for a nap yet.

Their a-bu seemed to know A-hue and like her very much. Their a-bu was always very friendly and treated all their friends nicely, but not in the way she treated A-hue. Their a-bu patted A-hue's head when A-hue greeted her. Then, she asked A-hue if she wanted to have a bottle of Yakult to drink.

While A-hue was drinking the Yakult, she looked around the house and was curious about everything. Even though Mei-Ling and Mei-Ai's parents owned a restaurant, the business was not doing well at the time. In other words, their family was not in poverty but had some financial difficulty. Therefore, there was nothing special or fancy to see in the house, but A-hue seemed to see it as a wonderland.

After A-hue finished drinking the Yakult, Mei-Ling and Mei-Ai's a-bu gave her an apple. A-hue was extremely thrilled. She said to Mei-Ling and Mei-Ai's a-bu, "I always want to eat apples, but my a-bu said that apples were too expensive. Now, Bao-Yun Mama said if I behaved like a lady, she would buy me apples."

It is true that apples weren't cheap back then. Only occasionally could Mei-Ling and Mei-Ai have an apple to share. That was why Mei-Ling and Mei-Ai were in a huge shock when they saw their a-bu give a whole apple to A-hue. However, they were even more astonished to see their a-bu with tears in her eyes while they were listening to A-hue talking about how much she loved apples.

That afternoon, Mei-Ling, Mei-Ai, and A-hue had a wonderful time. A-hue not only liked to talk but also loved to tell stories. When Mei-Ling and Mei-Ai played Barbie, they usually just put different clothes on Barbie or sang songs and danced with Barbie. A-hue did more. She made Barbie become Cinderella and told the whole story.

A-hue was a fantastic storyteller. She made Mei-Ling and Mei-Ai laugh and feel touched. At the same time, she also scared them a little. A-hue did not only let Cinderella's stepmother talk nasty and make Cinderella work. As a matter of fact, A-hue used a pencil as a stick to hit Cinderella and raised her voice to yell.

"You are a bad girl! Deserve to be punished! Finish the work or no dinner!"

After the stepmother left, Cinderella cried. Mei-Ling didn't know whether it was Cinderella or A-hue crying. Mei-Ai looked sad and handed a tissue to A-hue. Of course, in the end, the three little girls were happy because the prince found the poor miserable Cinderella and was going to give her a great life.

In Mei-Ling's feelings, A-hue was like Cinderella. She always showed up from nowhere unexpectedly and left without a word most of the time. Strangely, Mei-Ling, Mei-Ai, and other kids never really saw her walk out the door from that gangster's house. Neither did anyone ever see her walk into the house. It was like a fairy bringing her to them and coming to take her, so she could show up just like that and disappear in a second.

That summer Mei-Ling was ten and Mei-Ai was eight, they had A-hue over twice.

The second time, they decided to play paper dolls. Again, A-hue was very excited. She said that her mom never gave her money to buy the whole set of paper dolls. She begged but had no luck. Her mother always replied to her, "We don't have money." Hence, she drew and made paper dolls herself.

Despite the financial difficulty, Mei-Ling and Mei-Ai's a-bu still gave each of them an allowance of NTD 30 (about ninety cents in US dollars) every week. Mei-Ling usually would buy two pieces of candy to enjoy herself every day, but Mei-Ai did it only every other day. There were many things that Mei-Ai wanted to have, so she learned to save money by eating fewer candies. Barbie was one of her achievements, of course, with a little help from her a-bu.

The set of paper dolls was cheap; therefore, Mei-Ling and Mei-Ai didn't need to save money to get them. They usually bought a double-A4-size set, made by paperboard, and it was only NTD 5 (about seventeen cents). After they bought one set home, they took the dolls, hair, clothes, shoes, purses, and other items down carefully and put them in a box. They took very good care of them. They put different sets in different boxes; they wouldn't mess them up.

That day, when Mei-Ling and Mei-Ai took out several boxes of paper dolls, A-hue was speechless. She was in shock but was thrilled. Well, she couldn't speak for only a few seconds, and then she started to play and tell stories like last time, very busy.

While the three girls were busy playing the paper dolls, Mei-Ling and Mei-Ai's a-bu brought three bowls of ice-cold sweet mung bean soup for them. It was interesting that A-hue did not take it immediately as she had last time when Mei-Ling and Mei-Ai's a-bu gave her the Yakult and an apple. In fact, A-hue said, "Chen mama"—*Chen* is Mei-Ling and Mei-Ai's family name—"it's dangerous to have mung bean soup here. Sorry, we can't have it right now. We have to eat it later."

Mei-Ling and Mei-Ai's a-bu smiled and said, "No problem." However, Mei-Ling and Mei-Ai looked at each other and couldn't believe what they had just heard. What a hot day! A bowl of ice-cold mung bean soup would cool them off right away. Who would turn it down? Well, A-hue had. The two sisters surely knew the reason. Thus, they felt funny and appreciated at the same time.

That summer, Mei-Ling and Mei-Ai thought that they had a new friend in A-hue. However, two weeks before the summer vacation ended, A-hue didn't show up again to play with them. Other kids probably did not have any feeling of it. Outside kids just came and went naturally. A-hue was just another one. No big deal. However, it mattered to Mei-Ling and Mei-Ai.

After inviting A-hue to their home and playing with her twice, Mei-Ling and Mei-Ai liked her very much and regarded her as a friend in their hearts. They wanted to play with A-hue again and again. A-hue told stories with great imagination and emotion. Her tone could bring them to all situations easily. She amused them and brought so much fun to them. No doubt, A-hue was the best storyteller they had ever met. Furthermore, although A-hue was a little wild and thought about things a little differently from others, Mei-Ling and Mei-Ai found that she was sweet and thoughtful in her own way. They thought that A-hue might be able to become their bosom friend. How exciting just thinking of it!

The excitement turned into a disappointment. Mei-Ling and Mei-Ai didn't understand why A-hue wouldn't come to play with them anymore.

"Did she not have a good time playing freeze tag with everybody?"

"Did she not want to play Barbie and paper dolls with us again?"

As a matter of fact, Mei-Ling and Mei-Ai had both planned to give A-hue one set of paper dolls that they had had for a long time.

"Why does she not come?" the two little sisters asked each other so many times.

"Can't she go out anymore?" Sometimes, both of them looked at the gangster's house and asked.

Couldn't they just go to knock on the door and ask for

her?

No! They couldn't do that!

That was a gangster's home!

He was the most powerful gangster in the town and owned several te-tiam-a (brothels). Although Mei-Ling and Mei-Ai didn't know all facts about that gangster at the time, they had learned how horrible those gangsters were. Furthermore, they promised their a-bu that they would never be near any te-tiam-a and the gangsters' homes. Therefore, they wouldn't go to knock on the door and ask for A-hue.

Besides the disappointment, there was one thing that bothered the two sisters very much whenever they looked at the gangster's house. Mei-Ling and Mei-Ai hadn't met A-hue's father before, but they had known how frightening those gangsters were because the two punks who came to their parents' restaurant regularly were gang members. They did not understand why a gangster's daughter could be so nice and sweet, which was completely different from her father.

3

Dog, Dragon, and Bei-bei

One punk, O-gau (黑狗, in Taiwanese), was tall and thin. He came to the restaurant more often than the other one, A-Leong (阿龍, in Taiwanese), who was shorter and fatter. Not only did they know each other, but they also worked for the same boss.

O-gau often came drunk and very hungry; in fact, he was on drugs sometimes. Generally, he would order a large bowl of soy-stew minced pork over noodles and a small bowl of wonton soup. One day, when Mei-Ling and Mei-Ai's a-ba (阿爸, "father," in Taiwanese) brought the noodle and soup to O-gau, he became mad and raised up his voice.

"Why is the wonton soup so small?"

"You always have a small bowl of wonton soup. This is small!"

"I am very, very hungry today and want to have a large bowl!" O-gau glared at Mei-Ling and Mei-Ai's a-ba and yelled.

"But you didn't say you wanted to have a large bowl before. In fact, you said, 'As usual.'" Mei-Ling and Mei-Ai's a-ba felt mad too.

"I say *large* now. Now!" O-gau stood up, and his right fist was in the air already.

Anyone knows how easy this thing is, including children. Just cook a few more wontons, and then a small bowl of wonton soup would become a large one. It is very simple. That was why Mei-Ling and Mei-Ai did not understand why O-gau got so angry.

Another time, he complained that the noodles were too

much. "Why do I get a large bowl of noodles?" he furiously questioned Mei-Ling and Mei-Ai's a-bu, who had brought the noodles to him.

Mei-Ling and Mei-Ai's a-bu smiled and said, "Not so hungry today?" Then she went to get a bowl and tried to get some noodles out.

O-gau turned to criticize Mei-Ling and Mei-Ai's a-bu. "So fucking cheap. Even taking away that little amount of noodles. Are you going to sell those noodles to another customer?"

It seemed no matter what Mei-Ling and Mei-Ai's parents did, they were always wrong and had to take the blame. The customers in the restaurant all thought that O-gau was a lunatic, but no one stood up and said anything. Nobody wanted trouble; they just came to enjoy a meal, after all. They did say something to support Mei-Ling and Mei-Ai's parents eventually, but only after O-gau left.

"No wonder his nickname is O-gau; a mad dog likes to bark at people."

In the Taiwanese language, o means "black," and gau means "dog."

Mei-Ling agreed with that comment completely. To her, in fact, crazy dogs wouldn't just bark. They would bite people right on the bottom—very, very dangerous.

How about A-Leong? Was he the same?

A-Leong was a quiet guy. If he did not talk, he looked like a fine young man. Because his name, Leong, means "dragon," he got a dragon tattoo on his left arm.

The first time Mei-Ai saw the tattoo, she got scared and went out of the restaurant to find Mei-Ling at once. She described it to Mei-Ling with her arms and hands as if she saw a real snake on A-Leong's arm.

Like most societies in the world, snakes are not liked or welcomed by most people in Taiwan. Snakes are related to the idea of evil. However, you might find that it is interesting how people's minds work to make bad become good.

Dragons are seen as symbols of good fortune, nobility, power, and success; therefore, no doubt, most people in Taiwan love dragons. Since the appearance and movement of snakes are similar to dragons, why not see them as little dragons? As a matter of fact, calling snakes "little dragons" will decrease the fear that people have for snakes. Besides, when people call snakes "little dragons," they will grow big and become real fortune dragons. It is like a self-fulfilling prophecy. So, you see, if you are positive and give chances, an evil snake can become a fortunate dragon.

Then why was Mei-Ai frightened of a dragon tattoo?

Back then, most people who had tattoos were gangsters, and the gangsters usually had dragon tattoos. As a result, the dragons that were tattooed on the gangsters' bodies had changed into evil snakes in people's subconscious. Mei-Ai got scared because she realized that A-Leong was a gangster after she saw the dragon tattoo on his arm. Moreover, it was her first time seeing a gangster's tattoo this close. It was like seeing a crime happening right in front of her face; it was very frightening. At the same time, Mei-Ai was extremely surprised that a gangster looked so handsome and normal.

Well, maybe A-Leong was handsome, but he definitely wasn't normal. If anyone got a chance to see A-Leong fight, oh boy, they would be terrified. Mei-Ling and Mei-Ai's parents saw him fighting one time, right outside of the restaurant. It wasn't easy to forget his brutality. They wished their daughters would never see him fight.

Maybe A-Leong was a violent gangster, but at least, thank goodness, A-Leong didn't act like O-gau in the restaurant. Never once did he come drunk or on drugs. Usually, after he ordered the food, he would go to the back of the restaurant and sit in the corner quietly. Since Mei-Ling and Mei-Ai's parents couldn't refuse to serve any gangsters, they wished they could all behave like A-Leong, because some customers wouldn't walk into the restaurant if they saw O-gau was there.

It would be even better if the gangsters didn't show their tattoos.

However, if speaking as a mother, Mei-Ling and Mei-Ai's a-bu preferred those gangsters to show their tattoos all the time so her daughters could easily recognize them and keep themselves away from the danger. Thank heavens, another group of people, Chinese bei-bei, whom she also deemed as threats to Mei-Ling and Mei-Ai, were not too hard to recognize.

Ordinarily, people who live outside of Asia can't see much difference in appearance between people from each country in Asia. It is like many Asians often can't tell apart the people from European countries. Only when people live closely and interact frequently will they learn the uniqueness of each group of people. Hence, since Mei-Ling and Mei-Ai were very little, about five or six years old, they had already been able to recognize those Chinese bei-bei by their accents.

In 1913, Mandarin became the official language in China. However, each province, even cities or villages, in China has its own local dialects; as a result, people have their own accents when they speak Mandarin. In 1949, when the Chinese Nationalist Party fled to Taiwan and settled their sovereignty, the Republic of China, in Taiwan, they made Mandarin the official language too. The Taiwanese people also have their own languages: Taiwanese (Hokkien), Hakka, and aboriginal languages. Thus, at the time, many Taiwanese people had strong accents when they spoke Mandarin. But as time goes by, fewer and fewer Taiwanese people speak Mandarin with accents.

Mei-Ling and Mei-Ai spoke very little Mandarin but mainly Taiwanese before they went to elementary school. However, very soon after they began elementary school, they couldn't speak Taiwanese well anymore. Perhaps the two sisters have ears for language. Thus, they picked up Mandarin fast and well. More importantly, they needed to be competitive with their peers and didn't want to be punished for speaking Taiwanese. It turned out both Mei-Ling and Mei-Ai could speak Mandarin perfectly in the first semester of first grade. Moreover, from third grade, Mei-Ling were picked to represent her class for the speech contests and won the trophy every single time.

Wait a minute!

A student would get punished if they spoke their primary language?

Wasn't it too harsh?

Wasn't it ridiculous?

What kind of punishment?

Basically, there were three kinds of popular punishment: fine, corporal punishment, and wearing a Speak Mandarin sign around the neck. The person who wore a Speak Mandarin sign around his or her neck would have to find someone who spoke the other dialect, Taiwanese (Hokkien), Hakka, or aboriginal languages, and then give the sign to the person to wear. There was not a doubt that it successfully promoted the use of Mandarin in school. However, it gradually made many Taiwanese students feel ashamed to speak their parents' tongues. In fact, the schools and the government made the people on the island feel that the people who spoke Mandarin were superior and the people who spoke other dialects were vulgar. That linguicism affected Taiwan society profoundly. It made most Taiwanese people have low self-esteem in every aspect of their lives, such as customs, music, cuisine, and so forth—and made them believe that Chinese culture was better than Taiwanese culture. Well, it is so hard to detox and remove the poisonous idea, even though the Ministry of Education finally started having all the dialects taught at the schools in 2001. Moreover, despite the new government's effort, a lot of the younger generation now still can't speak their parents' tongues, and those languages are in danger of extinction. Alas and alack. Is there a remedy for this bitterness and sorrow that was caused by the Chinese Nationalist government's stupidity and brutality?

In 1913, Mandarin became the official language in China. The Chinese Nationalist government did not have a chance to push the Chinese people to speak Mandarin the way they did in Taiwan, due to the chaotic political situations and, later, a war with Japan. That explained why those Chinese bei-bei, who came to Taiwan after 1945, had various heavy accents. They did not have a fear of being punished at schools as Mei-Ling, Mei-Ai, and many other Taiwanese people did. As a result, they might learn some Mandarin but probably spoke their parents' tongues most of the time when they were young. Therefore, Mei-Ling, Mei-Ai, and many people in Taiwan had a hard time understanding them, but it didn't matter to Mei-Ling and Mei-Ai at all.

Oh, why?

Besides the gangsters, those Chinese bei-bei were another group of people whom Mei-Ling and Mei-Ai's a-bu considered dangers to her daughters. She wanted them to have as little interaction with those Chinese bei-bei as possible, and Mei-Ling and Mei-Ai were obedient completely. Hence, it really didn't matter to the two little girls if they could understand those Chinese bei-bei or not. Ironically, those Chinese bei-bei's strong accents also became the best way for the two sisters to recognize them.

Honestly, a lot of those Chinese bei-bei were very friendly, though. Some of them were very gentle and generous to the young kids. There were two Chinese bei-bei, for example, who came to Mei-Ling and Mei-Ai's neighborhood quite often. Those two Chinese bei-bei not only liked to see them play but also brought cookies and candies for them. Most kids accepted the sweets from them, including A-hue.

That summer, the time that Mei-Ling and Mei-Ai had a

lot of fun playing with A-hue, one day, when Mei-Ling saw A-hue taking candies and cookies from the old man, she was very anxious and wanted to tell her not to take them, but it was too late. A-hue was happily eating her cookies already. As a matter of fact, Mei-Ling burst out laughing when she saw A-hue using her new front teeth to bite cookies like a little rabbit. As a result, she forgot her worry totally. It was lots of fun to see A-hue eating cookies and sucking on candies. Because of the dental transitional period, Mei-Ling could see a candy rolling around in A-hue's mouth when she opened her mouth to talk. Several times, A-hue almost spat the candy out, so she used her hand to cover her mouth.

Of course, it would have been more fun to have cookies and candies than to see others have them, but Mei-Ling and Mei-Ai just wouldn't take anything from strangers. Since they were little, their a-bu had told them not to take and eat any food, cookies, or candies from strangers. Moreover, she had particularly pointed out those Chinese bei-bei.

"Yes, A-bu."

No matter how many times she had reminded Mei-Ling and Mei-Ai, they always replied to her like the first time she warned them. Mei-Ling and Mei-Ai's a-bu was glad to see that her two beautiful little girls seemed to understand her warning. Living in the area that was right next to the red-light district made her worry so much all the time. How she wished they were boys so that she wouldn't have to worry this much. Her husband wished they were boys, too, for a different reason, and she hated the reason badly.

4

Shim-bu-a:
Ciou-Lian and Ciou-Jyu

Having a son in a family was extremely important in Taiwanese society back then, and it is now still essential to many families. Moreover, it is better to have more than one son so that the family won't worry that no one can carry the family name if something happens to the only boy. It is not only a sin if the bloodline ends, but it is also an enormous crime to a family. The family members would feel guilty and anxious because they wouldn't be able to face their ancestors after they die.

In the past, when a couple couldn't give birth to a boy and the husband was the only son in the family, often, the husband and his family would consider that it was the wife's problem. It was she who couldn't give a son to the family. In general, some husbands would think of getting a mistress so they would have an opportunity to get a son. Usually, most husbands' families would silently accept their doing so. However, in many cases, the husband didn't want to get a mistress, but his parents actually pushed him to do it. Imagine how much sorrow, anger, and tears those wives would need to swallow down to their hearts. Were their hearts strong enough to hold the feelings for a lifetime?

Why couldn't a daughter carry the family name and be an heiress?

Well, a daughter would eventually get married and wouldn't be a family member anymore, so she wouldn't be able to carry the family name. Furthermore, according to the culture, her husband owned her after she married him. Therefore, if she could inherit her father's money and property, the inheritance would all go to her husband. Well, which family would like this idea?

In the Japanese colonial period (1895–1945), the law allowed daughters to have a right to inherit under the condition that there were no male heirs, brothers. Even though daughters still didn't have equal right on inheritance, it was a giant step, no doubt. Later, the Civil Code of the Republic of China was practiced in Taiwan after the Chiang Kai-shek regime fled to Taiwan in exile. Finally, all daughters have the same legal right on inheritance as sons. However, the old custom dies hard. Before the recent two decades, most daughters inherited almost nothing after their parents died. Even now, some parents still would ask their daughters, married or not, to sign a paper to give up their right to the inheritance. Apparently, an idea can be as stubborn as a rock. In this issue, the idea, which is sexism, grew into an unbeatable social culture. Even the law can't beat it. Fortunately, the new generations who were born after the 1970s are more and more liberal, and some older people are changing their minds. Thus, the idea that sons are more valuable and superior to daughters has been challenged. Furthermore, most daughters now can inherit money and property even though, in many cases, they don't get the same amount of inheritance as their brothers.

She, Mei-Ling and Mei-Ai's a-bu, was born in 1949, the year that the Chinese Nationalist Party was defeated by the Chinese Communist Party and exiled to Taiwan. Her name is Lin Ciou-Tao (林秀桃), but she was Wang Ciou-Tao (王秀桃) before. The change of her family name was due to an adoption. That year, she was seven years of age.

Under the social influence of gender bias, Ciou-Tao's parents tried very hard to have more sons, but they didn't get their wish to come true. They had only one son. Eventually, Ciou-Tao's parents stopped trying to have more babies. After all, they were too impoverished to have more. In fact, they had to give three daughters away. Ciou-Tao was the seventh and also the last child in the family, and she was one of the three daughters whom the parents gave away. In a way, Ciou-Tao was luckier because she was adopted to be a daughter. Her two elder sisters were adopted to be *shim-bu-a* (媳婦仔, in Taiwanese).

There was a famous old saying, "Raising a daughter is a losing-money business," which was related to the idea that a daughter would eventually get married and wouldn't be a family member anymore. Therefore, why not just give her away when she was little? Let her future parents-in-law raise her so the parents didn't need to spend money to nurture her and prepare a dowry for her wedding. Those future daughters-in-law were called shim-bu-a. Shim-bu-a is Taiwanese, and the term in Mandarin is *ton-gyan-gxi* (童養媳).

In the position of adoptive families, there were some good reasons for taking a shim-bu-a.

Some families felt that raising their future daughter-in-law themselves from the time she was little would make her more obedient when she grew up.

Some families deemed that taking a shim-bu-a could result in less expense for the future wedding. Moreover, the shim-bu-a could become a helper with housework. Therefore, in many cases, it was more like selling daughters and getting servants. The adoptive family would pay a sum of money to the girl's parents for the adoption.

To some families that hadn't had any sons yet, taking a shim-bu-a was a symbol of bringing a son to the family. This logic was way beyond imagination and showed how far many people would go to get a son in the old time.

The fates of shim-bu-a were various. Some adoptive

families were very kind to shim-bu-a, cherishing them as their own daughters and even sending them to school. On the contrary, some adoptive families were mean and ruthless. They treated their shim-bu-a as servants or laborers, and the act of physical abuse was practiced quite often. Furthermore, they let their shim-bu-a eat poorly—but not because the families were poor. Some were, but often it was solely an abuse.

There was a famous Taiwanese expression: "Women are like rapeseed and linseed; they grow on wherever they fall." It perfectly described shim-bu-a's lives—they had no right to make decisions about their own lives. However, they were also human, weren't they? They also had feelings. Surely, they might be eager for love when they got to their late teens, and what if a shim-bu-a did not have feelings for her arranged husband?

Oh, romance.

It is the true passion from one's heart; it can't be pretended.

It is an honestly exciting and mysterious feeling.

No one can resist the charm of romance. They pursue and adore it.

Oh, romance.

It illuminates one's life; it makes one see direction.

It brings one to places one hasn't been.

Oh, romance.

Assuredly, both the shim-bu-a and her arranged husband would desire romance and would want to marry for love, as others did. Could they?

Sigh for the tragedy.

A shim-bu-a and her arranged husband were like brother and sister growing up together. Thus, many of them did not have romance in their hearts. Moreover, many shim-bu-a were a lot older, maybe ten years older, than their arranged husbands. She wasn't just like his big sister. Since he was little, she might have been taking care of him, so she was also like a mother to him. Thus, he might like her dearly but have no romantic love for her.

Often, they married when the boy entered into puberty. In many cases, no matter whether the shim-bu-a gave a son to the family or not, her arranged husband still might get another wife after he grew up, marrying for love if he wanted to. Some of those husbands might stay in that marriage and have concubines, but some would divorce their wife, the shim-bu-a, regardless of their family's objection.

Undoubtedly, some of shim-bu-a's arranged husbands would refuse to marry them. Some parents were fine with it, but some weren't. The parents felt that it wasn't right and fair to the shim-bu-a. However, their sons thought that it wasn't right and fair to either the shim-bu-a or him to have no right to marry for love. Hence, some parents let the shim-bu-a go back to her original family (which was rare), or arranged for her to marry another man, or officially adopted her to be their daughter.

Ciou-Tao's father, Fu-Sheng (福生), was a farmer who owned a small piece of land that he inherited after his father passed away. The oldest brother had a duty to carry the family name and privilege to inherit the house, but the land was shared by all brothers. Because there were four brothers to share the land, each of them had only an acre of land. Moreover, Fu-Sheng was the youngest one, so he got the worst piece of land.

Having an acre of barren land, how could Fu-Sheng support his family? Not to mention that he had a big family. Fu-Sheng and his wife, Li-Jhu (麗珠), were mighty happy when they had their firstborn. It was a baby boy. They thought that it was a good sign and they were going to have more sons, but it didn't happen. One girl after another, they had six girls. Although Fu-Sheng felt disappointed, he loved his girls. They were beautiful and adorable. However, they were born into this poor family. Where were their futures? He felt awful that he couldn't be a better father to give them a good life, so he at least gave them a good name.

In the old time, when a family wanted to get a son but continuously got daughters, they would give their daughters names such as Jhao-Di (招弟), Wang-Shih (罔市), or Wang-Yao (罔腰). Jhao-Di means that a sister waves her hands to get her younger brother to come. Wang-Shih and Wang-Yao both have the same meaning: "Oh well, unfortunately, it's a girl. We bear the great disappointment to nurture her." Once a girl learned the meaning of her name, she would get greatly upset and feel embarrassed without a doubt. As a matter of fact, most girls carried shame throughout their entire lives. They felt that they were not wanted and were angry. Their names were invisible tattoos. However, each time people called their names, at once, the invisible tattoos became identifying marks—embarrassing them and shaming them publicly. Some eventually changed their names, but many of them did not.

Fu-Sheng saw his daughters as lovely flowers, so he and his wife, Li-Jhu, gave them names that were related to flowers. The eldest daughter's name was Ciou-Ying (秀櫻). *Ciou* means "beautiful," "elegant," and "handsome." *Ying* means "cherry blossom."

The second daughter's name was Ciou-Guei (秀桂). *Guei* means "Osmanthus."

The third daughter's name was Ciou-Mei (秀梅). *Mei* means "plum blossom."

The fourth daughter's name was Ciou-Jyu (秀菊). *Jyu* is a chrysanthemum.

The fifth daughter's name was Ciou-Lian (秀蓮). *Lian* is a lotus.

The youngest daughter name was Ciou-Tao (秀桃). *Tao* means "peach blossom."

A poor farmer who had a wife and seven children eventually had to give in. It was a certainty that there was no hope for their daughters to stay with them. Fu-Sheng and Li-Jhu thought that their daughters might have a great chance to have a better life with new families. It was painful to give away their daughters, but they believed that it was the best for their daughters. As a result, besides Ciou-Tao, Ciou-Jyu and Ciou-Lian were another two daughters who were given away.

It was 1956. Ciou-Jyu was ten years old, and Ciou-Lian was eight. They both were taken to be shim-bu-a. Their parents did not want to take money from the adoptive families. Since the two adoptive families were wealthy, Fu-Sen and Li-Jhu wished they could let their daughters go to junior high school and senior high school after the six-year compulsory education. That was all they wanted. However, the two adoptive families both insisted that Fu-Sheng should take the money. Fu-Sheng finally took the money and thought that Ciou-Jyu and Ciou-Lian were going to be treated well.

Ciou-Lian's adoptive family did let her go to junior high school and have a higher education. As a matter of fact, they saw Ciou-Lian as their own daughter. The fact that they did not have any daughters of their own might be the reason that they loved her very much, but the truth was that they were decent people who had a good reputation in the town.

Sadly, Ciou-Jyu suffered.

A servant, a friend of Fu-Sheng and Li-Jhu who worked for Ciou-Jyu's adoptive family, told them that Ciou-Jyu had a lot of work to do every day both before and after school. She needed to help in the kitchen and feed pigs, chickens, and ducks. Fu-Sheng and Li-Jhu felt upset and worried, but they tried to think positively. "At least Ciou-Jyu can have a bowl of rice to eat and a piece of meat sometimes."

In spite of the fact that Fu-Sheng was a farmer, his family did not have a bowl of rice to eat. At the time, the families that were in poverty could only have sweet potatoes at every meal. Some families that were in better shape could have sweet potatoes and rice congee—of course, a lot of sweet potatoes and little rice. Those families that were a lot better off ate solid rice but still mixed with sweet potatoes. If people could have a bowl of rice, just rice only, it meant they were very wealthy.

Ciou-Jyu's adoptive family was wealthy and ate rice, but only family members could. Furthermore, servants and workers ate differently. Workers worked very hard in the field, so they could have a bowl of solid rice mixed with sweet potato. Servants only deserved to have sweet potatoes and rice congee, and Ciou-Jyu ate with them. Of course, Fu-Sheng and Li-Jhu learned this fact eventually, but they comforted themselves by thinking this way: "At least she is not just eating sweet potatoes like us."

Ciou-Jyu was a gentle girl with great fortitude. The kitchen work and livestock feeding made her very busy— exhausted sometimes—but it wasn't a problem for her. The problem, perhaps, was that the three brothers in the adoptive family all loved her. The two elder brothers were older than Ciou-Jyu, and the youngest one was the same age as her. This family did not have any daughters either; therefore, the three brothers adored her a great deal. Maybe their mother got a little jealous and saw a potential problem, so she did not like Ciou-Jyu completely. Then, you might think that Ciou-Jyu couldn't continue going to school after she finished elementary school because the adoptive mother did not like her. Well, not exactly.

In the old days, most people believed that there was no need for women to get an education. At the time, what society expected was obedient women, so they didn't like a woman who was educated. Education, we all know, would open one's mind to think. Moreover, it would enhance one's courage to challenge unfairness, which meant a woman wouldn't be obedient anymore. Therefore, all a woman needed was to learn how to manage a household and be a quiet and respectful lady who could give birth to a son. Since the adoptive mother believed those ideas about women, after the six-year compulsory education, Ciou-Jyu stayed at home and did more work every day, naturally.

At the time, any kid who wanted to go to junior high school needed to take an entrance examination. The test wasn't easy; only the smart kids could get into junior high school. However, being intelligent wasn't good enough. Their families had to be able to afford the tuition; otherwise, it was in vain. Well, Ciou-Jyu was one of the three top students in her class, and her teacher was confident that she could pass the entrance examination easily and get into junior high school. However, her adoptive mother believed that she did not need more education, so Ciou-Jyu didn't even take the test. It was very vexing. In 1968, the six-year compulsory education was extended to nine years, but Ciou-Jyu graduated from elementary school in 1958. If she were born ten years later, she would have happily enjoyed her right to education.

The three brothers—Wen-De (文德), Wen-Zhi (文智), and Wen-Hua (文華)—did not agree with their mother's viewpoints about women. Perhaps because of age and life experience, Wen-De was much more strongly against those ideas than his two younger brothers. He helped Ciou-Jyu do homework sometimes. He knew how smart she was. She learned fast and loved to ask questions. He believed that Ciou-Jyu should continue going to school like Wen-Hua, who was the same age as Ciou-Jyu. He talked to his mother, but it didn't change anything. He was quite angry. Several times, he looked at Ciou-Jyu and wondered if she had ever asked herself why she wasn't born as a boy in a wealthy family. She would've had everything in life and would be outstanding and successful for sure.

The same year Ciou-Jyu graduated from elementary school, Wen-De attended university in autumn. Before Wen-

De went to university, he studied at a boys' high school for six years, so he didn't have much opportunity to interact with girls. The first year at university, he met some girls and got to know them. He found that they were charming and brilliant. "Why do men want them to stay at home and breed only?" Wen-De hated that people treated women unjustly. That gender bias destroyed women's lives and wasted their intelligence.

"Since you can't go to school, let the knowledge come to you." Wen-De believed that a person could be educated and knowledgeable by self-learning. Hence, Wen-De bought books for Ciou-Jyu and asked Wen-Hua to help her.

Why Wen-Hua?

Wen-Zhi was in the last year of junior high school. Thus, he was very busy with preparing for the senior high school entrance examination. Besides, Wen-Hua and Ciou-Jyu were the same age. He would be a better learning companion for her.

Oh, he was so attentive.
He must love her.
As a brother,
perhaps?

Wen-Hua loved to help Ciou-Jyu. Although Wen-De bought Ciou-Jyu books, he still shared his school textbooks with her. He found that Ciou-Jyu, indeed, was smarter than him. "If we both went to junior high school, she would be the one to help me with my homework."

Wen-Hua did not understand why Ciou-Jyu was not allowed to go to school. Practically, she was their sister, since his parents had taken her in and told them that Ciou-Jyu was their sister. She should have lived the same way as he and his elder brothers.

Well, Mother said, "Can't."

She said, "Ciou-Jyu is a shim-bu-a; she is not the same as a daughter. Besides, she is a girl; she doesn't need an education.

40

That is men's privilege."

"Men's privilege?" Wen-Hua got extremely mad when he heard what Mother said. He almost spat out, "Bullshit." Instead, he said, "Nonsense." After all, he was a well-educated young man.

"What does that mean, 'She is not a daughter'? Ciou-Jyu is Wen-Zhi's future wife, which means she is the daughter-in-law. Therefore, she is a *daughter*!" Wen-Hua wished he had guts to challenge Mother.

He, too, hated the idea of shim-bu-a.

"A girl doesn't even know the boy and is arranged to marry him. Not to mention that they are just little children who know nothing about marriage." The first time he heard Mother say, "Ciou-Jyu is Wen-Zhi's wife," he was shocked and confused. He knew the meaning of the word "wife," but Wen-Zhi was twelve and Ciou-Jyu was only ten.

"Are they going to get married this year? But they are so little!" At the time, Wen-Hua hadn't heard of the term *shim-bu-a* before. After all, he was ten years old like Ciou-Jyu.

"Of course not. They will get married later, when they grow up."

"Then why doesn't she come after she grows up?"

"Well, that's just the way it is. My silly son, stop asking questions. Don't you like to have a sister? She is pretty, isn't she?"

"But why does she need to work in the kitchen and feed the pigs, chickens, and ducks?"

"No more questions. Silly goose! Go to play with your brothers!"

Yes, he liked to have a sister like Ciou-Jyu. She was so pretty and sweet. She was like a princess to Wen-Hua. She reminded him of the German fairy tale "Rapunzel" because Ciou-Jyu had long beautiful hair and liked to tie it into two braids. However, gradually, he found that Ciou-Jyu was more like Cinderella. Seemingly, Mother didn't like Ciou-Jyu. Otherwise, she wouldn't have so much work to do.

Wen-Hua liked to help Ciou-Jyu with her work, but it had to be secretly. If Mother saw it, she would be displeased and say, "That's servants' work. You are a master." Thus, he asked all the servants not to tell Mother.

Wen-Hua found that feeding livestock was quite interesting. Especially, it was fun to see Ciou-Jyu talking to those animals and telling them not to fight for food. "There's plenty." She always said that.

There was not plenty of food on the table in Ciou-Jyu's family. Ciou-Jyu told him some stories about her family. Wen-Hua felt so sad to know that her family lived in poverty and ate sweet potatoes every day. He had sweet potatoes once in a while. They were not bad, but he wouldn't like to have them in each meal every day. Hence, Wen-Hua liked to share cookies and candies with Ciou-Jyu. He knew that Ciou-Jyu certainly had not had them before, and he had plenty to give. Later, he started bringing chicken legs or hard-boiled eggs for her after he found out that Ciou-Jyu didn't eat like them. Wen-Hua was extremely angry and went to tell Wen-De and Wen-Zhi.

Wen-De said, "I know, so we have to take good care of her."

Wen-Hua nodded his head.

Wen-Zhi said, "I know. I have brought her chicken legs and hard-boiled eggs sometimes."

"I have too." Wen-Hua laughed and said, "We've got to take turns, or Ciou-Jyu will be too full."

Wen-Zhi smiled but felt bitter. Wen-Zhi loved Ciou-Jyu, his future wife. It pained him to know that Mother did not treat her properly.

Wen-Zhi went to query Mother. "Ciou-Jyu is my future wife, not a servant. Why does she work with them and eat meals with them?"

"It's a process of learning," Mother calmly said.

"Learning for what? Being a maid? She is going to be a mistress of the family. She doesn't need to learn how to do servants' work!"

42

"It's the way it is." Mother looked serious.

Wen-Zhi knew that Mother was not pleased to be asked those questions, so he stopped and left Mother's room. He also knew that it was useless to say more. It was not going to change anything but would provoke Mother.

Wen-Zhi couldn't wait to grow up so he could marry Ciou-Jyu and give her a good life. He was fourteen years old. In four more years, he would be able to let Ciou-Jyu have a better life.

Besides bringing her chicken legs and hard-boiled eggs, Wen-Zhi took Ciou-Jyu to the seacoast by bicycle to see the sunset sometimes. Ciou-Jyu loved the sunset. She said to him, "The colors of the sky and the shapes of clouds construct unrepeated dreamy pictures every day. It is full of imagination and beauty. It's like people's lives. Each person's fate is different."

Wen-Zhi once heard people saying that young people shouldn't love the sunset. "The sunset, it's peaceful and graceful, but it's the end of the day. It's full of pity and sorrow. Young people should appreciate the sunrise. It's better for them to be stimulated by hope and energy. They need ambition, not peace and contentment."

"How is it possible for Ciou-Jyu to love the sunrise? She left home to be a shim-bu-a. She can't continue her education even though she is intelligent. She loves Wen-De, not me, but she will have to marry me. Where is her hope of a sunrise?"

Both Wen-Zhi and Wen-De loved Ciou-Jyu as more than just a sister. Well, who wouldn't be attracted to an extraordinary young girl who was handsome, charming, and sweet? Wen-Zhi felt lucky that he was the one to be engaged to Ciou-Jyu, but unfortunately, Ciou-Jyu's heart was engaged to Wen-De. He felt sad, but he also knew that it wasn't right to make one marry someone whom he or she did not love.

Wen-Zhi learned that Wen-De and Ciou-Jyu had feelings for each other when he was fifteen, Ciou-Jyu was thirteen, and Wen-De was nineteen. That year, Wen-De left home and went to Taipei to study at university. Both Wen-De and Ciou-Jyu were sad. At the time (1959), even with the express train from the town to Taipei, it was a four-hour train ride at least. Therefore, besides the intensity of university courses, Wen-De wouldn't be able to come home every week, not even every month. Coming home twice in one semester would be the most, which meant Ciou-Jyu and Wen-De would be apart from each other for a long time.

That summer, Ciou-Jyu was extremely sad about the coming separation. Before Wen-De went to university, several times, Wen-Zhi saw that Wen-De was talking to Ciou-Jyu, and she was weeping. Wen-De used a handkerchief gently to wipe her tears away and kissed her on her lips. Wen-De surely gave Ciou-Jyu a great sense of security. He was older, mature, and reliable. In fact, Wen-De was not only like a brother but also a father to her in a way. Who, in this world, could be more alone than Ciou-Jyu? She needed a person whom she trusted and loved, who could give her a free world. Wen-De was the one.

However, it was too hard for Wen-Zhi; it took him three years to make up his mind. Wen-Zhi told Wen-De his thinking when Wen-De came back from Taipei during the winter break.

Wen-De was very surprised. He had never expected that Wen-Zhi would want to break off the engagement with Ciou-Jyu. He knew how much Wen-Zhi loved Ciou-Jyu.

"But you love Ciou-Jyu very much."

"That's why I have to break off the engagement."

Wen-De was touched. He didn't know if he could be so unselfish like Wen-Zhi. He also felt guilty. He was the selfish one who had taken away his younger brother's beloved.

"Don't be. About love, we have to be honest."

Wen-De was so grateful, and he knew that Ciou-Jyu would be too. He felt that his life was like a summer rose garden, warm and sweet. Wen-De, the happy man, determined to give Ciou-Jyu a great life. However, he forgot that it was winter. It was too cold for roses to bloom.

Of course, before going to Mother, Wen-Zhi had to tell Ciou-Jyu first. He wanted to take Ciou-Jyu to the seacoast for the talk, but this time, he wanted to go in the early morning.

"Ciou-Jyu, would you go to see the sunrise with me one time?"

Ciou-Jyu laughed and said, "Of course I would love to. People say that it is almighty beautiful when the sun rises from the ocean, but I have never had an opportunity to see it. Can we go on Sunday? It will be easier for me. I usually have less work to do in the kitchen on Sunday."

"My goodness! How stupid I am! It's plainly not because she loves the sunset very much. It's because she has to work from four thirty in the morning every day. In the late afternoon, she finishes most of her work, so she can have a little break to enjoy the sunset." Wen-Zhi felt awful about his careless mind.

That Sunday morning, Ciou-Jyu walked out of the house with a straw hat that Wen-De bought for her. Wen-Zhi honestly thought that Wen-De was the best person for her. He always could see Ciou-Jyu's needs—for instance, that straw hat. Ciou-Jyu had lots of outdoor work to do. A straw hat could protect her face from the sun. Moreover, there was a fake chrysanthemum on the hat. *Jyu* is "chrysanthemum," after all.

While riding a bicycle, Wen-Zhi started singing an English song, "Young Love." The song was first released in 1956, the same year that Ciou-Jyu came to Wen-Zhi's family. It was very popular in the United States and became Wen-Zhi's favorite song a year later.

They say for every boy and girl
There's just one love in this whole world

And I know I've found mine
The heavenly touch of your embrace
Tells me no one could take your place
Ever in my heart
Young love (young love), first love (first love)
Filled with true devotion
Young love (young love), our love (our love)
We share with deep emotion
Just one kiss from your sweet lips
Will tell me that your love is real
And I can feel that it's true
We will vow to one another
There will never be another
Love for you or for me
Young love (young love), first love (first love)
Filled with true devotion
Young love (young love), our love (first love)
We share with deep emotion

The first time Wen-Zhi sang this song was also on the bike with Ciou-Jyu. Intentionally, he confessed his love to her through the song. However, Ciou-Jyu didn't understand. After all, she was a girl from an impoverished family and wasn't allowed to go to junior high school. How could she know any foreign language? After Wen-Zhi finished singing the song, he translated the lyrics into Mandarin for her. Ciou-Jyu smiled and blushed. She looked like a delicious peach. How Wen-Zhi wanted to kiss Ciou-Jyu on her cheek, but he just couldn't. He had to be a gentleman and respect her.

Wen-Zhi stopped singing "Young Love" when he took Ciou-Jyu to the seacoast on the bicycle after he learned of the love between Ciou-Jyu and Wen-De. He didn't want to make Ciou-Jyu feel uncomfortable and guilty. Then, Ciou-Jyu started singing a beautiful Taiwanese song, "If I Open the Door and Window of My Heart" (阮若打開心內的門窗). The song was first performed in 1957 by a male choir in Taipei, and it became popular in Taiwanese society after that. The composer was Lu Chuan-Sheng (呂泉生, 1916–2008), a famous musician in Taiwan. The author who wrote the lyrics was a talented dentist and writer, Wang Chang-Syong (王昶雄, 1915–2000). Up to the present, the song is still popular; many people love it exceedingly.

Ciou-Jyu sang the song well and with the feelings from deep inside of her heart, which moved Wen-Zhi. Perhaps it was her song.

If I open the door of my heart, I can see the colorful spring light.
Therefore, even though spring won't last forever, my bitterness still can be eased right this moment.
Where is my spring light?
I wish it will be in my heart forever.
If I open the door of my heart, I can see the colorful spring light.

If I open the window of my heart, I can see you, my beloved one.
Therefore, even though you have left and the house is empty, my heart is comforted.
Where is my beloved one?
I wish you will be in my heart forever.
If I open the window of my heart, I can see you, my beloved one.

If I open the door of my heart, I can see my homeland.
Therefore, even though the home is so far away, it makes me really want to go home right this moment.
Where is my homeland?
I wish it will be in my heart forever.
If I open the door of my heart, I can see my homeland.

If I open the window of my heart, I can see my dream of

youth.

Therefore, even though I can't see the hope of my future, it can stop me from complaining.

Where is my dream of youth?

I wish it will be in my heart forever.

If I open the window of my heart, I can see my dream of youth.

That morning, Ciou-Jyu was a bit surprised that Wen-Zhi sang "Young Love," because the last time he sang the song was three years ago. She knew that it wasn't because Wen-Zhi did not love her anymore. Probably, it was because he had found out that she had fallen for Wen-De.

Ciou-Jyu loved the three brothers so much, even more than her blood brother. No one had ever taken such great care of her. They were her guardian angels. Therefore, even though she had been taken in as a shim-bu-a and had so much work to do every day, she was very grateful and felt lucky in a way.

She knew it was wrong that she had fallen in love with Wen-De. She was arranged to marry Wen-Zhi; she should be faithful to him. "But who can control how their feelings grow and develop?" Ciou-Jyu screamed in her heart countless times. "Arranged marriage is just so wrong and inhuman. Haven't they seen their daughters and sons are crying and in despair?"

Ciou-Jyu surely did not want to hurt Wen-Zhi, but love came softly, so she couldn't resist the romance and allowed Wen-De to kiss her. She was aware of the evil thoughts in her mind. "Just kisses. That's all. I am never allowed to be myself freely. I don't possess anything, including myself. God, forgive me. Just let me have kisses from someone whom I love. I won't ask for more." Furthermore, she convinced herself with a bitter and naive idea. "It will end soon. Once Wen-De goes to university, he will meet some pretty and educated girls and completely forget about me. He will go on with his life, and I will marry Wen-Zhi."

Wen-De did not forget her. In fact, the more girls whom

he got to know at university, the more he felt that Ciou-Jyu was a remarkable person. Although she behaved obediently as a shim-bu-a, her mind was full of modern ideas. She was a thinker; Wen-De admired that. However, in a conservative society, a woman who had a liberal mind wasn't a good thing at all. Her soul would suffer if she didn't fight, but her heart would be wounded if she fought.

Wen-De and Wen-Zhi knew that Ciou-Jyu would never try to fight for her own happiness. Thus, they wanted to strive for her. They were smart young men born into a wealthy family and had never encountered any difficulty or misfortune. In a way, they didn't know what fear was. They believed that nothing couldn't be conquered, so there would be a solution to each problem.

"There will be a happy couple in the world because of my sacrifice." Wen-Zhi strongly believed that he was doing the right thing, even though the pain was like a huge rock lying on his heart. Moreover, since it was the right thing to do, he felt, "Let it be done beautifully." Therefore, Wen-Zhi planned a morning trip to the seacoast. He wanted Ciou-Jyu to know that she could hope, dream, and smile.

On the way to the seacoast, Wen-Zhi sang "Young Love" one last time and wished that Ciou-Jyu would remember his love for her. When he finished singing, they arrived at the spot down where they usually sat. Ciou-Jyu said to him, "You're really a great singer."

"You are too. Can you sing 'If I Open the Door and Windows of My Heart' for me, please?" Wen-Zhi had a big smile on his face.

Then, Ciou-Jyu smiled and sang, but Wen-Zhi interrupted it when Ciou-Jyu sang the lyric, "Where is my beloved one?"

"Ciou-Jyu, I know you love Wen-De, and he loves you too."

Ciou-Jyu looked uneasy.

"Don't worry. I am not mad or trying to confront you or anything of the kind." Ciou-Jyu's face turned red. Wen-Zhi took her left hand and held it with his two hands.

"I told Wen-De that I am going to end our engagement and let you and him marry."

Ciou-Jyu turned her head and looked at Wen-Zhi in surprise. "No…" she said in a light voice.

"Yes. It has to be done in this way. I love you truly without a doubt in my heart, but you and Wen-De love each other; that's all that matters."

Ciou-Jyu couldn't believe what she heard, so she decided to confess.

"Wen-Zhi, I did love you before. Honestly, I didn't expect that you would be such a nice person." Ciou-Jyu laughed with tears. "Before I came here, I heard so many terrible stories about shim-bu-a's lives. Thus, I came with fear. You have no idea what you and your brothers' kindness and friendliness meant to me in the first two months. I felt that I was the luckiest shim-bu-a in Taiwan.

"However, I was ten when I got here. I was too young to understand the meaning of romance. Simply, since I am arranged to be your future wife and you're so perfect and nice, a handsome young man, naturally, I fell for you right away. Who wouldn't? So I did love you before, with all my heart."

He couldn't help it—Wen-Zhi kissed Ciou-Jyu on her left cheek for several seconds. He wished he could freeze time and stay at this moment forever.

"Then, I got to know the three of you more and more as time went by. Things changed. Perhaps because my life is so broken and doesn't belong to me, I am attracted to an older man. Wen-De fulfills my needs. Next thing that I knew, there was an unexpected romance growing between Wen-De and me."

Ciou-Jyu couldn't stop crying. Wen-Zhi leaned closer and held her.

"Wen-Zhi, I am very sorry. Please, forgive me. I am so

ungrateful and unfaithful to you. Please do not cancel the engagement. It is necessary to keep the promise that our parents have made. Otherwise, we will embarrass them a great deal. In addition, it is impossible for a brother to take his brother's fiancée to be his wife. It is not morally right. People will laugh at and criticize it. It's too cruel for your parents. They are well respected in society. We can't shame them like this just because we want to be true to our hearts."

"Oh, Ciou-Jyu. Have your parents and my parents thought about your feelings? Why should you think of them? Do you really want to ignore your own feelings? I think that you should be brave and pursue your own happiness. Now, I am willing to give up my precious privilege, and it's time for you to master your life because you have a chance."

Who was right? Ciou-Jyu or Wen-Zhi?

Perhaps they both were right. Ciou-Jyu was politically correct. Wen-Zhi was humanly correct. However, it was so sad and frustrating. If one desired to survive in a conservative society at the time, he or she—she, particularly—had to be politically correct.

What should Ciou-Jyu, Wen-Zhi, and Wen-De do?

Wen-Zhi and Wen-De decided to make it their problem; nothing was related to Ciou-Jyu. In other words, they took the blame entirely. Thus, Mother wouldn't be mad at Ciou-Jyu and think that it was her fault.

"Of course it is her fault. She is one hundred percent guilty." Wen-De and Wen-Zhi's mother was furious. "A woman who disturbs the peace between brothers in a family is not a good woman. She won't be a good wife, either, because she is a seductive woman. I saw this situation coming two years ago, and it's happening now."

"Mother! How can you not know her? Ciou-Jyu is a simple, sweet girl. In fact, she is a self-respecting person, and you almost described her as a prostitute." Wen-De couldn't believe what Mother had said about Ciou-Jyu, which made him very worried.

"Mother, it's my problem. I want to marry for love. I do love Ciou-Jyu but in a sibling's way. I happened to know that Wen-De loves her, so I thought it would be a great solution if I cancel the engagement and let them marry. I learned that some families did it in this way. It shouldn't be an issue." Wen-Zhi still hoped that he could convince Mother.

"Mostly, it was because the fiancé died that the other brother took the shim-bu-a. Normally, people just don't do that. We are a well-respected family in this town. Why do we want to do something disgraceful?"

Mother made up her mind. "Anyway, Ciou-Jyu is just not good for this family. She has to go."

"What does that mean, 'She has to go'? Go where?" Wen-Zhi hadn't expected this, but Wen-De had worried that this situation might happen when he heard Mother saying that Ciou-Jyu was a seductive woman.

Mother's words scared the two brothers greatly. Immediately, Wen-Zhi told Mother that he honestly wanted to marry Ciou-Jyu. "Please forget everything that we said." However, Mother's heart was hard like steel. She insisted that Ciou-Jyu had to leave their family. Wen-Zhi and Wen-De begged Mother to let Ciou-Jyu stay as a servant, but Mother refused and said, "We can get any servant we want to have. Why do I want to have a seductive woman to work in the house? You're too young to understand that a troubled woman can ruin a family."

"Mother!"

"Say nothing more. The decision has been made." Mother told them to leave her room.

Wen-De blamed himself. "How stupid I was! I let my desire take control of my senses. Now, not only can't I give Ciou-Jyu a good life, but also, we will lose her. I am older and should've known better. How could I be so naive to believe that Mother would allow Wen-Zhi to end the engagement and let Ciou-Jyu marry me?"

"It's all my fault. Mother is very old fashioned and conservative. I've always known that, but I actually thought about challenging it. Oh God. What have I done to Ciou-Jyu?" Wen-Zhi regretted it so much that he couldn't eat or sleep.

"Maybe I will be sent home. That will be great. I finally can reunite with my family." Ciou-Jyu talked to Wen-De and Wen-Zhi with a smile even though she knew that it was almost impossible to send a shim-bu-a home, traditionally.

The two brothers had never been so quiet, but what could they say? They just looked at Ciou-Jyu feeding those ducks and wished for a miracle.

Two weeks later, sixteen-year-old Ciou-Jyu married a man who was thirty-five years of age. The man was a widower and had five children, ages fifteen, thirteen, ten, nine, and seven. His name was De-Sheng (德生). *De* means "virtue" and "morality." *Sheng* means "born." This man who was expected to be born with morality was an absolute scumbag.

De-Sheng had a small grocery store, but he often left the store to his thirteen-year-old daughter, Shu-Fen (淑芬), to manage. The fifteen-year-old son had to go to school, and a daughter didn't need more schooling after six-year compulsory education. Thus, she could watch the store.

De-Sheng demanded that his daughter watch the store not because he had other business to do but because he went to the gambling house. He liked to gamble very much. When he lost, which was quite often, he would drink. When he got home drunk, he used to hit his children. He stopped hitting them after marrying Ciou-Jyu. He beat Ciou-Jyu and raped her instead.

One day, about three months after De-Sheng and Ciou-Jyu were married, a Chinese man who had arrived in Taiwan after 1945 came home with De-Sheng. De-Sheng said to the Chinese man, "You want to do it here or take her home?"

"It's better that you don't hear it, don't you think?"

"It doesn't matter to me."

"Well, I can do it here if you really don't mind. She is gorgeous. I can't wait!"

Then De-Sheng told Ciou-Jyu to take the Chinese man to their room and do her best to please him.

De-Sheng's thirteen-year-old daughter, Shu-Fen, yelled at him, "Are you out of your mind? She is my stepmother, your wife!"

"Shut the fuck up! Or you do it for her. Your stepmother is a whore. She was fooling around with two brothers. People all know it. It's her luck that I took her. Who would marry a whore?"

"But she is your wife now. You know that she is not like what people said. She is a good woman." Shu-Fen fought back fearlessly.

"Well, a good woman will help her husband to pay his debt."

Ciou-Jyu was standing aside with tears. It was too much to bear. "A person can be poor, work like a dog, and have little food to eat, but he or she just can't live without dignity." These words were running around in her head, but Ciou-Jyu didn't say them out loud, because an animal wouldn't understand.

"I won't do it." That was all Ciou-Jyu said. She looked at De-Sheng and the Chinese man with bright, piercing eyes. "Today, you mind the store. Shu-Fen and I are having a walk."

"You come back, bitch!" De-Sheng couldn't believe that Ciou-Jyu hadn't obeyed him.

Soon they walked out the door and got to a quiet spot. Ciou-Jyu and Shu-Fen held each other and cried. They had become dear sisters after Ciou-Jyu came to this family. They understood each other as bosom friends; after all, the age gap between them was only three years.

A short while later, Ciou-Jyu and Shu-Fen both stopped crying. Shu-Fen suggested having a bowl of noodle soup.

"How? I don't have any money with me."

Shu-Fen had one NTD 5 paper bill in her hand and waved. They both laughed and went to have a bowl of noodle soup. That's right. Only one bowl—they shared.

That night, Ciou-Jyu made a decision. The next day, after De-Sheng left home, she also went out. She went to Wen-Zhi's high school and pretended to be a servant from his family and asked to see Wen-Zhi.

"It's urgent." They believed her and called Wen-Zhi out.

Wen-Zhi was extremely surprised and was speechless for a few seconds. How he missed his sweet rose, but looking at her, he could tell she was not doing well.

They walked to the seacoast naturally without communication.

"How is everyone?" Ciou-Jyu asked.

"Everyone is good. We are just terribly lonesome without you. You wouldn't believe that even the pigs, chickens, and ducks all told me so."

Ciou-Jyu laughed happily for the first time in three months. "Seriously, are you guys OK?"

"Not really. Wen-De hasn't come home since Mother arranged for you to marry that man. He didn't call home either. Of course Mother worries and misses him, but she is also angry and thinks that Wen-De is ungrateful.

"Wen-Hua is mad at Mother too. He actually didn't talk to Mother for two months. He is still very cold to Mother and keeps a distance from her. He came to me and cried several times. He cares about you very much and sends a servant to get news of you every week, so we know that you are suffering." Wen-Zhi's eyes became very red and were full of tears.

"Ciou-Jyu, I am very sorry. It's my fault. I should've listened to you. Apparently, Wen-De and I were dreamers with good intentions but lacked acquaintance with the real world. We didn't bring you to heaven but put you in hell. Oh God, I can't forgive myself."

Wen-Zhi began to cry. Ciou-Jyu gently put her right hand on Wen-Zhi's head and rubbed his hair. "Don't cry, my prince. Don't blame yourself. All I remember is that I am a lucky girl who is loved by three princes. Yes, you are my princes, because you made me feel like a princess in your family, and I know that I will always have your love and care. I don't blame you and Wen-De at all. What I keep in mind is love, not a mistake we made. That's right. It's *our* mistake, not just yours."

"Oh, Ciou-Jyu, you are too kind and sweet. If I—"

"Wait, wait. Wen-Zhi, listen to me. We, girls from impoverished families, have no hope. We depend on whom we meet to get a good life or not. At least I had a taste of heaven before living a life that many women have. Now, I hope you can do me a big favor. To help a girl who is in danger. She is my stepdaughter, Shu-Fen. She is only thirteen years old, but I believe that her father might sell her to be a prostitute. Can you find a way to take her to be a maid or a servant in your family? Please."

"Ciou-Jyu, you are in misery yourself, but you think of others. Where do you get your strength? Of course, anything that you ask, I will do it for you. Don't you need anything for yourself?"

"Don't worry about me. I have my own plan."

"What plan? Don't you want to tell me?"

"It's a secret, but you will know eventually."

"OK. I wait for the day."

"Wen-Zhi, I can't keep you any longer. You should go back to school, and I need to go home too."

"When can I see you again? Wen-Hua surely wants to see you too."

"I am sorry. I can't say a date or time. We will see each other when we can. Please send my love to Wen-Hua and Wen-De."

The next day, Wen-Zhi went to Mother and asked her to take a maid.

"Why?" Mother said.

"Because you owe us." Wen-Zhi let Mother know how Ciou-Jyu was.

"We need a maid and can help the girl at the same time. Why not? Do you want to see her being sold to be a prostitute?"

Mother finally agreed and took Shu-Fen in as a maid. She knew that she had to do it; otherwise, she might not get her three sons' hearts back.

After Shu-Fen became a maid in Wen-Zhi's family, Ciou-Jyu disappeared. No one knew where she went, but her husband, De-Sheng, didn't look worried. However, one thing was very odd, which aroused the suspicion of his fifteen-year-old son, Cing-Cai (慶財), and the neighbors.

There were four or five Chinese men who had arrived in Taiwan after 1945 had come to the grocery store every day since Ciou-Jyu disappeared. Once a Chinese man came to the grocery store, De-Sheng took him to the storage house that was in the back of the house. At first, neighbors thought that those Chinese men came to buy some goods. After a few days, it looked strange to them, because those Chinese men didn't take anything with them when they left. One week later, there were more Chinese men coming to the grocery store every day. Moreover, some Chinese men began coming in the night-time.

In the beginning, when neighbors told Cing-Cai this situation, he couldn't do anything to find out what was going on because he was at school. During the weekend, he was waiting for them to come, but no one came at all. He went to check on the storage house, but it was locked, and he couldn't find the key. One night, while he was studying, through his window, he saw a Chinese man coming. He sneaked out of his room and hid behind a tree that was next to the storage house. He couldn't believe what he saw. His stepmother, Ciou-Jyu, was in the storage house. She was tied up and half-naked. Moreover, her mouth was stuffed and tied up with a cloth, so she couldn't scream to get help.

"How could he? He kidnaps Ciou-Jyu and makes her be a prostitute! He is a fucking animal!"

Cing-Cai ran. He ran very fast, fast like the wind. He ran to find his younger sister, Shu-Fen, because there was only one person who could help Ciou-Jyu.

When he saw Shu-Fen, he asked her to get Wen-Zhi right away. From seeing Cing-Cai out of breath, Shu-Fen guessed that something must be crucial and related to Ciou-Jyu, so she went to find Wen-Zhi without asking her brother anything. Unfortunately, Wen-Zhi was out for a walk, so Shu-Fen went to get Wen-Hua. After Cing-Cai told them that Ciou-Jyu had been kidnapped and forced to be a prostitute, he and Wen-Hua ran to his home at once. Shu-Fen, crying, ran out to find Wen-Zhi.

When Cing-Cai and Wen-Hua got to the storage house, they pushed the door open and saw a Chinese man who was on top of Ciou-Jyu raping her. Ciou-Jyu was crying and looked helpless. Wen-Hua pulled the Chinese man up and gave him a hard punch to his face. Cing-Cai untied Ciou-Jyu and covered her up with a thin blanket that he picked up from the ground. Then, he took Ciou-Jyu back into the house.

The Chinese man screamed and ran out of the storage house without his trousers on. While he was putting the trousers on, De-Sheng came to see what was going on from hearing a loud noise. He got furious from seeing the scene and shouted at Wen-Hua.

"What are you doing on my property?"

"What filthy thing are you doing?"

"It's none of your business. It's *my* wife and *my* property. I do what I am pleased to do!"

"You can tell this to the police and judge yourself!" Wen-Hua couldn't bear it anymore, so he punched De-Sheng's face. Wen-Hua wanted to beat him up, but he was more concerned with Ciou-Jyu's situation. Thus, he left De-Sheng whimpering on the ground and rushed to the house.

When Cing-Cai took Ciou-Jyu back to the house, he told his ten-year-old sister, who looked frightened, to take care of Ciou-Jyu.

Ciou-Jyu surely was weak and hurt, but she had no desire to stay in this house anymore. Therefore, she washed herself and changed clothes quickly. When Wen-Hua walked into the house, she was almost done with changing.

Wen-Hua was worried about Ciou-Jyu and called her name, and Ciou-Jyu came out.

"Oh, my Lord, where is your kindness?" Wen-Hua screamed in his heart, and his eyes were full of tears. This girl, his dearest sister, whom he loved and cared for, was devastated. She was still beautiful but with a broken soul and a bruised body. Wen-Hua was heartbroken. He walked toward Ciou-Jyu and held her gently.

"Ciou-Jyu, let's go." Wen-Hua's voice was shaking, but his mind was determined. No matter what Mother would say, he decided to protect Ciou-Jyu for the rest of his life from this moment.

Ciou-Jyu was so weak and hurt that she couldn't walk normally. Wen-Hua held her; they walked together slowly. When they were about to walk out of the house, De-Sheng told them to stop.

"Let them go, A-ba." Cing-Cai wished he could've found out his father's animal behavior earlier so Ciou-Jyu wouldn't have suffered for that long.

"Go where? Ciou-Jyu is my wife. What is his position to take my wife away? If he wanted to take her home and fuck her, he had to pay first."

"If you weren't my father, I would certainly beat you up!" Cing-Cai yelled loudly in his mind. However, he and Wen-Hua said nothing. It was pointless talking to an animal.

"Stop! You two just stop right there! Ciou-Jyu, stay, and you get out!"

Ciou-Jyu and Wen-Hua kept walking and ignored him. Suddenly, De-Sheng ran toward them with cloth-cutting scissors in his right hand. Cing-Cai screamed out loud, "Watch out! He has scissors!"

It was too late. The scissors were stuck in Wen-Zhi's abdomen.

Wen-Zhi?

Shu-Fen had found Wen-Zhi at the seacoast and told him the terrible situation. At once, Wen-Zhi ran toward Shu-Fen's home. He had an unbearable heartache. He did not understand why he was always unable to save Ciou-Jyu.

"She said that she had a plan. It must be a plan for running away. Why didn't I give her some money? Then she wouldn't be here and tortured." Wen-Zhi's tears were flying in the air.

When he got to Shu-Fen's home, he saw the scumbag holding a pair of scissors and running toward Ciou-Jyu and Wen-Hua. He ran over and tried to stop him. The crazy bastard meant to stab Wen-Hua, but he stabbed Wen-Zhi, who was running toward him instead.

That scumbag must have wanted to kill Wen-Hua, because the scissors were stuck deeply in Wen-Zhi's abdomen. The blood poured out of Wen-Zhi's body like a spring.

That crazy scumbag was stunned when he saw the blood. Cing-Cai ran out of the house to the police station immediately.

"No!" Ciou-Jyu screamed and screamed. She and Wen-

Hua helped Wen-Zhi to lie down, and her tears dropped down on Wen-Zhi's face.

"My sweet rose, don't cry." After Wen-Zhi said that, he passed out.

A few minutes later, the police and an ambulance came. The police arrested De-Sheng, and the ambulance took Wen-Zhi to the county hospital.

Wen-Hua wanted to take Ciou-Jyu home, but she insisted on going to the hospital. As matter of fact, Wen-Hua found that Ciou-Jyu had signs of a nervous breakdown. "Maybe it's better for her to be in the hospital. She might be able to calm down if she is near Wen-Zhi, and also, a doctor can examine her." Thus, Wen-Hua took Ciou-Jyu to the hospital.

On the way to the hospital, Ciou-Jyu kept mumbling.

"Wen-Zhi, I love you. Please don't die.

"It's all my fault. I am not a good woman. I bring bad luck to people.

"Wen-Zhi, sorry. I shouldn't be unfaithful to you.

"Wen-Zhi, I am a whore now. Will you still love me?

"Wen-Zhi, I can't live without you.

"Oh, I should leave you alone so you won't die."

Wen-Hua got more and more worried. Besides her mumbling, Ciou-Jyu's eyes were unfocused. Sometimes, he had to stop her from hitting her head or pulling her hair. Wen-Hua was very afraid that he might lose two people whom he loved.

Wen-Zhi was in critical condition. Doctors had little confidence that he would survive. The scissors had pierced through Wen-Zhi's liver and stomach. Even though he was lucky that no one had tried to take the scissors out before he was sent to the hospital, he still had to fight with the God of Death.

While Wen-Zhi was fighting for his life, the doctor told Wen-Hua that Ciou-Jyu had suffered a nervous breakdown. She needed to be hospitalized. Moreover, she was pregnant.

Wen-Hua had never felt so helpless and hopeless.

"What if Wen-Zhi dies? Mother and Father are going to grieve for the rest of their lives. How about Ciou-Jyu? Because of Wen-Zhi's situation, Mother and Father definitely wouldn't allow Ciou-Jyu to come home with us. She is having a baby, and one of those bastards is the baby's father. If she knows it, she will go crazy. How to tell her? She can't even talk normally now. Oh, what should I do? What can I do?"

Before Wen-Hua had answers for those troubling questions, Mother and Father came.

"How is your brother? Is he going to be OK?" Father was quiet as usual but looked very serious. On the contrary, Mother was so worried that she had to talk to ease her nerves.

"What did I tell you? She is not a good woman. She brings trouble to our family."

"Mother!" Wen-Hua really couldn't bear to hear those hateful words. Why couldn't she just be quiet like Father? Wen-Hua tried not to hate Mother, but he did at this moment.

"What? Am I wrong? I had married her away, but your brother still got affected by her. Remember what I said? She is a seductive woman. She is. That's why her husband made her be a hooker."

"Mother, stop! It's you. All because of you, the tragedies happened. If you let Ciou-Jyu and Wen-De marry, none of this would have happened at all. You are the person who created the problems, not Ciou-Jyu!"

"Wen-Hua, you can't talk to your mother like that. Show your respect and apologize." Father finally opened his mouth.

Wen-Hua said nothing as an act of refusal and objection.

"It's Mother's fault. As a woman who was born and grew up in a conservative society, she certainly knows how women are treated as secondary human beings, lower than men. I am not asking her or other mothers to be revolutionaries to fight with men, but at least, do not use the little power that they have in their hands to make young girls, other mothers' daughters, suffer. Don't they, victims of patriarchal society, want to stick together, not harm one another?"

Wen-Hua knew that it was not the time to fight with Mother. They needed to stick together to pray for Wen-Zhi, but Wen-Hua just couldn't go against his viewpoints to apologize to Mother.

The next morning, Wen-Zhi passed away. Everyone was in shock. Mother fainted after learning the news from the doctor. No parents could accept the fact that their children had died before them, especially if they died young.

Ciou-Jyu died the same day, in the late afternoon. She hanged herself. She wrote a letter to Wen-Hua. She thanked him for rescuing her, but she was too tired to live her life.

"I have fought to live my life the best way that I can. However, I can't win. I just can't win. Fate is like ocean waves. It always comes back and hits the land or rocks. I try to be a rock so I won't be washed away. Unfortunately, I have learned that I am the land. So many pieces of me have been taken away. I am not me anymore. I don't know how to live my life. Where is my home? Where do I belong? The worst thing is that I killed Wen-Zhi, who loved me, who was willing to give me the whole world. I love him. I do love him. I was blind with the desire of fulfilling my needs, so I turned my back on my true love. I should be punished for my selfishness, ignorance, and ungratefulness. Hence, I shall leave with Wen-Zhi. I can't leave him alone again this time. Goodbye, Wen-Hua. You are like my twin brother. I love you. Finally, please send my love to Wen-De for me. I love him too."

Wen-Hua cried his heart and soul out.

5

Ciou-Tao

After Ciou-Jyu died, Wen-Hua went to see Ciou-Tao. Besides bringing the sad news, the most important thing was to check on Ciou-Tao. Ciou-Tao was Ciou-Jyu's younger sister. She was one of three daughters who had been given away. Ciou-Jyu had always cared about her little sister and worried if she had food to eat. In the suicide note, Ciou-Jyu had asked a favor of Wen-Hua: to perform her duty for her. Ciou-Jyu was his dearest sister, and he loved her so much. Of course he would do anything for her. More importantly, looking after Ciou-Tao was the last connection he could have with Ciou-Jyu. He cherished it.

Ciou-Tao had been adopted by the Lin family as a daughter, not a shim-bu-a. The Lin family wanted to adopt a daughter because the mother was ill, and the father needed a helper. Oh my Lord. To get a daughter to help out their family! What kind of life could Ciou-Tao have? Not to mention that she was only seven years of age when they adopted her.

Thank goodness the adoptive father, Ming-Cheng (明城), was a nice man, quiet and kind. He was a carpenter who didn't make much money. Ming-Cheng's wife had tuberculosis. He was too poor to give his wife proper treatment. The only thing he could do was to get a helper to ease his wife's worry that she couldn't take care of her four children and housework. A seven-year-old girl was indeed too young. Ming-Cheng wanted to get an older girl, but he liked Ciou-Tao the first time he saw her. He felt a connection with Ciou-Tao, so he decided to adopt her.

When Ciou-Tao was sent to the Lin family, the four brothers were six, five, four, and three years old. Although Ciou-Tao wasn't much older than them, she was very mature. She knew her responsibility to the family, so she did her best to do all the things that she thought needed to be done. After a short time, Ciou-Tao wasn't a helper anymore. She became a mother. Any time the little brothers had any problems, they all went to her. Perhaps they knew that it was useless to go to their mother, who was lying in the bed the whole day every day. Ciou-Tao was amazing, though. She could always solve their problems and satisfy their needs, except for one thing: hunger.

Bringing money home was Ming-Cheng's duty, but he couldn't get a regular job and make enough money. Well, not making enough money and having too many mouths to feed was a terrible combination. Ming-Cheng had an account in a nearby grocery store, and he owed the owner of the store quite a lot of money. Even though the owner didn't hurry him to pay the bills, he was too embarrassed to go to the store. Thus, he sent Ciou-Tao. In fact, Ciou-Tao sometimes went herself without Ming-Cheng's order. She had to. There was nothing she could cook for her brothers and they were hungry, but Ming-Cheng wasn't at home. However, later, when Ciou-Tao learned that the bills piled up like a skyscraper, she stopped going to the grocery store as often as before and started to take the four brothers with her to hunt for food almost every day.

Hunting for food?

It sounds ridiculous.

What does that mean?

How could children who weren't even ten years old go out hunting?

Well, it wasn't real "hunting." It was a bit like a treasure hunt. They walked all over the town and dug through people's garbage cans. They picked up some valuable metal stuff, plastic bottles, and anything that they could sell to the recycling company. Of course, Ciou-Tao and her brothers couldn't find something valuable every time, or they did get something, but they didn't have enough stuff to sell. Thus, they kept the stuff at home and went out to hunt more until they had enough to sell. It is not so hard to imagine how little money they could earn from selling that stuff. Therefore, to Ciou-Tao and her brothers, finding real food in the trash cans was much better. That was an immediate solution for their hungry bellies.

Back then, most people were poor, so there was not much food to be found in garbage cans. However, once in a while, Ciou-Tao and her brothers still could get surprises, such as a partial putrid pear, moldy papaya, tangerine, cabbage, or carrot. Those were items of food that the Lin family couldn't afford to buy. They were like many families that were also in poverty, eating sweet potato and rice congee. Sweet potatoes were shredded and cooked with a little amount of rice for each meal. Thus, Ciou-Tao and her four little brothers enjoyed the food that they found in the garbage cans very much.

Once in a blue moon, Ciou-Tao and her brothers got a treat—for instance, canned pineapple. Mm, yum! They ate the pineapple, drank the juice, and licked their hands, arms, and lips. After that, they played a game with the can. They kicked it like a soccer ball. The sound from kicking the can was like a bell ringing from heaven.

Sometimes, Ciou-Tao took her brothers to the outside of town to pick wild vegetables. It was a bit far away from home, but the four little guys didn't complain because they thought it was fun.

Mostly, Ciou-Tao took her brothers to the ditch to catch fish and frogs. Well, the ditch was only five minutes away from home on foot, so they could go there often. Moreover, the boys liked frogs more than vegetables. Of course, they couldn't catch frogs or fish every time, but they still had so much fun.

After all, they were just little children; they loved the water and nature innately. However, Ciou-Tao felt stressed when she took them to the ditch. She was afraid that they might fall into the water and drown. Picture that. Didn't Ciou-Tao look like a mother, think like a mother, and act like a mother?

By the time Ciou-Tao was ten years of age, she became a mother completely in a way. The adoptive mother passed away. Besides the sadness, there was little difference to the children, since their mother had been unable to be their company and take care of them. Sadly, there was an awful change. Ming-Cheng started drinking every day after he lost his wife. He had known that it was coming, but it was just so hard when he really couldn't see and feel his beloved anymore.

Ming-Cheng's bitterness and sorrow brought more burdens to Ciou-Tao. Because he drank every day, the money that was supposed to be used to buy food became less. Nearly one-third of the money was now spent on liquor. Moreover, who would want to hire or recommend a carpenter who came to work with a hangover? Therefore, their financial situation got worse. Little Ciou-Tao worried very much.

Thank heaven for one thing. Ming-Cheng, at least, wasn't the kind of person who had a bad temper and would beat up children after getting drunk. He only just fell into his own thoughts, and then he fell asleep. Twentysomething years later (it was no coincidence), Ming-Cheng died from having liver cirrhosis. Tragedy repeated. Another thirty-plus years later, his two sons died for the same reason. They both were heavy drinkers. Perhaps they inherited their father's personality. They broke down when they encountered problems in life. They did not learn from their adoptive sister, Ciou-Tao, who was tough and resilient, who always tried to find a way out when she was confronted with problems.

Besides hunting treasure in garbage cans, picking wild vegetables, and catching fish and frogs in the ditch, Ciou-Tao went to the train tracks to pick up the coals that fell from the train. She thought that it was too dangerous to bring her four brothers; therefore, she went by herself.

At the time, in the 1950s, most people in Taiwan used wood or coals to cook. Clearly, the Lin family couldn't afford to buy them, since they couldn't even buy enough food. Luckily, Ciou-Tao could get them free. After typhoons or rainstorms, she would go to the seacoast to pick up wood that was brought down by the water from the mountains. On regular days, she picked coals.

Picking coals from the train tracks was very dangerous, but it could help a family a lot. That was why all the kids from the impoverished families went to train tracks to pick coals. Since there were a lot of competitors, those kids soon became professionals after they started picking coals. Their eyes would search for other coals while their hands were picking one. At the same time, they paid attention to see if the train was coming. They all heard of one or two sad stories that a girl or a boy got hit by a train and died, and their parents always told them to come home safely. Hence, they all knew that they had to be very careful. However, no matter how careful they were, tragedies still happened. Some kids got seriously injured, losing a leg or an arm, for example. Therefore, the police forbade anyone to pick coals.

The police patrolled the train tracks very often. They took kids back to the police station if they caught them. The kids they brought back would be punished to stand by a wall or a corner for an hour or so. Well, which kids would want to be caught by the police and get disciplined? Thus, they shouted a warning to one another and ran when they saw a policeman coming. Surely, they were competitive when they were picking coals, but they immediately united as a team when the police chased after them.

Ciou-Tao got caught one time, but it wasn't a bad experience.

That time Ciou-Tao got caught, she was eight and was new to coal picking. When the policeman came, she was sort of away from other kids. By the time she finally saw the policeman, it was too late to get away. Moreover, she tripped and fell. She wounded her right knee.

On the way to the police station, Ciou-Tao was crying. The policeman thought that she was in pain, so he comforted her. He did not know that Ciou-Tao was crying for two reasons: the pain and being arrested.

That policeman was a nice man. After he took Ciou-Tao back to the police station, he immediately cleaned the wound on her knee and put salve on it. Then, he told Ciou-Tao to wash her face and hands. While Ciou-Tao was standing by the corner of the police station, he went to buy several steamed pork buns. When he came back, he gave Ciou-Tao one.

On the way back to the police station, the policeman heard not only Ciou-Tao's crying but also the noise that her stomach was making. He knew that she must be very hungry. "What a poor girl!" He felt sad. "If her family wasn't impoverished, she wouldn't need to take a risk to pick coals from train tracks." However, as a police officer, he couldn't say to her, "Be careful when you are picking coals." He had to tell Ciou-Tao the same thing that he told other kids whom he caught. "Do not go to train tracks to pick coals anymore. It is too dangerous."

The happiness totally made Ciou-Tao forget about the shame of being punished and lectured at the police station. Ciou-Tao was smiling and eating the steamed pork bun. It was like winning the lottery, an unexpected surprise. Moreover, this surprise brought her back to the great memory of having her first steamed pork bun.

One afternoon, two weeks before Ciou-Jyu, Ciou-Lian, and Ciou-Tao were sent away, their dearest uncle made three big steamed pork buns for them.

"Uncle, it smells different from those buns that you gave us." Once Ciou-Jyu took the bun, she could tell that it was a different bun.

"Uncle, why does this steamed bun look different?" Ciou-Tao asked.

"I think there is something inside the bun." Ciou-Lian pressed the bun a little.

"Girls, just have a bite." Their uncle had a smile on his face.

"Oh my God! It's meat!" Ciou-Tao was very surprised. She and her sisters could only have meat to eat three or four times a year, on those big holidays, such as the Mid-Autumn Festival (中秋節) and Lunar New Year's Eve.

"Uncle, it's so yummy."

"Dope, say thank you to uncle!"

Ciou-Tao hadn't thought that she could have a steamed pork bun again in her life. Even though she thought the steamed pork buns that her uncle had made for her and her sisters were better than this one, she was very grateful to have her second steamed pork bun. Thus, she was eating the bun with a big smile.

The policeman pleasantly looked at Ciou-Tao, who enjoyed her steamed pork bun with a smiling face, and he fell into his own thoughts. "Life is too rough to chew; even adults choke from it. Can this little girl survive the hardship?"

Ciou-Tao's original family was in poverty, but no matter whether she was tired of eating sweet potatoes or not, at least she had food to eat. After all, her parents were farmers.

Besides hard work, farming relies on the weather. Thus, Ciou-Tao's biological parents looked at the sky and prayed all the time. They, of course, knew that it is impossible to have good weather all the time, but they only asked for a peaceful life without hunger and debts. However, even if the weather was always good, their situation would be still very much the same. A small piece of barren land just couldn't provide a large family, two adults and seven children, with enough to live. As a result, they had to give three daughters away to improve their situation. Even though it was sad that they had to do so, they had been glad that Ciou-Jyu and Ciou-Lian were adopted by two wealthy families. Without a doubt, they would eat better and not feel hungry. It must be asked, then, why they gave Ciou-Tao to a poor family?

At the time, including the Lin family, there were three families willing to take Ciou-Tao. None of the three families were well off, but these families' financial situations were a little bit better than the Wang family's. Fu-Sheng and Li-Jhu decided to give Ciou-Tao to the Lin family because they liked Ming-Cheng. Ming-Cheng was a simple, nice man. He might not talk much, but Fu-Sheng and Li-Jhu could see and feel his kindness and sincerity when he talked to them. More importantly, he wanted to adopt Ciou-Tao as a daughter, not a shim-bu-a. Thus, Fu-Sheng and Li-Jhu strongly believed that Ciou-Tao would be loved and treated well in the Lin family.

Fu-Sheng and Li-Jhu were right. Ming-Cheng and his wife loved Ciou-Tao and saw her as their own daughter. However, later, the Lin family's financial situation had gotten so bad that Ciou-Tao had to find food to bring home all the time, which was completely out of their imagination.

Surprisingly, Ciou-Tao understood and accepted reality very quickly, and she did very well, considering her age. She knew ways to survive and keep the Lin family going. Believe it or not, in that situation, she even made sure that her younger brothers all went to school. It wasn't because Ciou-Tao understood the importance of education. Simply, she knew the rule: all kids had to receive six-year compulsory education, and making sure that her younger brothers all went to school was her duty. Well, who could deny that she indeed was a little lady of the house?

Unlike Ciou-Jyu's and Ciou-Lian's, Ciou-Tao's academic performance was poor, and so were the four brothers'. The four brothers were mediocre students and disliked school learning, but Ciou-Tao's situation was different. She had liked school very much before the adoption. Perhaps the hardship of daily economic issues occupied and consumed her young mind a great deal; therefore, she couldn't concentrate on learning at school and eventually lost interest. However, even if Ciou-Tao or her four brothers liked school and wanted to go to junior high school, how could the Lin family afford the tuition, since they were barely able to pay the elementary school tuition? Little Ciou-Tao knew the reality very well, but she did not pity herself and her brothers for having hardship in life. She just intelligently followed her instinct to live, and surviving the hunger was the top priority that she worked hard on.

The day Ciou-Tao was caught by the policeman was supposed to be a bad day, but Ciou-Tao left the police station with a big smile. When the policeman lectured her not to pick coals, the way Ciou-Tao nodded her head and said, "Yes, sir," made the policeman want to laugh. He knew that Ciou-Tao wasn't going to obey anything that he said. However, Ciou-Tao sincerely responded like she was going to quit the coal picking from that very day. Somehow, she didn't even look phony. When he was about finishing talking to her, Ciou-Tao said to him, "I am sorry, Officer. Can I go home now? I need to go home to cook for my brothers; otherwise, they will starve to death." What she said brought out his sadness and compassion, so he said, "Of course," and gave Ciou-Tao two steamed pork buns to bring home.

Eight-year-old Ciou-Tao laughed and hugged the policeman. Then she opened her mouth with two missing front teeth to say, "Thank you." Hugging was not popular in Taiwanese society at the time, so Ciou-Tao surprised him and touched his heart at the same time. He touched Ciou-Tao's head gently and told her to go home safely.

That day, Ciou-Tao's four brothers had a very late dinner, but they didn't complain. They thought that their sister was the greatest magician in the world. She always could find something for them to eat, and this time was unbelievably super steamed pork buns!

The next day, after school, Ciou-Tao picked some flowers by the ditch while her brothers were catching fish and frogs. When they were done, Ciou-Tao told her brothers to go home by themselves. She had business to attend to.

What? Business to attend to?

Ciou-Tao went to the police station. When she got there, she just stood outside by the wall and leaned to the right to sneak a peek to see if the policeman who had given her the steamed pork buns was in the station. Unfortunately, she didn't see him. Then she waited and sneaked a peek once in a while. About ten minutes later, one police officer saw her and asked her, "Do you need help?"

Ciou-Tao hesitated; she didn't know what to say. Suddenly, a sound came from behind her.

"Ciou-Tao, are you coming to see me? Are those flowers for me?"

"Yes, sir." Ciou-Tao flushed and spoke in a low voice.

The policeman laughed out loud, walked toward her, and touched Ciou-Tao's head gently like yesterday.

Ciou-Tao finally relaxed and gave the flowers to the policeman with a pretty smile. "Thank you for the steamed pork buns that you gave me yesterday. My brothers loved them very much. They said that they have never had such delicious food."

The policeman laughed out loud again. "Where did you get the flowers?"

"The ditch."

"I thought so. I love these flowers. Thank you. Be careful when you and your brothers go there fishing."

"How do you know we fish there?" Ciou-Tao was amazed that he knew.

"Everybody in the town went there fishing when they were kids. I went there to catch frogs too. Do you like frog meat?"

Ciou-Tao shook her head and said, "I am afraid of frogs. They are ugly and like to jump."

"Like to jump? Ha, ha, ha...they jump because they are frogs, sweetie. Ha, ha, ha. Try a bite next time. You will find it yummy. In fact, it tastes like chicken."

"Maybe..." Ciou-Tao really couldn't love those frogs. She loved her fish, and her brothers knew that. Therefore, whenever they caught a fish, they would say, "Sis, I got you a fish."

"Good girl. Don't you need to go home and do your homework? Come to visit me once in a while. Thanks again for the flowers."

Ciou-Tao nodded her head and smiled. She walked and jumped, jumped and walked, all the way home.

Maybe Ciou-Tao didn't like learning at school, but she was learning all the time from the people who lived around her, whom she saw, whom she encountered. In addition, when she was little, four years of age, she had learned that there were nice people out there. They were kind and generous. Hence, she trusted people.

6

Uncle Huang

There was a very amiable Chinese man in his midthirties who lived near Ciou-Tao's original family, and he was Ciou-Tao's favorite person in the village. The Chinese man was a soldier who had come to Taiwan in 1948.

After World War II, the second Civil War (第二次國共內戰, 1945–1950) immediately started in China. The Chinese Communist Party defeated the Chinese Nationalist Party in most battles. The Nationalist troops had been evacuating from the north of China to the south. Eventually, the Chinese Nationalist Party began sending troops to Taiwan.

Taiwan was freed from Japan's colonial rule (1895–1945) after World War II, and China had trusteeship on Taiwan. However, the Chiang Kai-shek regime occupied Taiwan as a shelter and its territory after being defeated by the Chinese Communist Party. They made Taiwan become their land of hope and opportunity so that they had a place to stand up and fight back against the Chinese Communist Party.

When the Chinese people were exiled from their country, most of them lost almost everything that they had in their lives. They might be able to buy new things to replace the ones that they lost or couldn't bring with them. However, they couldn't do the same with the family members whom they left behind in China. Imagine how sad they would be. When every holiday and anniversary came, how could they not feel pain and miss their families bitterly?

That Chinese man, Ciou-Tao's favorite person in the village, did feel sad and lonely. However, his life in Taiwan changed after he met Ciou-Tao.

The first time Ciou-Tao met Uncle Huang (黃), she was four years old. She was too little to understand many things, but she would be very happy when people played with her or sang to her. Uncle Huang seemed to understand little children's minds well. That was what he did, sang to her, when he met Ciou-Tao for the first time.

That day, four-year-old Ciou-Tao and five-year-old Ciou-Lian were playing hide-and-seek at home. Ciou-Tao hid outside of the house, behind a tree. While she was laughing about Ciou-Lian not being able to find her, Uncle Huang was resting by another tree.

"What a pretty girl! What's your name?"

"Ciou-Tao."

"How old are you?"

"Four."

"Are you playing hide-and-seek with your friends?"

"No, just with my sister Ciou-Lian. And she won't find me."

"How come?"

"Because I am hiding outside of the house."

"Your sister will come here to find you eventually."

"No, she won't."

"Why?"

"Because I am not supposed to be here."

"You mean you are cheating?"

Ciou-Tao smiled and nodded.

"What a bad girl! You are not playing a fair game." Uncle Huang couldn't stop laughing. He hadn't felt so cheerful for a long time. He had almost forgotten how much fun it was to talk to little kids. He always believed that kids were the greatest gifts from God. They made his life beautiful, joyful, and meaningful.

Uncle Huang had a wife and two daughters, but they didn't come to Taiwan with him. He was in the army service;

he came to Taiwan in 1948, of course, by order. He didn't want to leave China at all, but he had no choice. He tried to comfort himself: "Hang in there. I will be home soon." However, the situation got worse; the Chinese Communist Party was winning the war, and more Chinese Nationalist troops were coming to Taiwan. At the end of 1949, when the Chiang Kai-shek regime was exiled to Taiwan, Uncle Huang cried.

Time went by so fast. Uncle Huang had been in Taiwan for five years when he met Ciou-Tao. "Will the Generalissimo, Chiang Kai-shek, take us home?" Uncle Huang often thought about it, but he couldn't talk about it with anyone, including his comrades. One would be deemed as a traitor or a spy if he or she had a doubt that the Chinese Nationalist Party could defeat the Chinese Communist Party. They couldn't have any doubt about their country, the Republic of China, and the party. They needed to firmly believe that they were going to win the Civil War and get their sovereignty back from the Chinese Communist Party. Hence, all his thoughts needed to be kept to himself; otherwise, Uncle Huang would be like one of his comrades who was charged with treason and died in a foreign land, Taiwan. Uncle Huang intended to go home alive, so he had to be very careful. He could think whatever he wanted, but he just couldn't tell anyone his ideas and feelings about the war.

What a lonely, depressed man! No wonder he didn't feel so amused for a long time. In fact, Ciou-Tao brought the feelings and joy of being a father back to Uncle Huang, which made him want to play with her, so he sang an amusing song, "Two Tigers," to her.

You might have heard of a French song, "Frère Jacques." Here is the English version:

Are you sleeping, are you sleeping,
Brother John? Brother John?
Morning bells are ringing! Morning bells are ringing!
Ding, dang, dong. Ding, dang, dong.

During the period of Northern Expedition (中國國民黨北伐, 1926–1928) in China, in 1926, the National Revolutionary Army took the melody of the song "Frère Jacques" to write Chinese lyrics to make it a temporary national anthem. Later, about 1939, the son of Chiang Kai-shek, Chiang Ching-kuo, sang a new version of "Frère Jacques," with different lyrics, called "Two Tigers." It has become a popular children's song since then in the Chinese language world.

> Two tigers, two tigers.
> Run very fast, run very fast.
> One has no eyes; another has no tail.
> Real strange, real strange.

Even today at preschool, teachers in Taiwan often like to teach students to sing "Two Tigers," and most kids find it very interesting and amusing because of the lyrics and the cute little dance that comes with the song.

Ciou-Tao felt the same. She laughed very hard while Uncle Huang was singing and dancing. In fact, she said, "Please, again," after Uncle Huang finished the song. The second time, Ciou-Tao followed. Well, because they were having so much fun singing, dancing, and laughing, people who were miles away could hear them. Therefore, Ciou-Lian found Ciou-Tao.

"Got you! You broke the rule, and you are going to be punished."

Ciou-Tao was still laughing happily like a little daisy.

Uncle Huang became a friend of the Wang family soon after that day. It was 1953, which was a time when it wasn't easy for many Taiwanese people and Chinese people to become friends.

After World War II, the Allies handed temporary administrative control of Taiwan to the Republic of China (ROC) after Japan gave up the ownership of Taiwan. In a short time, the Taiwanese people became resentful of the Chinese Nationalist authority because they did not treat the Taiwanese people fairly and respectfully, as Taiwanese people expected. In fact, the Chinese Nationalist government behaved worse than the Japanese government. They were so corrupt and cruel, which were the same reasons that the Chinese Nationalist Party lost its sovereignty to the Chinese Communist Party. They arbitrarily seized private properties and destroyed the economy in Taiwan. For instance, they shipped tons and tons of food and stuff that they needed in the Civil War from Taiwan to China, which caused bankruptcy, unemployment, inflation, poverty, and hunger. Moreover, the Chinese Nationalist government and their troops were poorly disciplined. Some of them robbed and stole. Some of them molested and raped women. As a result, Taiwanese people's rage built up, and a public uprising began on February 28, 1947. At the beginning of this chaos, many Chinese civilians were beaten by Taiwanese people, mostly local gangsters, but at the same time, many Taiwanese people protected the Chinese civilians. There were nearly eighteen hundred Chinese civilians hurt and killed in the Incident. Immediately, the governor-general of Taiwan, Chen Yi (陳儀, 1883–1950), made a request, and thirteen thousand Chinese Nationalist soldiers were sent from China to Taiwan to suppress the uprising. Then the massacre started. The massacre ended on May 16, 1947, and tens of thousands of innocent Taiwanese people were brutally killed. As a result of this Incident, Taiwan had been ruled under martial law for thirty-eight years and fifty-six days, from 1949 to 1987, and people on the island had lived in fear of White Terror (白色恐怖).

The next year, 1948, Uncle Huang came to Taiwan. He and his comrades were warned by other soldiers, "The Taiwanese people are violent and hate the Chinese people."

However, very soon, Uncle Huang and some of his comrades found that what they were told wasn't true. Most Taiwanese people were friendly and kind. When Uncle Huang was in China, he learned that a revolt against the Chinese Nationalist government happened in Taiwan, but he knew few details. He suspected that the blood had flowed through the island like rivers; otherwise, he wouldn't see the anger and fear mixed in some Taiwanese people's faces when they looked at the Chinese people, soldiers in particular. Of course, it was impossible for Uncle Huang to learn the whole truth of the February 28 Incident. Thus, he kept his mind and eyes open.

There was one thing that Uncle Huang was very sure of, though; he was so tired of killing after all those years of fighting with the Japanese and the Chinese Communist Party. He believed that fighting with the Japanese was a reasonable and necessary action as the Chinese nation was invaded, but fighting the Chinese Communists?

"Aren't we a nation? Can't we talk instead of fighting and killing?" He thought about it often. "Perhaps it's impossible. After all, the two parties embrace different political ideas."

That explained why Uncle Huang applied to retire after the Chiang Kai-shek regime was exiled to and settled in Taiwan. Maybe he couldn't go back to China anytime soon, but he wanted to stop living a life that was only filled with fighting and killing. At the time, the Chiang Kai-shek regime, the Chinese Nationalist government, was still preparing for fighting with the Chinese Communist Party, so they needed a well-trained and younger military force. In 1952, the Chinese Nationalist government decided to let older or wounded soldiers go. Lucky for Uncle Huang, he was thirty-six years old; he was permitted. However, when a man who had no property and little education—and was unskilled—asked for retirement from the army service, how could he live on such a small pension?

Believe it or not, Uncle Huang and his comrades were even unable to rent a place to live. They were low-ranking and dirt-poor Chinese soldiers. When they were still in service, they had stayed on the base. Thus, that hadn't been a problem. However, if some of them got married or retired, where could they go?

The Chinese Nationalist government was supposed to take care of *all* its soldiers, but it only took very good care of the high-ranking officers by giving them nice houses that were taken from the Japanese people without compensation. To the low-ranking soldiers and veterans, they gave only a piece of land—which might be by a river, train tracks, or a cemetery—to build their own houses. Yes, the Chinese Nationalist government was not only incompetent but also heartless. The government didn't even bother to try to build some decent houses for the low-ranking soldiers and veterans, while they used those beautiful houses that they stole from the Japanese people to please the high-ranking officers. This was so sad. A lot of the land that was given to the low-ranking soldiers and veterans to build houses belonged to the Japanese people or some wealthy Taiwanese people, too, but it didn't matter, because the Chinese Nationalist government owned the whole of Taiwan.

Those low-ranking soldiers and veterans actually were very grateful that they could have their own places. Although the houses that they built with their own hands were very shabby, at least they had a place that they could call "home." Besides, those Chinese veterans were willing to take any job, since their pension was next to nothing. Some of them worked as janitors at schools. Some people did construction work. Some, like Uncle Huang, made steamed buns or bread to sell.

Uncle Huang's steamed buns were really good. Ciou-Tao and her family loved them very much. The first time that Uncle

Huang met Ciou-Tao was in the afternoon. He was on the way home after selling the steamed buns. He always left one bun for his lunch and dinner. That day, he gave the bun to Ciou-Lian and Ciou-Tao, and they shared the bun with their family. Even though everyone could only have one bite, they all loved it.

The big steamed bun is a traditional food in northern China. It became popular in Taiwan after people learned how good it is. To make this plain chewy bun requires the use of sourdough instead of yeast and good kneading, which is the reason that this steamed bun tastes excellent and is different from others.

Perhaps the steamed bun brought a good feeling to the Wang family. The next day, Ciou-Lian and Ciou-Tao's a-bu, Li-Jhu, gave them three sweet potatoes and told them to give the sweet potatoes to Uncle Huang if they saw him pass by.

That day, the two little girls weren't in the mood to play. They just sat by the door, looked, and waited. When they saw Uncle Huang, they stood up and started to sing and dance "Two Tigers." That was the most beautiful and unexpected sight to Uncle Huang. It had been too long. He could only hear the crying, screaming, wailing, and groaning. All he could see was blood and then more blood and death. Uncle Huang hadn't known that he could have a little piece of happiness like this again. Hence, he ran—ran to Ciou-Lian and Ciou-Tao, the way that he used to run home to his two daughters.

"Ciou-Lian! Ciou-Tao!" Uncle Huang was running and calling their names.

After finishing singing the song, Ciou-Lian and Ciou-Tao picked up the sweet potatoes to wave.

"For you, Uncle," Ciou-Tao said.

"My mother wants to give you these sweet potatoes to thank you for giving us a delicious steamed bun yesterday. My parents grew them. They are very yummy, like your bun." Although Ciou-Lian was only five years old, she spoke well.

"I am sure they are great. They look beautiful. My parents grow sweet potatoes too. I love them. I am going to have a nice dinner today. Please tell your parents that I appreciate it very much. By the way, I have one bun left again. Do you mind having it?"

"Not at all!" Ciou-Tao immediately responded with a big smile, and Ciou-Lian pinched her arm.

"Ouch! Why did you pinch me?"

"We can't take people's food all the time."

"Why not? Uncle said it's left over, and it's very yummy."

Uncle Huang enjoyed the two little girls' conversations very much, and he tried not to laugh too loudly.

"Well, Ciou-Lian, Ciou-Tao is right. No one wanted to buy this bun, so I decided to go home. Since you all like it, it will be my pleasure to share it with you."

Ciou-Tao looked at the bun that was in Ciou-Lian's hand and said, "I wish I could eat it right now."

"Dope! Say thank you to Uncle." If her hands were free, Ciou-Lian would definitely have pinched Ciou-Tao again.

After Uncle Huang received three sweet potatoes from the Wang family, he presumed that he was welcomed by this family. He was thrilled, so he decided to save three buns every day: one for himself and two for the Wang family. He wished he could give them more; in fact, if he could, he would have liked to give each person a bun. It was always a great frustration that he couldn't do what he desired to do, especially when they were just small things.

He wished he could go back to China, hug his wife and daughters, and work in the field with his parents again. These were simple joys that he hadn't seen as being special before, but now, they represented priceless happiness that no longer belonged to him. Politics had taken away his freedom. His right to go home to his family was denied. Besides, ironically, the reason that he had joined the army was because of extreme poverty. By going to the battlefield, he had wished to earn some money to let his family live better. However, after all these years, he was still dirt poor. He couldn't even make nine buns for the Wang family every day.

"Two buns a day, then."

Uncle Huang had learned to put down his wishes and accept the reality of life. He had to; otherwise, how could he live this bitter life?

Fu-Sheng and Li-Jhu knew how much the two buns were worth to a poor man. No, no. Even just one bun, it meant a great deal. They were also in poverty, so they knew. A poor man gave them two steamed buns a day. "He certainly loves our two young daughters very much," Fu-Sheng said to Li-Jhu.

Fu-Sheng and Li-Jhu also knew that Uncle Huang was a lonely man. Maybe he had his comrades' company, but he needed more than that. He needed a family and friends. Thus, they didn't care what their friends and neighbors might think or say. They made friends with Uncle Huang. It started in a sweet way. Uncle Huang gave them two steamed buns every day, and they gave him one or two kinds of vegetables every day, such as two sweet potatoes, one carrot, two eggplants, a small bunch of spinach, or a tomato. Uncle Huang's dinner table became lovely and finally had colors, and so did Uncle Huang's life.

Ciou-Lian and Ciou-Tao took Uncle Huang to the field to meet their parents about ten days later. Standing on the land made Uncle Huang miss his parents so much. They had taught him how to plant and be a good farmer. He could tell that Fu-Sheng and Li-Jhu were very good farmers too. However, "What's the use of being a good farmer? We never live a good life. We always suffer from poverty. People all need to eat, but who really cares about our misery?" Uncle Huang screamed in his heart as he asked for justice from God.

Uncle Huang, Fu-Sheng, and Li-Jhu were simple people who didn't know fancy talk; therefore, after greeting, exchanging names, and speaking a few words, they said goodbye.

Nevertheless, the three hearts were at ease. Uncle Huang liked the couple, and Fu-Sheng and Li-Jhu felt that Uncle Huang was a decent man. Later, Fu-Sheng and Li-Jhu felt so grateful because Uncle Huang not only taught Ciou-Lian and Ciou-Tao many things but also looked after their daughters.

Uncle Huang didn't have much education, but he was a very knowledgeable man. He went to school for only a few years, and then he had to stay at home to help his parents work in the field. However, those few years of learning at school had given Uncle Huang a skill for self-learning. During the daytime he worked hard in the field, and at nighttime he read and practiced writing new words that he learned. He was exhausted but happy. One of his good friends thought that he was crazy and said to him, "What's the benefit of reading and learning words for a farmer? Drink a few cups of liquor and go to sleep. That's what you really need!"

Uncle Huang didn't try to explain to his friend how he felt about learning words and reading. Although he thought that reading and learning words were necessary and he got so much pleasure from them, he also knew that everybody saw things differently. The impoverished farmer's top priority would be surviving. Reading and learning words were useless for surviving unless they intended to change the fate of their family. They would try very hard to hang in there for their son's education. Well, yes, it was the son, not the daughter.

Anyway, Uncle Huang was learning for his own interest. Therefore, it lasted as a lifelong habit. This habit helped him survive during wartime in China. He had his mind rest by reading. When he read, he could leave the world where he was for a better place. Besides, because he could read and write, he could write to his parents, wife, and daughters. Many of his comrades couldn't read and write, so they asked him to write letters to their families for them. Uncle Huang didn't mind at all, but he felt awful for them. There was no privacy to ask a person to write a letter for them. It was awkward, but they had no choice. Thus, they might not feel free to tell all the thoughts and feelings in their hearts. That was why Uncle Huang took it, writing for them, seriously. He saw it as his honor.

If Uncle Huang had a diploma, he certainly could teach in Taiwan like many other Chinese soldiers. In fact, Uncle Huang would be a better candidate because he spoke understandable Mandarin.

At the time, Taiwan was in the transition period from being a Japanese colony to becoming an occupied land of the Republic of China. Some Taiwanese people might be able to speak Mandarin, but most Taiwanese people on the island spoke Japanese, Taiwanese (Hokkien), Hakka, and aboriginal languages. After the government of the Republic of China was exiled to Taiwan in 1949, they soon made Mandarin the official language on the island. Since it was a policy, it made Taiwanese people start to learn Mandarin. Furthermore, the six-year compulsory education was practiced at the time. Once children went to elementary school, they immediately were asked to speak Mandarin only. Of course, those Taiwanese kids struggled at the beginning because their primary language wasn't Mandarin. Nonetheless, it didn't take a long time; very soon, they all could speak Mandarin. However, many Chinese people had strong accents when they spoke Mandarin. Therefore, most Taiwanese people had a hard time understanding them. As a matter of fact, around the 1950s and 1960s, students barely understood some teachers' Mandarin. Those teachers were from different provinces of China and spoke Mandarin with heavy accents. Actually, Generalissimo, Chiang Kai-shek, and his son Chiang Ching-kuo were great examples. If watching their speeches on the television without subtitles, most Taiwanese people couldn't understand them completely. Thus, not only were those poor Taiwanese students forced to learn a new language, but later, many of them had to figure out what some of their teachers were talking about after they finally could speak Mandarin.

Surprisingly, when Ciou-Tao's daughters, Mei-Ling and Mei-Ai, went to university in the 1990s, they complained to Ciou-Tao that they really had difficulties understanding one or two professors. Ciou-Tao laughed with complicated feelings. She couldn't believe that after all these years, something hadn't changed; unqualified teachers still had their spots. Maybe they were very knowledgeable, but what was the use if students couldn't understand them? How could they learn?

After Uncle Huang met Fu-Sheng and Li-Jhu, he spent more time with Ciou-Lian and Ciou-Tao. He taught them songs, drew with them, read to them, and told them stories. It was like a miniature private preschool with one teacher and two students, so Ciou-Lian and Ciou-Tao learned a lot, especially of the language, Mandarin.

The Wang family spoke Taiwanese (Hokkien) and some Japanese; therefore, their children had to learn Mandarin when they went to elementary school. Fu-Sheng and Li-Jhu did not worry whether they could pick up the language. "Leave it to school to worry." They thought that it was a teacher's job to teach students to speak the language, not them, since the government made the policy of asking them to speak Mandarin.

When Uncle Huang met Ciou-Lian and Ciou-Tao, Ciou-Jyu was in the first grade. Although her three elder sisters were in the sixth grade, fourth grade, and third grade, it didn't mean Ciou-Jyu had learned Mandarin from them before she went to elementary school. As a matter of fact, her sisters spoke only Taiwanese at home. Back then, most parents did not worry about their children's future success as parents today do. They didn't have the concept of helping their kids to lead the race right from the beginning. They wouldn't push their children to learn different things, such as foreign languages, math, ballet, music, and so on before they went to elementary school. It was an era in which most people were impoverished, and most young children needed to help their parents to do some work at home, particularly a farmer's family. Therefore, Ciou-Jyu's elder sisters had to finish their homework quickly after school, before the daylight was gone. Then, they hurried to clean the house, feed the pigs and chickens, and cook. As a result, Ciou-Jyu was struggling with learning Mandarin like most Taiwanese students in the first grade. She loved school. She was smart and eager to learn. Unfortunately, learning a new language and having a teacher with a little accent made it difficult to enjoy the learning, and she felt frustrated.

Wait a minute!

Obviously, Uncle Huang and the Wang family spoke two different languages, so then how did Ciou-Lian and Ciou-Tao communicate with Uncle Huang when they first met? Or how could their parents and Uncle Huang understand one another?

Well, Uncle Huang could speak Taiwanese. Although his Taiwanese was less than perfect, he could communicate with people very well. He started to learn Taiwanese after he came to Taiwan in 1948. When he met Ciou-Lian and Ciou-Tao, it was 1953. If one determined to learn a language, he or she would be able to learn something in five years. The reason for learning Taiwanese was simple. Uncle Huang wanted to know people; he fancied making friends with Taiwanese people. That was another reason that Fu-Sheng and Li-Jhu trusted and liked Uncle Huang: he could speak their language.

"How's school?"

"OK."

"What's the matter? It seems you don't like the school."

"I like school. I just..."

"Can't understand your teacher completely?"

"Uncle, how do you know?" Ciou-Jyu was amazed that Uncle Huang knew her trouble.

"Ciou-Lian and Ciou-Tao told me."

"Of course. I should've known that."

"Do you have housework to do now?"

"No."

"Do you want to read with me?"

"Uncle, aren't you going home?"

"Silly, I can go home anytime. Get your book out. Let's read."

Ciou-Jyu's eyes lit up. She had learned that Uncle Huang was a great teacher from Ciou-Lian and Ciou-Tao. In fact, her whole family knew. Ciou-Jyu envied Ciou-Lian and Ciou-Tao because they wouldn't struggle like her in the future.

Reading with Uncle Huang was fun to Ciou-Jyu. Firstly, Uncle Huang had great patience. He always let Ciou-Jyu try to spell and read herself. Once she pronounced correctly, he would say, "Great, wonderful, perfect," or "What a smart girl," which made Ciou-Jyu feel happy and gain confidence. Secondly, if Ciou-Jyu really couldn't figure out how to read some words, Uncle Huang would give her some hints or examples. He just wanted Ciou-Jyu to succeed by her own effort so she learned and remembered. Thus, the last thing that Uncle Huang would do was tell Ciou-Jyu the answer directly. In fact, a kid like Ciou-Jyu liked to learn in this way very much. She was smart and liked challenges. She hated to give up easily, and Uncle Huang knew it.

Getting Uncle Huang's assistance was a surprise and happiness that Ciou-Jyu didn't expect, and Uncle Huang got his own surprise and pleasure too. While Ciou-Jyu was reading with Uncle Huang, Ciou-Lian and Ciou-Tao went to the field to tell their parents. They were like two happy sparrows—they couldn't stop talking. Their parents were happy too. They deeply appreciated that Uncle Huang was very nice to their daughters.

Honestly, like many Taiwanese, Fu-Sheng and Li-Jhu didn't have good feelings for the Chinese people who came to

Taiwan after 1945, the Chinese soldiers in particular. Maybe most Taiwanese people wouldn't publicly talk about the February 28 Incident of 1947 because of fear, but it didn't mean that people forgot about it. How could one forget the massacre if she or he had witnessed the brutality?

The Chinese soldiers made nine people put their hands in the back and used a long iron wire to drill through each person's palms and ankles. Then the victims fell into the river together and drowned after the soldiers shot them with machine guns. The harbor was eventually covered with floating corpses.

Wu Hong-Ci (吳鴻麒, 1902–1947) was a judge who hated the corruption of the Chinese Nationalist government. He was particularly hard on the cases of corruption. His wife found his body and took him home. His coat, watch, and shoes were missing. He had wounds all over his body, and his testicles were cut off and put into his mouth.

Wang Tian-Deng (王添灯, 1901–1947) was a provincial councilor and a chairman of the newspaper who criticized the corruption of the Chinese Nationalist government officials. The Chinese soldiers poured gasoline on him and burned him alive. Then they dumped his body in the Tamsui River (淡水河).

The Chinese soldier used the gunstock to beat Siao Chao-Jin (蕭朝金, 1910–1947), a reverend, and forced him to kneel down, but he refused. He said, "I only kneel down to God, never to people." Then they shot him to death.

Ye Ciou-Mu (葉秋木, 1908–1947) was a city councilor and a chairperson of "the 228 Incident Settlement Committee" in Pingtung County. The Chinese soldiers cut off his nose, ears, and sex organ, and then they took him to parade through the streets. In the end, they shot him to death.

Huang Ma-Dian (黃媽典, 1893–1947) was a doctor who treated the poor free of charge. He was also one of the founders of the Chiayi Bus Company and the chairperson of the Automobile Corporation. After World War II, he became the president of the chamber of commerce in Tainan County. In 1946, he was elected to be the Tainan County councilor. He was accused of being the leader of insurgents in the 228 Incident. The soldiers put a sign on his back and tied him up. Then they chained him to a jeep. He ran and fell after the jeep. Eventually, he couldn't run anymore, so he gave in. The jeep dragged him to Chiayi Circle, and the soldiers executed him by shooting.

They tortured him all night to get the list of names of Taiwanese elites and students. He never gave in. His ribs were broken, and his fingers were swollen. After they put a sign on his back and tied his arms to his back, they took him to parade in the street. Before execution, the soldiers kicked him and forced him to kneel down. He refused. He shouted and yelled at the soldiers. The bullets flew through his nose and forehead. His blood and brains were everywhere, but he stood still with eyes that glowered for a while. Eventually, he fell on the ground, his eyes still wide open. He saved thousands of Taiwanese intellectuals with his life. His name was Tang De-Jhang (湯德章, 1907–1947), a lawyer who often defended people against Japanese people's bullying at a low fee or for free.

However, Fu-Sheng, Li-Jhu, and many Taiwanese also knew that not all the Chinese people were evil and brutal, so they tried to keep their minds open, thank goodness. That is always where the hope is born and grows.

Maybe the steamed buns brought the friendship to the door of their hearts, but mostly it was because of Uncle Huang's love and sincerity that knocked the doors of their hearts open. They saw a beautiful soul loved their daughters and made them laugh and feel happy. How much more did a person need to prove that he was a good man? In fact, if one looked into Uncle Huang's eyes, he or she would know how this decent man had suffered but still believed in love.

"Go ask Uncle to stay for dinner with us. Try your best to make him stay. Can you do that, girls?" Fu-Sheng said.

"Then go to tell your sister to make sweet potatoes congee and tomato scrambled eggs," Li-Jhu said.

Sweet potatoes congee and tomato scrambled eggs! A feast!

"Yeah!" Ciou-Lian and Ciou-Tao were too happy to speak. That was double happiness; Uncle Huang would dine with them, and they would feast.

After that, two little sparrows flew back; they interrupted Ciou-Jyu's reading.

"Uncle, my parents would like you to stay for dinner with us. Please stay," Ciou-Lian said, standing straight.

Uncle Huang thought that Ciou-Lian's eyes were so beautiful; they were like two stars in the black sky. Looking at her eyes, he smiled.

"Uncle, stay. We are going to have a feast: sweet potatoes congee and tomato scrambled eggs!" Ciou-Tao thought that a feast could make Uncle Huang stay.

"Dope, you are not supposed to tell what we are going to eat. What if Uncle didn't like the dishes and decided not to stay?"

"I don't think so. Whenever we gave Uncle sweet potatoes and tomatoes, he always smiled and said, 'Great.' And you tell me who wouldn't like eggs?" Ciou-Tao was very confident with her thinking.

"Dope, you simply just don't tell!" Ciou-Lian gave Ciou-Tao a look.

"OK, girls. I will stay. It is a great honor that your parents invite me. How can I not stay?"

"Stay! Stay! Stay! Uncle stays!" Ciou-Tao was jumping up and down, and Ciou-Lian went to the kitchen to tell her eldest sister, Ciou-Ying, what their parents said.

Uncle Huang looked at them and smiled. Ciou-Lian was gentle, thoughtful, and very smart. Ciou-Tao was outgoing, warm, caring, and full of imagination. The two sisters were very different, but they both were well-mannered kids. "Fu-Sheng and Li-Jhu have done a great job," Uncle Huang praised in his heart.

Then Uncle Huang continued helping Ciou-Jyu to read. After Ciou-Jyu was done with the reading, Uncle Huang said to her, "You know, besides reading, we can discuss any problem with your schoolwork, if you like." Ciou-Jyu nodded with a big smile. She loved her uncle Huang.

Frankly speaking, that dinner was an ordinary meal. Sweet potatoes congee, tomato scrambled eggs, and stir-fried sweet potato leaves. It wasn't just simple; in fact, it was very shabby. However, Uncle Huang enjoyed it very much. He felt like being home. His family was also very impoverished, so he fit in. Moreover, the atmosphere at the dinner table was great. It was warm and happy. The children were talking about their day, and Fu-Sheng and Li-Jhu just listened and smiled. Of course, the younger ones were more talkative. Probably the older ones were exhausted from working a lot.

After dinner, Fu-Sheng and Li-Jhu told Uncle Huang something that made him cry.

"Old Huang, dine with us every evening from now on." Uncle Huang's comrade also called him Old Huang, but it sounded different when Fu-Sheng and Li-Jhu said it. It was sweeter.

"No, I can't do that. Another pair of chopsticks, more burden to you."

"What burden? Do you hear yourself? How about two steamed buns a day for us? Isn't it a burden? Let's stop talking about burdens. Be friends and family."

"Family?" Uncle Huang had tears in his eyes. He couldn't believe what he had heard.

"Yes, family. You are the kids' beloved uncle. Of course, we are not your real family, not the same, but since they are not around, let us be your family," Fu-Sheng said.

"Old Huang, eating alone every day is too lonely." Li-Jhu looked into Uncle Huang's eyes.

"Think this way. You just bring your dinner to eat with us." Fu-Sheng tried to persuade Uncle Huang. "Of course, you won't be tied down. You stay whenever you like. Sometimes you might want to hang out with your comrades, and you just go."

"I know. I...I'm touched and don't know what to say. You two are the kindest people in the world. I don't know why I am so lucky."

"Old Huang, we are lucky, too, so just say *yes*," Li-Jhu said.

The invitation made Uncle Huang extremely thrilled. He was no longer a loner; he had a home and a family in Taiwan —he belonged to the lovely Wang family.

Oh, what a happy man!
The happy man started to sing.
He walked with a spring in his step.
He smiled more and looked cheerful.
Oh, who was the happy man?

Uncle Huang's comrades saw his change. Some of them

were happy for him, but some warned him to be careful.

"Taiwanese people dislike us. They don't see us as their own people. They won't truly trust you."

Uncle Huang thanked them for their concern, but he felt sad. The February 28 Incident had destroyed the trust between most Taiwanese and Chinese people. He deemed that the Chinese Nationalist government had to take the responsibility to heal the wound. They should sincerely apologize and do something to earn the Taiwanese people's trust. In addition, if the Chinese civilians could reach out first, it would be a great help. Otherwise, it would be hard for many Taiwanese and Chinese people to be friends, and there would be no chance that the two groups of people would unite as one nation.

For quite some time, Uncle Huang had been very sick and tired of politics. It was the politics that made his life miserable. They, the Nationalist Party and the Communist Party, both said to the Chinese people that they would build a better China and everyone would have a good life, but they lied. As a matter of fact, they forbade him and the rest of the Chinese people to pursue their own happiness. They couldn't live a simple and peaceful life with their families.

The acceptance from the Wang family made Uncle Huang realize how much he had lost. How little he actually wanted, but it was so hard to get. The day he left home to join the Chinese Nationalist troops, he thought that he would be home soon. Thus, he had not seriously said a decent goodbye to his parents, wife, and daughters. Uncle Huang regretted it deeply. Now, he didn't even know whether or not he and his comrades could go back to China to see their families in their lifetime.

The hell with politics!

Uncle Huang stayed to have dinner with the Wang family almost every day, and the Wang family loved Uncle Huang having dinner with them. They enjoyed listening to Uncle Huang's life stories at the dinner table. Those stories weren't all pleasant; in fact, some stories that were related to the war made everyone feel upset or cry. However, they still asked Uncle Huang to tell them stories all the time because Uncle Huang was their family. They loved him and wanted to know his life.

Of course, the dinnertime was so joyful, not just because Uncle Huang told stories. Everyone talked. The diversity of talk was like the flowers in the garden; they were different but all so pretty.

Since they were family and enjoyed one another's company, they naturally celebrated holidays and festivals together. Besides the aboriginal people, the Taiwanese and Chinese people shared a lot of culture but were not entirely the same. Therefore, the Wang family and Uncle Huang had a lot to share and talk about, which also meant it was tremendous fun for them.

Hundreds of years ago, in about the seventeenth century, many Chinese people who lived on the southeast coast of China tried to improve their lives and immigrated to Taiwan. People said that it was almost like a death challenge to cross the Taiwan Strait. Many of them didn't survive the journey. As a result, in the early times, almost no Chinese women came to Taiwan with those Chinese men. Only single young men, who had no responsibility to anyone but themselves, would be willing to take the risk to seek their fortune. Besides, at the time, the Qing dynasty forbade people to bring their families to travel with them. Thus, there is a famous Taiwanese expression, "There was only Chinese great-great-grandpapa, no Chinese great-great-grandmama" (有唐山公，無唐山媽), precisely telling the early immigration history of Taiwan.

People live in the culture that their ancestors created. They also reform the culture with new beliefs, customs, knowledge, and lifestyles. Since we all live in a certain culture, it is not difficult to understand why people would enjoy, appreciate, modify, or fight against their culture. When the early Chinese immigrants settled in Taiwan, they, too, brought their traditions and customs to Taiwan. Maybe the Taiwan Strait is not very wide, but it was wide enough for the Chinese immigrants to be isolated from China and develop a new culture that was based on the old one they had lived in. Take the language, for instance. The ancestors of the Taiwanese people who speak Taiwanese were from the south area of Fujian province (福建省), known as Minnan in China, and spoke the language called Hokkien or Minnan language. However, hundreds of years went by; the Taiwanese language is not the same Hokkien dialect anymore. The same situation happened to the Taiwanese people who speak Hakka. There is little similarity between Hakka and Cantonese now.

Uncle Huang was from the north of China; he and his family were like the other northern people in China, who loved to eat steamed buns and noodles. The Wang family was like any other Taiwanese family; they loved their rice. However, both Uncle Huang's family and the Wang family ate sweet potatoes most of the time due to the extreme poverty.

The big chewy steamed bun was a new food for the Wang family, but they loved it after they tried it. That was why they, particularly the children, were excited and happy to get more after the first time that Uncle Huang gave them a bun. On the other hand, sweet potatoes and rice congee were new but familiar to Uncle Huang. It reminded him of millet congee. He and his family loved millet congee very much. They also put sweet potatoes in the millet congee, sweet potatoes a lot more than millet, of course. The winter in northern China is mad, so a bowl of millet congee would always bring them to heaven. Ciou-Jyu, Ciou-Lian, and Ciou-Tao were very excited to hear this story, because Taiwan is in a subtropical weather zone. They had never seen snow before. They had no idea about how cold it could be in that kind of winter, so they asked Uncle Huang many funny questions: "Did you go out in winter? How many clothes did you wear? How did you drink water since everything was frozen? Where did pigs and chickens stay? Did you give them blankets?"

Well, you see, the cultural similarity and diversity brought a lot of pleasure to the Wang family and Uncle Huang. Gradually, they also became more thoughtful and open-minded in the process of learning from another culture.

The Lunar New Year is the most important holiday in both Taiwanese and Chinese societies. Most people would be eager to go home to celebrate with their families. Since Uncle Huang and his comrades couldn't do so, they usually got together to celebrate in one person's broken little house. Each of them chipped in some money to buy some food, such as roast chicken or beef. They also made big bread, steamed buns, noodles, and other good foods. They drank, ate, and talked—not too shabby. Not surprisingly, they all talked about the life that they missed in China. It was good to have someone who understood their loss and suffering to talk to, but it was very depressing to talk about it on Lunar New Year's Eve. When the Wang family invited Uncle Huang to have dinner together on Lunar New Year's Eve, Uncle Huang accepted the invitation without hesitation. Besides the fact that he liked to spend time with the Wang family, Uncle Huang wanted to escape from the gloomy dinner on Lunar New Year's Eve with his comrades.

On that first Lunar New Year they celebrated together, Uncle Huang gave the Wang family a big surprise. He made dumplings.

Eating dumplings on Lunar New Year's Eve is a tradition of many northern Chinese people. Of course, they eat dumplings on regular days, but they eat dumplings on Lunar New Year because of what dumplings symbolize. The shape of the dumpling looks like ancient Chinese money. Therefore, eating dumplings is wishing fortune would come to the family in the coming new year. Furthermore, the stuffing that they use represents some wishes, such as being healthy, wealthy, happy, or having peace. When people eat those dumplings, it means that those wishes will come true in the new year.

In addition, many families would make it more fun to eat dumplings together. They would put a coin in one of the dumplings that they made, and the person who got that dumpling to eat would have great luck for the new year. In brief, that is a fortunate dumpling. Some families actually would make several fortunate dumplings. They wish everyone in the family to start a new year with good luck.

When Uncle Huang made dumplings, he made ten fortunate dumplings even though he only made thirty dumplings. He wished everyone in the Wang family, including himself, could get a special dumpling. No doubt he told everyone about the fortunate dumplings before eating them. Surely, he wouldn't want anyone to break their teeth. Everyone was tremendously excited because it was another new food for them and looked delicious. Furthermore, they all fancied getting a special dumpling.

Honestly, the dumplings that Uncle Huang made weren't luxurious. The stuffing was mostly cabbage, some scallions, and very little ground pork. However, that was a poor man's best offer, the best gift that everyone in the Wang family had ever had at a Lunar New Year.

While everyone was crazy about the dumplings, Uncle Huang was interested in radish cake (蘿蔔糕). He hadn't had it before but had heard of it from a comrade. He took a piece of radish cake and dipped it into the sauce, a mix of chopped garlic, soy sauce, and sesame oil. It smelled really good with the sauce. They, the northern people in China, loved garlic. They ate it raw with everything, steamed buns, noodle soup, dumplings...anything!

He had a bite. "Well, it's my kind of food." Uncle Huang had a conclusion. Everyone in the Wang family was happy that he loved the radish cake, and Ciou-Jyu, Ciou-Lian, and Ciou-Tao couldn't wait to tell the symbolic meaning of eating radish cake.

"Uncle, do you know why we eat radish cake on Lunar New Year?" Ciou-Jyu asked.

"I know. I know. I know the answer." Ciou-Tao was like a student waiting for the teacher to pick her to answer the question.

"Of course you know." Ciou-Lian skipped the "dope." It is a tradition that people can't say any bad words on New Year's Eve and New Year holidays.

"To have good luck?" This was an intelligent guess. Perhaps the bitter living had left scars in their lives. Most people in Taiwanese and Chinese societies wished to have luck and loved to pursue fortune.

"Uncle, you are right, but do you know why eating radish cake can bring people luck?" Ciou-Jyu asked a further question.

"I have no idea!"

"I know. I know." Well, it was Ciou-Tao again.

This time, Ciou-Lian only gave her a look, but she wished she could pinch her. Again, people can't have any negative behaviors on such an important holiday.

"Uncle, you know the word 'radish' in Taiwanese, right? It sounds like the phrase, 'A good omen.' That's why we eat radish cake."

"Oh, that is brilliant and interesting! If I don't know the language, I'll never enjoy the idea."

That was what the Wang family and Uncle Huang did all the time, sharing their life experiences and their own traditions and customs, which brought them closer and closer.

Alas. Somehow, happy times are always too short. The happiness that Uncle Huang and the Wang family had together only lasted three years.

One day, after dinner, Fu-Sheng asked the children to leave the room because he and his wife had something essential to tell Uncle Huang.

"Old Huang, we are going to give away Ciou-Jyu, Ciou-Lian, and Ciou-Tao."

"Old Wang, no! You can't do that!"

"We have to. We have debts."

"Oh no."

"We have tried very hard to hang in there for years. Now, we have to do something."

"By giving your daughters away?" Uncle Huang immediately regretted what he said. "I am sorry, Old Wang. I had two sisters given away."

Uncle Huang remembered the day that his sisters were taken away; he cried terribly. He was eight years old. He didn't understand why his sisters were going to be some people's wives, since one sister was ten and another one was only seven years old.

"They're just children," little Uncle Huang had screamed.

"This is a custom. They won't get married until they grow up. They are *tong yang xi* [童養媳, shim-bu-a in Mandarin], the future daughters-in-law." Uncle Huang's father tried to make him understand.

Shortly afterwards, Uncle Huang learned that it wasn't a custom. It was a poor people's custom, and for girls only.

"Old Wang, is it really that bad? I have some money, very little, of course. I can give it to you. If it is still not enough, I can borrow some money from my comrades. I'm sure that we can figure out something. Please don't send our girls away." Uncle Huang saw Li-Jhu crying. Her tears dropped on the clothes that she was sewing. Suddenly, the needle jabbed into his heart.

"Actually, the debt is one thing. It's because they are not going to have a future if they stay with us. Look at their elder brother and sisters. They are going to be exactly like my wife and me, having a hard life without prospects. No matter how hard we work, the good life just doesn't belong to people like us."

"Sigh."

Uncle Huang now knew that Old Wang had thought the whole thing through. He just needed some support. After all, most people would have a guilty conscience when they gave away their daughters. They wouldn't go to jail for it, but they would imprison themselves in their minds.

However, what was the use of having emotional support here?

"After crying for two or three weeks and hearts aching for a few months, everyone would go back to their lives as if nothing happened. They might have several scars on the bottom of their hearts, but they'll keep on living. People won't talk or think about the disgrace that the most intelligent creatures in the world have to give up their own daughters to survive. The ones who take the price and suffer a great deal are those daughters, not the parents or sons." The anger rushed out of Uncle Huang's heart like steam. He had to try hard to keep these thoughts in his mind, because he couldn't hurt his good friends' feelings.

"Old Huang, my wife and I don't even want to take the money from the two wealthy families that are going to adopt Ciou-Jyu and Ciou-Lian. I don't want people to think that we are selling daughters to pay our debts. Li-Jhu and I seriously think about their future. We are awful parents. We can't give them a good life, so let others do it for us."

"Oh God. How is it possible that they would love them as their own daughters?" Uncle Huang still talked in his mind, but he couldn't control himself to be calm anymore. He cried.

Li-Jhu cried even harder. In the Taiwanese language, people refer to their children as parents' hearts and livers. If a mother cried her heart out first, would it be easier to let her heart go?

At last, Uncle Huang stopped crying, and he told Fu-Sheng what he knew. "I know the two families. Indeed, they are very wealthy. I have seen the boys from the two families once or twice. They are well-educated young men, no arrogant temperament. But I am a bit worried about the family that is going to adopt Ciou-Jyu. People say that the mother is an arrogant and mean person."

"I heard about that, too, but they are a well-respected family in town. They won't do stupid things, I suppose." Fu-Sheng also worried, but he tried to be positive.

"Maybe it's just a rumor." Uncle Huang didn't believe the words that came out of his mouth. However, he also wanted to be hopeful with Old Wang. After all, it was about their sweet Ciou-Jyu's future.

"Old Huang, I think that Ciou-Jyu and Ciou-Lian should be able to continue their education after they graduate from elementary school. In fact, they might have a chance to go to senior high school too. Even just finishing junior high school, it's still better than staying with us."

"No, it's not true! It's better to stay with their family!" Uncle Huang shouted in his heart.

"How about Ciou-Tao?"

"Sigh. I don't know if Li-Jhu and I have made a good decision."

"How so?"

"The Lin family's financial situation is not bad like us, but it is not very good either. Mr. Lin is a carpenter, a simple and amiable man. He and his wife have four little boys. His wife is sick in bed…"

"No, Old Wang! No!" Uncle Huang interrupted impatiently. "She will surely suffer, Old Wang. She is only seven years old, too young to take care of others. Unquestionably, she's not going to have a better life like Ciou-Jyu and Ciou-Lian. Let me take her." Uncle Huang had a sudden daze for a few seconds after he said, "Let me take her."

"Old Huang, in our minds, you are the best candidate in the whole world to be all my daughters' father. Without a second thought, I would let you take Ciou-Tao to be your daughter, but…"

"But I am too poor and have no future."

"No! It's not that! You might go back to China next year or a year after. Who knows? Then what should you do? Take her with you to go back to China? Besides, when the day comes, you will have your own family to take care of, so you need to save money to prepare for it right now.

"Old Huang, I wouldn't mind my daughter eating only steamed buns with you every day because I know that she would be happy under your care. Moreover, she would be educated like you. Do you know how many times Li-Jhu and I talked about you while we were working in the field? We thank God for sending you to us. You have spent time playing and teaching our daughters, which is our duty but which we are unable to perform. We are very grateful. Many times, you said that we give you a home and family and you are thankful. As a matter of fact, it's our honor to have your friendship. It's we who couldn't wait to pull you into our family. That's why we must tell you our pathetic decision before they are given away. And we need your help."

"Help?" Uncle Huang did not understand.

"Would you talk to them for us? Of course, we will tell them first, but they won't understand and will resist. I am not good at talking to children, and Li-Jhu, who carried them for nine months, who brought them into this world, has no strength to tell the reason why we have to send them away... oh, my good Lord! Listen to me! What a loser! I can't even convince myself!" Fu-Sheng began to weep.

Uncle Huang said to himself, "How can we convince the girls that they are given away because we love them? Instantly, the word 'abandon' will appear in their minds. The rejection, confusion, resistance, and anger will come right after. Telling them to accept it? Saying that we really love them very much? Asking them to be understanding? Or begging them to forgive us?"

"I'll talk to them," Uncle Huang said to Fu-Sheng.

The painful conversation ended here, but Uncle Huang's mind couldn't rest while he was on the way home. "We poor people shouldn't have so many children. Having babies and being able to feed them are two different things. Except for a fool, everyone knows it. Those stupid ideas—only sons can keep the family name, daughters are no longer family members after getting married—create sexual inequality and countless tragedies. Why do people still stubbornly believe those hateful ideas? Why?"

That night, Uncle Huang drank and made himself horribly drunk. The next morning, with a hangover, he bitterly made steamed buns. He wanted to make three buns, just for Ciou-Jyu, Ciou-Lian, and Ciou-Tao. No, no. He wanted to make steamed pork buns, a super big pork bun, a lot of meat in there, for his little girls. Uncle Huang wished he could give them many things, the beautiful things. Perhaps a home was what he wanted to give them the most, but he couldn't. It was like he couldn't free his wife and two daughters from hunger; it was the same. "I am a useless man." Uncle Huang was angry and depressed.

Five days later, the ugly moment powerfully came.

After Fu-Sheng and Li-Jhu told Ciou-Jyu, Ciou-Lian, and Ciou-Tao about the adoption, Ciou-Jyu and Ciou-Lian both quietly cried. Ciou-Tao, oh, Ciou-Tao, she was mad and screamed.

"Why? Why? Why?" That was all she said.

Of course, their parents had no explanation for them. Fu-Sheng looked into the distance with no focus. Li-Jhu looked at them and cried. Uncle Huang couldn't talk to them in this situation, so he decided to take them out.

"Let's go to the pond."

Crying and walking. Walking and crying. All of them. All the way to the pond.

The pond was the three girls' favorite place. It was like a mini paradise. There were a lot of things that they could see, explore, and play. Ciou-Lian and Ciou-Tao always asked Ciou-Jyu to take them to the pond after she finished whatever work that she needed to do. Therefore, mostly it was between four and five o'clock in the afternoon, before dinnertime.

It was a naturally beautiful farm pond. There were tadpoles, shrimps, frogs, fish, field snails, crabs, dragonflies, damselflies, and many kinds of insects living in the water or surrounding area. Consequently, kids in the neighborhood would come to catch fish, frogs, or field snails to add one more dish to their dinner tables. Generally, Ciou-Jyu, Ciou-Lian, and Ciou-Tao came here for fun. They would look for grasshoppers, observe ants' movement, or make grass rings and wreaths. They never got bored. They complained only that they couldn't stay as long as they wished.

Additionally, farmers' ducks would come to the pond, too, which brought a lot of fun for the three girls. Ciou-Jyu, Ciou-Lian, and Ciou-Tao liked to see ducks swimming in the pond very much. Perhaps it started from Ciou-Tao, who laughed about the ducks' movements. "Look! They pretend they are not busy. They lie. Look at their feet, paddling like they got to run. They are phony ducks." These words then stuck in their heads, and they would laugh when they saw ducks swimming. Later, Ciou-Tao even imitated the ducks' movements, which cracked Ciou-Jyu and Ciou-Lian up. Who knew this amusement would later become an important memory to make them smile when they were apart living their own lives?

"Girls, you are probably thinking about why your parents want to send you away and why you."

After they arrived at the pond, they found a spot that was under shade to sit down. With Uncle Huang, Ciou-Lian, who was a quiet kid, would become talkative, but that afternoon, even chatty Ciou-Tao didn't want to talk.

"First, please don't think that your parents don't love you anymore. They do love you; in fact, they do this because of love."

"It doesn't make any sense." Surprisingly, it was Ciou-Lian speaking.

"Uncle, you have two daughters. Would you give them to other families?" Ciou-Jyu asked.

"Alas. Honestly, I wouldn't. However, the situations are different. Your parents have seven children."

"Then why don't they send my elder brother and sisters away?" Ciou-Tao was still very mad.

"You are younger and need more care. Besides, your parents hope you all can go to junior high school and senior high school after you finish elementary school, but it will be impossible if you stay with them."

"We don't need more education after we graduate from elementary school. We want to stay at home and work with them." Ciou-Jyu still had tears in her eyes.

"That's right! We don't need to go to school. We can learn with Uncle. As a matter of fact, Uncle is a lot better than our teachers. You can teach us a little something every day." Time went by fast. Ciou-Tao had been a first-grade student for two months.

"I agree. Who needs a teacher to learn?" Ciou-Lian had gotten this idea from her role model, Uncle Huang.

"Girls, it's more complicated than that. Your parents feel upset that they can't feed you well and still have debts. They can't give you anything but suffering. They have found families that can give you a good life."

"But we won't be their daughters anymore." Uncle Huang had found out a long time ago that Ciou-Lian was very sharp.

"She's an excellent thinker. Hopefully, the family appreciates her qualities." Uncle Huang was indeed worried that Ciou-Lian wouldn't be liked because of her intelligence.

"Ciou-Lian, you are still your parents' daughters. Think this way. You all, including your elder sisters, will eventually get married and leave home. You only leave earlier."

"I stay. I will not get married ever. I don't like boys." Because of her new experience at school, Ciou-Tao had come to a conclusion. She looked certain and sounded determined, which made Ciou-Jyu, Ciou-Lian, and Uncle Huang laugh.

The laughter was powerful. It pushed some of the clouds away, and then the heat burned them.

"Girls, let's get Popsicles. We need to cool down your cute little red faces." However, no one got excited like they used to.

"Come on. I know you still have something to say. Let's get some Popsicles first. What do you think?"

"OK." Even though Ciou-Tao was upset, she wouldn't reject a Popsicle.

"Not OK, dope. You forgot what A-bu said? We can't ask Uncle to buy candies and stuff."

"Oh God. Ciou-Tao is going to miss Ciou-Lian's lectures badly." Uncle Huang spoke in his heart.

"They are not going to be our parents anymore. I won't listen to them or follow any rules."

"Ciou-Tao, take your words back." Ciou-Jyu wouldn't allow her to disrespect their parents.

"Ciou-Tao, you don't mean it, right? You feel angry and hurt, so you resist, right?"

Ciou-Tao nodded with tears, and Uncle Huang held her tightly. "Oh, my little peach blossom is going to be all on her own." There was an enormous pain in Uncle Huang's gut.

"Girls, since we are not happy, we should do something to make us happy. Thus, we will remember this afternoon as the happiest time ever. What do you think?"

"I agree." Ten-year-old Ciou-Jyu understood Uncle Huang's thinking.

"I want a Popsicle."

"Yeah, you surely need one for your puffy eyes." Would Ciou-Lian miss this kind of conversation with Ciou-Tao?

Yes, she did miss it very much later. Why wouldn't she? In her adoptive family, she had to be a lady and only had three elder brothers. Hence, she never had a chance to talk in that way again. However, she wouldn't want to talk to anyone in that fashion either. After all, that was an elder sister's love that only her dearest younger silly sister, Ciou-Tao, was entitled to.

"Uncle, how come you never try a pineapple-flavored Popsicle?" After Ciou-Tao got her favorite pineapple-flavored Popsicle, she seemed to forget the adoption subject.

"I am afraid of pineapple."

"Really?" The three girls couldn't believe what they heard.

"Why?" Ciou-Tao was very curious.

"In the war, one time, after we didn't have food to eat for days, we got a lot of canned pineapple. We were extremely thrilled even though it was fruit, not real food. I have to say that the canned pineapple tasted heavenly good, but I started to get sick when I was eating the third can. Perhaps the canned pineapple wasn't agreeable to an empty stomach. I wasn't the only one, though. Several of my comrades got sick too."

"Poor uncle and your friends." Ciou-Jyu was a compassionate person.

"So, Uncle, you are not going to eat pineapple for the rest of your life?" Ciou-Tao just finished her Popsicle, and she was talking and licking her lips.

"Well, probably." Uncle Huang also finished his Popsicle. It was a dried-plum flavor, sweet and sour, and many Taiwanese people loved it.

"What a pity! I love, love, love my pineapple."

"Ciou-Tao, I know you *love* your pineapple. How about this: if one day I try a piece of fresh pineapple, I'll go to tell you."

"Really? Uncle, you will come to tell me even though I am in the new home?"

"Yes, I will. I promise."

"Yeah!" Ciou-Tao jumped to Uncle Huang and clung to him.

"Uncle, do you know if my parents will come to visit us? Or can we go home visiting them once in a while?"

"Ciou-Lian, I can't answer for your parents. In my personal experience, my two sisters were sent away, and I have never seen them again. China is enormous, and they were sent to another town. It was impossible to visit or bump into each other on the street..."

"Or they were prohibited from seeing your family?" Ciou-Jyu had heard of shim-bu-a and understood the reality more than her younger sisters.

Uncle Huang tried very hard to avoid hurting them more, but he didn't want to lie either. "Yes. Some adoptive families would forbid their adoptive daughters to visit their original families and wouldn't want their parents to visit them either."

"So I was right. We are not going to be our parents' children anymore. I am not going to apologize this time." Ciou-Tao said this while looking at Ciou-Jyu.

"We are abandoned." Ciou-Lian concluded. Her voice was low but powerful. Uncle Huang saw the rage in her eyes.

The eyes that he loved were brighter because of the raging fire.

Ciou-Jyu leaned over to hold Ciou-Lian, and then they cried their hearts out.

"Sis, I won't be able to see you anymore." Ciou-Tao joined the crying.

"I am going to lose my family again," Uncle Huang said to himself.

One week after that afternoon, the day came.

At first, each adoptive family was going to send a person to pick up Ciou-Jyu, Ciou-Lian, and Ciou-Tao. However, Uncle Huang asked Fu-Sheng to let him take the girls to their new homes. He wished to walk with and talk to the girls one more time. Fu-Sheng immediately agreed because he knew that Uncle Huang loved his daughters and always could help them with problems. They trusted him, listened to his opinions, and loved him dearly. Since he had no guts to take them to their new homes, why not let their beloved uncle do the job?

Uncle Huang planned to take the three girls to leave home together and send them to their new homes one by one. He thought that this way might be better for them. There might be less crying and fear if they were leaving together. More importantly, they would have a little bit more time to be sisters.

Ciou-Jyu, Ciou-Lian, and Ciou-Tao had been weeping every day for the last week, but they did not cry when they said farewell to their family. Perhaps they realized that there was no chance for a miracle and stopped hoping.

They looked pale and forlorn. Li-Jhu held them together with tears and told them to behave in their new homes. The three sisters just nodded.

Then they started their journey. They looked back after they walked a few steps. Everyone was crying. A few seconds later, they turned back and kept on walking.

"We will go to Ciou-Tao's new home first," Uncle Huang

said weakly.

"Why me first?"

"Because I want your sisters to know where you will live so they can check on you if they have a chance in the future."

"I want to know where they will live, too, so I can go to see them if I have a chance."

"Listen, Ciou-Tao. Your adoptive parents are nice people. I don't think that they would refuse to let your sisters visit you. However, your sisters' adoptive families are different. They have a lot of rules for everyone in the families, including servants. It wouldn't be a good idea if you, even me or your parents, go to visit them. We might give your sisters some trouble."

"Uncle, you mean my sisters' new parents are not nice people?"

"They are nice people, but every family is different. It's like you and your sisters are unique; you like and dislike different things. We, outside people, wouldn't know the rules in each family. Moreover, your sisters are adopted by wealthy families, so there are more rules to follow. We want them to have no trouble in their new families, right? Thus, we don't make problems for them."

"So I can only wait for them to come to me."

"That's right. Besides, did your parents tell you that your adoptive mother is very sick?"

"They did. Will she die?"

"Ciou-Tao, you can't say something like that!" Ciou-Lian was very worried about her "dope."

"It's OK, Ciou-Lian. Ciou-Tao is just concerned. Ciou-Tao, honestly, I don't know how ill your adoptive mother is, but she will need your assistance. It might help her get well. Can you do that, Ciou-Tao?"

Ciou-Tao nodded and said, "How come I don't get a wealthy family and servants?"

"Because you like to be free, don't you?"

"Yeah, I don't like to be asked to behave by many rules. Sis, you both are in trouble now."

Ciou-Jyu laughed, of course, with a little bitterness.

"Dope, we won't get trouble if we don't break the rules. Don't worry about us. It's you who need to learn to behave and talk properly so you won't get disciplined."

"I won't make trouble. I have promised A-bu."

"Good, good. You are my champion girls. I know I can always be proud of you." Uncle Huang was glad to see that the three girls' strength was mightier than he had thought.

Well, the first stop, the Lin family, was right in front of them. Wang Ciou-Tao would be Lin Ciou-Tao from today.

Mr. Lin, Ming-Cheng, was waiting by the door when they arrived.

"That's a good sign and good start." Uncle Huang was glad to see it.

Ming-Cheng shook Uncle Huang's hand and thanked him. He asked all of them to come into the house and have a drink of water. They went in but only stayed a few minutes. There were two more stops to go.

Before they left, surprisingly, Ming-Cheng told Uncle Huang to come to visit Ciou-Tao once in a while. "She just has another family. Why can't she have family visit?"

Uncle Huang was touched by Ming-Cheng's warm thoughts. He knew that Ciou-Tao wouldn't have a good material life, but she would be happy and loved in the Lin family. That was plenty.

Ciou-Jyu and Ciou-Lian were excited. They could tell that their little sister would be treated well, so they felt relieved. Furthermore, they could come to visit Ciou-Tao if they were available. Hence, they said farewell but did not cry.

"Now, we are going to Ciou-Lian's new home. It's about twenty minutes' distance. Are you all right, my girls?"

"Uncle, Ciou-Tao is young and naughty. She also talks too much sometimes. I was worried that her new parents wouldn't like her, but now, I feel relieved because Ciou-Tao's adoptive father is nice."

"Ciou-Jyu, I understand what you are saying totally, but I wish Ciou-Tao could always be herself. She is an honest person who has a good heart. She might say something that could make people mad, but the words would all truly be from her heart. Don't worry. She will learn how to express her opinions in a better way bit by bit. Uncle has confidence in her."

"I hope so. I don't want her to be punished." Ciou-Lian looked concerned.

"Ciou-Lian, how about you? Are you worried that you might be punished in the new family?"

"There are a lot of rules at school, too, but I have never gotten any punishment yet. I am more afraid that they won't like me as Uncle does."

"Oh, it won't happen, Ciou-Lian. You are a thoughtful girl. You think before you speak and act. Who wouldn't like a smart and considerate girl? Give people some time to get to know about you. Be patient."

"OK, Uncle."

Uncle Huang stopped walking and gave Ciou-Lian a hug. He had pain in his gut again. "Who wouldn't want to be liked and loved? My dear God, I am begging you to let Ciou-Lian's wish come true, to be liked and loved." Uncle Huang prayed in his heart.

Then he said, "Ciou-Lian, I always believe that you can accomplish anything if you set your mind to do it. But I hope you can learn not to be too hard on yourself."

That was a blessing, to have Uncle Huang to take Ciou-Jyu, Ciou-Lian, and Ciou-Tao to their new families. In tough times, people all need strength to get through the hardship, and the young ones need some encouragement to assure their mind and build their confidence. Who could do a better job than Uncle Huang in this sad situation?

When they arrived at Ciou-Lian's new home, she seemed

to relax more. A friendly old man was waiting for them. Later, the old man and Ciou-Lian became very close. He was like Ciou-Lian's grandpapa. She could tell him anything in her mind, and he could always comfort her. Ciou-Lian called him "Beard Man," as everyone did.

The Beard Man took them to see the lady of the house, Ciou-Lian's adoptive mother, the future mother-in-law. She was an elegant lady; she was also very friendly. Once she learned who Ciou-Lian was, she walked to her and held Ciou-Lian's hands and called her name. Then, she told Uncle Huang, Ciou-Jyu, and Ciou-Lian to sit down and have a cup of tea.

"My Lord, I thank you." Uncle Huang was relieved. He was pretty sure that Ciou-Lian's adoptive mother wasn't acting to be nice.

Ten minutes passed.

"Thanks for the tea, madam. I am sorry that we can't stay any longer."

"What a pity. Please bring those desserts with you." Immediately, a servant made a small parcel for them.

"Thank you, madam. You are very kind."

Before they left, Uncle Huang looked into Ciou-Lian's eyes and nodded.

When they walked out of the house, Ciou-Jyu cried.

"Uncle, we all are alone now."

"Oh, Ciou-Jyu. Cry it all out. You are entitled. You have been so strong to be a good example to your sisters." Uncle Huang held her tightly and dropped his tears on Ciou-Jyu's hair.

Ciou-Jyu had beautiful shiny hair. It was like black silk. She usually made it into two braids because she had a lot of work to do. Uncle Huang wished she could put her hair down in the future. She could sit down and read, not have a lot of work to do.

"Ciou-Jyu, do you have a fear for your new life?"

"Yes, I do, Uncle. I am also afraid that the people in my new family won't like me."

"You have several good friends at school, and you have been elected to be a model student every year. You are liked and recognized for your good qualities. You should be confident."

"But, Uncle, it's different. I'll be a shim-bu-a in the family. You know very well that most people do not treat their shim-bu-a well. In fact, they see shim-bu-a as second-class people."

"What you said is true, but it's not the whole truth. We just met Ciou-Lian's adoptive mother, and she is a nice lady. She won't be the only good adoptive mother in the world. There are always good and bad people around us. Ciou-Lian is fortunate, and we are happy for her. Be honest. I did try to get some information about your adoptive parents and brothers. People said that the three young men, your adoptive brothers, are very nice. Their father is a quiet man, and the mother is a critical person. I think that you should be fine with your adoptive brothers and their father. Just be more alert and respectful to your adoptive mother. Sometimes, people are critical because they have higher standards and like to pursue perfection."

"Uncle, thanks for looking after us. I may not have an easy life, but I am prepared for it now. I will always keep your words in my mind to make you proud. In my heart, you are my father too."

"Oh, my beautiful little chrysanthemum. I have seen you girls as my daughters. How I wish I were a wealthy man so that I could take you all home. All I have are words. What's the use? I can't help your parents to keep you all."

"Uncle, I love your words. They are so precious and powerful, which helps my sisters and me all the time."

"So take this to your heart. You are an outstanding person, and you can conquer all the challenges."

Then the last stop was right in front of them, and they saw three young men standing there with beautiful smiles.

"Hi, we are your new brothers. My name is Wen-De. He is

Wen-Zhi, and this is Wen-Hua."

"Hi, my name is Ciou-Jyu, and he is Mr. Huang, my uncle."

"Nice to meet you, Uncle Huang and Ciou-Jyu." The three brothers spoke like they were singing.

"My girl has three guardian angels. My Lord, I am very grateful." That was a bright golden afternoon, and Uncle Huang smiled like the sun.

After that day, taking three girls to their new families, Uncle Huang got ill and couldn't get out of bed for days. He was like an empty man. His heart and liver were gone, and even his soul was torn apart. He had lost his family again, and this time, he sent them away himself. He did not have a family in Taiwan anymore.

"Why is it so hard to keep your family with you?" On the way home from taking Ciou-Jyu, Ciou-Lian, and Ciou-Tao to their new families, Uncle Huang kept repeating that thought in his mind.

Uncle Huang came to Taiwan in 1948, and he couldn't write any letters to his family who were in China after the Chiang Kai-shek regime, the Chinese Nationalist government, was exiled to Taiwan in 1949. Of course, it wasn't because he didn't want to write to them. The Chinese Nationalist government forbade him, his comrades, or anyone in Taiwan to send letters to China. In fact, according to martial law, sending letters to China was a crime—treason. Many Chinese people went to jail or got the death penalty for sending letters to their families in China. However, a lot of Chinese people still took a risk to try. They sent the letters that they wrote to their families to their friends who lived in or were exiled to Hong Kong, the United States, or Canada. When their friends received the letters, they sent the letters to their families in China for them.

It was exciting for people to receive messages from their families so they knew that their beloved ones hadn't died in the war. However, the people in China also got severe punishment when the Chinese Communist Party discovered that they had contact with their families who escaped to Taiwan. How cruel was that? Frankly, the Chinese Nationalist Party and the Chinese Communist Party were the same, treating the Chinese people in the same heartless way.

Uncle Huang was well aware of the danger, so he didn't try to contact his family in China. However, the Chinese Communist Party still harshly punished many Chinese people only because they had family members who escaped to Taiwan. In fact, if their family members were Chinese Nationalist soldiers, the Chinese Communist Party assuredly made those people prefer death to life. Therefore, Uncle Huang not only missed his family but also worried very much about their safety.

It was true that Uncle Huang's life became brighter and had color after he found a family in Taiwan. This new and unexpected joy comforted his soul and eased some of his pain, but he suffered more when the happiness was gone. It was like a double loss, so he sank into deep despair. He couldn't stop thinking about what was wrong with this world.

"Why aren't we allowed to be with our families?"

"Why is it so hard to keep my family with me?"

The questions beat him to be sick.

That evening, Uncle Huang was supposed to tell Fu-Sheng and Li-Jhu how things went after he sent Ciou-Jyu, Ciou-Lian, and Ciou-Tao to their adoptive families. However, Uncle Huang never showed up. Two days later, there was still no sign of him, so Fu-Sheng decided to visit Uncle Huang.

"Old Huang, are you home?" In front of a broken little house, Fu-Sheng knocked on the door. After he called Uncle Huang several times, a neighbor of Uncle Huang came out of the house and told Fu-Sheng that Uncle Huang was sick. While that comrade of Uncle Huang was talking to Fu-Sheng, they heard a movement from inside the house.

"Old Huang, it's your friend, Old Wang." That comrade had a loud voice and a heavy accent.

"Coming."

From hearing the voice, Fu-Sheng could tell that Uncle Huang was very weak, but Fu-Sheng was shocked when Uncle Huang opened the door. After only three days, Uncle Huang looked a lot thinner. He had been thin, but now he looked like a stick.

"Old Huang, what happened? Are you OK?"

"Come in, Old Wang. You sit, but I have to lie down."

"Of course. Want me to help you?"

"I am all right. Sit, sit. Don't worry about me."

"Don't worry about you? We haven't seen you for three days. We're worried to death. See, you have been sick, and we didn't even know. How awful!"

Even just lying down took Uncle Huang quite some effort.

"I am sorry. I promised that I would go to tell you and Li-Jhu how things went after I sent our girls to their new homes, but I was too upset to remember that you and Li-Jhu were waiting for me, and I just came home."

Fu-Sheng sighed; he felt so awful. He shouldn't have agreed to let Uncle Huang take Ciou-Jyu, Ciou-Lian, and Ciou-Tao to their new homes.

"Old Wang, I thought I would be fine, but it was so hard to walk away from them one by one. Even though I have learned that some people in their new families would take good care of them, I can't help being sad. You know that I see them as my own daughters. I feel that I have lost everything again."

"Old Huang, you still have us. You are our family. Come home with me. Let us take care of you. You are too sick to be alone."

"Old Wang, everyone in your family is busy. Why add a

burden to you? My comrades will check on me. We look after one another.

"Three years ago, I was vastly happy and grateful that you and Li-Jhu accepted me and allowed me to be part of your family. Of course, without Ciou-Jyu, Ciou-Lian, and Ciou-Tao, we are still family, but it's not the same anymore. I feel that I got knocked down by a big punch. Old Wang, I am a useless and weak man."

"Old Huang, I am the useless and weak man, not you. I can't keep my whole family together. I didn't even have the guts to take Ciou-Jyu, Ciou-Lian, and Ciou-Tao to their adoptive families. You did the job for me. You are brave."

"Alas. Old Wang, I have been hanging in there to wait for the end of the war so I could go back to my family in China. But now, I have lost strength and belief. Perhaps, that afternoon, taking our three girls to their new homes reminded me that we are powerless civilians. I don't think that I can see my family again."

"Old Huang, don't say that. Be hopeful. It might take some years, but the day will come. You will see your family again. Besides, don't tell anyone what you just said to me, including your comrades. You might get into trouble. Your Generalissimo, Chiang Kai-shek, and his government don't like to hear this."

"I know, Old Wang. I know. I have heard and seen as you have."

"So go home with me. Did you see yourself? You need to be taken care of."

"Old Wang, I will be fine. Thanks for your offer. I am touched. But I even have difficulty lying down. How can I walk to your home? Besides, I am not completely alone. Maybe my comrades and I are alone without our own families, but we're one another's family. The one you just met, Cannon Jhang [張大砲], has cooked for me these several days. Thus, I will be fine here. I will go to visit you and Li-Jhu when I get better. It won't take long. In a few more days, I will recover."

"Well, since you have someone to take care of you, I should let you be."

"Thanks, Old Wang."

"Goodbye, Old Huang. I'll see you soon."

"See you."

Two weeks later, finally, Uncle Huang had a full recovery. He went to visit Fu-Sheng and Li-Jhu and brought them a piece of news.

"I am leaving next month."

"What? What does that mean?" Fu-Sheng was shocked.

"Why? Where are you going?" Li-Jhu couldn't believe that Uncle Huang was leaving.

"I am going to join the Veterans' Engineering Corp for the Central Cross-Island Highway construction [修築中橫]."

"No, Old Huang, don't go. It's very dangerous." Fu-Sheng couldn't agree with Uncle Huang's decision.

"I need a change of scenery."

The three of them fell into silence. Fu-Sheng and Li-Jhu knew the reason very well.

Taiwan is a mountainous island. The Central Mountain Range is the principal range of mountains in Taiwan. It runs from the north to the south, which divides Taiwan into the west and east. Although it is called the "Central" Mountain Range, it is located a lot more to the east of the island. Therefore, even with a few more mountains in the west, the western side is still wider and is mostly plains. The eastern side, where most of the population live, is called Huadong Valley (花東縱谷), which is in between the Central Mountain Range and Haian Range (海岸山脈), which parallel the east coast. Now, try to picture it: How difficult is it for people to travel from one side to another side? It would take a long time. Thus, the need for a road that connects the east and the west was naturally revealed. However, imagine it, how dangerous it could be to build the Central Cross-Island Highway through those mountains?

"Old Huang, the pain will go away eventually. Please give yourself some time." Fu-Sheng tried to persuade Uncle Huang.

"Old Wang, some pain will never go away. People have to get paralyzed with their feelings and pretend that they are healed because the problems can't be solved and the pain is huge. I have been painfully hanging in there for eight years. Now, somehow, I just don't know how to ignore the feelings of massive sadness and helplessness. Thus, I have to make a change in my life."

"By putting your life in danger?" Fu-Sheng was very emotional. How he wished he could help Uncle Huang to ease his pain. If changing scenery could help, he wouldn't mind losing his dear friend's company. However, Uncle Huang was going to work in a highly dangerous environment, so Fu-Sheng unquestionably disapproved of it.

"Old Huang, don't you want to go back to China to your family? You need to be safe and sound for them because they are waiting for you." Li-Jhu thought that Uncle Huang would change his mind for his beloved family.

"How do I know if they are still alive? I was a soldier of the Chinese Nationalist Army. The Chinese Communist Party would definitely punish them. I might have lost them already." Uncle Huang had become very negative after being sick for more than two weeks.

"If that really happened, you would still have us. We are your family and care about you. Once you told us that you love this town. You can't leave the town that you love. Stay."

"Old Wang, I do love everything here, including those

mountains. Now, I am going to climb those mountains. How exciting! Besides, precisely speaking, I am not leaving our town. I'm just going to another part of our town for a while."

"Alas. Old Huang, obviously, you have made up your mind." Li-Jhu felt that the frustration and sadness had taken Uncle Huang away from them.

"Then be very careful." Fu-Sheng knew that no one could change Uncle Huang's mind at this moment.

The project of the Central Cross-Island Highway construction started on July 7, 1956. Mainly, the government employed Chinese veterans to be road builders. However, they needed a larger workforce, so the military and regular criminals, civilians, unemployed young men, and the private-sector employees joined in the construction later.

Actually, the need for a road to connect the west and east of Taiwan was recognized in the Japanese colonial period (1895–1945). However, mostly, it was a political need.

In 1895, the Qing Empire (大清帝國, 1636–1912), which was in the land of modern China, lost the Sino-Japanese War (甲午戰爭, 1894–1895) and signed a treaty, called the Treaty of Shimonoseki (馬關條約), giving Taiwan and several islands to Japan. In 1895, Taiwan began to be ruled by the Empire of Japan (1868–1947), but the Taiwanese people organized resistance groups to fight with the Japanese soldiers. Eventually, the Japanese government suppressed all the Han people, but the aboriginal people still troubled them a great deal.

There were more than ten groups of aborigines in Taiwan, and they all lived in the mountains. Hundreds of years ago, when the Chinese people, the Han, immigrated to Taiwan, they had forced the aboriginal people to move to the mountains and taken over their lands. Perhaps the harsh environment made the aboriginal people tougher. Furthermore, inside the mountains was more complicated and dangerous than the Japanese government and troops could have imagined. They had great difficulties to conquer the aboriginal people. Therefore, one of the significant reasons that the Japanese government desired to build a road to connect the west and east of Taiwan was to vanquish the aboriginal people. The Truku, known as the Taroko, was the last group of aborigines who surrendered in 1914. In this last war, the Truku War, which was brutal and bloody, around two thousand of the Truku warriors fought against twenty thousand of the Japanese soldiers for three months. They failed with glory.

In 1956, the Chinese Nationalist government took the road that the Japanese government built as a foundation to design and improve to become the Central Cross-Island Highway, but its reasons for building the highway were very different from those of the Japanese government.

Firstly, it was for national defense. Secondly, the Chinese Nationalist government wanted to utilize mountain and forest resources to develop the national economy. Thirdly, the Chinese Nationalist government said that they had to take care of the Chinese veterans, which was the most important reason, and explained why most road builders were Chinese veterans.

It sounds nice that the government wanted to take care of its veterans. However, if you learn some facts, you might have a different opinion.

The Chinese Nationalist government claimed that they didn't have money to build the highway, so they handed over this project to the Veterans Affairs Council. At the time, many Chinese soldiers were asked to retire, but most of them were still young, in their thirties and forties, which meant those soldiers needed to get a job after they retired. Consequently, the Chinese Nationalist government thought that it would be beneficial for both the government and the veterans if those veterans joined the project of the Central Cross-Island Highway construction, the engineering team.

At the time, there was no modern technology and equipment to be used. Moreover, the terrain was inaccessible by machinery. Therefore, the dynamite and pickaxes were the only tools that the workers used to smash through rocks. In such severe working conditions, it was not so hard to foresee that workers would be injured or killed easily. Therefore, it is not difficult to imagine that the civilians wouldn't want to take the job even if they were impoverished and the wage was high. Then, one might want to ask, "Why did the Chinese veterans want to take the job?"

Believe it or not, many veterans who joined the project of the Central Cross-Island Highway construction were the reserve soldiers, not the retired veterans. At the time, there were two kinds of retirement for those Chinese soldiers. The real veteran completely left the army service and took the full pension. Another kind of veteran, who left the troops but stood by for the order from the Veterans Affairs Council and received about 80 percent of their original salary, should have been called reserve soldiers. In other words, those reserve soldiers didn't join the project voluntarily. On the contrary, it was their duty to join the project when the Veterans Affairs Council gave them an order. After all, they were still federal employees. Thus, wouldn't you say that those poor and unskilled Chinese veterans, reserve soldiers, who had no property and families in Taiwan, were the best candidates for the road builders?

Well, was it *taking care of* or *taking advantage of*?

Uncle Huang was a real veteran, but he chose to join the project. All his comrades told him not to go because he might not be able to come back.

"Are you crazy?"

"Maybe I am."

"Do you need money?"

"No."

"You might get killed."

"It's OK. I am already dead."

Before Uncle Huang left for the job, he went to visit Ciou-Tao.

Even though Ciou-Tao's adoptive father, Ming-Cheng, didn't mind her original family coming to visit her at all, Fu-Sheng and Li-Jhu thought that it would be better not to visit Ciou-Tao at least for six months. It would help Ciou-Tao settle down sooner. However, they worried about Ciou-Tao more than they did about Ciou-Jyu and Ciou-Lain. After all, she was only seven years old. Then Uncle Huang happened to ask them if he could visit Ciou-Tao before he went to the mountains to work. They gladly agreed. They thought that it was a great chance to find out how Ciou-Tao was in her new life.

It was the end of autumn, but it was still pretty warm on the island. If Uncle Huang were in China at this time of year, he would have been wearing a jacket. Since the weather was still warm, Uncle Huang planned to take Ciou-Tao to get a Popsicle. In fact, he intended to spoil her that afternoon because he didn't know when he could give her a treat again. While Uncle Huang was walking and thinking of his plan, suddenly he saw Ciou-Tao's happy face. Ciou-Tao was talking to a man in front of a broken house like Uncle Huang's.

Uncle Huang could tell that the man was one of his own. Perhaps he had also retired from the army service. However, Uncle Huang didn't like him. He could tell the man wasn't a good person. Uncle Huang felt uncomfortable to see Ciou-Tao being around him.

Ciou-Tao looked very happy, though. It seemed the change in her life had not taken away her smile.

"Ciou-Tao!" Uncle Huang waved to her, and Ciou-Tao ran to him right away.

"Uncle! You came to see me as you promised. You ate

pineapple?"

"What?"

"You said that you would come to tell me if you ate a piece of fresh pineapple."

"No, not yet. I haven't got my courage ready for the pineapple. I came because I miss you and want to talk to you."

"Uncle, I miss you badly, and my sisters too. We used to read and play with you during this time of day. Before, I was on the way home and met that man. I was thinking of you and that Chinese man showed up. He reminded me of you, so when he said hi and talked to me, I talked to him. I know that I shouldn't do that. I still remember everything that you told me. Just say hi to strangers. Do not get into conversations immediately. But that man was nice like you." Uncle Huang looked at the direction where the man was, and that man was still there. Uncle Huang gave him a nod.

"OK, Ciou-Tao. I am glad that you remember my words, but try to remember to do it."

"OK, Uncle."

"Let's go back to your home first so I can ask your adoptive parents' permission to take you out."

"Yeah! Where are we going?"

"How about the seacoast?"

"Yes! I want to go there all the time, but my new father doesn't let me take my little brothers to go there. He said it's too dangerous."

"Well, Ciou-Tao, your adoptive father is right. You are too young to go to the seacoast without adults' company."

"So can we take my little brothers to go with us? They will be very happy if they can come with us. My new father is too busy to take us out."

"Sure, we certainly can do that if your adoptive parents agree."

"My new father is not at home, but I am very sure that my new mother will say OK because she is very nice."

"Ciou-Tao, you call them new father and new mother?"

"No. I call them A-ba and A-bu."

"Well, it's interesting to me to hear you call them new father and new mother, but others might not feel the same way. Some people might think it's rude."

"Don't worry, Uncle. I won't say it in front of others."

"Good girl."

Ciou-Tao's adoptive mother was on the bed, so Uncle Huang waited in the living room when Ciou-Tao went inside to ask her adoptive mother's permission.

"Sure. You kids have fun."

Mrs. Lin, Chun-Ying (春英), knew almost everything about Ciou-Tao's life, her original family, and Uncle Huang. Chun-Ying enjoyed listening to her children talking to her. Not only was she bored from lying on the bed all the time, but she also wanted to know her children's thinking and feelings, especially Ciou-Tao. She couldn't be their mother physically, but she wanted to be close to them mentally. She felt guilty that she couldn't be a mother to her boys and adoptive daughter, Ciou-Tao. In fact, Ciou-Tao was doing her job, taking care of her four sons. Thus, Chun-Ying was also very grateful. She thanked God for sending Ciou-Tao to them. She and Ming-Cheng loved sweet and talkative Ciou-Tao very much.

The four little boys felt the same way. Since they had Ciou-Tao to be their elder sister, they felt that their life was so much more fun. Now, her uncle Huang was taking them to the seacoast. How wonderful and exciting!

Before they went to the seacoast, Uncle Huang took them to buy Popsicles. The boys were so happy and excited because it was their first taste of Popsicle. In the beginning, they felt weird that their sister's uncle spoke a strange Taiwanese. "Why?" The question popped up in their minds, but soon, the Popsicles occupied their minds and tongues entirely. They forgot their curiosity about Uncle Huang's unique Taiwanese completely.

When they arrived at the seacoast, the boys went to

play on the sand. Uncle Huang and Ciou-Tao sat on two different rocks and talked.

"How is your new life, my sweetie?"

"OK."

"What does that mean?"

"Everyone is nice. I like them. But I miss my family, Ciou-Jyu, Ciou-Lian, and Uncle."

"Sure, you do. I would too. I like your little brothers. They are cute."

"But they create trouble sometimes."

"Everyone did when they were little."

"I did not."

"Ha, ha, ha…" Uncle Huang thought about the first time he met Ciou-Tao, who was cheating on playing hide-and-seek. He laughed so loud that the boys turned back and looked at him.

"Besides that, any trouble?"

"I worry that the new mother will die."

"What makes you think that?"

"She lies on the bed all the time and coughs very often. She looks pale and weak. I have never seen anyone like that. I am so afraid."

Uncle Huang leaned over and held her. "Do not be afraid, my girl. People get sick. Some people get well, and some don't. It's life, and eventually, we will all die."

"So is my new mother going to die?"

"Maybe. But if you do some work for her at home, it might help her."

"Like bathing my brothers?"

Uncle Huang said nothing and just nodded. He had heart pain. Maybe Ciou-Tao was capable, but was she too little to be a mother. So soon, his little peach blossom had lost her childhood.

"Ciou-Tao, I am leaving…"

"To where? Are you moving away? Why?" The word, *leaving*, had just come out of Uncle Huang's mouth, and at once, Ciou-Tao got very emotional and excited.

"Ciou-Tao, I will still be in our county. I got a job to work in the mountains. That's all. I am not going anywhere."

Immediately, Uncle Huang knew that he had scared Ciou-Tao and felt bad.

"Ciou-Tao, look at the mountains behind us. Aren't they beautiful?"

"They are super beautiful. I always love them." Actually, Ciou-Tao had told Uncle Huang a million times.

"I feel the same way. Now, I finally have an opportunity to go there and look inside of them. Don't you think it's exciting?"

"Yeah, it's quite exciting. So Uncle's new job is to look around the mountains?"

"Well, not exactly. My job is to build a highway to connect the east and west of Taiwan."

"Uncle, you mean, in the future, we can take a bus to the other side of the mountains?"

"Yes."

"Wow, that's really cool! But isn't it hard to build a road in the mountains?" Even an eight-year-old girl could picture the difficulty of building a highway in the mountains.

"It's not easy for sure, but I would like to try something different because…"

"My sisters and I are not around anymore, so you are bored and sad."

Uncle Huang didn't know how to respond. What Ciou-Tao had said was his feeling, but she might talk about her own feelings too. He felt that he had to be strong for his little girl, but he had never lied to her and intended never to do so. Thus, he tried hard to be positive.

"Yes, I do feel bored and sad without you guys around. But it's also because I really want to see Taiwan. Don't you want to know what our homeland looks like? Taiwan is my second home, and I want to see and know her. Now, I can see a part of Taiwan that I haven't seen before and get paid. Isn't it great?"

"It does sound terrific, but I am afraid."

"Afraid of what?"

"I feel building a road in the mountains is dangerous."

"I see. I promise, I will be very careful." Uncle Huang held Ciou-Tao tightly, as he would keep his words firmly.

"Guys, let's go to get some snacks!"

"Yeah!" The four boys were thrilled.

"What snacks are we going to have?" It seemed that Ciou-Tao forgot her worry.

"What do you feel like, sweetie?"

"I miss Uncle's steamed buns."

"Sorry, I should've thought about it and made some for you. How about this? Let's try some other food that my family in China also loves very much."

"What?" Ciou-Tao got very excited. Anything that was related to Uncle Huang she was interested in.

"Big bread [大餅]."

"I heard you talking about it before. I would like to try it. Uncle, let's go. I am hungry now."

"Me too," the four brothers all agreed.

"OK, big bread for hungry kids. Perfect!"

Perhaps feeling happy made them have a great appetite. After finishing one big bread, Ciou-Tao and her four brothers still felt hungry, and so did Uncle Huang. All of them agreed that they should buy another big bread to share. Talking and eating. Eating and talking. They had a wonderful time together, and the four brothers finally understood why their adoptive sister loved Uncle Huang that much.

Well, before they went home, Uncle Huang took them to a grocery store to buy lollipops. He really popped these kids' minds open that day, but why not? Uncle Huang was going to make twice as much money soon, and he didn't know when he could see his peach blossom again.

On the way home, when they passed by the ditch, Uncle

Huang suggested sitting by the ditch for a while. Everyone agreed. Who wouldn't? Obviously, four little boys had no intention to sit down at all. Before Uncle Huang and Ciou-Tao found a spot to sit down, the boys were already playing with frogs.

There was a reason for sitting by the ditch. There were some important things that Uncle Huang needed to tell Ciou-Tao.

"Sweetie, have you ever seen some women who dress beautifully and wear heavy makeup in this area?"

"Yes, I have. Some of them are very nice, but I don't like how they look."

"How they look?"

"Their clothes are not ugly, but I won't wear them when I grow up. I like lace. I want to look like a lady."

"Oh, I see."

"And I don't like the way they talk to people. It's very strange that they like to stand by their houses and only talk to men. Some of them would lean against the window and tell men to come in. Why don't they invite other women or me?"

"Oh no. Sweetie, *never* go into their places. Promise me. Those are not good places."

"How come? There are a lot of beautiful lights outside of those houses. It might be very pretty inside."

"Listen to me, Ciou-Tao. Listen carefully. The owners of the houses are very bad people. They treat those ladies awfully. They make money by forcing those ladies to sleep with strange men."

Sleeping with strange men! Ciou-Tao might not know the real meaning of "sleeping with," but she felt wrong to make a girl to sleep with strangers.

"They have to? Can they go home?"

"No, most of them can't go home, not until they pay off the debts."

"Uncle, you mean they owe people money and are punished by sleeping with strangers?"

"Something like that."

"That's not right. What if the strangers smell and snore?"

"Ciou-Tao, it's more serious than that. They will be beaten up if they don't do what the owners want them to do."

"They should run away and tell the police."

"They can't. Most of them can't go out."

"Uncle, you mean they are locked up?"

"Yes. They are not free."

"Oh my God! Really?"

"Ciou-Tao, I am sorry that I told you these terrible things, but I have to. People said that some owners of those houses kidnapped young girls sometimes. I am not sure if it's true or a rumor, but I want you to be aware of it, since you are living right next to this area. Moreover, remember what I always tell you: don't get too friendly with strangers. Would you promise me?"

"Yes, I would. I'll keep Uncle's words in mind all the time."

"Good girl!"

"But what if the stranger is a policeman?"

"Well, as I told you before, there are always good people and bad people out there. Same with the policemen; there are some good and some bad."

Ciou-Tao nodded, and suddenly, she laughed. "Uncle, don't worry. I will be very careful. Besides, I have four little soldiers with me. They will protect me."

"Yes, we will protect our sister." The oldest boy happened to hear what Ciou-Tao said.

"Ha, ha, ha…" Uncle Huang looked at the sunset and felt that it was a fantastic afternoon.

"Well, let's go home, or your parents will worry."

The next day, Uncle Huang told Fu-Sheng and Li-Jhu that he couldn't only say goodbye to Ciou-Tao. He loved and cared about Ciou-Jyu, Ciou-Lian, and Ciou-Tao equally.

"The two girls will be very upset when they learn that I only went to see Ciou-Tao before I leave the town to work in the mountains. I can't do that."

"But, Old Huang, the other two families are very different from Ciou-Tao's adoptive family. Do you think they would like the idea that you or even Li-Jhu and I go to visit Ciou-Jyu and Ciou-Lian?"

"No, I don't think so. That's why I didn't plan to visit them in the first place."

"Old Huang, I completely agree with you. You can't leave here without saying goodbye to Ciou-Jyu and Ciou-Lian. The two girls will feel hurt. They love you and trust you so much."

"Fu-Sheng, I thought about it last night. If I go to wait outside of their schools, I can talk to them while walking them home."

"Old Huang, that's a good idea. People meet on the street. You're their uncle. You meet and walk and talk. It's natural." Li-Jhu wished she could do that. Oh God, how she missed her little girls!

"I agree with Li-Jhu. Old Huang, do it. Check on our two girls for us."

The next day, Uncle Huang went to Ciou-Lian's school and waited outside the school by a tree. Before Ciou-Lian walked out of the school, she saw Uncle Huang. She ran to him with a big smile and tears.

"Are you OK?"

"Yes, I am OK, Uncle."

"So those are happy tears?"

"Yes."

"I know you need to go home right now, so let's walk and talk."

Ciou-Lian smiled and nodded.

"Ciou-Lian, how's your new life?"

"It's OK. Without everyone, it's not great like before."

"Oh, my beautiful lotus, it will be eventually. Believe me." Uncle Huang held Ciou-Lian's hand tightly.

"Actually, my adoptive parents and brothers are very nice to me. I like them."

"Wonderful." Uncle Huang was thrilled. "Ciou-Lian, I came to tell you that I am leaving and going to work in the mountains."

"Uncle, you mean those mountains?"

"Yes."

"So I won't see you anymore?"

"Silly girl. I will be back when we finish building the road."

"Uncle, please don't go. It's a dangerous job."

"Ciou-Lian, I will be fine."

"It will be very different if you're not living in this town with us."

"Ciou-Lian, it's the same. In fact, it's probably better. When you miss me, you can look at the mountains. You might see me waving to you."

Ciou-Lian laughed. No matter how good a person's vision was, no one could see a person waving in the mountains. She knew that her dearest uncle just wanted to make her laugh, and that was his way to tell her not to worry.

The next day, another school.

"Uncle!" Uncle Huang's sweet chrysanthemum was running to him. No tears! Great!

"Ciou-Jyu, do you go home alone?"

"No, I usually go home with Wen-Hua."

"I was right. Where is he?"

"I just saw him chasing and playing with his friends."

"I see."

"Uncle, I miss you so much."

"I miss you very much too. How is your new life?"

"Different."

"I am sure it is."

"The three brothers are nice and interesting."

"Interesting?"

"They are like Ciou-Lian, Ciou-Tao, and me, the Three Musketeers."

"Brothers and sisters can support and protect one another; that is a beautiful thing."

"But looking at them makes me miss Ciou-Lian and Ciou-Tao more."

"I understand. But don't think you lost one another. Uncle thinks that your love will last forever and you girls will reunite one day."

"Hi, Uncle Huang!" Wen-Hua showed up with a little shortness of breath.

"Hello, little fellow. Did you have fun with your friends?" Uncle Huang looked at him and smiled.

"Yes, I did. But when I told them that I have to go home and my sister is waiting for me, they made fun of me. Some friends they are!"

"They just didn't want you to leave. They had a good time with you too."

"I guess so."

"Let me walk you two home."

"Uncle Huang, Ciou-Jyu misses you very much."

"I have told Uncle already."

"And she told me that you and your brothers treat her very well."

"Have to. She is our sister."

"Then I won't need to worry about her when I go to work in the mountains."

"Uncle, what do you mean? You're leaving?" Ciou-Jyu's smile disappeared at once.

"Yes, I am. I am going to work in those mountains. Therefore, practically, I am not far away from you."

"Uncle, it's very far to me." Ciou-Jyu cried.

"What kind of work will you do in the mountains, Uncle Huang?"

"Wen-Hua, I am going to build a highway with many people."

"Uncle, don't go. Building a road in the mountains is too dangerous."

"I agree with Ciou-Jyu."

"I can't lie. It is a dangerous job, but I will be very careful. After all, I still want to come back to see you guys."

"Uncle, let's make a pinky promise that you will come back to us safely." Wen-Hua put his hand out.

Uncle Huang put his hand out right away, but Ciou-Jyu couldn't stop crying.

"Come on, Ciou-Jyu! We make Uncle promise, and he will be back. You told us that Uncle is the greatest man in the whole world. A great man always keeps his word."

"OK." Ciou-Jyu couldn't help laughing a little. Wen-Hua always knew how to make her laugh.

"Promise!" They said it under a tree with thousands of golden shooting stars falling through the tree leaves.

"Wow..." That was all Uncle Huang could say in his heart at first. Standing inside the mountains, the power of nature was so big that he felt himself becoming small and trivial, but that power was truly gentle to him, like a mother to her child. For the first time in over a decade, Uncle Huang's soul rested at last. However, his mind was still unable to rest.

Every day after work, Uncle Huang and his team workers went back to their campsite. The campsite was not far from the worksite. In other words, they were in nature the whole day every day. After a shabby dinner of congee, dried peanuts, dried radish, and dried baby fish, their entertainment was chatting, and the topics were mainly related to war. Well, what else could they talk about? Virtually, their lives were war.

Uncle Huang was tired of talking about war and listening to war stories, separation, hunger, robbery, rape, trauma, massacre, and death. However, while others were talking, he couldn't help thinking about his own misery. One night, Uncle Huang laughed bitterly because he finally admitted that war had dominated their present and future lives and they had little chance to escape from it. Under the moonlight, he looked at the million-year-old mountains that surrounded him, and he wondered how many sad stories these mountains had heard or witnessed. Undoubtedly, the Chinese people's sufferings were new to the mountains.

"Would you speak to God for us since you are so close to the sky, near heaven?"

"Please speak to God for us. He will listen to you if he let you beautifully stand here forever."

"Please beg God for us. We want to go home. Let us go back to China."

They became Uncle Huang's good-night prayers. Alas, what could the poor man do as the night fell and the darkness covered everything? Asking for hope was sensible.

Thank God, at the crack of dawn, everything was different. Uncle Huang saw life. The birds' chirps reverberated through the gorge. The hawk was hovering and waiting for a mindless bird to be its breakfast. Furthermore, some big animals were still active. Uncle Huang had seen Formosan monkeys (台灣獼猴), sikas (梅花鹿), and serows (山羊), and he wanted to see Formosan Reeve's muntjac (山羌) very much. His workmates told him that Formosan Reeve's muntjac has a unique howl. It sounds like cursing, the f-word in Taiwanese. One of his workmates imitated the sound, and Uncle Huang couldn't stop laughing. "Oh, my good Lord, where did they learn that word?" Uncle Huang wished he could tell Ciou-Jyu, Ciou-Lain, and Ciou-Tao about Formosan Reeve's muntjac, and he knew that Ciou-Tao would laugh louder than anyone else.

In the daytime, besides birds and various insects,

butterflies were the most attractive scenery in the gorge. Uncle Huang was amazed because he had never seen so many different kinds of butterflies in his life.

According to a book that was published by the Japanese in 1960, there were about 200 species of butterflies in Europe, 260 species in Japan, and 400 species in Taiwan and 55 of them were endemic.

In 1918, during the period of Japanese rule (1895–1945), Taiwan started the butterfly specimen business. After World War II, Taiwan became the biggest supplier of butterfly specimens in the world; therefore, the island was recognized as the Butterfly Kingdom internationally. In the peak period, 1968 to1975, Taiwan exported about 1.6 million butterfly specimens and crafts every year. Many impoverished families in the countryside improved their finances by selling butterflies that they caught. This national treasure became many Taiwanese people's fortunes.

Uncle Huang knew about the butterfly trade. He worried that the business would decrease the numbers of butterflies and might ultimately lead to the extinction of some butterflies. He felt that it was so wrong to make butterflies that should fly in the sky lie down in the boxes. He believed that if people could come here, Taroko Gorge, to see butterflies, they would be charmed by their beauty and want to see them alive more than ever.

Uncle Huang slowly acknowledged that nature could comfort his body and soul. He wished he could have much more time to explore and appreciate nature. However, the construction team could only work in the daytime, so they didn't have much time to have a break. Moreover, once they began working, they needed to be focused 100 percent. The first day at the job, before Uncle Huang started to work, the supervisor of the site warned him to be cautious all the time while working. As a matter of fact, Uncle Huang had comprehended the danger the first day he arrived and saw others working. Right after he started working, he felt that he had almost no control of his life. Thus, when later he learned that people in other sites were hurt or died, he wasn't too surprised. Nevertheless, Uncle Huang was extremely shocked and terrified when he saw his workmate strike by a rock and fall into the gorge. Just like that, so easy, a life ended.

Whenever Uncle Huang and his workmates learned of a worker's death, some of them sighed with a great deal of sadness, and some cried. Often, someone would say, "He made it through the wars with the Japanese and the Communists, but he couldn't survive in this job. Why?"

Why?

The question was resounding in the gorge, but no one answered it. Probably, they were too scared to say the truth out loud: they had lost the right to life.

Then shouldn't Uncle Huang run away from this job?

Alas. Uncle Huang had known how risky this work could be before he decided to join the team. However, he didn't have a fear until he started working. Knowing is one thing and doing is another, which is a perfect description for this case. While Uncle Huang was standing on a rock and holding a pickax to hit and break the rock without protection, and behind him was the gorge, the threat and danger was right in front of him. It was a similar feeling that he had on the battlefield years ago, but this time, the enemy was the mountains that he loved. Hence, it might be hard to believe that Uncle Huang didn't feel regret and had no intention to withdraw himself from the project. Put it this way: for over a decade, Uncle Huang had been away from home and seen too many dark sides of humanity, cruelty, greed, lying, corruption, and evil. Since he couldn't go home and had lost his new family, he didn't want to see and hear those things anymore. He wanted to have a break, and nature was the best choice.

Uncle Huang felt that rocks, trees, wind, clouds, water, sun, moon, and all the lives in the mountains were his soul mates. He could talk to them, and they understood him. They told him to relax, to be gentle to himself, and to allow them to embrace him. He particularly loved clouds and the wind more than others. He liked to sit on a cloud and let the wind take him to travel. Of course, the wind was the key. Without a cloud, the wind still could take him to anywhere that he wished to go: the top of the mountain, the bottom of the gorge, Ciou-Jyu, Ciou-Lian, Ciou-Tao, and home.

Boom! The dynamite was set off, and the rocks were flying like rain.

Uncle Huang was flying. This time, he was flying with rocks.

"I am going home..." That was what Uncle Huang said before he landed on the bottom of the gorge.

"Who?"

"Who?"

"Who was that?"

They asked this same question the second time of the month.

"Old Huang."

On May 9, 1960, the entire road was opened to vehicles. About 12,000 people had worked on the project, and 226 people died in total. If it wasn't that the death of an engineer in 1957 brought the public attention to the loss of those workers, they would be forgotten as if they had never existed. In 1958, a memorial, Eternal Spring Shrine (長春祠), was built. It memorialized 212 veterans who died during the construction. Now, people can see all 226 deceased's names in the Eternal Spring Shrine. Surely, no one knows who they were, but they are remembered as whole, poor men who were in exile and gave Taiwan a beautiful highway with their lives.

7

Two Sad Souls:
Ciou-Tao and Wen-Hua

Thank goodness Uncle Huang had prepared.

"Old Wang, if you are reading this letter, which means I have died..."

"Oh no..." Everyone in the Wang family was crying terribly.

It was Uncle Huang's comrade Cannon Jhang who went to give the letter to the Wang family after he learned of Uncle Huang's death. He was the one who had taken care of Uncle Huang before when Uncle Huang was sick in bed over two weeks. Fu-Sheng was shocked and profoundly sad. He told Cannon Jhang that he wanted to have a funeral for Uncle Huang.

Cannon Jhang cried. He finally comprehended how close and deep was the friendship and love between this family and Old Huang. He was happy for Old Huang. They, Chinese soldiers or veterans who came to Taiwan alone, were not going to have any family or friends to mourn for them when they died in Taiwan. Maybe a few comrades, but that was all they could have. Perhaps that was fair. Old Huang had opened his heart to the land and people of Taiwan, and they loved him back.

Cannon Jhang wiped his tears and told Fu-Sheng that he could prepare a picture of Old Huang for the funeral. He also had a request. "Can you be so kind to let other comrades come?"

"Of course! We all are Old Huang's family and friends.

We should get together to say goodbye to Old Huang. He will be very happy if he sees all of us at his funeral." That was how the Wang family had a few more Chinese friends after Uncle Huang's funeral. They were nice, but they weren't Uncle Huang, the special and nicest man in the world.

The very next day, Ciou-Ying went to tell Ciou-Jyu, Ciou-Lian, and Ciou-Tao about the death of Uncle Huang. There was no good time to tell the sad news. Ciou-Jyu, Ciou-Lian, and Ciou-Tao were very close to Uncle Huang. It was impossible not to tell them the sad news right away. In fact, it would be very wrong to hold up the news, even just one day. However, how to tell Ciou-Jyu and Ciou-Lian was a hard task. "Let Ciou-Ying go. An eldest sister's visit wouldn't cause too much attention," Li-Jhu told Fu-Sheng.

As Li-Jhu and Fu-Sheng predicted, Ciou-Jyu couldn't come back for the funeral, but surprisingly, Ciou-Lian could. The Beard Man came with her. Ciou-Tao, of course, could come. Furthermore, her four little brothers came with her. They asked Ciou-Tao to bring them. They liked the coolest Uncle Huang. In fact, Ming-Cheng would have come to pay his respects if he didn't need to work.

It was a simple funeral. Li-Jhu lit incense sticks for everyone, and they held the incense sticks and bowed to the picture of Uncle Huang. Everyone was quiet but talked to Uncle Huang in their hearts. When they were done, they gave the incense sticks to Li-Jhu to put in the censer.

After the praying, Ciou-Lian and Ciou-Tao held hands and cried. They didn't know what to say. However, it was essential that Ciou-Lian and Ciou-Tao mourn Uncle Huang together. They held hands and said nothing, but they had communicated. Through their hands, they said to each other, "I know. I know. I know how you feel because I feel the same." That was the kind of comfort and support that the two sisters needed.

Ciou-Jyu also needed that "I know," but she couldn't

have it. Although Wen-De, Wen-Zhi, and Wen-Hua had learned so many things about Uncle Huang as if they had known him for years, they did not have the love that the three sisters had for Uncle Huang. Thus, they couldn't give the same support and comfort that Ciou-Lian and Ciou-Tao could give to Ciou-Jyu.

Goodbye! Goodbye!

People say goodbye all the time, to friends, classmates, colleagues, lovers, family, and the deceased.

After saying goodbye to Uncle Huang, Ciou-Lian and Ciou-Tao had to say farewell to their parents, brother, and sisters.

"A-ba, A-bu, we are going home."

"Home. They are going back to their homes." Li-Jhu and Fu-Sheng could see the changes in their daughters.

It was true that the two girls weren't the same people anymore. In just a year and a half, they had grown so much, physically and mentally. They knew very well who they were and where they belonged. In brief, they had accepted reality.

Rationally, Li-Jhu and Fu-Sheng were glad that Ciou-Lian and Ciou-Tao had fit into their new lives well, but emotionally, they felt a sense of loss. In a way, the two little girls were no longer their daughters anymore. They felt that they would lose them totally after this funeral. Uncle Huang's death also was the end of their old lives.

"Take care of yourself." That was all Li-Jhu and Fu-Sheng said.

Ciou-Lian and Ciou-Tao nodded and said, "I will." Then they left.

The Beard Man said, "Let's walk you guys home." Nobody objected.

The Beard Man was a kind and thoughtful person. Ciou-Lian loved him and saw him as her grandpapa. He loved Ciou-Lian too. He knew how much Ciou-Lian missed Ciou-Tao, so he wanted to give them more time to be together by walking Ciou-Tao and her four brothers home.

"Sis, your dress is nice. You look like a princess," Ciou-Tao praised sincerely.

Ciou-Lian didn't know how to respond for a moment. She always knew that Ciou-Tao hadn't gotten a better life than she did. Ciou-Tao had gotten taller but thinner. Her clothes were shabby as before. No, no. It was worse, because no one sewed the holes for her. Ciou-Lian wondered if Ciou-Tao would feel that their parents not only abandoned her but also treated her unfairly and question why they hadn't given her to a wealthy family as well.

"Sis, if we played games together like old times, you would be Cinderella's stepsister, and I would be Cinderella. Perfect! And I will get a prince, but you can't. Ha!"

"There, my dearest dope. She is still the same." Ciou-Lian knew that she wouldn't need to worry about the difference between them.

"Oh, yeah? The way you talk, it's more like Cinderella's stepsister, not me. And plus, you said you didn't like boys. Since when you want a prince?"

"OK! OK! Take the prince and marry soon!" After finishing talking, Ciou-Tao stuck her tongue out at Ciou-Lian and ran. Then Ciou-Lian and the four little brothers, who didn't know what was going on at all, chased after her.

Soon, so very soon, there was another goodbye to say, but none of them was sad. They had just had a moment of good time; why should they feel upset? In fact, it is better to say farewell happily, isn't it? It was supposed to be a sad and somber occasion, but the two sisters found comfort and joy unexpectedly. Later, when Ciou-Lian and Ciou-Tao grew older, they thought that it might have been dear Uncle Huang's plan and gift for them. He wanted them to know that there were a lot of misfortunes, troubles, setbacks, or tragedies in life, but at the same time, there were hopes and joys just around the corner waiting for them. Life wasn't all bad.

It was true that Ciou-Tao didn't feel her new life was all bad. Although she ate poorly and needed to work a lot, she felt loved. Everyone in the Lin family loved her, especially the four little brothers. That was enough for her. This concept, "Love is more important than anything," had grown in her mind from being Lin Ciou-Tao, and she brought the idea to her own family ten years later. However, her trust for people had been severely challenged several times. She began to keep a distance from some groups of people, but fortunately, she never gave up on love or lost her compassion for people.

What were those challenges? Why were they so influential?

After Uncle Huang died, Ciou-Tao missed him so much. She had some sort of transference. She was extra friendly to the Chinese men, especially the one whom she had met on the day that Uncle Huang went to see her before he went to work on the project of building the Central Cross-Island Highway. The man lived near Ciou-Tao's home, so she could meet him quite often. More importantly, the man seemed amiable. Well, who wouldn't like a nice person?

One beautiful afternoon, Ciou-Tao went to pick coals. After half an hour or so, she finished picking and didn't get chased by the police, so she was happy. On the way home, she walked the alley that she could walk by that Chinese man's house because she particularly missed her uncle Huang that afternoon. Ciou-Tao happened to see a Chinese man selling steamed buns when she was on the way to pick coals. She was sad for a moment, but immediately, all the happy memories of eating Uncle Huang's steamed buns appeared and chased the sadness away. Thus, she did not cry this time.

However, she cried later.

The man was sitting in front of his house and smoking a cigarette. When Ciou-Tao saw him, she waved to him. The man waved too. Then, the man stubbed out the cigarette on the ground.

"Hi, Uncle Ye [葉]."

"Hello, Ciou-Tao. I can see that you just came back from picking coals. It's hot today. Come in and have a glass of cold dried plum juice."

"Uncle, I can't take food or drinks from strangers."

"You called me Uncle, so I am not a stranger. You know me, right?"

"Hmm."

Although they said hi to each other all the time, they only knew each other's names. Nothing more.

Ciou-Tao went into the house, and she felt so familiar. It looked like Uncle Huang's house. Of course the two houses looked alike. All those impoverished Chinese veterans built their own houses.

"Wow, this dried plum juice is great!"

"You want more?"

"No, thank you."

"Why? Because we are strangers? Just have one more glass!"

"Thank you, Uncle."

"No problem, good girl."

"Uncle, did you build this house yourself?"

"Yes. My comrades and I did it together. How do you know?"

"My uncle also built his own house."

"Oh, the man I saw before, right?"

"Yeah. He died."

"How awful! Come here. Let Uncle give you a hug."

Then Ciou-Tao stood up and went over.

The man held Ciou-Tao, and Ciou-Tao pretended that she was holding Uncle Huang. However, the man wasn't Uncle

Huang, a righteous man. He began to touch Ciou-Tao and kiss her neck. Ciou-Tao knew that it was wrong, so she screamed and tried to push the man away. Ciou-Tao was struggling because the man was strong and powerful. She couldn't fight to win, to escape.

Help!

Help! Help!

Ciou-Tao despaired; she wished someone could help her. She cried and screamed, louder and louder.

"Leave her alone!" Someone heard Ciou-Tao and ran into the house to rescue her. He pulled the Chinese man away from Ciou-Tao and punched him in the face.

The man was younger and stronger than the Chinese man, so the Chinese man begged for mercy. Too bad! The young man put handcuffs on him!

"No, you'll go to the police station with me."

Now, Ciou-Tao could see. It was the police officer who had caught her picking coals and given her steamed pork buns about five months ago.

Thank God people could easily hear voices from that broken house. That was why the police officer heard Ciou-Tao's scream while he was on patrol.

"Ciou-Tao, don't cry. You are safe now." The police officer used his handkerchief to wipe her tears.

"Can you go home alone?"

Ciou-Tao nodded.

"Come to the station to see me tomorrow. Can you do that?"

"Yes, sir," Ciou-Tao answered with a low voice.

The officer saw Ciou-Tao walk away. When Ciou-Tao walked to the end of the alley, she looked back and waved to him.

Ciou-Tao didn't tell anyone what had happened to her after she got home. As a matter of fact, she never told anyone this horrible incident until five years later. She finally understood Uncle Huang's warning after that terrible experience.

She also realized that not all the Chinese men were nice like Uncle Huang. Indeed, she learned the lesson.

The next day in the morning, Ciou-Tao went to the police station. It was summer vacation, so she didn't need to go to school. She could have gone to the police station at any time of the day, but she arrived there at 8:30 a.m. The reason was pretty simple. She was still suffering from the shock and needed a sense of security from the police officer. Luckily, the police officer was there; he was on the early shift.

"Come in, Ciou-Tao."

Honestly, Ciou-Tao didn't know how to enter the police station. At school, when a student needed to go into the teachers' office, he or she had to stand politely in front of the door and say, "Bao-gao" (報告, Reporting as ordered. Do I have permission to enter?) Then the student could go into the office after any teacher said, "Come in."

How about the police station? "Just walk in, or should I do the same as at school?" Ciou-Tao felt very troubled. Therefore, it was good that the police officer saw her and told her to come in.

"Did you have breakfast?"

Of course she didn't, but Ciou-Tao didn't want to tell.

"I have a sesame flatbread [燒餅] that I couldn't finish. Can you help me out?" The officer knew that Ciou-Tao surely hadn't had breakfast, but he didn't want her to feel embarrassed.

"OK, sir. I can help, but what is sesame flatbread? I have never heard of it before." What a poor girl! Never heard of the bread before but agreed to eat it.

"That's Chinese bread. It's very yummy. Have a bite and drink some soy milk with it. It's a perfect match." The officer gave Ciou-Tao a piece of sesame flatbread and a cup of cold soy milk.

"Wow! It's really good. I like it." The way Ciou-Tao ate showed how hungry she was.

"Good, good. I am glad you like it."

"Sir, you like Chinese food?"

"Ciou-Tao, you can call me Uncle Lai [賴]. I do like Chinese food. It is yummy."

"I like Chinese food, too, especially the steamed buns. My uncle made them really good."

"You have a Chinese uncle?"

"Yeah. But he died."

"Oh, I am sorry, Ciou-Tao."

"My sisters and I called him Uncle Huang. He was the greatest man in the whole world. He was a soldier. He couldn't go home and had to stay in Taiwan. After he retired from army service, he sold steamed buns. He made the best steamed buns in the whole world and dumplings too. But he got a new job in the mountains and fell into the gorge and died..." Ciou-Tao began to cry.

"Ciou-Tao, don't cry." Officer Lai leaned over and rubbed her head.

"Ciou-Tao, you were very lucky to have a wonderful uncle, but do you know that not everyone is good like Uncle Huang?"

Ciou-Tao nodded and said, "Yes, I do. Uncle Huang told me before."

"You should remember what he told you. Don't be too friendly to strangers."

"Uncle Huang told me that too."

"He was really a great uncle. He told you all the important things that you need to know. He must care for and love you very much."

"My sisters and I also loved him very much. He taught my sisters to do homework. He was a very smart man."

"No wonder you miss him so much. Is that the reason you trusted that Chinese man yesterday?"

Ciou-Tao looked sad and nodded.

"Ciou-Tao, whenever you miss your uncle Huang, just think of everything that he told you. He would like you to do that very much. Besides, do you know there are some strange houses in this area? The women stand by the door or lean by the window."

"I know. Uncle Huang told me that they are locked up and can't go home. They owe people money, so they have to sleep with strangers. Uncle Huang told me not to go to that area. I might get kidnapped…"

Officer Lai felt pity that Ciou-Tao had lost her guardian angel. She had been taught everything that she needed to know to survive, but she was just too young to comprehend the severity of reality.

"Ciou-Tao, again, please do what Uncle Huang told you to do. He would be very happy to know that you listen to him and remember his words. Moreover, anytime you need help, just come here. If I am not here, you still can ask my colleague for help."

"But Uncle Huang also said that not all the policemen are good. I have to be careful too."

"Ha, ha, ha…true, true. He was right. But the policemen in this station all are good. I promise."

"OK. I believe you, Uncle Lai, because you are a good person."

It was a marvelous day; not only was Ciou-Tao's shock from the horrible attack eased away, but she also got a new guardian angel in her life. From that day, Ciou-Tao started keeping a distance from the Chinese men, the veterans specifically. Five years later, Ciou-Tao completely hated that group of people after she learned a piece of heartbreaking news.

It was a beautiful afternoon. A thunderstorm had just passed by, and the sky was perfectly clear blue. A handsome young man who looked pale came to call on Ciou-Tao. He was Wen-

Hua. He brought her dreadful news: the death of Ciou-Jyu.

Ciou-Tao was shocked and speechless.

"Ciou-Jyu died? Ciou-Jyu died?" Ciou-Tao's mind went blank.

Before coming here, Wen-Hua had first gone to Ciou-Jyu's original family to tell them of the tragedy, and then he went to visit Ciou-Lian. Each time, when Wen-Hua explained how and why Ciou-Jyu died, he felt a sharp knife stabbing into his heart again and again. Wen-Hua wished he didn't need to tell the whole ugly story over and over again; however, Ciou-Jyu's family had a right to know. Furthermore, it was his family who put Ciou-Jyu in hell and caused the tragedy, the deaths of Wen-Zhi and Ciou-Jyu, but his parents, especially Mother, didn't think that they had any responsibility on that matter. Thus, he believed that he had a duty to take the blame for his family. It was a difficult task, no doubt, but surprisingly, no one screamed or yelled at him, which bothered Wen-Hua more.

There were some heavy thoughts running in Wen-Hua's mind. He couldn't hold them any longer but had no courage to say them out loud either. "It's our fault. Blame us! Yell at me! Please don't stay quiet. Is it because we are rich people that you feel useless to fight and keep silent? No, we also make mistakes and do shameful things. We're rich and freaking arrogant and heartless." It was the first time Wen-Hua hated that he was born in his family.

Ciou-Tao surprised Wen-Hua in many aspects.

After Wen-Hua told Ciou-Tao the whole thing, she said, "Thank you for taking care of and protecting my sister, and I am sorry about your brother."

"But..."

"You were unable to save her?"

Wen-Hua did not know what to say and was impressed with Ciou-Tao's sharpness.

"Who can save us? Poor girls from poor families can only follow fate."

"No! You shouldn't believe that."

"Shim-bu-a have no control over their own lives. If they tried to fight with their fate, they would certainly get hurt."

Wen-Hua looked at Ciou-Tao, who was three years younger than him, and sighed in his heart, "She is so honest and mature. Clearly, hard life forces her to grow up fast."

Indeed, the hard life made Ciou-Tao grow very fast. She wasn't the same Ciou-Tao who had been attacked by a Chinese man five years ago, whose adoptive mother had died three years ago. Maybe she was still a young girl, thirteen years old, but she thought more like an adult now.

"Who will hold the funeral?"

"Her…"

"Husband."

"No, no. He is in jail now. His family will hold the funeral."

"That's right. He killed your brother and my sister. He belongs in jail."

"Ciou-Tao, I tried to persuade my parents to exercise their power to hold the funeral, but they said that they have to respect the custom. The stupid custom!"

"But it's true that Ciou-Jyu is not related to your family. Even if she were your parents' daughter, your parents still had no right to hold the funeral, because Ciou-Jyu was married, and her husband owned her. It's so not fair that he still owns her after she died. Why can't we own ourselves?"

"Ciou-Tao, I am sorry. I wish I owned the world so I could change the damn rules. Set everyone free to be themselves, to be equal."

"Wen-Hua ge [哥, elder brother], no need to feel sorry. It's not your fault. By the way, I need to thank you. I wanted to but never had a chance."

"For what?"

"The chicken legs and hard-boiled eggs."

"What?"

"Ciou-Jyu used to come to see me once in a while. She

wanted to know if I was OK and always brought me some chicken legs and hard-boiled eggs. She told me that you and Wen-Zhi ge gave her chicken legs and hard-boiled eggs frequently. Sometimes, you both gave her on the same day, and she couldn't consume them all so wanted to give me some. However, I suspect that she didn't eat any and gave me all she had. She was always worried that my little brothers and I might not have food to eat. Of course, she couldn't always come and give me chicken legs and hard-boiled eggs whenever she had many. Therefore, she would share with the servants when she had plenty of chicken legs and hard-boiled eggs. She was a sweet girl, wasn't she?"

"Yes, she was. She was very kind and also beautiful and intelligent."

"I wish I had all those qualities. She and Ciou-Lian are perfect like princesses. I would never grow up like them. Like people said, I am an ugly duck, and they are beautiful swans."

"Well, you know, they also said that the ugly duck will become a swan eventually."

Ciou-Tao burst out laughing.

"Me? Impossible!"

That was the first time Wen-Hua met Ciou-Tao, but he felt that he had known her forever because of Ciou-Jyu. He had learned that she was funny, naughty, and full of imagination, but it was very different to talk to her in person. Better! Wen-Hua felt that Ciou-Tao was like the Taiwan blue magpie (台灣藍鵲), not delicately beautiful but toughly handsome. The Taiwan blue magpie is endemic to Taiwan; Ciou-Tao was a unique individual. He found that Ciou-Tao was an amazing and charming girl. He liked her very much.

"Wen-Hua ge, I can stay to be a duck forever. I am fine with it. What's wrong with being a duck?"

"True. You are right."

"Besides, I heard people saying that the roast duck is quite yummy."

Well, what a logic that Ciou-Tao talked about the value

of being a duck! Ciou-Tao's funny sense lifted up Wen-Hua's spirit. "What? But there will be no chance that you would know how it tasted if you were roasted."

"Wait! We just met for the first time, and you already want to roast me?" Ciou-Tao actually liked Wen-Hua's humor.

"I am entirely innocent here! Think slowly; who brought up the roast duck first?"

Just like that, they were supposed to be sad and cry, but they laughed loudly. At that moment, Wen-Hua finally understood why Ciou-Jyu looked so happy and laughed a lot when she talked about Ciou-Tao.

Wen-Hua also thought, "Ciou-Tao is like sunshine. She doesn't like to be covered by clouds, especially dark ones. She might be pulled down in a sad situation, but she would try to come back with a smile. She wants to survive and live her life." Wen-Hua was inspired. "Ciou-Tao surely lives in poverty, but she is fine. Better than fine and better than me. Ciou-Jyu asked me to look after Ciou-Tao, but I think I can only offer food for her stomach."

"Ciou-Tao, can we be friends?"

"Nope! You are my brother. You are my dear sister's brother, so I am your sister too. Then you have to look after me. Ha!"

"Well, my dear little sister, it's my honor to look after you. As a matter of fact, I have to do so. It's Ciou-Jyu's order. She also said that I have to discipline you if you are bad."

"Did she really say that? I don't believe you. She was too nice to say such a thing. I think she probably said, 'Give Ciou-Tao some chicken legs or hard-boiled eggs because she is very poor.'" Ciou-Tao laughed like a sunflower.

Wen-Hua became serious. "Ciou-Tao, please be honest with me since we're brother and sister. How bad is the situation in your adoptive family? Do you eat every meal? You look too thin."

"Wen-Hua ge, perhaps you have known that my stepmother died three years ago. After that, my stepfather is not the same anymore. He doesn't work as hard as before. Moreover, he drinks more than before. We can't eat three meals a day. My four poor little brothers are hungry all the time. After all, they are boys. They need more food than I do. But don't worry. We are surviving. There is food in the ditch, frogs and fish. Even in people's garbage cans we can find something."

Eating trash? It pained Wen-Hua to hear that.

"Oh, Ciou-Tao…" Wen-Hua really didn't know what to say.

"Wen-Hua ge, honestly, this isn't a good life. It's bad, in fact. But this is our life, and we deal with it. In three more years, I will be sixteen; then I can get a job. Everything will be better. In the meantime, if you have extra chicken legs or hard-boiled eggs, I wouldn't mind having them."

"Sure, I'll bring you chicken legs, hard-boiled eggs, and anything you need."

"I'm just kidding."

"No, I would like to help."

"OK. But, don't do it regularly, only when you come to see me once in a while. That'll be a treat, much nicer."

"It's a deal, then." Wen-Hua wanted to respect Ciou-Tao's feelings. He didn't want to make her feel uncomfortable.

"Ciou-Tao, I have to go home now. I will see you soon. And come to me anytime when you need help or want to talk. Anything at all."

"Wen-Hua ge, thank you so much. I know you will do anything for me because I am Ciou-Jyu's sister. I am very grateful. I have heard many great things about you and your two brothers, so I am happy that I finally can meet you. I wish it could've been on a happy occasion, not because of my sister's death. Life is tough, and we have to be tough. It's not going to be easy. I have been there before. I lost my dearest uncle Huang, I am sure that you know him, and my stepmother."

"Ciou-Tao, I understand what you're saying because I am already in hell. It is so unbearable to lose my brother and Ciou-Jyu. They were so important to me, and I loved them very much..." Wen-Hua started to cry.

"Wen-Hua ge, we will be fine. I don't know when, but I know we will in the end." Ciou-Tao looked at the wall as she spoke. She was afraid that she would also cry if she looked at Wen-Hua. Then she reached out her hand and found Wen-Hua's hand. The two hands held, and they said, "I know, I know."

After Wen-Hua left, Ciou-Tao ran out of the house.

She was running and crying. She was running in the direction where her other loved one lived.

The tears were blurring her eyes. She almost couldn't see anything, but she was still running in the direction where her heart belonged.

Ciou-Tao needed Ciou-Lian.

She also wanted to tell Ciou-Lian not to leave her alone in the world.

Ciou-Tao saw Ciou-Lian sitting next to the Beard Man and crying, so she ran faster.

"Ciou-Lian! Ciou-Lian!"

Ciou-Lian heard. She knew that was her dearest dope, so she stood up and ran to Ciou-Tao.

The two sisters held each other so tight that they became one. They cried their hearts out. They couldn't talk. There were no words between them. What to say? Death had defined everything.

Then the Beard Man went to them. He was an old-fashioned man. Hugging and patting weren't his ways. He only talked.

"Let's go there to sit down."

They listened.

After the two sisters sat down, they finally stopped crying. However, they still couldn't talk. What to say? The pain had expressed everything.

"Girls, we can't cry too much and too hard; otherwise, the deceased wouldn't be able to leave our world. When our sadness is too mighty, we might pull them back, and they will be lingering beside us. Some of them might become wandering ghosts. That's not good. The spirits should go to where they belong so they can face their judgment and go for their reincarnation. Ciou-Jyu was a wonderful person. She will be judged to have a better next life. We should pray for her. Let her arrive at God's place soon."

This wasn't the first time Ciou-Lian and Ciou-Tao heard these folk ideas of death. However, it was Ciou-Jyu whom they had lost. How could they not cry hard? Nevertheless, they did not want Ciou-Jyu to become a wandering ghost, either, so they tried to hold back a bit of their sorrow and keep their grief in their hearts, not let it out with their tears. It was hard, but they had to do it for their beloved Ciou-Jyu.

Finally, the two sisters could talk.

"Ciou-Lian, you need to promise me one important thing."

"What?"

"To live to one hundred years old."

"Why? I don't want to live that long. It's too old."

"It *is* too old. Ninety, then."

"Still too old."

The Beard Man was glad to see that the two sisters had calmed down and were having funny conversations. He always enjoyed listening to them talk.

"Then, you say, how long do you want to live?"

"Sixty years."

"Only sixty years? Can't. You can't only live sixty years."

"Why?"

"Because I believe I will live longer than sixty years."

"Why are you so sure?"

"I just know."

"You know, or you wish?"

"Both. Anyway, you just need to live longer than me."

"Why?"

"I can't live without you."

"Me either."

"Then what should we do?"

"Dope. We can die on the same day."

"That's a deal. Sis, I have another thing to tell."

"What's it about?"

"Well, I hate Chinese people!"

"But Uncle Huang was Chinese."

"I know. But don't you hate them?"

"Maybe a little bit."

"Just a little bit?" Ciou-Tao almost screamed.

"I do hate those Chinese men who hurt Ciou-Jyu, but they weren't the only people who hurt her. Her husband abused her too. In fact, he is the evilest one of all. He is Taiwanese. Are you going to hate all Taiwanese people now? Don't you remember Uncle Huang told us that there are always good and bad people in any group?"

"Of course I remember everything that Uncle Huang said. But don't you remember that all the Chinese people in Taiwan can't go back to their families in China because of the Chinese government's prohibition? I think they are generally not nice, treating people horribly like their government is treating them."

"But still, not all Chinese people are bad. Don't hate people in this way."

"Do you know I was almost raped by a Chinese man? Almost like Ciou-Jyu! Have you ever seen that many Chinese men go to te-tiam-a all the time? They are simply bad people." Ciou-Tao spoke with rage.

"What? What does that mean, you were almost raped?" Ciou-Lian was shocked. The Beard Man too.

"I trusted a Chinese man who lived in my area. He tried to rape me, but a policeman came to rescue me. So I was fine."

"When did it happen?"

"Several weeks after Uncle Huang died."

"And, what's te-tiam-a?"

The Beard Man immediately interfered. "Ciou-Lian, a lady does not need to know the place."

"A bad place, anyway." Ciou-Tao knew that the Beard Man didn't want her to tell Ciou-Lian what a te-tiam-a was.

"Oh." Ciou-Lian realized she did not know many things that happened in Ciou-Tao's life. In fact, the world that Ciou-Tao saw was different from the world in which she lived. She was an adoptive daughter of a wealthy family, but Ciou-Tao lived in poverty. She had good food and nice clothes and even could go to junior high school, but Ciou-Tao had to find food to eat all the time. She had a great life with good prospects, but Ciou-Tao impatiently wished her sixteenth birthday could come earlier so she could get a job. They loved each other very much, which would never change, but in a way, they were no longer in each other's lives, since they were adopted by different families.

Ciou-Lian always knew that Ciou-Tao's life wasn't easy, but she didn't expect something terrible would happen to her. She now understood why Ciou-Tao hated the Chinese people so much. She had been taken advantage of by a Chinese man. "Oh, she was so little. It must have been very scary. Ciou-Jyu's death brings the horrible memory back to her. How can she not feel angry? She, for sure, understands Ciou-Jyu's misery more than anyone else. Oh, my poor dope. How can I feel unhappy that she hates the Chinese people? She is entitled."

Ciou-Lian hugged Ciou-Tao tightly. She wished Ciou-Tao could stay with her so she could protect her and give her a better life. However, she couldn't. She couldn't even hold on to this moment longer.

"Ciou-Lian, I have to go home. Otherwise, my brothers would think I was kidnapped."

Her dope still had her sense of humor to joke about it. It was good and sad.

"Ciou-Tao, wait. I have apples for you."

"Apples again? Don't you have anything else? Ciou-Jyu used to give me chicken legs and hard-boiled eggs, and you always give me apples. Well, how come you two couldn't use your imagination and give me something else?" Ciou-Tao, of course, was kidding. That was her being little sister in front of her dearest sister, and Ciou-Lian knew it and liked it.

"Well, too bad. Take them or leave them. Have you ever heard that an apple a day keeps the doctor away?"

"No, never heard of it. But I am glad that you told me now. Since you have apples often, you are going to live longer than me for sure. That's great!"

Ciou-Lian made a face and ran into the house to get apples. When she came back, she had two bags with her.

"Two bags of apples?" Ciou-Tao pretended to be very surprised and feel troubled, but the truth was that she always loved to get apples from Ciou-Lian and chicken legs and hard-boiled eggs from Ciou-Jyu. No matter how many chicken legs, hard-boiled eggs, or apples she got, even just one, she always felt very happy. Those chicken legs, hard-boiled eggs, and apples were the love from her beloved sisters, which proved that Ciou-Jyu and Ciou-Lian still cared about her as they did in the old days. Yes, poor Ciou-Tao had a great appetite—both her stomach and her heart needed to be fed.

"No. When I went to my room to get apples, my a-bu came to give me a piece of cooked pork belly meat. She told me to give it to you."

"Really? She is so nice. Thank her for me. I love her. How does she know I dream of eating pork? She is a super wonderful lady."

"I give you apples all the time. Why don't I get 'super wonderful' ever?" Ciou-Lian tried to act like she was mad, but she couldn't. In fact, she laughed out loud. She felt that Ciou-Tao was too funny.

"That's because you're beautiful." Ciou-Tao tried to act serious, but she failed.

"See, I don't believe you. You are not even serious."

"You *are* beautiful. Also, very kind. I love you the most in the world." Ciou-Tao always loved Ciou-Jyu and Ciou-Lain equally. They were the people whom she loved the most in the world, but now, only one was left.

"OK. For the 'beautiful and kind,' I'll give you two more apples next time."

The two sisters laughed. They were laughing so loud that Uncle Huang, Ciou-Jyu, and Wen-Zhi might be able to hear them in heaven with big smiles.

That day, the darkest day, Wen-Hua walked Ciou-Tao home after Ciou-Jyu's funeral.

"How come a married woman can't be buried in her original family plot?"

"Bad luck, perhaps."

"It's so not fair that women have to obey those ridiculous ideas and rules."

There was one rule that bothered Ciou-Tao a great deal. Although Ciou-Tao's adoptive father loved her the same as his sons, once she married, she wouldn't be able to go home to see her adoptive father and brothers anytime she wanted to.

Why?

There were two popular explanations. A daughter would bring bad luck to her original family if she went home often. Furthermore, people would gossip about it and think that she had a bad marriage and so came home often. Well, old-fashioned people had a great fear of bad luck and a bad name. Therefore, in some strict families, their married daughters could come home only once in a year, on the second day of the Lunar New Year, and they asked their daughters-in-law to do the same.

"I am not going to get married, so I can be buried with

my family after I die." Ciou-Tao was happy that she had figured out a way to live without others' control.

"Well, Ciou-Tao, I think you don't know a custom. An unmarried woman can't be buried in her family plot. In fact, they can't even be buried next to any other family members' graves."

"What? Bringing bad luck again?"

"You got that right."

"I can't believe it. This is outrageous! This world is really against women. Asking women to behave and do every-thing in high standards and unreasonable ways. They treat them as a piece of meat. They chop them, cook them, and toss them in whatever way they want."

"Ciou-Tao, it's not that I disagree with you, but not every man is like that. At least, I don't and I won't treat women like that."

"Wen-Hua ge, sorry. I know you are not that kind of person. The other day, Ciou-Lian told me not to hate a group of people just because a few or many of them are bad. But sexual discrimination is different. It's like the whole society is against women. More ridiculously, many women treat their daughters or daughters-in-law as if they are enemies."

"I know. It's so wrong."

"How come they don't stick together to tell men to treat them fairly?"

"I have no idea." Wen-Hua was very mad about how his mother had treated Ciou-Jyu. He did not understand why his mother didn't like a sweet girl who was smart and worked hard. As a matter of fact, she chose Ciou-Jyu to be Wen-Zhi's future wife. "Didn't she like her and so adopted her?" He asked himself this question a million times.

"Wen-Hua ge, you are going to university in two years. Maybe you should study the human mind. To see what's wrong with people. Maybe you can change the world."

"Well, I don't know if I can get into medical school. I am not smart like my brothers. Even if I am lucky to get in, I don't

163

think I can cut people's heads open to study their brains."

"It does sound bloody scary. OK, study something else. By the way, which school do you want to go to?"

"Cheng-Kung University [成功大學] in Tainan [台南]."

"Tainan? So I won't be able to see you anymore."

"Ciou-Tao, I still have one year and half in high school, so we still can see each other often. Besides, I will come home on holidays and winter and summer breaks after I go to university."

"But Tainan is so far away, on another side of the mountains. You won't want to come home often when you think about taking more than eight hours to come home. Why don't you want to go to a school in Taipei?"

"Ciou-Tao, to be honest with you, I want to be away from home. My parents disappointed me, and I lost my brother and Ciou-Jyu. My heart hurts. Sometimes, I feel I can't breathe from thinking of them. It doesn't mean I want to forget them by being away from home. I am not going to forget them ever, but I have to find a way to forgive people and make peace with myself."

"Wen-Hua ge, I have no peace in my mind either. I hate Ciou-Jyu's husband and the Chinese people. In fact, I would never like any Chinese people for the rest of my life."

"But, Ciou-Tao, Uncle Huang was Chinese, and he was a very nice man. You might meet some Chinese people like him in the future."

"Can't. I just can't like any Chinese people anymore. They practically killed your brother and my sister. Furthermore, once I was almost raped by a Chinese man. They are just bad people. They like to rape women. Do you know te-tiam-a? Those places lock women up, and many Chinese men go there and pay to rape those poor women all the time. Uncle Huang was exceptional. He is the greatest man I have ever met. I love him like my own father. He will always stay in my heart."

"Oh, Ciou-Tao. I am sorry to hear about what happened to you. I think I can understand your feelings. The hatred that

164

I have in my heart probably is the same degree as yours. But we have to be very careful. Don't let that angry monster eat us up. It's not worth being ruined by those bastards. That's why I want to go to the university in Tainan. To find myself again and to be a better person."

"I see. You want to help yourself by changing the scenery. Wen-Hua ge, I hope your dream comes true, and thank you for sharing your feelings and thoughts with me. It helps me. I don't want to be a person who has tons of hatred in the heart, either, but I have no way out. Now, I will try to find a way to calm my mind."

"That's great, Ciou-Tao. Don't let those people hurt us more."

8

The Alley

The last year in senior high school was very stressful for the students who wanted to go to university, because only about one-third of students in Taiwan could get in. Wen-Hua was too humble. He was one of the top students at his school. Perhaps he compared himself to his elder brothers, Wen-De and Wen-Zhi, who didn't need to spend a lot of time studying but got good grades all the time, so he felt that he wasn't intelligent. However, teachers believed that Wen-Hua would do very well on the entrance examination and get into medical school. He had indeed been a little bit interested in medicine but was not anymore after Wen-Zhi was stabbed to death and Ciou-Jyu killed herself in the hospital. He wanted to be away from anything that would remind him of the death of Wen-Zhi and Ciou-Jyu.

Then what did he want to study at university?

Mathematics or physics.

Wen-Hua had an interesting math teacher in the first year of senior high school. He didn't just teach math but talked about math. He told them how different mathematicians described mathematics, the science of formal systems, all mathematics is symbolic logic, a self-evident truth, the queen of sciences, which charmed Wen-Hua a great deal. Then the physics teacher said, "Physics is to understand how the universe behaves, and mathematics is its inseparable partner." Well, how could Wen-Hua resist the two beautiful subjects? Thus, he spent a lot of time studying them and found them very interesting. As a result, he thought about majoring in them at university, but at the same time, he thought about medicine too. Later, the death of Wen-Zhi and Ciou-Jyu helped him to make a decision.

Since the goal was clear, Wen-Hua felt relaxed. He worked very hard. He wouldn't go to bed until one o'clock in the morning almost every day. However, he was happy. He felt that he was getting closer to Tainan.

After the funeral, Wen-Hua began to go to see Ciou-Tao once a week. It was always a pleasure to visit Ciou-Tao. She made Wen-Hua forget schoolwork and exams and made him laugh. Ciou-Tao's life was considerably different from his, but it was fascinating to him. Even though many stories that he heard from Ciou-Tao were sad or bitter, Wen-Hua still enjoyed listening because he was interested in how people lived and thought about things. He felt that he was living in a beautiful small world without most people in it. He wasn't aware of it until he learned a lot about Ciou-Jyu's life in her original family. Gradually, his desire of getting to know the people in the real world got stronger and stronger, but his mother thought that the people in the real world were vulgar and there was no need to have any association with them. Wen-Hua deemed that his mother was mistaken. Wealth did not make people respectable and honorable, and poverty wouldn't make people have less virtue either.

Wen-Hua was impressed by Ciou-Tao and her neighbors' generosity. He presumed that Ciou-Tao's neighbors all knew that his family was very wealthy. However, there was always someone who would give him a guava, a mango, a peach, a passion fruit, a Java apple, or a piece of watermelon. Wen-Hua could tell that some of them might not be poor like Ciou-Tao's adoptive family, but they were not well off either. However, they shared and gave. A middle-aged woman would loudly call Ciou-Tao from her home, two houses away from Ciou-Tao's home, which usually meant she had something for Ciou-Tao. Mostly, it was food that she had just cooked. It could be some sweet potatoes or pancakes. Honestly, those were simple food, which his family seldom ate them at all, but Wen-Hua found that they were so delicious. Perhaps it was the love that made them taste so good.

Not to mention Ciou-Tao's generosity. She gave Wen-Hua a whole Fuji apple. Wen-Hua was extremely shocked. A Fuji apple? That was a very expensive fruit at the time in Taiwan. Because of the weather, apples couldn't grow in Taiwan. It was an imported fruit and so was very expensive, and only rich people could afford to buy it. Wen-Hua's family was wealthy, but they only had apples once in a blue moon. Of course, Wen-Hua knew that the apple must have come from Ciou-Lian. Ciou-Lian's adoptive family was richer than his family, so they could afford to buy apples often. Even so, shouldn't Ciou-Tao save the apple for herself? No, she shared. A girl who lived in poverty and had to find food in people's garbage cans gave him a fancy apple. She astonished him.

Another quality that Wen-Hua liked very much about those people was their caring. In his mother's opinion, those people were nosy. Wen-Hua couldn't say his mother was completely wrong. It was true that a few of them were solely nosy and liked to gossip, but most of them were caring. Perhaps they were in the same boat, working hard to survive and make their lives better, so they inquired of each other how things were going and offered assistance if they were able. After they learned that Wen-Hua was preparing for the university entrance examination, they encouraged him and also told him to take care of his health. They hoped his dream would come true. The middle-aged woman who gave Ciou-Tao sweet potatoes and pancakes went to the temple to pray for him and asked a talisman from God of Culture and Literature—Taiwanese people call him Wenchang Dijun (文昌君)—who can help students to do well on exams. She gave that talisman to Wen-

Hua. All the things that they said to him or did for him were simply because he was Ciou-Tao's friend.

Hurrah!

Wen-Hua got a very high score on the university entrance examination, so he got his wish to study mathematics at Cheng-Kung University in Tainan. He was happy, but his parents weren't.

"Why did you lie to us?" Wen-Hua's mother was very angry that Wen-Hua hadn't put the Taiwan University College of Medicine on the list of the university department choice order of preference, because Wen-Hua could go to any university and study any subject according to his scores.

"Mathematics? What are you going to do after you graduate?"

"I like math. It's very interesting."

"Fun won't bring you a great career and money."

"Mother, why does everything have to be about money and social status?"

"Have you ever thought about why you can have everything that you have right now?"

Wen-Hua couldn't deny that he was lucky to be born in a wealthy family, so he could have almost anything that he wanted. Especially after learning how Ciou-Tao and her neighbors lived, he was very grateful about what he had.

"Next year, you have to transfer to Taiwan University and a subject that will have career prospects—civil engineering, for example."

In Mother's eyes, only graduating from Taiwan University would give him a bright future. Once, Wen-Hua had been eager to follow Wen-De's steps to study at Taiwan University, the best university in the country, Taiwan's Harvard. However, the death of Wen-Zhi and Ciou-Jyu had had a tremendous impact on him, so Wen-Hua walked off the path that he had planned to go, going to Cheng-Kung University in Tainan instead of Taiwan University in Taipei.

On the contrary, in the alley, Ciou-Tao's world, people's reaction from knowing that Wen-Hua got into university was entirely different.

Since Wen-Hua started to visit Ciou-Tao once a week after Ciou-Jyu died, gradually, he found that he had become a member of a small community in that alley. Not only had the people accepted him, but he also felt attached to them. Every time Wen-Hua walked into the alley, it felt like going home. Therefore, since Wen-Hua was officially free, no summer school, no homework, no exams, after the university entrance examination, he went to visit Ciou-Tao more often, almost every other day. Believe it or not, soon, people in the alley would get concerned if he didn't come to see Ciou-Tao for more than two days, and he would feel weird on those days that he didn't go to visit Ciou-Tao. Then there was no surprise that the people in the alley were vastly happy when they learned of Wen-Hua's good news on the result of the university entrance examination.

The release of the result of National University Entrance Examination was a big thing in Taiwan. Almost everyone was concerned about it, no matter if they had children, nephews, or nieces who took the university entrance examination or not. The next day, after the day that the results were released in newspapers, Wen-Hua went to tell Ciou-Tao the result. However, before he saw and told Ciou-Tao the good news, people in the alley had asked him first, and in seconds, everyone knew which university he had gotten into. They were so happy for him even though they didn't know what mathematics was and what one could do after graduation. They applauded for him and congratulated him. They felt as proud as if their son, nephew, or grandson had gotten into university.

While everyone in the alley was cheering for Wen-Hua's

good news on the university entrance examination, Ciou-Tao's youngest brother came back from the ditch with his friends. Once he understood why the alley was filled with merriment, he immediately ran to Wen-Hua and gave him the frog that he had just caught in the ditch. He said, "Congratulations, Wen-Hua ge! A gift for you."

Well, that wasn't the only gift that Wen-Hua got.

A granny gave Wen-Hua a tie. She said, "That's my husband's tie. He died. No one can use it. For you. You will need it in college."

An old man who was smoking gave Wen-Hua a cigarette and said, "Have one; you are a man now." Wen-Hua couldn't take that, but he thanked him.

The middle-aged woman who went to the temple to pray for Wen-Hua and gave him a talisman was so happy. She said, "What did I tell you? Wenchang Dijun is very powerful and kind. If you ask him sincerely, he will make your wish come true." Then she gave Wen-Hua a pineapple. It was huge, and Wen-Hua felt that he couldn't take such a big fruit from her. He suggested taking a piece of pineapple, not the whole. However, she said, "Pineapple in Taiwanese language sounds like 'Luck comes to you.' I don't want others to share your luck away."

There were too many gifts to bring home, but not one from Ciou-Tao. In fact, Ciou-Tao looked a little bit unhappy that day.

"What's the matter? Are you OK?" Wen-Hua was concerned because that wasn't the Ciou-Tao he knew.

"Well, you are leaving. We are not going to see each other often anymore."

"I know. But, you know, we can write to each other if you want."

"It's a good idea, but it's still not the same. Besides, you will read my ugly handwriting. It's bad."

"My handwriting isn't good either."

"Really? I can't believe what I heard. I thought smart

people have beautiful handwriting."

"Where did the idea come from?"

"Ciou-Jyu and Ciou-Lian both have elegant handwriting. They are smart."

"Well, my brother Wen-De is remarkably intelligent, but his handwriting is worse than mine. Ha, ha, ha!"

"Thank God they don't judge handwriting on the university entrance examination. By the way, Wen-Hua ge, congratulations. I am so happy for you. I have a gift for you."

It was a fountain pen. No doubt, Ciou-Tao got it from a garbage can, but it looked brand new.

"I was very lucky last month. I got several good things from the trash cans. A watch, an antique mirror, a pair of sneakers, and this fountain pen. I am very sure this pen is good, but you need to buy some ink."

"That's wonderful, Ciou-Tao. I like this gift. I am going to use it to write my papers, of course, and to write to you too. I'll buy some ink later on the way home."

"How? With all the gifts? It's impossible. Ha, ha, ha..."

"No. I will only bring this pen and that tie home. The rest of them are yours now."

"All for me?"

"That's right."

"What if they ask?"

"They wouldn't mind that I gave them to you, because you're their sweetheart."

"OK. Thanks."

"I got to go."

9

White Terror and Freedom Fighters

Two months later, at the end of September, Wen-Hua left for Tainan. Tainan was new for him. He wanted to get to know the city a little bit, so he left one week before school began.

Tainan is the oldest city in Taiwan and is also known as Capital City because Tainan had been the capital of Taiwan for nearly three hundred years. The Dutch occupied Taiwan from 1624 to 1662. In the beginning, they only had control in the south and built a defensive fort, which was called Fort Zeelandia (熱蘭遮城), in Tainan. Two years after the Dutch's occupation of the southern Taiwan, the north of Taiwan was under Spain's control (1626–1642). It was the Dutch who kicked the Spanish out of Taiwan. Later, the Dutch were pushed out of Taiwan by a Chinese prince, Zheng Chenggong (鄭成功), as known as "Koxinga" (in Dutch). In Mandarin, Koxinga pronounces as Guo-xing-ye, which means "lord of the loyal surname." That is how the Cheng-Kung University got its name, to memorialize Zheng Chenggong. Hence, the Capital City, Tainan, has much history and culture to share with the people who come to it.

Wen-Hua loved Tainan right away. He found that Tainan was a charming city, and he fell in love with the food completely. He wrote to Ciou-Tao and told her everything in great detail. Ciou-Tao replied and asked him not to talk about food anymore. She got very hungry from reading his letter. Of course, Ciou-Tao was kidding. She loved to hear anything from Wen-Hua. Besides, she couldn't travel to anywhere, but she could have many Tainan trips through Wen-Hua's eyes and words.

Knowing Wen-Hua seemed to enjoy his life in Tainan made Ciou-Tao happy. The deaths of Wen-Zhi and Ciou-Jyu and the university entrance examination had stressed Wen-Hua so much. He needed some free air. People like her had learned and understood the cruelty of the world very well since they were young. She could handle disasters and tragedies much better than Wen-Hua; therefore, Ciou-Tao had worried very much about Wen-Hua in the past year. It seemed Wen-Hua's decision, going to Cheng-Kung University, was correct. From reading his letters, Ciou-Tao always felt that she could see Wen-Hua smiling.

The history and culture of Tainan were very charming indeed, but the life at university was even more lovely. The classes and professors were great, and Wen-Hua met some delightful people in the student clubs. However, he didn't join any clubs in the end but went to a private reading group instead.

Private?

Yes, it had to be very private because they were reading some books that were banned by the Chinese Nationalist government, the Chiang Kai-shek regime. As a matter of fact, some people were put in prison or got the death penalty because of that.

Oh my God! Didn't Wen-Hua know that?

He knew.

Then why did he want to join the group and read those books?

Because he wanted to know things.

What things?

Anything. Everything that the Chiang Kai-shek regime forbade.

Sometimes Wen-Hua shook his head and laughed after he read some banned books. Those were classic literature, excellent essays, poems, and novels. They were banned only because those Chinese writers were in China or didn't flee to Taiwan with the Chiang Kai-shek regime—or because they were Russian writers. Wen-Hua couldn't believe that a writer's good work was denied entirely because he or she lived in the land that was controlled by the Communists. Moreover, why did the Chinese Nationalist government think that they could judge better than everyone else in Taiwan and decide what books people could or couldn't read?

Well, the Chinese Nationalist government probably didn't think that they knew better and so decided what books people in Taiwan could read or not. More than likely, it was because Communism was a threat, a big one, to the Chinese Nationalist government, the Chinese Nationalist Party, the Chiang Kai-shek regime. From the First Civil War (1927–1937) to the Second Civil War (1945–1949), the Chinese Nationalist Party was helpless in fighting with the Chinese Communist Party. The Chinese Communist Party really knew how to survive, escaping and hiding, pretending to surrender, acting willingly to unite with the Chinese Nationalist Party to fight with the Empire of Japan, and utilizing the Second Sino-Japanese War (1937–1945) to recover and get stronger. Eventually, the Chinese Communist Party kicked the Chinese Nationalist Party out of China. As a result, Taiwan was the last piece of land that allowed the Chinese Nationalist Party to catch their breath and place their hope on, so one day they could win the war and go back to China to be the authority again. Hence, the Chinese Nationalist Party definitely couldn't lose the last land as they lost China. They mustn't let it happen again. Consequently, Communism and anything that was related to Communism had to be banned, banned, banned.

However, Communism wasn't the only threat to the Chiang Kai-shek regime. Well, think about it. Which intelligent people who had a conscience would like a dictatorship? Not Lei Zhen (雷震, 1897–1979). Not Ying Hai-Guang (殷海光, 1919–1969).

They were both editors and writers of the *Free China Journal*(自由中國), a magazine that was founded in 1949. In the early time, the position of the magazine was on the Chiang Kai-shek regime's side because the people who founded the *Free China Journal* were some famous Chinese scholars and politicians who were against Communism and pursued democracy. However, they saw the evil of Chiang Kai-shek gradually, how he gave himself absolute power in the Chinese Nationalist Party and the country, the Republic of China, a Chinese exiled regime. The magazine began to review the problems that happened in Taiwan and criticize and advise the government.

In 1954, Lei Zhen pointed out the crisis of education; the Chinese Nationalist Party interfered in education and entered schools to develop their affairs. President Chiang Kai-shek, the chairperson of the Chinese Nationalist Party, got extremely mad and gave an order to expel Lei Zhen from the Chinese Nationalist Party. Later, Ying Hai-Guang supported Lei Zhen's opinions with two articles and said that education and academics should be free from political influence.

In October 1956, the magazine published a special issue to ask Chiang Kai-shek to obey the law and constitution and criticize the government's policies with sixteen articles written by scholars and politicians in the name of celebrating Chiang Kai-shek's seventieth birthday. After that, from July 1957, for eight months, the *Free China Journal* published a series of editorials to discuss the use of US aid, the need of an opposition party, freedom of the press, and the impossibility of striking back at mainland China. Well, weren't they brave—or, you may say, crazy—to write something that would provoke a dictator? Believe it or not, they talked more.

In 1960, the Chinese Nationalist Party proposed to freeze the law and let Chiang Kai-shek run for president a third term. How could Lei Zhen and other fellows in the magazine bear that idea? It was unconstitutional. They opposed it and criticized the Chinese Nationalist Party for controlling the country. Hence, Lei Zhen strongly believed that an opposition party was needed, and he acted. Lei Zhen was Chinese, but he looked for and gathered the important Taiwanese and Chinese people in Taiwanese society to found a party. Immediately, the three newspapers that belonged to the Chinese Nationalist Party attacked Lei Zhen as a traitor who worked for the Chinese Communist Party, who wanted to create riots in Taiwan and overthrow the government. Three months later, on September 4, 1960, Lei Zhen was arrested for distributing the Chinese Communists' propaganda and covering up for the Chinese Communists' spy. Chiang Kai-shek gave an order, "Must sentence for at least ten years in prison, and the primary verdict can't be changed in the second and third trials." Of course, the magazine, the *Free China Journal*, died with the incident.

Luckily, Ying Hai-Guang didn't get arrested. However, he got severe punishments. Most of his books were banned, and the scholars who spoke for the Chiang Kai-shek regime called him a fake liberalist, a traitor, and a liar. In 1966, Taiwan University cancelled the renewal of his employment as a professor in the Department of Philosophy at Taiwan University under the government's pressure. In 1967, Harvard University invited Ying Hai-Guang to be a research scholar, but Chiang Kai-shek's government forbade him to go. Moreover, any professors who were associated with Ying Hai-Guang in the Department of Philosophy at Taiwan University lost their jobs. Besides, the government had people to keep a watch on him. Thus, in a way, he was in prison too. A great educator and a philosopher, Ying Hai-Guang died in 1969. He was only forty-nine years of age and didn't have a chance to see his friend Lei Zhen, who, after being released from prison, still fearlessly spoke out his care for Taiwan and expectation to the government. Nine years later, in 1979, Lei Zhen died at the age of eighty-two.

That was the fate of those people who wanted to speak from their hearts and tell the truth and right and wrong in Taiwan during the White Terror period, from 1949 to 1991. To Chiang Kai-shek and his party, shutting those people up was a job that must be done so their authority wouldn't be challenged and the Republic of China wouldn't die in Taiwan after they were kicked out of China by the Chinese Communist Party.

"Outrage!"

Wen-Hua got very excited when he learned Lei Zhen and Ying Hai-Guang's remarkable stories and suffering. Actually, that wasn't the first White Terror story that Wen-Hua had learned, but he had the same strong reaction, upset and angry, as always. Moreover, he felt remarkably ridiculous that people around him had never talked about some big shocking things that happened in Taiwan, as if those things had never happened before. For instance, Wen-Hua was born in 1946, and the February 28 Incident, which was known as the 228 Incident or the 228 Massacre, happened in 1947. He had never heard his parents, neighbors, teachers, or friends talking about that massacre. At school, from elementary school to high school, not a single history textbook mentioned the 228 Incident. The day that Wen-Hua learned of the 228 Incident in the private reading group, he was shocked and speechless. However, Wen-Hua's mind was very busy.

"How could it be possible that not a person around me talked about that massacre?"

"It's a huge brutal incident in Taiwanese history. How can schools not teach or talk about it?"

"Aren't people angry? Why don't they say something?"

Well, perhaps Wen-Hua was too astonished to be able to think with common sense, but soon he got his rationality back.

"Which criminal would voluntarily tell their crimes to the public?"

"What can people do while the murders are the government?"

"The best is to put their heads down, lock the pain, anger, and sadness in the bottom of their hearts, shut their mouths, and live."

Nothing that Wen-Hua had learned shook his trust in the government as much as the 228 Incident. He agreed with English-born American political activist, philosopher, political theorist, and revolutionary Thomas Paine that "government, even in its best state, is but a necessary evil; in its worst state, an intolerable one."[1] He also believed that government mustn't be evil to the degree that the Chiang Kai-shek regime had been.

After the government agents used the barrels of their guns to hit a middle-aged widow Lin Chiang-Mai (林江邁), on February 27, 1947, who had illegally sold smuggled cigarettes, Taiwan fell into chaos. In order to resolve the conflict between the Chinese Nationalist government and Taiwanese people and help the society restore peace, the local leaders, intellectuals, elites, and provincial councilors had tried to negotiate with the Chinese Nationalist government. With the permission of the governor-general of Taiwan, Chen Yi (陳儀, 1883–1950), on March 1, the officials and provincial councilors formed the 228 Incident Settlement Committee (二二八事件處理委員會). There were twenty-seven committees across Taiwan. The Committees had collected public opinions and asked political reform. Chen Yi showed friendliness and promised to improve the situation. At the same time, Chen Yi sent a telegram to Chiang Kai-shek to request for sending more troops to Taiwan. On March 8, the troops landed at Keelung (基隆), the massacre started. On March 9, the 21st Division headed to the south, and the whole of Taiwan began to be slaughtered. Of course, most members of the 228 Incident Settlement Committee were accused of rebellion or treason and executed.

After Wen-Hua's trust in the government was shaken, his eyes and mind opened. Finally, he could see that something he had felt to be normal was actually abnormal or wrong.

"The criminals don't want to tell their crimes—for example, the 228 Incident—which is normal, but why don't they teach us more Taiwanese history and geography, since we are living on this island?" This was a question that Wen-Hua had never asked before. In fact, he and his peers in high school had never felt strange or wrong about the fact that they learned so much Chinese history and geography but so little Taiwanese history and geography. Now, Wen-Hua could see how abnormal it was that all students in Taiwan knew the major rivers and mountains in China but knew barely any rivers and mountains in Taiwan.

Well, if following the Chinese Nationalist government's logic, it wasn't abnormal at all. Taiwan was a part of China, a province of China. Chinese people learn Chinese history and geography. What was there to question? Moreover, equally introducing each province of China by a few pages in a textbook—what was wrong with that? In fact, it would be very wrong if schools taught more Taiwanese history and geography.

No matter how logical it was, assuredly, it is wrong if people know nothing about their land because of the government's will. Sadly, at the time, students in Taiwan were trained to listen to the teachers, not question teachers' ideas, so very few of them had a habit, ability, or courage to question and challenge the things and ideas around them. Unless those young people had a chance to learn Taiwanese history and the truth of the Chinese Nationalist government from their families and acquaintances, or by reading banned books, most of them grew up to become obedient citizens who loyally loved their fatherland, China, and government as the Chinese Nationalist government wished.

Indeed, Wen-Hua's eyes and mind opened because he got acquainted with thinkers in the private reading group and read banned books. However, he had always been a thinker since he was little. That was why he was interested in the private reading group and eagerly desired to join it after he had an intelligent conversation with a senior student in a student club.

Wen-Hua had started to think and ask questions since Ciou-Jyu came to his family. In the beginning, he was happy to have a sister. Soon, he loved this beautiful sister very much. Ciou-Jyu was very caring, so even though they were the same age, she was more like his elder sister. One sweet memory was always vividly in Wen-Hua's mind. Every day, Ciou-Jyu would make sure that Wen-Hua brought everything with him before they went to school together—the water bottle, especially. Ciou-Jyu would say to him, "You need to drink more water. It's good for you." Weeks later, he learned that Ciou-Jyu was a shim-bu-a, Wen-Zhi's future wife. He was shocked. He had never heard of shim-bu-a and so didn't understand why Ciou-Jyu had to come to their family before she and Wen-Zhi could get married. She was ten years old, like him. He couldn't imagine that he had to leave his family to live with another family. It must be scary. Besides, he couldn't understand why Ciou-Jyu had to do so much work. It seemed she was a servant, not Wen-Zhi's future wife. He actually told his mother that Ciou-Jyu should be treated like him and his brothers because she was his sister, a future sister-in-law. However, Wen-Hua's mother said, "You are wrong. She is a shim-bu-a, so she is not equal to us." It shocked him a great deal to know his mother's thinking. Of course he was upset, too, which led him to think about fairness. Thus, in a way, the manner in which Wen-Hua's mother treated Ciou-Jyu brought a thinker to the world.

However, the thinker grew very slowly and mostly thought about the subjects that were related to Ciou-Jyu. Later, the deaths of Wen-Zhi and Ciou-Jyu made Wen-Hua grow very fast. For the first time, he had a taste of despair. The people whom he loved were gone in the blink of an eye. He suddenly lost a sense of purpose in his life and wanted to be away from home, a place that disappointed him and caused his loss. Thank God Wen-Hua had a duty, looking after Ciou-Tao, which turned out to be a pleasure and comforted his soul. Thus, he stopped being negative. He began to ask himself, "Since life is like a shooting star, what do I want in life?" Ciou-Tao and her neighbors showed him the answer. He found that Ciou-Tao and her neighbors just wanted to live, but they struggled. They didn't give up, nor even complain, and they just kept on going and wished tomorrow would be better. Wen-Hua realized, "I did lose a great deal, like many people who also lost their beloved ones, but I still have plenty, more than most people, to live." That was why, a year later, reading those banned books and magazines fit his need: to know things and broaden his views and mind.

Those banned articles, books, and magazines, especially the *Free China Journal*, helped Wen-Hua to learn the concepts of freedom and democracy, which were completely different from what he had learned from textbooks, teachers, or government. The freedom in Taiwan was the Chiang Kai-shek regime's definition of freedom. The democracy in Taiwan was the contrast to the Communism. They weren't real freedom and democracy. There was no freedom and democracy in Taiwan under the Chiang Kai-shek regime's control. Wen-Hua eventually came to his own conclusion. "Taiwan is the Chiang Kai-shek regime's shelter as they prepare to strike back at China. China is their home. Taiwan is not. They trust the Chinese people more than the Taiwanese people, but anyone, whether Chinese or Taiwanese, who is deemed as an enemy of the Chiang Kai-shek regime is guilty. Chiang Kai-shek is as bad as any dictators in the world, such as Adolf Hitler [希特

182

勒, 1889—1945], Joseph Stalin [史達林, 1878—1953], and Mao Zedong [毛澤東, 1893—1976]. The Chinese Nationalist Party is not any better than the Chinese Communist Party. Moreover, how they try to remind the Taiwanese people of the brutality in the Japanese ruling period is an ironically hideous joke."

Ciou-Tao noticed the change in Wen-Hua from reading his letters. It wasn't because Wen-Hua told her those thoughts in the letters. As a matter of fact, he couldn't do that. It was too dangerous to write down those kinds of ideas and send them to people. Undoubtedly, Ciou-Tao wouldn't report him, but what if the mail was lost? Wen-Hua couldn't imagine the possibility of consequence. However, Wen-Hua still didn't tell Ciou-Tao that he joined a private reading group and read banned books when he came back to the town during the winter break, because he didn't want to put Ciou-Tao in danger. He knew Ciou-Tao very well. She would surely want to read those banned books. In fact, Wen-Hua very much wished that he could give Ciou-Tao all the banned books that he had. Not only did he want Ciou-Tao to know those forbidden things, but he also wanted to know her opinions and have discussions with her. Maybe Ciou-Tao had little formal education, but she was an intelligent self-learner and a thinker. Wen-Hua valued Ciou-Tao's opinions. Many times, he was inspired by Ciou-Tao's ideas. However, Ciou-Tao lived in an open environment, which meant she couldn't secretly read banned books. Then why did he want to bring trouble to Ciou-Tao?

After the winter break, Ciou-Tao found more changes in Wen-Hua. In the letter, Wen-Hua said, "I consider a transfer to Taiwan University to study philosophy or political science. I think that mathematics can't help to solve people's problems."

Ciou-Tao replied, "Didn't you tell me that math is the queen of science? Then why do you want to leave the queen for the servant?"

"Ha! Ciou-Tao, you are so brilliant! Politics are the public affairs, and politicians like to call themselves the public servants."

In the letters, they were still the same old Wen-Hua and Ciou-Tao.

In the end, Wen-Hua didn't transfer to Taiwan University and study philosophy or political science. Something happened.

One day, Wen-Hua got a message. A military education instructor (教官) asked Wen-Hua to see him in the military education office. "Why does the military education instructor want to see me?" Wen-Hua was very surprised at first and got worried later.

In 1912, the government of the Republic of China started military education at schools in China. All students in senior high schools and universities had to learn military science and be trained on foot drill, shooting, and military fitness. After the Chiang Kai-shek regime fled to Taiwan in exile, they also practiced military education in senior high schools and universities. It began in 1951 and has never stopped since then. Usually, there are about three to six military education instructors in each school, which depends on the size of the school.

When the Chiang Kai-shek regime was exiled to Taiwan, the army that came with the government was called the Chinese Nationalist Army. Practically, they were Chiang Kai-shek's troops. Therefore, they were loyal to the Chiang Kai-shek regime and his party, the Chinese Nationalist Party. However, the regime needed more loyal people; in fact, the young people were better ones. What to do? Easy. Send their people, the military officers, to be military education instructors in senior high schools and universities, and help young people to become patriots. At the same time, of course, they could spy on everyone on the campus, which assured the whole of Taiwan was under control.

In recent years, many people in Taiwan, including students, have asked the military education instructors to step out of the schools. However, there are some people who disagree with the idea. They say that military education instructors are safeguards and mentors to students. They can keep schools safe. Perhaps when a bird has been kept in a cage too long, it forgets how to fly and the taste of freedom.

The military education instructor, who called Wen-Hua to the office, watched everything at school with his colleagues. He and his colleagues specifically disliked student clubs. In their viewpoint, that students got together to plan activities was potential trouble, and that students gathered to read was the worst kind of all situations. They knew that there were always some students who liked to read banned books. Thus, they were sure that there must be some private reading groups on campus. To them, it was very easy to watch students and acquire information. Most students were naive, so they just walked around campus and listened to students talking quietly and could get a lot of information. Furthermore, they had students who worked for them would provide them a lot of information. In addition, some patriotic students would come to report something too. Hence, it was very easy to find out the problem students.

"Yes, sir. Do you need me in service?" Wen-Hua tried to be calm.

"Someone told me that you are reading banned books. Is that true?"

"Of course not, sir. Everybody knows what banned

books mean. It's a crime to read them. I won't risk my future to read some poisonous books."

"Then how come people said that you are reading them?"

"I don't know, sir. It must be a mistake. If you want, you can come to my place to check. We can go right now." Wen-Hua had guessed the reason why the military education instructor called him, so he had prepared.

"It's good to know that you didn't read banned books. Don't read them in the future either. Otherwise, as you said, there won't be a future for you."

What a threat! Those plain words could terrify anyone profoundly.

Wen-Hua considered himself very lucky. He could have gotten a severe punishment, such as having major demerit, parole, expulsion, or stripping of academic standing, which was very common, but he didn't get any. Furthermore, Wen-Hua knew a case that had happened in the 1950s. A young lady named Ding Yao-Tiao (丁窈窕, 1927–1956), who read banned books, was reported to Taiwan Garrison Command (台灣警備總司令部), a state security department, by an evil man, and then she was sentenced to death. Hence, Wen-Hua felt fortunate because all he had gotten were cruel words. Wen-Hua saw it as enormous mercy from that military education instructor.

Ten years later, in the 1970s, two students of law at Taiwan University were also as lucky as Wen-Hua.

The two students were a couple, Hong San-Syong (洪三雄) and Chen Ling-Yu (陳玲玉). They read a lot of Ying Hai-Guang's books and realized that people in Taiwan had no freedom and democracy. Then they founded a student club, NTU Law Societas and published *NTU Law Societas*. They held a series of forums and speeches to discuss freedom of speech, which were so popular that caused trouble. Some of their friends were arrested by the secret police from Taiwan Garrison Command, and Hong San-Syong was going to be arrested too. However, the chief military education instructor in Taiwan University, Jhang De-Pu (張德溥), fought very hard to keep Hong San-Syong, because he knew that if he did not keep Hong San-Syong with him, Hong San-Syong would be imprisoned or might die in the prison. Thus, Hong San-Syong was saved, but he got a major demerit, and his girlfriend, Chen Ling-Yu, got two minor demerits, which was the chief military education instructor's decision.

After Hong San-Syong graduated, he couldn't find a job for a long time because of the mark on him. The couple blamed the chief military education instructor for bringing the misfortune. Later, Chen Ling-Yu graduated and passed the bar examination. Then, after they were married, the couple went to the United States to work and settled there eventually. Eighteen years later, they got a chance to meet the chief military education instructor and learned the truth. The chief military education instructor, Zhang De-Pu, was sent to rectify Taiwan University by Chiang Kai-shek's son, Chiang Ching-kuo, but he didn't do the job that he was assigned. On the contrary, he protected those students who pursued freedom of speech. As a result, he couldn't go back to the army and be promoted to become lieutenant general.

It was shocking and touching. The person whom they blamed and were mad about before wasn't a bad person at all. In fact, he was a brave man.

Being brave was almost impossible in the White Terror period. Brave people paid prices, losing friends, jobs, properties, health, or their lives. Thus, most people kept silent, put their heads down, and lived. Wen-Hua didn't approve of that. He believed that the civilians' silence enhanced the evil government's power. However, Wen-Hua became quiet himself after seeing the military education instructor.

"Who reported me to the military education instructor?" Wen-Hua wondered. He couldn't believe that he had been reported. Their reading group was very secret, and the leader wouldn't let strangers join easily unless he was very confident about the person's reliability. It couldn't be the members of the group. Then, who?

Wen-Hua never found out. At first, he really wanted to know who had reported him, but very soon, he wasn't interested anymore. That he had no clue was one reason, but more importantly, it was because he didn't know what he wanted to do if he found out the person. Yell at or beat the person? What was the use? In fact, the person might report him again, and Wen-Hua would get into real trouble. Alas. Autocracy brought out the worst in people. The weak people couldn't make the right decisions, the evil people perfectly fit into the situation, and most good people withdrew.

Although the anger came strongly, it didn't stay long. The fear came gradually and quietly, and then it lingered and changed Wen-Hua.

Besides Wen-Hua, the other two members of the reading group were called to see military education instructors too. Unfortunately, one of them got a minor demerit. He didn't admit that he read banned books, but he questioned the military education instructor, "What's wrong with reading those books? Many people say that they are great books."

"Well, who are those people?" the military education instructor asked him.

"I don't know."

"Really? Suddenly, you don't know. Maybe you and your reading pals are the many people."

"What reading pals?"

"Don't try to get smart with me. I won't argue with you. I know you are reading banned books, and you show no regret but arrogance. Therefore, you will get a punishment, a minor demerit."

"A minor demerit?"

"Yes. And you will be on probation next time if we find out that you read banned books again. Now, dismissed."

Frankly, their private reading group wasn't private anymore. They might be watched, so it was better they stopped gathering to read and have discussions. That was the end of the private reading group, and they couldn't even have a farewell party. Simple. Everyone was scared.

Maybe they were ambitious, critical, and passionate and felt that they could do something to change Taiwan. However, after the incident, they realized that they couldn't even fight with military education instructors. They crushed them like a human being using one finger to press ants to die, so easy.

Wen-Hua finally understood how it felt and why most people kept silent. Thus, he also put his head down to live. He no longer wanted to transfer to Taiwan University and study philosophy or political science. He just wanted to study mathematics, a world that respects logic and truth.

"Wen-Hua ge, I have a gift for you!" Ciou-Tao looked thrilled.

"A gift? Why?"

"To congratulate you on the transfer." Ciou-Tao was very confident that Wen-Hua had gotten the transfer.

A pain passed through Wen-Hua's heart.

"What's the matter? Are you OK? You seem upset."

"Ciou-Tao, it's a long story. Are you busy? Can we go to the seacoast to talk?"

"Let's go."

"They are bastards!"

"Ciou-Tao, don't get excited. It's over now."

"Something like this just makes me angry. I hate rats. I just don't understand how much harm a book can do to the country. If you don't like the ideas, you fight back. Banning books, what a loser!"

"Ciou-Tao, many banned books not only talk about good ideas but also reveal the truths of the government."

"Worse! When criminals got caught, they were punished, but when the government got caught, they banned books."

Wen-Hua laughed. He truly admired Ciou-Tao for her intelligence and sense of irony.

"Ciou-Tao, it's very sad. Some of those brilliant authors are in jail."

"What? Not only are their books banned, but they are also in prison? Just because they wrote something that the government doesn't like? I can't believe it! Are they Taiwanese writers?"

"Some of them are Chinese."

"I don't like the Chinese people, but I dislike this government more. You know, Uncle Huang wasn't allowed to go home because of the Chiang Kai-shek regime's order. If he and his comrades tried to go back to China, they would be seen as traitors or spies and killed. What a great Chinese government!"

"Ciou-Tao, you know you can't talk about this to people, right?"

"Otherwise, I might be reported to the secret police? I don't think so. My neighbors are good people. Besides, we are very careful. We only talk in the house if we want to complain or criticize that greatest Chinese government."

Wen-Hua couldn't believe what he had just heard. Ciou-Tao and her neighbors did not like the government either. He learned the Chinese Nationalist government's brutality and crimes from reading banned books and magazines. How about Ciou-Tao and her neighbors?

Well, Wen-Hua didn't know that it was the power of oral tradition. In human history, a lot of knowledge, ideas, culture, and historical events have been preserved and transmitted orally, and the government's brutality surely is the thing that people won't want to forget.

"Ciou-Tao, please don't always think you are safe. My friends and I are great examples. We thought we were safe and no one would know our reading group, but the government just found out."

"Then I shouldn't trust my neighbors anymore? I can't do that! They are like my family. We care for and trust each other. How awful would it be if people couldn't trust their friends anymore?"

"Ciou-Tao, I fully agree with you, but—"

"You are afraid and lost your faith in people?"

"Ciou-Tao, you know me well, or I should say that you know humanity well. Honestly, two months ago, I almost collapsed emotionally. My reading friends and I once were happy and enjoyed the reading and discussion. We were inspired a great deal by those banned books. We eagerly wanted to do something for Taiwan. However, one day, suddenly, we had no right to read those books anymore after seeing military education instructors. At first, I felt very angry that they took away our freedom to read. Then I felt terrified because I thought about that they could've put us in prison or killed us in the name of reading banned books. I feel better now but have difficulty trusting people. There must be someone who reported us to military education instructors; otherwise, how could they know our private reading group?"

"Wen-Hua ge, I am sorry. I should've been more thoughtful. If I were in your circumstance, I couldn't be calm like you for sure. I would go nuts, couldn't concentrate on schoolwork, and would just want to find out the dirty rat. You did great. I admire you."

"Ciou-Tao, I shouldn't laugh, because you are so sweet. But picturing you going nuts and trying to find out the rat. I am amused."

"Laugh! Laugh harder! I hate to see you looking serious and sad."

"Ciou-Tao, you just swept away all my negative feelings and thoughts."

"Good! And I'm going to find the rat and give it some lessons with the same broom!" Ciou-Tao looked determined.

"Thank you, ma'am." Wen-Hua stood up and bowed.

Both Ciou-Tao and Wen-Hua laughed out loud. So loud

and so free.

10

She:
A Warrior

A year later, Ciou-Tao was sixteen years old and got a job in a clothes store. The owner of the store was Ciou-Tao's adoptive father's distant relative, so he was willing to take Ciou-Tao on. He and his wife weren't nice people, but they had no complaints about Ciou-Tao's work.

Ciou-Tao's job was selling clothes. When a customer came into the store, Ciou-Tao would observe what styles of clothes that customer liked. Then Ciou-Tao would take out similar styles of clothes and show them to the customer. Therefore, knowing how to talk to customers was also very important in this job.

Well, talking to people happened to be Ciou-Tao's interest; in fact, she was great at it. Even someone like her boss's wife, a difficult and mean person, admired Ciou-Tao's ability and paid compliments. However, Ciou-Tao preferred the boss's wife to pay her a higher wage instead.

Since Ciou-Tao had a job, the financial situation in her adoptive family was improved. No more debts. No need to find food from trash bins anymore. Although they still ate poorly, Ciou-Tao felt so relieved. Finally, she was like a grown-up making money, and she could control her life. She liked the feeling. In fact, she thought that if all women could get a job, they would have more control over their own lives. Maybe they could decide how they wanted to live their lives. This idea wasn't born after Ciou-Tao got a job. Because of the hardship of her life and learning many women's miseries, she had given a lot of thought to this subject since she was little. Financial independence only confirmed and strengthened Ciou-Tao's belief.

Ciou-Tao had lived in the area that was right next to the red-light district since she was seven years old. In order to protect her, even though Ciou-Tao was too young to understand what sex was at the time, her dearest uncle Huang had tried hard to make her understand the danger of approaching those houses. After the neighbor aunts knew her, they warned her to be careful too. Unlike Uncle Huang's conservative way, Ciou-Tao's neighbor aunts talked openly. They told Ciou-Tao what French kiss, touching, intercourse, and rape were, and they would explain to her anything if Ciou-Tao asked.

Hmm...isn't it awkward to talk about sex in public?

No! They talked in private, and it was very casual. It could be two or three women chatting in one's home, and then Ciou-Tao came in and listened to them talking. They usually talked about news or gossiped of something. Believe it or not, Ciou-Tao enjoyed listening to them. Those neighbor aunts were considerate, you might say. Frequently, they would ask Ciou-Tao if she knew or understood something that they were chatting about. If Ciou-Tao did not know and shook her head, they would explain to her. Ciou-Tao also asked questions if she did not understand something that those neighbor aunts chatted about. Well, enthusiastic teachers and a curious student who liked to learn were a great combination. That was why eight-year-old Ciou-Tao knew that it was wrong when the Chinese man held her, touched her, and kissed her, and she screamed for help.

Ciou-Tao loved those neighbor aunts. In her heart, they were her mothers. Her adoptive mother was gentle and amiable, but she was very sick and died when Ciou-Tao was ten years old. Practically, Ciou-Tao didn't have a mother at all. Thank goodness Ciou-Tao had those neighbor aunts. They pitied Ciou-Tao and took care of her and taught her things like she was their daughter. Of course, to those neighbor grannies, Ciou-Tao was their granddaughter. That was the reason why Ciou-Tao knew so many sad stories that had happened in the red-light district. Those neighbor aunts always had new stories to tell, but most stories were quite similar: girls were sold to the te-tiam-a (brothels) by parents or abducted by strangers.

"How could their parents do that?" Ciou-Tao asked with rage.

"No way out!"

"What does that mean?"

"They are poor and have debts."

"But my parents didn't sell me to te-tiam-a. I think they don't love their daughters."

"Sometimes it's not they wanted to do that. It's the gangsters asked them to use their daughter to pay the debts. The gangsters would threaten to beat the father or rape the mother if they didn't pay the debts right away. Therefore, without parents saying anything, most of the time, the daughter would voluntarily go with the gangsters to save her family."

"I hate gangsters. They are monsters. They should be locked in jail." Ciou-Tao was really mad.

"There are some parents as bad as those gangsters."

"Really?"

"They like to drink or gamble and don't work. They owed people a great deal of money or wanted to get some cash in hand, so they sold their daughters to be prostitutes."

"They also need to be locked in jail."

"There are a group of people who need to be locked in jail too."

"Who?"

"Those people who would go to the aborigines' villages and look around to find some targets. If they see those parents who don't work but drink, they will tell them a way to make money."

"Selling their daughters to te-tiam-a?"

"No and yes. They lied. They told the parents that they could take their minor daughters to work at a factory in the city. Those parents believed them and let their daughters go with them. In the end, they were sold to te-tiam-a."

"This is beyond evil! I can't take it!"

"Ciou-Tao, who can take it? But it happens. Evil people are out there."

"How come all sold daughters?"

"Ciou-Tao, this is a man's world."

"It's not fair."

"You mean, they should sell sons too?" A neighbor aunt tried to joke with Ciou-Tao.

"That's not what I meant." Ciou-Tao laughed. Of course, no one should be sold. What Ciou-Tao despised was sexism.

"There is another kind of selling daughters. The parents married off their sixteen- or seventeen-year-old daughter to the Chinese man who is over thirty-five years old with a sum of money."

"How come they want to buy a person to marry them? Moreover, why did they choose girls who can be their daughters to marry?"

"They can't find one, so they buy one."

"What does that mean, 'They can't find one'?"

"Ciou-Tao, they are Chinese. Which Taiwanese family wants to marry their daughter to them? Maybe they have already had wives in China, or they might go back to China next year or in the next two to three years. Who knows? Not to mention that they are poor and no one understands them when they speak."

"Now that you mention it, the other day I heard a disgusting thing. Four Chinese men chipped in some money and bought a wife to share, and the girl was mentally disabled."

"No. You are kidding. I don't believe it. It's like animals, too ridiculous."

"But my uncle Huang is a great man."

"Ciou-Tao, you are right. Not all Chinese men are bad."

Besides listening and talking to the neighbor aunts, Ciou-Tao observed.

Ciou-Tao had many chances to observe the activities in the red-light district because she and her brothers went to the ditch to catch frogs and fish very often. The red-light district was right next to the ditch; therefore, Ciou-Tao could see that several dogs and gangsters were always sitting or standing outside of some houses and who went to te-tiam-a.

One thing bothered Ciou-Tao very much. It seemed some women weren't unhappy about being prostitutes.

Question? Ask the neighbor aunts!

"Oh, we didn't tell you that some of them volunteer to be prostitutes?"

"No, you didn't. Volunteer? How could it be?" Ciou-Tao was extremely surprised.

"Honey, poor. Their families are poor. They want to make quick and easy money. No shame."

"So they want to do it and decide to do it all by their own will?"

"Yes. Completely."

"Oh."

Actually, Ciou-Tao had some thoughts in her mind, but she didn't say them out. She knew that those neighbor aunts wouldn't like to hear them.

For the first time, Ciou-Tao learned that some women could make their own decisions to do what they wanted to do. How wonderful! However, she couldn't cheer for them, because the neighbor aunts would disapprove of it. It didn't mean Ciou-Tao approved of prostitution. She just loved the idea that a woman could master her life with her free will.

About the shame, Ciou-Tao also had some thoughts. Those women who volunteered to be prostitutes were seen as shameless, but how about the men who went to te-tiam-a and those parents who sold their daughters to te-tiam-a? Weren't they disgusting and sinful as well? However, it seemed people only criticized and looked down on those women but not those men and parents. Why? They also committed a shameful act, didn't they? Besides, if prostitution was illegal, how could te-tiam-a be everywhere in that part of town?

"Ciou-Tao, not all te-tiam-a are illegal."

"Really?" Ciou-Tao was very surprised. "How come?"

"Some of them have licenses."

"License? Permission to do that business?"

"Something like that."

"The government gave them licenses?"

"Yeah."

"I can't believe it!"

"You'd better believe it. In fact, some of them have a contract with the government."

"What does that mean? License and contract are different?"

"Having a license means you are qualified and so are allowed to do this business. The..."

"Auntie, wait! What does 'qualified' mean?"

"Do not have any girls under eighteen years old, and all the girls and women are healthy, for example."

"I see."

"Can I continue?"

"Yes, please."

"OK, having a contract with the government is more complicated."

"Let me tell. I can let Ciou-Tao understand easily."

"Good! Then I can go to make a fruit plate."

"Ciou-Tao, your uncle Huang and his comrades were soldiers from China, right? Most of them came to Taiwan without their families, so they are very lonely. They are veterans, so they are free to go to any te-tiam-a, legal or illegal. Those soldiers who are still in service go to those licensed te-tiam-a that the Chinese Nationalist government has a contract with."

"Because of loneliness, they need to go to te-tiam-a?

Uncle Huang didn't go."

"Ciou-Tao, maybe he went, and you didn't know."

"He was with my family all the time. I know he didn't go."

"See, that's why he didn't need to go. He had your family, so he was happy."

"But they have comrades."

"Ciou-Tao, do you like to be hugged?"

"Yes."

"Family or friends, which one you need more?"

"Family, I think."

"That's right. Maybe you have a lot of good friends, but you would need your family more. That's a different kind of love and affection. Moreover, they are grown men; therefore, they also need intimacy very much, and prostitutes could fulfill that need."

"But it's not the same. They are not their wives."

"Ciou-Tao, it's better than nothing."

"Oh..."

In Ciou-Tao's mind, she disagreed with the auntie's opinion. However, she was just a young girl who was in the early teens. She might learn some ideas of sex from the neighbor aunts, but she had no clue about romance and affection between a man and a woman. She believed that decent people wouldn't pay to have sex with young girls who were locked up by the owner of a te-tiam-a. If they were very lonesome and wanted to have a family, why didn't they find someone to marry? She believed that if they were as kind and gentle as Uncle Huang, many Taiwanese girls would be willing to marry them. It wouldn't be like what the neighbor aunt said: "Who wants to marry a Chinese man?"

Later on, Ciou-Tao learned of the 228 Incident from Wen-Hua, and she realized why many Taiwanese people wouldn't want to marry off their daughters to the Chinese men. It wasn't simply because the Chinese men were poor or weren't nice, or because they might have wives in China, or because there was a language barrier between the Taiwanese people and the Chinese people. It was more about hatred. How the Chiang Kai-shek regime and his troops brutally killed the Taiwanese people and seized their property made people furious. Ciou-Tao understood the anger completely. Her beloved sister Ciou-Jyu had been treated barbarically by her husband and many Chinese men who wanted to have intimacy and comfort from women.

The day when Ciou-Tao learned of Ciou-Jyu's death from Wen-Hua, she was shocked and sad but looked calm. She couldn't express herself completely to Wen-Hua, who was practically a stranger to her at the time. She hid her rage. After Wen-Hua left, she ran to find Ciou-Lian. Besides crying and running, she screamed in her heart, "Fuck those bastards who are crying about not being able to go back to China! I don't give a damn! They deserve their miseries."

This rage, later, became a tremendous fear when Ciou-Tao became a mother. She feared that her daughters, Mei-Ling and Mei-Ai, might be sexually harassed or abused by the Chinese men. Before Ciou-Tao met someone, she thought about leaving this part of the town so, in the future, her children wouldn't live in a scary and filthy place. However, she met a young man who had a small restaurant by the ditch, right next to the red-light district. Finally, she understood romance. She stayed. Perhaps love made Ciou-Tao believe that she could conquer any problems.

Ciou-Tao got the job in a clothes store at the age of sixteen, and she met that young man when she was eighteen. One day, Ciou-Tao walked into that young man's restaurant and ordered a bowl of braised pork over noodles, and the noodles were so delicious that she went back again. However, she didn't go to the restaurant often because of the same old issue, financial difficulty. Maybe she made money now, but she had a family to take care of with a small salary. Thus, she was very conservative. The fifth time she went, it was winter. The young man brought her a bowl of noodles and a bowl of wonton soup that she hadn't ordered.

"Sorry, I didn't order wonton soup."

"I know. I just thought that you wouldn't mind having a hot soup on a cold day."

"It would be wonderful to have a bowl of hot soup today, but I can't afford it."

"Oh, don't worry. It's free. I am sorry. I should've told you first."

"Free? Why?"

"It's embarrassing. I made a mistake on one customer's order. So I am asking you for a favor to have the soup."

"Oh, I see. No problem. I can help."

"Thank you."

"*Thank you!*" Ciou-Tao had a big smile.

Was it really a cook's mistake or affection? No matter what it was, he certainly got Ciou-Tao's attention. Ciou-Tao noticed, after talking to him so closely, that the young man had a handsome face. She also found that the young man had good manners and treated customers nicely. She liked that.

The next time Ciou-Tao went, the young man brought her a bowl of wonton soup again.

"Why? Making a mistake again?"

"No. This time, there's no mistake. It's that I want to give you a bowl of soup."

"Oh, why?"

"I want to go out with you."

Ciou-Tao almost fell off the stool.

"What do you think?" The young man had a big smile, and Ciou-Tao could see his teeth. They were very clean and white.

"OK." Ciou-Tao loved those white teeth.

"When do you have time?"

"I have to work every day, though."

"Like me?"

"You too?"

The two found common ground in their lives, which pulled them closer at once.

The young man, Chen Ming-Hao (陳明豪), was poor too. He was twenty-four years old. His father had died six years ago. He was the oldest son in the family, so naturally, he took the responsibility to take care of his three younger brothers and four sisters. Before his father died, he had worked with his father for six years. If you do the math, yes, he was only twelve years of age and started to work.

Ming-Hao's father was a farmer. After he was married and had a child, he decided to change his fate, being poor. He left the village for the town to find a job and left his wife and Ming-Hao to stay with his parents. He should've gone to a big city in another county. There was little opportunity to get a job in the town, so he only got a part-time labor job in the market at first. As time went by, he had some savings and had seen how people did business, so he got a food cart to sell noodles and wonton soup. Several months later, the business got steady, so he finally could bring his wife and Ming-Hao to stay with him in the town.

Once the family was united, babies came, one after another. Therefore, poverty came back. Even though they were not impoverished like others, who needed to send daughters away, he and his wife were struggling. As a result, Ming-Hao couldn't continue his education after he graduated from elementary school. Ming-Hao was sad about it because he liked school. However, he was acquainted with the reality. Ming-Hao put away his sadness and went to the market to help his father. Actually, in the beginning, he was hoping to get a job, but he was too young to be hired for a full-time job. Well, it didn't stop him from finding a way to make a few pennies. While Ming-Hao was working with his father, he got some manual work here and there, to move goods for some shops. Then he began to dream of having his own grocery store. However, the dream couldn't come true because of his father's death. Ming-Hao had to take over his father's business to take care of his family.

Working with his father for six years, Ming-Hao had learned everything that he needed to know to run the business. Thus, no transition issue. He felt stressed because the whole family responsibility fell on his shoulders. Although his four younger sisters stopped going to school one by one after they graduated from elementary school, Ming-Hao still needed to support the three younger brothers to finish high school. Preparing three people's tuitions and other school expenses was a huge burden, but in order to let his three brothers have a better future, Ming-Hao had to hang in there. Ming-Hao wished he could also let four younger sisters continue to go to school, at least finishing junior high school, because they liked school too. However, he just couldn't afford seven people's tuitions and school expenses at one time. More importantly, Ming-Hao wanted to break the chain of poverty in his family, so his brothers were the priority. His sisters, after all, would get married and become members of other families, so it wouldn't be a big problem if they didn't go to high school.

Two years after Ming-Hao took over the business, he heard a rumor that the local government wanted to rebuild the marketplace. Ming-Hao and other food vendors worried. "Where could we go?" They asked one another.

Surprisingly, the government thought about their benefits and gave them a place to do business. More amazingly, they didn't get a spot but a small house, which meant they could have their own restaurants.

Hurrah! What a great change!

Ming-Hao's business got better after moving to the new

place. In the marketplace, most people went there to shop for fruits, vegetables, meats, or grocery, and after one o'clock in the afternoon, the crowd would be gone. In the new place, the situation was completely different. In the morning and afternoon, most people on the street were residents. About four to five o'clock in the afternoon, people started to swarm in. Some tried to catch a 5:30 p.m. movie; some wanted to have a suit tailored; some wanted to have some fun in amusement arcades; some had a date in an icy and fruit punches shop; some came to eat; some went to te-tiam-a. It was like a sleeping area suddenly woke up. The neon and light lit up gradually. People talked, shouted, and sang. It seemed wrong. It was against nature. It was the end of a day, but everyone who came to this area was full of energy.

Hence, Ming-Hao changed the time to do business. He opened the restaurant at four o'clock in the afternoon and closed it at two o'clock in the morning, so he couldn't have a dinner date with Ciou-Tao as most people did. Luckily, it wasn't a problem. Ciou-Tao had very long working hours, from eleven in the morning to ten in the evening, so she couldn't have a dinner date either. Well, dating in the morning and having breakfast together, then. Under daylight, the romantic feeling was not any less, and they had the birds singing for them.

Besides dating in the morning, they saw each other again in the evening. Think about it. Ming-Hao's restaurant was by the ditch, and Ciou-Tao was living near the ditch, five minutes away on foot. Therefore, after work, on the way home, Ciou-Tao could go to the restaurant to see Ming-Hao. Well, very soon, Ciou-Tao didn't just sit and talk to Ming-Hao. She helped, cleaning the table after customers left or washing dishes.

One night, about 11:00 p.m., a pretty girl came into the restaurant, and she got Ciou-Tao's attention right away.

"Tomorrow is a regular school day. Shouldn't she be in bed already?" Ciou-Tao wondered.

The man who came with the pretty girl also caught Ciou-Tao's eye. He had a dragon tattoo on his right arm. "Is he her father?"

Then Ciou-Tao heard the pretty girl call him "uncle."

"Thank God. He is not her father." Ciou-Tao breathed a sigh of relief.

After they left, Ming-Hao told Ciou-Tao something shocking.

"They are from a te-tiam-a."

"The pretty girl is the owner's daughter?"

"No, Ciou-Tao. The girl was sold to the te-tiam-a."

"What?" Ciou-Tao couldn't breathe.

"She looks younger than her age. She is thirteen and going to work as a prostitute next year."

"How do you know?"

"People told me."

"Does she know that?"

"I don't think she knows, because she lives in the owner's house. She probably thinks that she is going to do some cleaning job or work in the reception."

"Oh no." Ciou-Tao felt powerless and weak suddenly.

Since Ciou-Tao started to work in the clothes stores, she had a chance to read the newspaper every day. Ciou-Tao had to work for eleven hours, but they did not always have customers in the store. She found that reading the newspaper was a great way to kill time, and she enjoyed it very much.

After finishing elementary school, Ciou-Tao hadn't gone to junior high school. Her adoptive family was too poor to let her get more education; however, even if she had a chance to go to junior high school, she would choose not to go. Poverty troubled her so much that her young mind couldn't concentrate on anything but hunger. That was how Ciou-Tao lost her interest in school learning. However, she still loved to read. She used to read anything that she got from garbage cans. She, of course, got newspapers sometimes, but they weren't like the one she had in the clothes store; it was brand new and on the day. Therefore, reading the newspaper in the clothes store was like five-star entertainment to Ciou-Tao, and she read the whole newspaper, including advertisements. That was how Ciou-Tao learned more brutal truths of prostitution in Taiwan. She believed that her neighbor aunts all knew those truths but didn't want to tell her. Probably, the aunties thought that it was too much for a young girl to acquaint with those ugly stories.

On March 24, 1965, *United Daily News* (聯合報) reported that a man from Taipei went to Hualien County to deceive a mother into believing that he could take her fourteen-year-old daughter to get a cleaning job in a contracted te-tiam-a. The mother got NTD 8,000 (about USD 200), and the man got NTD 4,000 from the contracted te-tiam-a. From the end of January, the owner had forced the girl to work as a prostitute. The girl didn't want to do it, and the owner beat her continually.

On July 27, 1965, *United Daily News* reported that in Taipei city, a nineteen-year-old girl had escaped from a contracted te-tiam-a and gone to a police station to ask for help. She said that her father had married her off to a forty-year-old man after her mother died. She was only sixteen. A year ago, she got divorced, and her father told a lie to persuade her to travel with him to Taichung. Her father sold her to a contracted te-tiam-a for NTD 20,000 (about USD 5,000).

On November 17, 1965, *United Daily News* reported that a Taipei City Juvenile Police team detected a case. A couple had deceived a fifteen-year-old girl into running away from home five days ago. After the husband raped her, the husband and his two friends sold her to a te-tiam-a. The manager of the te-tiam-a forced the girl to serve one hundred customers a week.

On March 30, 1966, *United Daily News* reported that the Tainan Police Department detected a huge prostitution scandal. A group of criminals had cooperated with a contracted te-tiam-a to deceive young girls into working in the te-tiam-a. Those girls were mostly about sixteen years old, and more than half of them were from aboriginal villages. Every one of them needed to do the service for at least thirty customers a day; otherwise, the people who worked for the owner would beat them badly. Moreover, they could only have one day rest when they had a period. If a girl was under fourteen years old and physically developmental delayed, they would inject the girl with hormones six times a week. When a virgin was forced to do the service for the first time, they forbade her to cry and scream. A gangster would be standing outside the room to guard. Not only did the girls not get any money from the owner of the te-tiam-a, but they were locked in the house with guards watching. The whole day, every day, they were imprisoned.

Ciou-Tao knew what was going to happen to that pretty girl she had seen in the restaurant. She was so upset that she thought about helping her. That thirteen-year-old girl was naive and friendly. The next time she came, she happened to be by herself, so Ciou-Tao had a small talk with her.

"Hello," Ciou-Tao started.

"Hi."

"You came alone today."

"Yeah. My uncle is busy, and I promised him that I would go home as soon as I get the food."

"You can't go out alone?"

"No, I am not supposed to. They are afraid that I might run away and go home."

"You miss home?"

"Very much."

"Where is your home?"

"In the mountains. Very far away. I need to take a train first and then a bus. After that, I still need to walk about twenty minutes."

"Wow, that's really far. So why are you here? For studying?"

"No. I am not that lucky. I came here to work."

"Work? What kind of work are you doing? By the way, how old are you?"

"Thirteen. They told me that I would get an easy job, but they said that I am too thin. In order to help me grow stronger, they have given me vitamins."

"I see. If you could go home right now, would you go?"

"No. I can't do that. I came here to make money for my family."

"I see. You are such a good girl. What's your name?"

"Lin Yi-Wen [林怡雯]."

"Here is your food, Yi-Wen. I am leaving too. Let me walk you home."

"Thank you. I like talking to you. You are a nice lady."

"A lady? Never. I talk loudly, eat loudly, and sing loudly."

Yi-Wen laughed and laughed, couldn't stop.

Then Yi-Wen's home was right in front of them. The uncle who had a dragon tattoo on the right arm was standing by the door with an unpleasant face. Before he opened his mouth, Ciou-Tao spoke.

"I am the girlfriend of the restaurant owner. I was going home when this young lady got her food, so I suggested we walk together."

The man said nothing and just raised his right hand as showing his appreciation. Then he and Yi-Wen walked into the house. Yi-Wen looked back and smiled.

"That house! That house! She stays in that house. Oh God. There is no way that I can help her!" Ciou-Tao felt so upset.

The owner of the house was the biggest gangster in the town and also the county councilor. People said that he might run for the mayor next time, but practically, he already was the mayor. He controlled the whole town.

Ciou-Tao never understood why a gangster, a big fat one, could happily do whatever he wanted to do and wouldn't get any trouble.

"Where is the law enforcement administration? Sleeping or blind? The neighbor aunts and people in the town all can see the crime, but it seems they can't. They can't, or they pretend that they see nothing?" Ciou-Tao was so mad about the death of justice.

"Easy. Money and power make the crime go unseen," Wen-Hua said.

"Ciou-Tao, have I told you that the Chinese Nationalist government uses the local gangsters to control Taiwanese society?"

"What?"

"It's their tradition. In fact, Chiang Kai-shek has a history of working with gangsters. In China, he used them to purge the political dissidents and control the financial institutions. That's why he, a nobody, could climb to the top of power."

"No wonder they lost China!"

"Ciou-Tao, you got that right. Since they fled to Taiwan in exile, Chiang Kai-shek's regime has sent gangsters to assassinate many people who pursued democracy and freedom."

"Bastards!"

"Ciou-Tao, remember the 228 Incident in 1947? It changed Taiwanese society completely. Before the massacre, many Taiwanese elites were involved in political affairs with beautiful expectation and passion for establishing a modern and democratic Taiwan. Sadly, in order to control Taiwan entirely, the Chinese Nationalist government killed most of them in the 228 Incident, which scares people and makes the local leaders keep themselves away from politics. It gives those gangsters a chance, of course, with the Chinese Nationalist government's support. The Chinese Nationalist government uses them to dominate Taiwanese society by allowing them to run for election, and those gangsters won the local election by bribery, threats, and violence. Then they embezzle. Corruption and evil are the names of Chiang Kai-shek and his party."

Ciou-Tao signed. "This is very depressing."

"Ciou-Tao, I know you are frustrated that you can't help the girl. But please be careful. Don't walk the girl home again. You might get trouble just because of that. I know I sound like a coward, but you know very well how those people are. I don't want anything bad to happen to you."

"OK. I promise you."

"You'd better keep your promise, because I would like to see my little sister dressing in a white gown and holding a bouquet."

"What white gown and bouquet?" Ciou-Tao blushed with happiness.

"I am serious. I hope I can go to your wedding before I go to study in the United States."

"The United States? When?"

"Next year, I assume."

"How about the three-year compulsory military service? Don't you need to finish the service before you go abroad?"

"I have severe myopia, so I will be exempt from the service."

"I see. Then why don't you go this year after you graduate?"

"You want me to go that bad?" Wen-Hua laughed.

"That's not what I meant."

"I know. I know. I am just joking. Anyway, I can't leave the country without the government's permission."

"That's right. We're *not* a free country. How can I forget! But I wish you wouldn't go." Ciou-Tao had a sad face. "You know that I love talking to you. You're the only one who understands me fully. I will be very lonely if you're not around."

"Oh, Ciou-Tao, you're very important to me too. In my heart, you're my family. All my friends know that I have a little sister, Ciou-Tao. I love and cherish every second that we're together. I'm going to miss this badly. We have been writing to each other for four years. Let's keep on writing. Try to think that I only go to another city to study, and the letters will be from the United States. What do you think?"

"You'd better write often."

"Yes, ma'am."

Although Ciou-Tao promised Wen-Hua to stop thinking of helping the pretty girl, Yi-Wen, she was still concerned about her. However, one week later, Ciou-Tao's worry went away entirely because something happened. Ciou-Tao nearly broke down.

Ciou-Lian died.

The world stopped from the moment that someone from Ciou-Lian's adoptive family came to tell Ciou-Tao of the death of Ciou-Lian. Ciou-Tao couldn't think and talk. She couldn't hear anything but the sound of her teardrops hitting the ground.

"Everyone whom I love has left me one by one."

This time was different. It was like game over.

"Now, I have no one in this world."

Unlike Ciou-Jyu, Ciou-Lian was adopted by a great family. Ciou-Tao never got jealous of her; in fact, she was exceedingly happy for Ciou-Lain. Ciou-Tao always believed that every daughter should be loved and treated like that. Ciou-Lian's adoptive parents, in Ciou-Tao's opinion, were the model parents. They gave Ciou-Lian everything the same as they gave to their own sons, so Ciou-Lian was as free to do things as her adoptive brothers. For instance, Ciou-Lian always wanted to be an elementary school teacher, so after junior high school, she went to junior teachers' college. Many of her adoptive parents' friends were surprised and disapproved because they thought that a lady from a wealthy family should go to finishing school, but Ciou-Lian's adoptive parents supported her 100 percent. Most importantly, they understood love and respect, so they didn't force their son and Ciou-Lian to get married.

Growing up together, Ciou-Lian and her adoptive brother, arranged husband, loved each other like siblings, no romance between them. Her adoptive parents respected their feelings, so they let their son and Ciou-Lian cancel the engagement, and then they officially adopted Ciou-Lian to be their daughter. Then you can imagine how much Ciou-Lian loved her adoptive parents. As a matter of fact, Ciou-Lian decided to stay single. She wanted to be their company and take care of them. However, her adoptive parents didn't want her to do so because they worried that she would have no one to take care of her if they died. They persuaded her and found a nice educated young man for Ciou-Lian, and Ciou-Lian liked him and eventually agreed. The adoptive parents were so happy and planned to give Ciou-Lian a beautiful wedding. However, Ciou-Lian had influenza and died, two weeks after the engagement. It was 1968, and she was only twenty years of age.

"What's wrong with God? He gave the best of every-thing to Ciou-Lian but forgot to give her health. Why?"
"Who is going to call me 'dope' for the rest of my life?"
Ciou-Tao was devastated.

Five months later, on a day in autumn, Ciou-Tao got married. Perhaps the loss of Ciou-Lian impacted Ciou-Tao too much. The needs of belongingness and family made her decide to marry Ming-Hao.

Ming-Hao was very sure about his feelings for Ciou-Tao. He believed that Ciou-Tao would be a good wife and a great mother to their children. However, Ciou-Tao had some doubts about Ming-Hao. Ciou-Tao couldn't deny that Ming-Hao was a good man who had a strong sense of responsibility for his family; in fact, she admired that quality very much. However, she didn't like the fact that he was very traditional and conservative. She saw potential problems.

Ming-Hao's idea and method of breaking the chain of poverty, in many people's opinion, including many women, sounded sensible. Ciou-Tao thought that the idea was great, but the method was wrong. She disapproved of the fact that the four sisters were the ones to be given up. It was so wrong to think that they would get married eventually, so they didn't need more education, which revealed Ming-Hao's beliefs: boys were more valuable and important than girls, and women were not equal to men.

"If we got married and had children, would he treat our son better than our daughter?" Ciou-Tao couldn't help being worried. Ciou-Tao wanted her future daughter to be loved equally to her brother and have the same opportunity to pursue her education and dreams.

"If we work hard to improve the finances and don't have many children, no kid will need to be sacrificed." Ciou-Tao thought that she found a solution and convinced herself to believe it. Then she married Ming-Hao.

Another five months later, Ciou-Tao was pregnant, and Wen-Hua was leaving for the United States. He was going to study statistics at Columbia University. Ciou-Tao cried hard when Wen-Hua went to see her and said goodbye.

"I know. I'm too emotional. Can't help it. Everyone is leaving me."

"Ciou-Tao, it's OK. They say that the hormones make pregnant women more sensitive than usual."

"You mean I am normal?"

"That's right."

"But I don't like myself not being me. Besides, the morning sickness is killing me. I can't imagine how my mother could have seven children. That was a lot of throwing up."

"Ciou-Tao, you are back. God, I am going to miss your funny talking and sense of humor very much. You will write to me, right?"

"Of course. But you'd better hope that I don't vomit on the letter."

"Oh no!" Wen-Hua made a dying face, and Ciou-Tao laughed.

Then Wen-Hua became a little bit serious.

"Ciou-Tao, I know that deep down in your heart, you're still very sad about Ciou-Lian's death. But Ciou-Tao, you still have me. You're not alone. Please remember it. Besides, now you have a husband. Everything is going to be fine if we allow time to heal us gradually."

"Wen-Hua ge, it's not the same. Ming-Hao is nice, but Ciou-Jyu, Ciou-Lian, Uncle Huang, and you are like the blood in my body. One by one, you all left me. You might say that you will come back to see me once every few years, but I have a funny feeling that I will lose you."

"Oh, Ciou-Tao, please don't be so negative. Taiwan is my home, and you are my dear little sister. I will be back. I promise."

"I guess I am too pregnant to be positive. I blame the hormones. Take care of yourself. It's you who are going to be very alone in another country. Don't bury yourself in the books all the time. Go out with girls sometimes. I hope you will bring a sister-in-law to come home with."

"What if she had blue eyes and blond hair?"

"It doesn't matter if she had blue eyes, red hair, or black skin. As long as you love each other, it's nobody's business. I will be very happy for you."

"Ciou-Tao, you'll be a great mother. Kiss the baby for me when she or he is born."

Then Mei-Ling (美玲) was born; it was 1970. Mei means "beautiful," and Ling is a light ringing sound.

Ciou-Tao could tell that Ming-Hao was happy but not wholly. In the culture, most parents strongly expected the eldest son could have a son to carry the family name even though they had several sons. Ming-Hao was the eldest son, and Ciou-Tao could tell that he wished himself to fulfill the expectation. Therefore, the moment that Ciou-Tao saw the baby, she swore to herself, "I am going to let her know that women and men are equally good."

A year and a half later, Mei-Ai was born; it was 1972.

This time, Ciou-Tao could see disappointment on Ming-Hao's face. Hence, Ciou-Tao decided to name the baby girl Mei-Ai (美愛). Ai means "love." Ciou-Tao wanted Ming-Hao to know that she loved this baby girl. She was not going to love her less just because she was a girl.

Indeed, Ming-Hao was very disappointed that he did not have any sons. He believed that he had a duty to have an heir to carry the family name. Actually, he shouldn't have felt so stressed, because he had three younger brothers. They might have sons in the future. But Ming-Hao worried, "What if they don't get any sons like me? Who will carry the family name?" After his father died, he acted and thought like a father in the family. In general, people just had more babies until they had a son. However, before Ciou-Tao and Ming-Hao got married, they had decided to have two children only. The reason was simple. They didn't want to put themselves into extreme poverty. They wanted to give their kids a good education. That was good thinking, but now they had two daughters, which made Ming-Hao feel he failed to meet the responsibility as the eldest son.

Ciou-Tao found that many people liked to imprison themselves in some unreasonable ideas, and she happened to marry one. Once in a while, when a chance came, Ciou-Tao would share some positive thoughts with Ming-Hao. For instance, "Daughters also carry our blood, and they would always be our children even after they get married." Ciou-Tao wished Ming-Hao could become more open minded and, eventually, love and cherish their daughters with his whole heart. Ciou-Tao found that it was so hard to change a person's mind on this issue. The idea, the importance and necessity of having sons, was like an ancient unbreakable rock. However, after sharing her ideas with Ming-Hao several times, she thought that maybe the idea wasn't unbeatable. Perhaps it was the people who were too stubborn. They defended the idea loyally like guarding the queen in the castle.

Ciou-Tao couldn't help wondering if people really didn't know that they hurt their daughters enormously and gave too much pressure to their sons. It brutally and repeatedly created wounded families for centuries, but it seemed most people had no intention to stop the uncivilized act. "It's OK. From me, I am going to protect my daughters from those poisonous ideas. They'll grow to be happy and confident women."

Before Ciou-Tao and Ming Hao got married, Ming-Hao's three younger sisters used to take turns to help in the restaurant, but after they were married, Ciou-Tao stopped working in the clothes store and worked with Ming-Hao in the restaurant instead. Ciou-Tao enjoyed working in the restaurant with Ming-Hao very much. To her, it was so much more fun to work in a restaurant than in the clothes store. There was always something that needed to be done, making wontons, cleaning tables, washing dishes, chopping vegetables, taking orders from customers, and so on. She preferred to be busy rather than to have nothing to do. Furthermore, it was also a job that she had to interact with customers. Thus, she was happy to have a better job.

Ming-Hao also felt happy. He liked Ciou-Tao's assistance very much. She was so efficient and got things done beautifully. Having her was like having two helpers. Ciou-Tao really knew how to manage to do things. She would do some preparation work—such as making wontons or checking on the soy sauce, white vinegar, and white pepper bottles on each table —while there was no customer in the restaurant. Moreover, after Ciou-Tao had worked in the restaurant for two months, Ming-Hao found that Ciou-Tao was ready to cook for customers, so he let Ciou-Tao try several times. Ming-Hao was right. Ciou-Tao did well, and customers paid her compliments. It meant Ciou-Tao could run a restaurant all by herself. For the first time in a long time, Ming-Hao felt that he might be able to take a break from work once in a while. Ciou-Tao also thought that it would be great if Ming-Hao could have a break sometimes, because he had begun to work when he was twelve years old. However, it became a disaster later. Abominably, Ming-Hao took advantage of Ciou-Tao's kindness, and it got worse when Mei-Ling and Mei-Ai both went to elementary school and could help in the restaurant.

There was a place called *tshing-te-kuan* (清茶館, "tea

217

house" in Taiwanese). In the Taiwanese and the Chinese language, tshing-te kuan sounded like a salon, where scholars, writers, and artists would gather together to drink tea and have intelligent and engaging conversations. In reality, it wasn't a romantic place; it was a gambling house.

There were several tshing-te-kuan in the area where Ciou-Tao and Ming-Hao lived. As a matter of fact, there was a tshing-te-kuan only a few houses away from Ciou-Tao and Ming-Hao's home. While Ciou-Tao and Ming-Hao were looking for a house after they had been married for five years, Ciou-Tao told Ming-Hao that she didn't want to buy a house near a tshing-te kuan, since she had compromised to live near the red-light district. However, there was no better choice. The house was very close to the restaurant and cheap, which fit their needs completely, so they bought the house in the end.

In Ciou-Tao's viewpoint, there was almost no difference between te-tiam-a (brothels) and tshing-te-kuan. Firstly, they had the same customers. Many people who went to tshing-te-kuan also went to te-tiam-a, and 99 percent of people in tshing-te-kuan were the Chinese veterans who were exiled to Taiwan with the Chiang Kai-shek regime. Secondly, the owners of the tshing-te-kuan were either gangsters or related to gangsters. Well, some gangsters actually owned both te-tiam-a and tshing-te-kuan. Anyway, in short, both te-tiam-a and tshing-te-kuan were hellish, filthy places!

In order to protect Mei-Ling and Mei-Ai, Ciou-Tao began to tell them to be alert to something and some people, particularly the Chinese veterans, after they moved into the new house.

Telling Mei-Ling and Mei-Ai not to be near those bad places—te-tiam-a, tshing-te-kuan, and gangsters' houses—was very easy. The word "bad" was powerful. Telling them that bad people did bad things immediately let the two little sisters have a full understanding of why they should not be near those places. Besides, Mei-Ling was only six years old, and Mei-Ai was four, so they trusted and listened to their a-bu completely.

On the other hand, telling Mei-Ling and Mei-Ai not to have any contact with the Chinese veterans was hard. First of all, the Chinese veterans were everywhere, so Ciou-Tao couldn't tell her two girls not to go to some specific places. Furthermore, who were the Chinese veterans? It was not easy to explain to the two little girls. Actually, that needed experience of interaction or close observation, which was against the warning itself. However, Ciou-Tao seemed to worry too much and underestimated her daughters' ability.

"A-bu, they're old and talk strange, right?" Mei-Ling asked.

"A-bu, we won't talk to them. We don't understand them at all." Mei-Ai put her hand by her ear.

Ciou-Tao laughed and felt relieved.

Then, one day, Ciou-Tao saw two Chinese veterans giving candies and cookies to the children in the neighborhood. She felt uneasy. At once, she demanded Mei-Ling and Mei-Ai not to take any food and sweets from those Chinese veterans even though she had told them not to accept any food from strangers a thousand times. Ciou-Tao's heart hurt after she warned her two girls. She felt that she denied and betrayed her dearest uncle Huang. She still remembered how happy she, Ciou-Jyu, and Ciou-Lian had been when Uncle Huang gave them food, candies, or cookies. They, of course, loved those treats, but they liked the feeling of being loved even more. From looking at Uncle Huang's smile and eyes, Ciou-Tao could tell that Uncle Huang loved them very much. Ciou-Tao felt so sad. Because of a few bad Chinese veterans, she didn't know how to tell Mei-Ling and Mei-Ai about Uncle Huang, the greatest man in the world.

Several years later, Ming-Hao broke the safety net that Ciou-Tao had built. After Ming-Hao became a regular in the tshing-te-kuan, he got some gambling friends. In the tshing-te kuan, people played four-person card games. Sometimes, people couldn't play because all the tables were full or they didn't have four people to open a table. Thus, some Chinese veterans who knew where Ming-Hao lived would go to knock on the door and asked him to join in the game. Ciou-Tao was furious. Gambling was bad enough, and then the Chinese veterans were right outside of their house. What would be next? Introducing Mei-Ling and Mei-Ai to them?

Ciou-Tao asked Ming-Hao to stop gambling, but he refused.

"I am doing this for our family. We have a mortgage to pay, but the business in the restaurant is slow. This is an easy and quick way to make extra money."

"You don't always win. You lost five thousand the other day."

"I have been working so hard since I was twelve. Can't I have some fun sometimes?"

"Then go fishing or something. Why does it have to be gambling? You are gambling away our money."

"I can't spend the money that I made?"

"We have two children to raise."

"They are girls. How much education do they need?"

"They are going to university."

"Ha, ha, ha...what for?" Ming-Hao walked out of the door and went to the tshing-te-kuan.

Ciou-Tao couldn't believe that Ming-Hao had changed. No! Maybe he hadn't changed; that was also him; only she hadn't seen this part of him before. Then what made this ugly part of him come out?

Perhaps frustration.

Ciou-Tao could tell that having two daughters but no son bothered Ming-Hao a lot. He probably felt that he was a failure and lost purpose to work hard. No matter what, it shouldn't become an excuse for gambling. Ciou-Tao believed that Ming-Hao had a gambling addiction. She had seen it before. A neighbor aunt's husband was addicted to gambling and said the same reasons why he wanted to gamble, so she knew how difficult it was to quit gambling. Thus, Ciou-Tao was angry and worried. However, she tried to forbid herself to think about it too much because the reality was merciless. If Ming-Hao intended to be like this, she would have to work harder in the restaurant.

11

A-bu and Daughters

One day in 1981, finally, there was something that cheered Ciou-Tao up. She received a letter from Wen-Hua. He was coming home! It had been twelve years since Wen-Hua had been in Taiwan. Even though they never stopped writing to each other—sending pictures too—Ciou-Tao missed her Wen-Hua ge enormously.

Wen-Hua had earned a PhD in statistics from Columbia University. Then he taught at Columbia University after graduation. Later, he married a lady who was also from Taiwan, and they had a son.

Ciou-Tao couldn't wait to see Wen-Hua, of course—and his wife and son too. However, she didn't get to see Wen-Hua at all, and Ciou-Tao cried her heart out.

Wen-Hua died.

Wen-Hua was found dead on the Taiwan University campus after he was taken away for the second inquiry by the secret police from Taiwan Garrison Command. The secret police took Wen-Hua to question for several reasons. Firstly, Wen-Hua had raised funds for *Formosa Magazine* (美麗島雜誌) when he was in the United States. Secondly, he had sent remittance to the manager of the *Formosa Magazine*. Thirdly, once, Wen-Hua had gotten people to translate articles from that magazine into English. Lastly, when Wen-Hua came back to Taiwan, he had discussed Taiwanese democratization with many people.

The government made an announcement. Wen-Hua

committed suicide because he was afraid that he was going to be arrested for the crime that he had committed. However, Wen-Hua's father told a journalist that Wen-Hua was tortured to death. It wasn't an accident or a suicide. He requested to watch a medical doctor do the autopsy and took pictures. Wen-Hua had nine rib fractures on one side and three on the other side and intra-abdominal hemorrhage. The whole lung was damaged. One kidney was ruptured, and another one was swollen. His stomach and intestine had no food. The pubis was broken, and ten fingers were curly and turned black. There was a more than ten-centimeter-long elbow-splitting wound and four lines of blood mark on Wen-Hua's back.

There was other evidence to prove that it was an act of murder. A brand new NTD 100 bill was found in Wen-Hua's shoe. That is a tradition that an executioner will do after he kills a person in order to let the deceased go with peace so won't come back to him for justice.[2]

"Murderers! This government is a criminal!"

Ciou-Tao was sad and angry, but she could scream only in her heart. She couldn't let neighbors hear her. Everyone was watched, and the government's thugs were everywhere.

"Oh, Wen-Hua ge…" Ciou-Tao could only cry.

Eleven-year-old Mei-Ling and nine-year-old Mei-Ai never saw their a-bu cry this way, so they were worried and scared.

They gave Ciou-Tao a handkerchief and a glass of water, and then they sat next to Ciou-Tao quietly. Slowly, the tears rolled down to their cheeks.

Ciou-Tao held them and wished she could tell Mei-Ling and Mei-Ai that the Chinese Nationalist government was an evil monster and a murderer. They were so much older and had good knowledge of the crimes that happened in society, but they also grew to love the Chinese Nationalist government very much after they went to school. Thus, Ciou-Tao didn't know how to let them understand the brutality and evilness of the Chinese Nationalist government. They probably wouldn't know how to react if she told them the truth. To believe what they learned at school or their a-bu's words? There would be a huge emotional conflict in their hearts, which was too much for children. Hence, Ciou-Tao decided not to tell the whole truth.

"A-bu, why are you crying?" Finally, Mei-Ling asked.

"Did someone hurt you?" Mei-Ai looked very sad.

"No one hurt me. It's Uncle Wen-Hua..." Ciou-Tao couldn't continue.

"A-bu, is it because he is not coming back, so you are sad?" Both Mei-Ling and Mei-Ai had been excited about meeting Uncle Wen-Hua. Because their a-bu talked about him all the time, they felt like they had known Uncle Wen-Hua forever.

"No, Mei-Ai, not because of that. Uncle Wen-Hua died."

"What? Where and how?" Mei-Ling felt like she had been struck by lightning.

"He died in Taipei. I don't know how." Oh, poor Ciou-Tao had to lie.

"A-bu, I am so sorry." Mei-Ai cried immediately, and then she said, "A-bu, Uncle Wen-Hua was a good person. He will go to heaven."

"Dope, of course he was a good man. Otherwise, he wouldn't be A-bu's good friend." Mei-Ling seemed to take out her anger on Mei-Ai. She was angry at God for taking away her a-bu's best friend—no, no, dear brother, actually.

"He was not just a good man. He was a righteous man."

"A-bu, what is a righteous man?" Mei-Ai asked.

"A person who is very honest, who cares about other people and wants things to be fair."

Ciou-Tao didn't remember when Mei-Ling began to call Mei-Ai "dope." It was funny to hear it at first. Ciou-Tao couldn't believe that the word, *dope*, which belonged to Ciou-Lian and her, had been passed on to Mei-Ling and Mei-Ai. Naturally, she enjoyed listening to it every time and found sweetness and comfort from hearing it, but this time, hearing the word was deadly painful. It reminded her that the last great person in the first half of her life had left her, so the first half of her life officially ended. Ciou-Tao found that her chest was hollow and dreadfully hurt. What now? A new life?

"But what kind of new life am I having?" Ciou-Tao felt bitter. She also felt lonely, like she had no one in her life. The person whom she spent her life with had changed so much. He was almost like a stranger to her. Furthermore, they had very different viewpoints on many things, so it was hard for Ciou-Tao to get support and comfort from Ming-Hao. In fact, he often hurt her feelings instead. When Ciou-Tao told him about the death of Wen-Hua, Ming-Hao immediately told her not to let people know that Wen-Hua was her good friend.

"We don't want to get into trouble," Ming-Hao said.

Ciou-Tao felt like she got a hard punch; she was dazed, hurt, and angry. That thinking— "We don't want to get into trouble"—was so disgusting and hateful! She found that Ming-Hao was not only a coward but also a cruel person. She regretted that she had gotten married in a rush and so hadn't found out Ming-Hao's nature before she married him. Actually, Ciou-Tao had been thinking about divorce for quite some time. However, it was the time that the court wasn't friendly to women. The judge usually gave custody of children to the father if the father did not have significant flaws due to the reason that most mothers were not financially independent. The reason was truth and fact but unfair. What could Ciou-Tao do? What choice did she have? She didn't want her daughters to be raised by Ming-Hao alone, so she had to stay in that unhappy marriage.

Ciou-Tao didn't go to Wen-Hua's funeral, but it was not because Ming-Hao didn't want her to go. Seriously, if Ciou-Tao determined to go, she would go, no matter what. She wasn't afraid to challenge Ming-Hao, but she cared about her daughters' feelings. Ciou-Tao didn't want them to feel anxious often because their parents fought. She decided not to go to the funeral because of an essential reason: Wen-Hua's parents, especially his mother, didn't like Ciou-Jyu. After Wen-Zhi died, his mother hated Ciou-Jyu greatly. Ciou-Tao didn't think that Wen-Hua's mother would like to see her. It was great sadness and tragedy. Wen-Zhi had been killed by a lunatic, and Wen-Hua had been murdered by the government. That poor father and mother deserved a moment of peace. Ciou-Tao didn't want them to get upset just because she wanted to go to the funeral. There were many ways to say goodbye to her Wen-Hua ge.

To the seacoast!

Uncle Huang had taken Ciou-Tao and her four little adoptive brothers to this seacoast once.

To the seacoast!

This seacoast was Ciou-Jyu and Wen-Zhi's place.

To the seacoast!

After Ciou-Jyu and Wen-Zhi died, Wen-Hua and Ciou-Tao came here often too.

To the seacoast!

This place allowed them to speak from their hearts.

The wave came and said, "Speak! Tell what's in your mind. I am listening."

Another wave came after and said, "Speak! Tell all your troubles. I'll take them to the bottom of the ocean."

This place also made them realize that there were many possibilities in life. The changes in the sky were various and couldn't be predicted, and the scenes wouldn't stay long but were unforgettable. Thus, they learned to cherish the moment that they had together. Those moments that they had in the seacoast were so beautiful and wonderful at the time and became ultra-precious to them later when they separated from each other. Alas, it was no longer "them" anymore. There was only one left.

Ciou-Tao didn't go to the seacoast by herself. She

brought Mei-Ling and Mei-Ai with her. She wanted to tell them some beautiful and fascinating stories, which was the way that she chose to memorialize the first half of her life and Wen-Hua and comfort her broken heart.

"What? Auntie Ciou-Lian also called you dope?"

"Sis, maybe you are Auntie Ciou-Lian."

"Dope, I am not Auntie Ciou-Lian. It's she was reborn to become me."

"OK, girls. That's called reincarnation."

"A-bu, 'carnation'? The Mother's Day flower?" Mei-Ai was totally lost.

"Dope, it's re-in-carnation, meaning reborn."

"Eating garbage?" The two sisters were astonished.

"We were too poor. No choice. But it was not really garbage. They were bad-quality fruit and vegetables. If you clean them well, you can get a feast."

"A-bu, no, no. That wasn't a feast and couldn't compare to Fuji apples, chicken legs, and hard-boil eggs." Mei-Ling disagreed completely.

"A-bu, did you say that apples were very expensive at the time? How come Auntie Ciou-Lian could give you Fuji apples often?"

"Because her adoptive family was very wealthy."

"But rich people are not nice. How come they gave Auntie Ciou-Lian apples?" Mei-Ai had a bad experience at school.

"Mei-Ai, not all the rich people are bad. Uncle Wen-Hua's family is very wealthy, too, but he was very nice. There are always good and bad people out there, no matter whether they are rich or not." Ciou-Tao wanted her girls to know this very much. "As a matter of fact, Auntie Ciou-Lian's adoptive parents were the best parents whom I have ever known. They loved your auntie, Ciou-Lian, very much."

"A-bu, why do you never tell us how Auntie Ciou-Jyu died?"

"That was a complicated, sad story. I will tell you one day when you grow up."

"Because we are not smart enough to understand?"

"What do you think, dope?"

"Stop calling me dope, or I won't get smarter."

"OK, dope." Mei-Ling stuck her tongue out and ran away. Mei-Ai chased after her.

"Wen-Hua ge, now you reunite with Wen-Zhi, Ciou-Jyu, and Uncle Huang and finally meet Ciou-Lian. Say hi to them for me. I miss you." Being alone, Ciou-Tao began to talk to Wen-Hua.

"They are Mei-Ling and Mei-Ai. Aren't they funny and sweet? It's too bad that you didn't get to meet them in person before you went to see Wen-Zhi, Ciou-Jyu, Ciou-Lian, and Uncle Huang. It's OK. We'll all meet in the end. But you have to wait for a long time, though, because I am going to live a long life to see the Chinese Nationalist government rust and perish."

Before Ciou-Tao came to the seacoast, she was worried that she might fall apart when arriving at the location where she and Wen-Hua used to sit down and talk. She did get emotional in the beginning, but her mood was cheered up after telling Mei-Ling and Mei-Ai the delightful and happy stories. Thus, Ciou-Tao had a wonderful time with Mei-Ling and Mei-Ai, which was a familiar good feeling that she used to have when she was with Ciou-Jyu, Ciou-Lian, Uncle Huang, or Wen-Hua. She liked it.

"A-bu, did you say you and Uncle Wen-Hua used to sit here and talk?" Mei-Ling wanted to confirm.

"Yes."

"A-bu, we found some wildflowers. We want to give

them to Uncle Wen-Hua." Mei-Ai's small hands held a little bunch of yellow and white flowers.

"That's very thoughtful of you. Here, here. Here is Uncle Wen-Hua's spot."

When Mei-Ai squatted and put down the flowers, the wind bellowed and moved the flowers a little bit. Mei-Ai got panicked and hopped like a frog to hold the flowers, and she said nervously, "Sis, stone! Get a big one."

Ciou-Tao wanted to have a big laugh, but she held herself still. Seeing how Mei-Ling and Mei-Ai interacted with each other often reminded Ciou-Tao of her childhood.

One afternoon in summer, Ciou-Jyu, Ciou-Lian, and Ciou-Tao went to the pond together. While Ciou-Jyu and Ciou-Lian were busy catching fish and frogs, Ciou-Tao was picking flowers. Suddenly, Ciou-Tao saw a frog, so she said, "Sis, a frog is here."

"Catch it!" Ciou-Lian said.

"I can't."

"What does that mean, you can't? Don't tell me you are still afraid of frogs."

"I am not afraid. It's just I don't like them," Ciou-Tao defended.

"Just use anything to cover it. Hurry, or it will be gone."

"Ciou-Lian, she is afraid of frogs. Don't make her do it." Ciou-Jyu smiled.

Ciou-Lian ran to Ciou-Tao.

"Oh my God! You used a rock?" Ciou-Lian couldn't believe what she saw. She could tell that Ciou-Tao threw the rock on the frog, not put it on the frog, because the frog was kind of flat and died.

"At least I didn't let it get away. We catch frogs to eat. I don't think it matters if it looks flat or round."

"OK. Then you eat this one tonight."

"That's enough for me. I have done my best to catch this ugly monster. I am not going to eat it. You are the one who

likes frog meat. You can have mine. Thank you very much."
Ciou-Tao ran away after finishing talking.

Ciou-Lian had a big laugh and couldn't stop for a long time.

"Girls, we have to go home now. We can come back another day."

"A-bu, can we come here often? I like it here. It's beautiful. No wonder Auntie, Uncles, and you liked to come here."

"I like it here too," Mei-Ai said.

"A-bu, this can be our secret place. Don't tell anyone," Mei-Ling suggested.

"Yeah, our secret place. Don't tell A-ba." Mei-Ai spilled out her thoughts accidentally.

"Mei-Ai, you don't want A-ba to come here with us?" Ciou-Tao asked.

"No," Mei-Ai answered with a low voice.

"I don't want him to come here with us either." Mei-Ling had an angry expression on her face.

"Why?" Ciou-Tao was shocked by knowing her two daughters' feelings.

The two girls were silent.

"You don't like A-ba?"

They shook their heads.

"How come?"

"He likes to gamble and let you work alone in the restaurant frequently," Mei-Ling said.

"He doesn't like Uncle Wen-Hua," Mei-Ai said.

"A-ba told you that he doesn't like Uncle Wen-Hua?"

"No, he didn't. But we heard he said to you, 'Don't let people know that you and Wen-Hua are good friends.'"

"How could he say that? Uncle Wen-Hua was like your brother. He was a good man, and A-ba doesn't like him, so

A-ba is the one who has problems." Mei-Ling and Mei-Ai had watched and listened quietly. They knew things.

"Kids know." Ciou-Tao was always careful. She had tried hard to hide some feelings and things that she thought were harmful for her daughters to know, but something like Ming-Hao's gambling was impossible to hide. She told herself, "Maybe it would be better to talk to them honestly so that Mei-Ling and Mei-Ai wouldn't feel helpless and anxious because holding those negative thoughts and feelings in their minds."

"I don't like your a-ba gambling either. He thinks it's a way to make more money."

"But he lost money often." Ciou-Tao really could see Mei-Ling's anger.

"That's true. Gambling is not a good thing, no matter what good reasons that a person has. But I can't change your a-ba's mind. Thus, I do my best to make sure that we have more and more money in the bank every month, not getting less."

"A-bu, you are super smart." Mei-Ai looked happy.

"About Uncle Wen-Hua. You are right. He was a very good man. I hope you both can grow up to become like him. I don't like the fact that your a-ba is so cold to Uncle Wen-Hua, either, but he has his own reason. We shouldn't blame him. I will tell you the reason when you grow up. That's our deal. What do you think?"

"Yeah, I like to have secrets with A-bu." Mei-Ai got very excited.

"When will you tell us, A-bu?" Mei-Ling was more realistic.

"How about after you graduate from college?"

"That's a long time!" Mei-Ling couldn't believe it.

"It's the best time. Like you only eat a peach when it's ripe."

"I can wait. My teacher said that you would get the best if you wait patiently." Mei-Ai looked happy, but Mei-Ling didn't. After all, Mei-Ling was two years older. She was more mature and could think deeper. She wasn't satisfied with Ciou-Tao's explanation, but she knew that she and Mei-Ai just had to wait.

Actually, Ciou-Tao liked Mei-Ling's spirit, thinking and asking questions endlessly, very much. However, she also had a fear. Being a thinker wasn't a good thing in Taiwan. Which thinker would approve of dictatorship? No, no, a lot worse than that. Which dictator wouldn't lock thinkers in jail or kill them? A beautiful human quality had become a crime in criminals' eyes. How ironic!

Two years ago, Mei-Ling and Mei-Ai met a new friend, A-hue, and instantly, Ciou-Tao learned from neighbors that A-hue was from that house. Alas, about twelve years ago, Ciou-Tao walked a girl, Yi-Wen, back to that same house. She couldn't believe that more than a decade later, there was still a little girl sold to te-tiam-a. As time went by, there were only a few te-tiam-a left in the red-light district, but as long as they were allowed to exist, many young girls like Yi-Wen and A-hue would be illegally sold to te-tiam-a.

Ciou-Tao wished she didn't need to tell Mei-Ling and Mei-Ai those horrible things, but she had to, since they lived in an environment that was full of danger. Ciou-Tao wanted them to be aware of the danger, just as, more than a decade ago, her uncle Huang and neighbor aunts wanted her to stay away from the red-light district. But she also wanted them to be children, happy and innocent. Thus, she tried hard to avoid talking about sex or to touch on the subject lightly if she had to talk about it. However, the two thinkers always had many questions and opinions, and Ciou-Tao didn't know how to respond sometimes.

"How come A-hue has two mothers?"

"I don't think she has two mothers. I believe she calls the lady who takes care of her Mother."

"Why? Shouldn't she call her Auntie?"

"Perhaps A-hue likes her and misses her own mother."

"A-bu, wait! Her mother is not living with her?"

"No. Actually, where A-hue lives is not her home."

"What? She is not the gangster's daughter?"

"No."

"Mei-Ai and I thought that she was the gangster's daughter. Thank God."

"Then why doesn't she just go home if she misses her mother?"

"She came here to work."

"Work? She is like my age. She has to work?" Mei-Ai opened her eyes wide in surprise.

"You two work. You both help me in the restaurant."

"But we stay at home."

"A-bu, what kind of work is she doing?"

"Probably like you two are doing in the restaurant, sweeping floors, cleaning the tables, or washing dishes."

"Which restaurant does she work in?"

"I don't know. Why do you want to know?"

"Because she hasn't come to play with us for a while. And, A-bu, you say that we can never go near the gangster's home, so maybe we can go to the restaurant to see her and ask her to come to play with us."

"But she works for the gangster's family, and you two can't go near any places that belong to gangsters."

"That's right. I didn't think about that."

"A-bu, how come a gangster would want to open a restaurant? Who would go to eat their food? Maybe they put poison in the food."

"Dope, they are not good people but wouldn't be so stupid to put poison in the food. They open a restaurant to make money, not for killing people. Otherwise, they would open today and go to prison the same day. Why would they want to go to the trouble of opening a restaurant just for one-day killing people? They could kill people as they usually do. Easier."

Mei-Ai laughed crazily after listening to Mei-Ling's analysis.

"A-bu, are those Chinese veterans as bad as the gang-sters?"

"Why do you ask?"

"Because you tell us not to go near them either. So they must be very bad too."

"They are different. The gangsters bully and kill people. Many Chinese veterans take advantage of women and children. Of course, not all the Chinese veterans are bad, but since you can't tell who the bad ones are, staying away from them is the best and safest way."

"How do they take advantage of women and children?"

"Do something disrespectful."

"Like what?"

"Touching and kissing."

"A-bu, touching and kissing is not good? But I like you hugging me and kissing me."

"That's different. What those Chinese veterans do would make a lady have a baby, but you will have a baby with someone whom you love and want to marry."

"Then why don't they find someone to get married?"

Ciou-Tao just shrugged her shoulders and smiled. That was another thing that she couldn't tell Mei-Ling and Mei-Ai. Thank God they didn't ask more questions.

Two years later, during the summer break, Mei-Ling and Mei-Ai finally saw A-hue again. That night, they were helping Ciou-Tao in the restaurant, and the business was very slow. It was too hot for people to have hot soup and noodles in a restaurant without air conditioning. While the sisters were bored and watching a soap opera with Ciou-Tao, two customers came in.

"Good evening, Chen mama," the pretty young lady greeted Ciou-Tao at once.

"You are…A-hue?"

"Chen mama, you remember me? I am so happy."

There she was, a completely different A-hue, a little taller and looking like a grown-up now. Her hair was long and curly. She had makeup and nails polished with apple red. A-hue drew Mei-Ling's and Mei-Ai's attention right away when she walked into the restaurant, but they didn't recognize her. Hence, Mei-Ling and Mei-Ai were shocked when they heard their a-bu call her A-hue, a name that they would never forget.

"Mei-Ling! Mei-Ai! Do you remember me?"

"Yes, we do." Mei-Ling felt a little bit uncomfortable. She and Mei-Ai couldn't tell that she was A-hue at all, but she didn't want to hurt A-hue's feelings.

"I thought you wouldn't recognize me, since I changed a lot. You two are still the same. I am glad."

It was an awkward moment. Mei-Ling and Mei-Ai didn't know what to say to A-hue, who had a scary guard standing right next to her. They never forgot her, but this wasn't the A-hue whom they remembered. They, now, were older and had learned what prostitution was. The moment that A-hue and that man walked into the restaurant, Mei-Ling and Mei-Ai knew that the man was a gangster and the young lady was a prostitute.

Even though they didn't have communication, A-hue understood the feelings that her two friends might have. She didn't blame them for not talking to her. She had changed so much. She couldn't recognize herself either. How could she expect Mei-Ling and Mei-Ai to interact with her as they had two years ago? She was grateful that they didn't deny their friendship and reject her. "They must be able to tell that I am a prostitute, but they still look at me with friendly, smiling faces. Who wouldn't be afraid and would know how to talk to a friend who is watched by a gangster?"

"Mei-Ling, go to get two bottles of Yakult and two apples." Ciou-Tao finished cooking the soups and noodles that A-hue and that gangster had ordered.

"Yakult and apples!" The three girls' hearts were trembling. Ciou-Tao, their a-bu and Chen mama, thoughtfully and powerfully pulled them together.

Can't cry.
Don't cry.
Smile like you were together playing.
Remember the best time that you had together.
You are friends forever.
You are my daughters.

Mei-Ling put the two bottles of Yakult and two apples in a plastic bag that Mei-Ai held. The two sisters looked at each other and smiled. Then, Mei-Ai gave the bag to Ciou-Tao.

Ciou-Tao gave the bag to A-hue with another bag of food.

"Chen mama, you still remember I love Yakult and apples?"

"Of course." Ciou-Tao had a big smile. "And cold mung bean soup."

When the gangster took out the money to pay, Ciou-Tao said to him, "It's on the house today, since we are so happy to see an old acquaintance. Come often."

When A-hue walked out of the store, she looked back and smiled. Mei-Ling and Mei-Ai immediately waved to her. The cloud of awkwardness was chased away by a soft summer wind. Three young girls were finally reunited.

"A-bu, did they inject A-hue with hormones?" Mei-Ling asked furiously.

"Certainly, they did." Ciou-Tao felt very tired.

"I am glad that A-hue remembers us, because I couldn't recognize her at all," Mei-Ai said. "A-bu, can we help her?"

"I don't think so."

"Why? We can report to the police." Mei-Ai trusted the law enforcement people.

"Mei-Ai, you are too naive. If you and I, two young girls, can see the crime is out there, don't you think the police know?"

"So, Sis, you mean they are afraid of gangsters like we are?"

Nobody wanted to answer that question. No matter what the answer could be, it would certainly be depressing.

12

Crisis or Hope

Well, there was something even more depressing, which bothered Ciou-Tao a great deal: Mei-Ling and Mei-Ai had become patriotic since they started junior high school.

Both Mei-Ling and Mei-Ai had been good students. Their academic performance was excellent, and they obeyed the school rules completely. In the teachers' eyes, they were model students. Therefore, there was no surprise that the two sisters expected themselves to go to the best high school in the town and a good university in Taiwan. Any students who wanted to go to the best high school in their town or get into a university must memorize everything in the textbooks that were written, edited, and published by the National Institute for Compilation and Translation under the Ministry of Education so that they could get high scores on the entrance examination. In other words, the textbooks were like the Bible. Most students, including Mei-Ling and Mei-Ai, not only read and studied them but also believed everything that was written in the textbooks. However, even without the stress of taking school entrance examinations, the influence of the school education and textbooks was still beyond imagination. Mei-Ling and Mei-Ai began to learn Chinese history in fifth grade, and they started to call themselves Chinese from then on.

Mei-Ling and Mei-Ai learned the same Chinese history and geography that their uncle Wen-Hua had learned at school two decades earlier. Not only was China their fatherland, but the Generalissimo, Chiang Kai-shek, and his son, Chiang Ching-kuo were great leaders. They freed and protected Taiwan from being taken away by the Chinese Community Party. Lies, all students in Taiwan learned were lies, but they didn't know. Those lies made most students patriotic. They loved their country, the Republic of China, and the great leaders, Chiang Kai-shek and Chiang Ching-kuo, loyally.

Ciou-Tao wished she could tell Mei-Ling and Mei-Ai the truth, but she couldn't. What should they do after they learned the truth? Stop studying? Then what should they do with the high school and university entrance examinations? Or would they even believe her? In the end, Ciou-Tao convinced herself that Mei-Ling and Mei-Ai would find out the truth later, as Wen-Hua had. Before that, she needed to be calm and hang in there. However, it was so hard to be calm when Ciou-Tao kept seeing that the Chinese Nationalist government's influence was everywhere in all students' lives.

After the Chiang Kai-shek regime fled to Taiwan in 1949, the government of the Republic of China started military education in senior high schools and universities in 1951. It was bad enough that the government sent the military people, so-called military education instructors, to stay at schools to make all students learn military science, foot drill, shooting, and military fitness—and spy on everyone on the campus. In 1952, Chiang Kai-shek's son Chiang Ching-kuo even established a youth organization, China Youth Anti-Communist National Salvation Corps (中國青年反共救國團). It also provided basic military training to youths by holding many camps with different topics in many places all over the island. In a stressful and boring young life, to students, those camps were fun and attractive. They could have exciting activities and meet people, especially the opposite sex. In junior high school, boys and girls were kept separate in different classes. Then, in senior high schools, girls and boys went to separate schools. Therefore, going to the camps was a good chance for senior high school students to meet friends from the opposite sex and, perhaps, to find a little romance. Maybe because boys and girls were discouraged from having contact, there were always more students who wanted to register for the camps than the actual number of people who could be accepted. The China Youth Anti-Communist National Salvation Corps would give each senior high school the quota of people in each camp, usually about two to three people. Therefore, students had to sign up first and wait to see if a military education instructor would call them all in to draw lots to decide who could go. Some camps were always very popular, for instance, the Cross-Island Highway Hiking Team (中橫健行隊), so the students who wanted to go to those camps would have to pray hard for good luck. Well, Mei-Ling also very much desired to go to that camp, the Cross-Island Highway Hiking Team. She tried to register for it in two semesters but didn't get any luck. Finally, the third time, she was lucky and could go.

"A-bu, I can go to that camp this time!" That day, Mei-Ling came home with great excitement.

"The Cross-Island Highway Hiking Team?"

"Yeah!"

"I don't understand why you're eager to go to that camp. We have gone to Taroko [太魯閣] and Tianxiang [天祥] every year since you were three." Yes, there was a reason to go there every year, to visit Uncle Huang, but Mei-Ling and Mei-Ai didn't know the reason.

"A-bu, that's different. We always go to the same area by riding motorcycles. This hiking team is going to take us to walk for a week, to deeper inside the mountains."

"Deeper inside the mountains...is it safe?" Ciou-Tao remembered how Uncle Huang died. Those beautiful mountains killed her dearest uncle.

"A-bu, are you still thinking of the old time when those Chinese veterans were building the highway? Since they finished the construction, it's safe now."

"Not that safe! Once in a while, you can see the news on TV about people who were hit by rocks. They were hurt or died." Ciou-Tao wasn't exaggerating, and her life had lost color for a long time because Uncle Huang was hit by a big rock and fell into the gorge.

"I know, A-bu. We will wear helmets, and the people who will lead the team have a lot of experience. I will be fine. I'll come home in one piece."

"That's not funny! We didn't even get to see Uncle Huang's body!" Ciou-Tao was very upset that they couldn't get Uncle Huang's body out from the gorge. Her beloved Uncle Huang just lay in there to let the water and rocks run over him every second and every day until he vanished.

"Who is Uncle Huang?" Mei-Ling had never heard of him.

"An old neighbor." Ciou-Tao was still not ready to tell her daughters about Uncle Huang.

"Oh, I'm sorry. A-bu, are you going to let me go to the hiking team or not? I hope you will."

"Go, go. Just be very careful."

Thank goodness it seemed Mei-Ling wasn't interested in politics. She liked to go to the winter and summer camps that were held by the China Youth Anti-Communist National Salvation Corps only because she wanted to meet new friends—specifically boys, of course. After all, she was a teenager. However, one year later, something unbearable and painful happened, which scared Ciou-Tao and made her worry very much. She was afraid that Mei-Ling might join the Chinese Nationalist Party.

On January 13, 1988, President Chiang Ching-kuo died. That was Mei-Ling's last year of senior high school. The government made everyone mourn for his death. The school teachers even gave every student a piece of small black cloth to pin on the left arm of their jackets. Ciou-Tao had a tremendous heart pain when she saw Mei-Ling and Mei-Ai coming home from school with a piece of small black cloth pinned on their left arms. She wanted to scream, "Take it down! He isn't your father or grandfather. In fact, he murdered your uncle Wen-Hua and many people. He killed and imprisoned people who had different opinions from him and pursued freedom and democracy. He does not deserve people's tears and grief!" However, Ciou-Tao kept quiet again, saying nothing. If Ciou-Tao could, she wouldn't hesitate for a second to tell Mei-Ling and Mei-Ai the stories about Wen-Hua, the 228 Incident, and the White Terror. Ciou-Tao knew her two daughters well. They had good hearts and couldn't bear any injustice situation. Surely, they wouldn't have peace in their minds after learning those horrible stories. Furthermore, they wouldn't be able to concentrate on their studies anymore because they would have doubts on everything that was written in the textbooks. Besides, Ciou-Tao had fears. The government and its thugs never stopped spying on people, so it would be safer if Mei-Ling and Mei-Ai remained unaware of the true face of the Chinese Nationalist government. In fact, they might get into trouble if the military education instructors knew that they were kind of related to Wen-Hua. However, Ciou-Tao had doubts about her silence. "Is it correct to keep silent, not telling Mei-Ling and Mei-Ai the truth? Does my silence take away Wen-Hua ge's justice?" Ciou-Tao couldn't help asking herself over and over again. In the end, as always, Ciou-Tao tried hard to hold herself back and not to get too excited. However, while most students, including Mei-Ai, pinned that piece of small black cloth on their left arms for a few days, Mei-Ling did it for more than one week. Ciou-Tao felt that she seemed to lose a daughter and betrayed her Wen-Hua ge.

Thank God, at least, Ciou-Tao didn't need to worry about Mei-Ai. She only pinned that piece of small black cloth on her left arm to mourn the dictator, Chiang Ching-kuo, for three days. Furthermore, she didn't like to go to those winter and summer camps. She loved to be alone and paint. So, clearly, Mei-Ai wasn't interested in politics and wouldn't join the Chinese Nationalist Party at all. However, surprisingly, it *was* Mei-Ai who asked Ciou-Tao if she could join the Chinese Nationalist Party. Ciou-Tao almost fell off the chair.

"What?" Ciou-Tao could hear herself speaking loudly, almost screaming.

"A-bu, I said I want to join the Chinese Nationalist Party."

"I heard you. But why?"

"If I join the party, I can apply for a scholarship."

"What does that mean?" Ciou-Tao sort of understood Mei-Ai's intention, but she needed more information about why Mei-Ai wanted to join the Chinese Nationalist Party.

"If I am a member of the party and my semester academic performance score reaches eighty, I can apply for a scholarship. I believe it's three thousand NT dollars [about USD 85]. Two semesters, a year, will be six thousand. It's great. Don't you think, A-bu?"

"Hmm..." Ciou-Tao didn't know how to react. "Good students like Mei-Ai deserve to receive a scholarship without a doubt. But from the Chinese Nationalist Party? No, no way. How can this party be this filthy? They use the money to buy young people's loyalty and get more new blood into their party. Chiang Kai-shek and Chiang Ching-kuo have died, but the Chinese Nationalist Party is still powerfully alive. They want to control Taiwan forever."

"Mei-Ai, I don't think this is a good idea. For a scholarship to join the Chinese Nationalist Party? Don't you think we should join a party because we agree with their ideas and principles?"

"But A-bu, that money will be a great help for us. I am sure you know very well that I am not interested in politics at all. I just want to have that money from them. Besides, as I know, they won't ask me to do anything after I join them."

"Mei-Ai, listen to me. I disapprove of this idea absolutely. Maybe we have financial difficulty, but we are OK without that scholarship. You should never compromise yourself to do something for money. Remember your friend A-hue? Her family compromised, so she lost her childhood, freedom, and dignity.

"There is one thing that I never wanted to tell you and your sister, but I must say it now. Please keep this in mind. The Chinese Nationalist Party is not a good party. It will be a disgrace to join them. Even if they want to give you a billion dollars right now without membership required, you still have to turn around and walk away with your chin up." Ciou-Tao thought about how her Wen-Hua ge had been tortured to death, so her eyes glistened with tears.

"Yes, A-bu." Mei-Ai was astonished to see the tears in her a-bu's eyes. She knew this was a serious matter. If taking a scholarship from the Chinese Nationalist Party would make her a-bu cry, she wouldn't want to have the money, not even a penny.

That night, while Mei-Ling and Mei-Ai were studying at home, Mei-Ai told Mei-Ling what had happened after she told her a-bu that she wanted to join the Chinese Nationalist Party.

"What? A-bu cried?"

"Not really, but her eyes were full of tears."

"That was serious."

"I thought so too."

"Do you believe what A-bu said, that the Chinese Nationalist Party is bad?"

"Yes, I do. All we know about the party is from the history textbooks and the media, and they are all positive. I believe that A-bu might know something different, but she doesn't want to tell us about it for some reason. A-bu never lies to us; therefore, I believe her. Besides, I don't want to upset her because of the three thousand NT dollars for each semester."

"I think you are right. Once I heard a classmate say, 'How

is it possible that a party is so great but was defeated by the evil Chinese Communist Party?' Well, the way that she stated it wasn't like a curious person who had a question in mind. It was like she knew something and satirized the Chinese Nationalist Party."

"Really?"

"She got into trouble, though."

"What?"

"The next day, she was called to see a military education instructor and got a warning."

"Just for saying that?"

"That's right."

"It's unbelievable."

"Mei-Ai, you'd better believe it. That's why I never want to join the Chinese Nationalist Party. I don't want to get involved in anything that might be complicated. I just want to get into university and enjoy my life, have fun."

"Me either. My friend told me that I don't need to do anything, and nothing is going to change after joining the Chinese Nationalist Party, but I can apply for the scholarship every semester. I thought, if it's true, why not?"

"Yeah, three thousand NT dollars is a lot of free money to spend, though. I don't blame you."

"I was very much touched by A-bu's words. Do not compromise yourself because of money. Sis, don't you think it's powerful?"

"Yes, indeed. I am going to use it in my writing next time."

"Hey, thief! That's mine. A-bu gave it to me."

"It's not stealing. People quote famous people's sayings all the time. It's borrowing."

"Yeah, right!" Mei-Ai stuck her tongue out.

"And you can write like this: once, a wise woman said…"

Then the two sisters laughed out loud.

That night, at the same time, Ciou-Tao couldn't laugh at

all.

"How come this Chinese Nationalist Party can't leave people alone?"

She was furious, and her mind couldn't rest, so she made mistakes on several customers' orders.

"Ciou-Tao, I ordered noodle soup, not dried noodles."

"Sorry."

"Boss, I ordered rice dumplings, not wontons."

"I am so sorry."

Ciou-Tao finally admitted that no one in Taiwan could escape the influence of the Chinese Nationalist Party. As a matter of fact, even the people who were in other countries, this government still had power over them. Wen-Hua once told Ciou-Tao that some people who were studying abroad were on the government's blacklist. They were forbidden to come back to Taiwan because of their political opinions, pursuing freedom, democracy, and Taiwan's independence. The Chinese Nationalist government knew things abroad, especially in the United States, because they had students to spy for them. Some of those student spies received the Dr. Sun Yat-Sen Scholarship (中山獎學金) that was provided by the Chinese Nationalist Party, and only the members of the party could apply.

"Now, my daughter is thinking about joining that party and getting their scholarship." Ciou-Tao knew the scholarship that Mei-Ai wished to apply for was different from the Dr. Sun Yat-Sen Scholarship, but she didn't want Mei-Ai to get money from a criminal organization.

"If she got a scholarship from them now, she might apply for the Dr. Sun Yat-Sen Scholarship in the future." Mei-Ling and Mei-Ai had both talked about studying abroad many times, and Ciou-Tao agreed. She believed that the experience of studying and living in another country would help them to open their minds. However, she and Ming-Hao couldn't afford the expensive tuition and other expenses, and Mei-Ling and Mei-Ai both knew it and said that they would find a way to support themselves, such as working for two or three years after graduating from university. Ciou-Tao knew her daughters well. Mei-Ling and Mei-Ai were honest and righteous girls who wouldn't do something dirty and evil, spying on others for the government. "But what if they really want to study abroad one day but do not have enough money? And the Dr. Sun Yat-Sen Scholarship can cover everything and let the student live very well, which can make a person compromise easily.

"Alas. The devils know human weakness well. They see opportunities in poverty and greed because many people would give up their dignity for money. It's scary. They can even attract a simple girl like Mei-Ai to join their party. Thank God my daughter trusts me and believes my words, so she won't join the party and get the dirty money that the Chinese Nationalist Party has stolen from the Taiwanese people."

Although Mei-Ai listened to Ciou-Tao and didn't join the Chinese Nationalist Party, Ciou-Tao was still worried once in a while. She finally realized how powerful the Chinese Nationalist Party could be. They had made a huge net to cover all the people on the island.

"Would Mei-Ling and Mei-Ai be the lucky ones, like Wen-Hua ge, who discover the truth of this government of the Republic of China? Do I make a mistake by not telling them all the ugly truths about this Chinese government in exile? Does my protection harm their souls?"

These questions occupied Ciou-Tao's mind and troubled her a great deal, which made her forget what she had always believed: raise children to have a conscience so they will find the right direction to live their lives. Soon, Mei-Ai reminded her well.

13

Hope

Because girls and boys were kept separate in different classes or schools beginning in junior high school, most boys and girls became shy and didn't know how to talk to each other. Believe it or not, many of them would feel wrong or even sinful to have interactions with the opposite sex. These feelings and thoughts weren't from nowhere. Many school teachers and parents constantly instilled those ideas in them. Those adults believed that romance was a distraction and thought that their kids or students were too young to know what love was. Thus, it would be better that they didn't have any contact at all. The purpose was to keep young kids focused on school learning so they could get a good score on the entrance examinations and get into the best senior high school in the town and a good university. That was why the students who were found to have a girlfriend or a boyfriend would get scolded by their teachers or military education instructors, and many parents approved of the discipline. In Ciou-Tao's opinion, that was sick thinking. Therefore, she didn't get mad when Mei-Ai told her that she met a boy and liked him.

Mei-Ai met the boy in the library. "A-bu, it was interesting," Mei-Ai told Ciou-Tao.

"I was reading the newspaper. Then I heard someone say, 'It's bullshit!' right in my ear. I got startled and turned back to see who was talking. A big tall guy was standing behind me. He giggled and said sorry. He said that when he walked by and saw one headline in the newspaper, he couldn't help commenting on it."

"What was the headline?" Ciou-Tao was curious.

"'All Taiwanese people happily celebrated Taiwan's Retrocession Day [臺灣光復節].'"

"Ha, ha, ha…" Ciou-Tao couldn't stop laughing.

His name was Lan Tian (藍天). *Lan* is "blue," and *Tian* is "the sky." Thus, his friends sometimes would joke about his name.

"Hey, are you blue today?"

"How come you are here, but it is raining?"

"Where is your white cloud?"

Lan Tian didn't mind his friends making fun of his name; in fact, he felt funny too. There was only one situation that he couldn't take it. After people learned his name, many of them thought that he was Chinese. There were not many Taiwanese people who would give their children a one-word name. People usually gave their children a two-word name, such as Ciou-Tao. Therefore, naturally, many Taiwanese people would think that Lan Tian was Chinese, and probably so did many Chinese people who had escaped from China to Taiwan after 1945. To be seen as a Chinese person bothered Lan Tian very much. There was an important reason behind it, and it was very personal.

Lan Tian's great-grandfather was a famous painter. He was born in an impoverished family. As a result, he had to teach at school after he graduated from college. Eight years later, he had finally saved enough money and went to study at Tokyo School of Fine Arts (東京美術學校, today's Tokyo University of the Arts). He graduated in 1929, and his work was admired by the Japanese art circle.

After his graduation in 1929, he went to Shanghai to teach in two art schools. Because of this factor, he developed a distinctive style that combined the essence of Chinese landscape painting with Western painting techniques. Furthermore, he liked to draw the scenery around his life.

In 1932, he went back to Taiwan. In 1946, he joined the Chinese Nationalist Party and got elected as a city councilor. When the 228 Incident happened in 1947, there was a conflict between the Chinese Nationalist government and civilians in the town. Several city councilors, including Lan Tian's great-grandfather, organized a local 228 Incident Settlement Committee to reconcile the dispute. However, when the six members of the committee went to meet the Chinese Nationalist Army at the airport, they were arrested at once. They were taken to the prison and tortured to confess that they had stirred up the riot. After the Chinese Nationalist troops, which was requested by the governor-general of Taiwan, Chen Yi, arrived, they took the six members of the committee to the train station. On the way to the train station, the Chinese Nationalist troops endlessly humiliated them. When they arrived at the train station, those soldiers raked the square that was in front of the train station with machine gun fire. People ran away, and the Chinese Nationalist Army pushed the six members out of the truck. At this very moment, Lan Tian's grandmother went to beg a soldier not to kill her father. The soldier kicked her away and shot her father to death.[3]

This kind of ugly, brutal crime happened everywhere in Taiwan during the 228 Incident. Some people's families were killed violently like Lan Tian's great-grandfather; some people witnessed the slaughter; some people heard the bloody stories. People on the island knew the massacre, but the Chiang Kai-shek regime and his party didn't want the people in Taiwan to talk about it. In fact, they were worried that the Taiwanese people would be against them again, so they oppressed all the people to be silent and obedient on the island.

No! We won't surrender.

Yes! We will tell our daughters and sons.

No! You won't be able to fool us again.

Yes! Our daughters and sons will tell their daughters and sons.

No! We don't believe the history that you write.

Yes! We are historians, to tell the truth.

No! You can't silence us forever.

Yes! We will tell our father's story to the world one day in the future.

That was also the bitterness that people could only express in the dream.

A-ba, rest in peace.

A-ba, I miss you.

I dream of you every night. You smile. Why?

Don't you hate them?

Do you regret welcoming the Chinese coming to Taiwan?

To Lan Tian's family, it was a tremendous tragedy to Taiwan that, after the Second World War ended, the Allies handed temporary administrative control of Taiwan to the Republic of China, the Chiang Kai-shek regime. The government of the Republic of China lied to the Taiwanese people about their ownership of Taiwan and claimed that Taiwan was retroceded to China by utilizing the Cairo Declaration:

"The several military missions have agreed upon future military operations against Japan. The Three Great Allies expressed their resolve to bring unrelenting pressure against their brutal enemies by sea, land, and air. This pressure is already rising.

"The Three Great Allies are fighting this war to restrain and punish the aggression of Japan. They covet no gain for themselves and have no thought of territorial expansion. It is their purpose that Japan shall be stripped of all the islands in the Pacific which she has seized or occupied since the beginning of the first World War in 1914, and that all the territories Japan has stolen from the Chinese, such as Manchuria, Formosa, and The Pescadores, shall be restored to the Republic of China. Japan will also be expelled from all other territories which she has taken by violence and greed. The aforesaid three great powers, mindful of the enslavement of the people of Korea, are determined that in due course Korea shall become free and independent.

"With these objects in view the three Allies, in harmony with those of the United Nations at war with Japan, will continue to persevere in the serious and prolonged operations necessary to procure the unconditional surrender of Japan."[4]

The Cairo Declaration was the outcome that was made in the Cairo Conference in 1943. It was an agreement without legal recognition by international law but was very important to the Chiang Kai-shek regime because it served as proof that they had territorial sovereignty of Taiwan. On October 25, 1945, the Japanese government handed over the ownership of Taiwan to the Allies' representative, the Chiang Kai-shek regime. The next year, the government of the Republic of China announced that October 25 was Taiwan's Retrocession Day. Maybe they just wanted to have the island in the beginning, but they began to need Taiwan more and more when they were defeated by the Chinese Communist Party during the second Civil War (1945–1950). Eventually, in 1949, they had nowhere to go but Taiwan, so Taiwan had to be theirs. After the Chinese Nationalist government fled to Taiwan in exile, they would have a big celebration on October 25 every year to instill the idea that the government of the Republic of China rescued the Taiwanese people from the Japanese government's brutality. It was marvelous that Taiwan was retroceded to the fatherland, China. Hurrah! Hurrah! Hurrah!

"Bullshit! Bullshit! Bullshit!"

Lan Tian wasn't afraid to express his anger after he told Mei-Ai his great-grandfather's story and the lie about Taiwan's Retrocession Day.

"Oh my God!" Mei-Ai was speechless because she had just learned something that really shook her mind a great deal. Somehow, she believed Lan Tian. Perhaps it was because her a-bu's words, "The Chinese Nationalist Party is not a good party," stayed in her mind vividly.

Seconds later, Mei-Ai said, "Last year, my a-bu told me that the Chinese Nationalist Party isn't a good party. That was all she said, so I didn't know they are such scumbags."

Lan Tian laughed. He had never met a girl who was so honest and expressed herself so directly.

"Thank you for listening to the story. My a-bu warns me not to tell the great-grandfather's story to others all the time. We might get into trouble or bring trouble to people. I guess you make people trust you, so I tell."

"Thank you for your trust. It always feels good to be trusted. Do you mind if I tell my a-bu the story? I think she would like to know a story like that."

"No problem. I trust you."

"I have to be honest with you. I am very much surprised by what I learned from you. It's like you have to read the history textbooks in an upside-down way—right is wrong, and wrong is right. Then you get the truth. However, while my trust for the country is shaking, my heart is fighting against it because I want to believe our government."

"Mei-Ai, have you ever heard of Thomas Paine?"

"No. Who is he?"

"He was an English-born American philosopher and political theorist and activist."

"I see."

"He said, 'Government, even in its best state, is but a necessary evil; in its worst state, an intolerable one.'"[5]

"So he deemed all governments are evil in nature."

"That's right. So you don't have to believe our government to feel safe or anything. Think of my great-grandfather and many people who were killed or imprisoned. They trusted the government of the Republic of China, but what happened to them?"

"It's very sad that you trust someone and they betray you. If someone did that to me, I would go crazy."

"Don't go crazy. Just go to the library." Lan Tian tried to cheer Mei-Ai up.

Mei-Ai couldn't stop laughing. "Do you come to the library often?"

"Almost every day. The library is my home."

"You must like to read."

"Yes. But I like to read some books and magazines that are not in the library more."

"Oh yeah, what are they?"

"That's a big topic. How about I tell you next time if you agree to go out with me?"

"I would love to know all about it, but I can't go out with you. You know my school. The teachers and military education instructors don't like us to make friends with boys. How about just like today? We meet in the library."

"That's a good idea. I don't want you to get into trouble either. Those people are pretty sick!"

"Believe it or not, that is exactly what my a-bu says about them. Ha!"

"I think you should bring your a-bu with you next time, because I am falling in love with her now."

"Hey, you, I'll tell my a-ba."

"So that Blue boy falls in love with me?" Ciou-Tao found Lan Tian interesting.

Mei-Ai laughed and nodded.

"A-bu, what Lan Tian told me is true, right?"

"To be honest, I do know the lie about Taiwan's Retrocession Day, but I have never heard of his great-grandfather's story before. Many people were indeed killed in the 228 Incident. Lan Tian has no reason to make up a story like this. I believe him." Ciou-Tao couldn't believe that Mei-Ai had learned the 228 Incident from a stranger. She felt nervous but also thrilled. She wanted to believe that it was God's plan.

"A-bu, it's really horrible. How could the government treat people like that? And how come you never told me and Sis these things?"

"Mei-Ai, we still have the same government, don't we? So how could I tell you and your sister these things? I don't want you two to live in fear." The crucial moment came unexpectedly. Ciou-Tao had no time to think what she should do but faced it honestly.

Mei-Ai still remembered what Lan Tian's mother told him all the time, "Not to tell the great-grandfather's story to people. We might get into trouble or bring trouble to people." Mei-Ai tried to imagine how it felt to grow up knowing those terrible things.

"A-bu, I can't wait to tell Sis these things. She will definitely fall off the chair."

"I am sure she will." Ciou-Tao knew her daughters well. In fact, she thought that Mei-Ling might scream and get very excited.

"A-bu, do you think Sis will learn the Taiwanese history at university since her major is history?"

"I don't know. She only told me that the classes are so boring right now."

"A-bu, I feel like studying history at university too."

"Mei-Ai, I understand how you feel. As a matter of fact, I am glad that you know some truths about our government, but at the same time, I am also afraid. I believe that you very much want to know about Taiwanese history now, and people should know their national history, so I won't and can't stop you from learning it. Just be very careful, please, since you have learned how evil and brutal the government is. And of course, the same as I told your sister, you can study whatever you like at university."

"Thank you, A-bu."

"Oh, by the way, if you want, you can bring Lan Tian to our restaurant."

"OK, A-bu."

The next morning, after Mei-Ai went to school, Ciou-Tao went to the seacoast alone.

"Wen-Hua ge, I can't believe that the day has come. Mei-Ai met a boy. His name is Lan Tian. He is a young man who knows Taiwanese history very well. I guess he has read those books and magazines that you read before. His family had a big tragedy. His great-grandfather was a famous painter and well-respected person in another town. He was killed in the 228 Incident. You might know him since you read and knew so much Taiwanese history. When Mei-Ai told me that Lan Tian's great-grandfather was tortured in prison and then killed in public, I thought about you immediately. I had to try very hard not to cry, because I am not ready to tell Mei-Ai your story. Wen-Hua ge, can you believe it? Just learning a person's story, her mind has been stirred very much. Moreover, she wants to study history at university now. Like you told me decades ago, truth is powerful, but I fear she might end up like you.

"After that dictator, Chiang Ching-kuo, died last year, the new president is Taiwanese. People said things might be different. But how? He is a member of the Chinese Nationalist Party too. In fact, he is the chairperson now. Although the two heads of the Chinese Nationalist Party have died, the party is still evil. Being a chairperson of that party, how good could he be?

"Wen-Hua ge, you always said that things would eventually change because there are many people in Taiwan working very hard to fight for freedom and democracy. I always admire those people, but I get weak when I see my daughter walking on the path that you had walked before. I am proud and fearful too. Wen-Hua ge, please help me to have the strength to guide her and protect her."

Seeing the waves coming and going, back and forth endlessly, Ciou-Tao suddenly realized that the water was so much closer to the coast. When she was young, she and her four stepbrothers could play on the sand. Now, most of the area was under the water. "Things do change. Maybe my daughter wouldn't get into trouble."

"Hey, Lan Tian. Tell me what books and magazines that you're reading at home."

"Mei-Ai, I just arrived. That hill is killing me. I need a moment to catch my breath."

"You walked?"

"No, riding a bicycle. It's easier if I walk. Riding a bike up a hill is tough, but I look forward to going home. I don't have to pedal all the way, and the bike is like flying in the air."

"You are very strange, my friend." Mei-Ai liked him, though.

"I *am* strange. Do you regret being my friend?"

"Are you kidding? It's not easy to get a funny friend these days."

"Am I the funniest one?"

"I don't know. I just know you. And plus, I haven't found anyone who is funnier than my sister yet."

"Well, you got me excited here. I want to meet your sister."

"Too bad. Mei-Ling is studying in Taipei now."

"I'll meet her when she comes back."

"Yeah, like you know she wants to meet you."

"Who wouldn't want to meet a funny guy?"

"Yeah, right! Funny guy, when will you tell me what books and magazines that you're reading at home?"

"Now! But we have to talk in a different place."

"Why?"

"Have to."

Lan Tian took Mei-Ai to the park that was next to the library. They found a quiet spot to sit down.

"Mei-Ai, do you know banned books?"

"What?"

"Books and magazines that the government forbids people to read."

"What's wrong with those books and magazines?"

"The government says that they are poison, not good for people's minds."

"Really?"

"Of course, it's bullshit!"

Whenever Mei-Ai heard Lan Tian say "bullshit," she couldn't help laughing.

"Can you believe this? For instance, if people say that they like the color red, the government might see them as traitors who love the Chinese Communist Party."

"So you can't read Karl Marx's books, right?"

"Nope! You're good. Learning fast."

"Anything else?"

"They ban any articles, books, or magazines that criticize Chiang Kai-shek, Chiang Ching-kuo, and the Chinese Nationalist Party—and punish the writers too."

"So does that mean people who read those books and magazines would get into trouble too?"

"Yes."

"And you like to read those books and magazines."

"That's right."

"You are not afraid?"

"If I say no, then it's a lie. I try not to think so much. Just be careful and read at home only. More importantly, do not tell any people about it."

"But you tell me..."

"I trust you."

"I hate this."

"I trust you?"

"Not that. I hate the government making people live in fear. Think of it. How disgusting is that? The textbooks that we read describe how good our government is, but they secretly have done many dirty things."

"Mei-Ai, they banned those books and magazines quite openly, though."

"It's a secret to me because I didn't know anything that you just told me."

"Your parents have never told you any horrible things that the Chinese Nationalist government has done?"

"Only one time, and it was a comment without any explanation. My a-bu seriously told me that the Chinese Nationalist Party is not a good party after I asked her permission to join the Chinese Nationalist Party. My sister and I assumed that my mother knew that the Chinese Nationalist Party has done a lot of dirty things, but she didn't want to tell us. But now, I know that she wanted us to live happily without worry and fear."

"Mei-Ai, why did you want to join the Chinese Nationalist Party?"

"For the scholarship. To be honest, my family is not poor, but we are not rich either. Any little bit of income helps."

"Mei-Ai, one of their scholarships is very disgusting."

"What does that mean?"

"They have one scholarship that is called Dr. Sun Yat-Sen Scholarship. It's for the students who graduated from university and are going to study abroad. They have to be members of the party and pass assessments. It is a lot of money, though. Students can live very well with it. They have to do some jobs for the Chinese Nationalist government. For instance, to steal those Taiwanese magazines that criticize Chiang Kai-shek, Chiang Ching-kuo, and the Chinese Nationalist Party from their schools' libraries."

"Really? What for? Most Americans can't read Mandarin. What are they afraid of?"

"They don't want those students who are from Taiwan to know the truth, their crimes."

"I don't understand one thing. In my thinking, anyone would hate Chiang Kai-shek, Chiang Ching-kuo, and the party if they learned the truths and facts. But how come so many people are on their side, support them, or even do dirty jobs for them?"

"Some of them are actually as bad as Chiang Kai-shek, Chiang Ching-kuo, and that party, and some others believe that they are saving the country, the Republic of China, from being overthrown. Therefore, those student spies do not feel guilty or ashamed that they took pictures of those Taiwanese students who marched for human rights and fairness in Taiwanese elections and called to threaten those Taiwanese students who got together to discuss the pursuit of freedom and democracy in Taiwan. Many students eventually are on the blacklist and forbidden to come back to Taiwan because those students who received the Dr. Sun Yat-Sen Scholarship spied on and reported them to the Chinese Nationalist government."

"Oh my God! To be forbidden to come back to Taiwan? That's brutal. Even though it's great to live in a free country, I am sure that those students want to come back home very much."

"That's why my a-bu doesn't want me to study in the United States after I graduate from university. She believes that I'll be on the blacklist for sure. Thus, she suggests that I should go to other countries—France, for instance. There will be less possibility to be spied on."

"I agree with your a-bu. Or you stay in Taiwan to get your PhD."

"So you see how this government deprives our freedom!"

"Now, you mention freedom. I realize something interesting but sad. Before you told me those horrible things, I never felt I wasn't free. I always believed that our country was free and democratic."

"Perhaps you believed everything written in the textbooks."

"Yes, I did. Very much."

"That's why you are one of the top students."

"Oh, please don't make fun of me. This is not a compliment now."

"I am sorry; I didn't mean that. My a-bu is right. I need to learn how to express myself correctly. I meant to say that you and your sister are loved and trusted, so you trust people, teachers, and the schools and believe what you learn. Moreover, you both are intelligent, so you learn well."

"Which is the type that the government loves, but I don't like them anymore. Lan Tian, lend me a few books."

"Are you serious?"

"Reading is beneficial to you. You've never heard of this from teachers?"

"Yes, I have. Man, you've got me very excited now. Finally, I have a reading buddy. For that, I am providing you with the best service. I'm going to make a reading plan for you, so you'll learn more systematically."

"Systematically? Like our government?"

"Ha! Very funny!"

As a high school student himself, Lan Tian knew that it was hard for Mei-Ai to spend a lot of time reading those banned books. Besides, they both had only three semesters left, so they had to study hard for the university entrance examination. Thus, Lan Tian picked a book that was very easy and enjoyable to read for Mei-Ai. He was sure that the book would open her eyes and shake her mind.

The book, *The Fig Tree* (無花果), was the author's auto-biography. The author, Wu Chuo-Liu (吳濁流, 1900–1976), was an influential Taiwanese journalist and writer. He lived through two different ruling periods, the Japanese era and the Chinese time, which was not easy for him and most Taiwanese people at the time. The use of language, the way of thinking, the attitude and manner of doing things, and the degree of tolerance for civilians' pursuit of freedom of speech and human rights were completely different between the Japanese and the Chinese government. This made the Taiwanese people think and compare their lives in the Japanese era and the Chinese time. Mr. Wu wrote honestly about his feelings and viewpoints on things that he had seen and been through, making the book valuable historical information. He told how the Taiwanese people were oppressed in the Japanese ruling time by his own experiences. He described what he saw in the 228 Incident and analyzed why the conflict between the Taiwanese people and the Chinese people on the island was hard to end and suggested what all the people on the island should do for a better future. Unlike most people, Mr. Wu was an educated man who reflected himself honestly, talked from his heart, and reviewed things from different angles. Even today, some people in Taiwan think the ideas that Mr. Wu had in the book still shine like the stars that can lead the people on the island to walk out of the darkness if people are willing to listen.

"What's the matter?" Ciou-Tao asked Mei-Ai, who had tears on her face.

"Nothing. This book is really good. Some stories make me feel sad."

"Is this the book that Lan Tian lent you?"

"Yes, it is."

"Can I borrow it to read when you go to school?"

"A-bu, take it. I just finished reading it. You will love it."

"I have no doubt."

"A-bu, the stories that I read in the book were from a

world that is unfamiliar to me. That's like a lost world to me, especially the Japanese time. However, calculating the time, A-bu, you were born in 1949, the year the Chiang Kai-shek regime fled to Taiwan, which means that your a-ba is like the writer who lived through two nations' ruling time. It wasn't that long ago at all, but I know very little about that period."

"Mei-Ai, do you think the stories that you learned in that book can be put in the textbooks?"

"Some of them can, like how bad many Japanese people treated the Taiwanese people, but some definitely can't, because they are ugly facts about some Chinese civilians, many Chinese soldiers, and the Chinese Nationalist government."

"The Chinese Nationalist government isn't the only government that doesn't want people to know their ugly crime, though. I believe that all the governments in the world are the same. They like to talk bad about all governments but themselves."

"A-bu, I just realize how important it is to write down all the stories that people have seen or been through in that period before they die. I hope some people are doing the job right now."

"I agree with you."

The next time Mei-Ai met Lan Tian, she told him about how she wished some people could write down the stories that happened in the period from the Japanese era to the Chinese Nationalist government time.

"We are losing the people who experienced significant historical events. The longer we wait, the more witnesses will pass away. I wonder if our historians are aware that we are racing against time."

"I am sure some of them are. Mei-Ai, believe it or not, we all can be historians ourselves."

"What does that mean?"

"That book is the author's autobiography. He talked about his own stories from little to grown up, how the people around him and some events had great influences on him and what his feelings and opinions were. Don't we all have our own stories to tell? In my case, my great-grandfather's tragedy didn't end with his death. It continues affecting our family tremendously, and I think it's important to write them down."

"I want to read your book when you finish it one day."

"See, if I wrote my family's stories and you read it, you would learn a partial Taiwanese history. All the stories that happened on our land are our history."

"All the stories that happened on our land are our history. True. It's so true. I like it.

"Lan Tian, when my sister and I were little, we loved our a-bu telling us her childhood stories. We felt closer to her after listening to those stories. Sometimes she wouldn't tell us something and would say, 'It isn't a good time to tell.' My sister and I would feel very disappointed. It felt like we couldn't go into some part of her world, and a small distance would appear between our a-bu and us at once."

"Mei-Ai, you just talked about a good concept here. We are connected not just because we are family or one nation. It's the life that we share and the things that we have been through together that bring us closer. Reading others' life stories or knowing what happened on our land also does the same to people. That's why it's important to know our history, and it's wrong that ninety-nine percent of what we learn at school is Chinese history."

"That's why I always think that I am Chinese. China is our country, and one day we will go back to that beautiful land. However, I was born and grew up here. There is no home to me in China. My homeland is here, Taiwan."

"That's why we should mainly learn Taiwanese history and geography."

"Lan Tian, do you think many older people have the same opinion as yours?"

"Probably. But what can they do or say? People fear the

Chinese Nationalist government."

"Those people who spoke from their hearts in their books are courageous."

"Yes, they are. I will introduce you to a brave man's articles in the future. His name is Lei Zhen. He was the writer and editor of the *Free China Journal*. He was charged with distributing the Chinese Communists' propaganda and covering up for the Chinese Communists' spy and sentenced to ten years in prison."

"Because of what he wrote?"

"That's right. And you won't believe this. After he was released from prison in 1970, he didn't keep his mouth shut like many others. He still spoke from his heart to the Chiang Kai-shek regime, asking for democratization in Taiwan and suggesting to change the name of the country from the Republic of China to the Chinese Republic of Taiwan."

"Holy cow! He is something else. You have to lend me the magazines."

"Sure. I'll bring you the magazines next time. He was an extraordinary man, no doubt. How many people in this world wouldn't fear autocrats? He was one of the few."

"I am afraid. Even just reading a banned book, I have fears."

"Mei-Ai, to be afraid is natural. I have fears too. It's just not as much as it used to be."

"It's funny. I can't put my a-bu and fear together. In my feelings, she is a super a-bu."

"Not my a-bu. She is always screaming, 'Cockroach!' 'Mouse!' 'Help!'"

Mei-Ai laughed. "Come on! That doesn't count. My a-bu is afraid of frogs in a way that you can't imagine, but my sister and I still think she is super."

"Really? It's hard to imagine your a-bu is afraid of frogs."

Then Mei-Ai told Lan Tian the story that Ciou-Tao threw a big rock to "cover" a frog after Ciou-Lian warned her not to let the frog jump away. Lan Tian laughed so hard that he almost choked to death.

Mei-Ai told Ciou-Tao the conversation that she had with Lan Tian when she got home.

"Lan Tian said that everyone can be a historian to write her or his family stories."

"Interesting viewpoint."

"It is an interesting viewpoint, but I thought about it on the way home. I don't think each family can contribute valuable materials to national history."

"Maybe they don't have to be the materials for national history. They can be stories only for their family and friends. Mei-Ai, don't you think it's nice to know our family's stories so we know who we are?"

"Yes, it is. But A-bu, my focus is on national history. I was shocked exceedingly after knowing some Taiwanese history that I have never heard of before, so I believe there must be many stories that no one knows and that should be written down. However, after thinking of it, I also believe that not all people's stories are valuable for national history. For instance, all the family stories that Sis and I have learned from you were interesting or bitter, but they are not essential materials for Taiwanese history. Thus, here comes the question: How do historians know where to find the families or people who have important stories to tell? Moreover, even if historians find the families or people who were the victims of the 228 Incident, for example, it doesn't mean they would like to talk about their stories. I believe that many people wouldn't like to tell their stories because of fear or pain. As a result, there must be some hidden victims around us, and no one knows about their existence. That is a shame."

Ciou-Tao fell silent for a few seconds because she didn't know how to respond. She did have plenty of valuable shocking stories to tell. She hadn't wanted to tell Mei-Ling and Mei-Ai when they were little; now, she didn't know how to start. Furthermore, even though Uncle Huang, Ciou-Jyu, Ciou-Lian,

Wen-Zhi, Wen-Hua, and neighbor aunts were trivial people, their lives were deeply affected by the government. Hence, Ciou-Tao didn't like Mei-Ai used the term "valuable materials." It sounded like the Chinese Nationalist government's way of speaking, to see civilians like faceless and valueless worms or ants. Of course, Ciou-Tao knew that it was not what Mei-Ai meant. She just believed that not all people's stories could be written in history.

Ciou-Tao winked at Mei-Ai and said, "I completely agree with you. There must be some hidden victims around us. Therefore, how do you know that I didn't hide some secrets from you and your sister? Something big and significant in Taiwanese history!" Ciou-Tao walked away after finishing talking. In the kitchen, she cried.

Two months later, the semester ended, and winter vacation came. It was the first time Mei-Ling and Mei-Ai separated from each other for more than four months. Even though Mei-Ling came home two times during the semester, it was too depressing to Mei-Ai. Mei-Ling also missed Mei-Ai very much, but she didn't have the same depressing feeling. After all, she was a freshman at university. Everything was new and fresh to her. For example, the parties at university were completely different from any parties that she had gone to before, so much more fun. Mei-Ling said to Mei-Ai, "You will finally know what party means after you go to a party at university." In short, Mei-Ling's life at university was full of fun things, and she was happy. Therefore, Mei-Ling came home with a million things to tell.

Mei-Ai also had tons of things to tell.

"Sis, I met a guy in the library."

"What? Before I get a boyfriend, you have got one already."

"Wait! It's not a boyfriend. He's just a friend, an interesting guy."

"Aren't you afraid of being scolded by school teachers or military education instructors?"

"What can they scold about? We're just friends. A-bu knows him and likes him too."

"Even so, be very careful. Those school people are annoying and crazy."

"I know, Sis."

"So you two only study together in the library?"

"Yes. And talking, too."

"Dope! Of course you talk to each other." Mei-Ai laughed. She missed Mei-Ling and being called "dope."

"Sis, do you know about banned books?"

"That's what you talk about in the library?"

"Yeah."

"I've heard of banned books but don't know what they are, actually."

"I just finished reading one, *The Fig Tree*. It's fantastic. A-bu loves it too. Sis, you should read it."

"You are reading a banned book? That guy lent you?"

"His name is Lan Tian. Yes, he lent me that book, and I can't wait to read the *Free China Journal*. He'd better bring it to me next time."

"You're crazy! There'll be many examinations in the last year of high school. You have to be ready for it. Otherwise, you won't be able to get a high score on the university entrance examination."

"That's why I am reading them right now while I still have a little free time."

"Good to know that you haven't lost your head. But why do you want to read banned books and magazines? Aren't they bad, so the government bans them?"

"No. On the contrary, they are super good, so the government bans them."

"Mei-Ai, you are not making any sense."

"The Chinese Nationalist government banned those books that criticize Chiang Kai-shek, Chiang Ching-kuo, and the party or talk about some topics and ideas that they don't like."

"Who likes criticism? Of course they got mad and banned those books."

"But they also punished those writers, imprisoned them. Don't they say our country is free and democratic?"

"Maybe they said something that hurt our country."

"Gee, you surely love the government!"

"No, I don't love the government that much. I just want to think and talk justly. It's you who sound like you dislike our government."

"You got that right!"

"Really?"

"Sis, you should read *The Fig Tree*. Your mind will be challenged by it."

Mei-Ling wouldn't define herself as a patriot, but she did love her country, the Republic of China, like hundreds of thousands of students in Taiwan. Why wouldn't they? According to what they learned from the textbooks, they had a great country, a democratic country, and the best leaders, Chiang Kai-shek and Chiang Ching-kuo. Although she had a little doubt on the government, overall, she loved the country. However, Mei-Ling was an open-minded person and trusted her a-bu and Mei-Ai very much, so she read *The Fig Tree*.

A corrupt government?

The February 28 Incident?

Mei-Ling couldn't believe what she read. That was a very different government from the one that she had learned from the textbooks and media.

Was the author a liar, so this book was banned?

It didn't seem so. His words were plain and simple. He thought deeply. He discussed problems uprightly. He didn't only talk about how depressing and upsetting it was to live under the Japanese rule, but he also told some good experiences that he had had with several Japanese people. Furthermore, he didn't just criticize Chinese people. He also pointed out the Taiwanese people's drawbacks. He wished to have a better Taiwan, one where the Taiwanese people and the Chinese people could get along.

"It's a great book," Mei-Ling told Mei-Ai and Ciou-Tao, who were sitting in the living room talking.

"I told you." Mei-Ai was very happy.

"I can't believe that the Chinese Nationalist government and its troops did so many horrible things after they arrived in Taiwan. A-bu, is that the reason you don't want us to have any contact with those Chinese veterans?"

"No. That's not the reason. I didn't know a lot of things that were written in the book until I read it."

"Then what's the reason?" Mei-Ai also wanted to know.

"Girls, that's a big long story to tell, and it's brutal."

"A-bu, please don't say it's not a good time or maybe another day. We are old enough to understand complicated things."

"That's right, A-bu. We have learned about the 228 Incident. What could be more brutal than a massacre? We can handle it." Mei-Ai joined in persuading Ciou-Tao.

Ciou-Tao knew that it was the time to tell those stories that she hid in the bottom of her heart. "OK. Girls, let's go to our place."

Mei-Ling and Mei-Ai looked at each other and smiled.

14

A-bu's Love and Pain

It was a damp and cold winter day. It wouldn't be nice to sit at the seacoast and talk, but who cared? The two sisters just wanted to listen to their a-bu's stories and know why their a-bu did not want them to have any contact with those Chinese veterans.

"Girls, do you remember once you asked me why we go to Taroko and Tienhsiang every Lunar New Year?"

"You said you like it there. It's beautiful."

"That's true, but the real reason that I go there is to visit my uncle."

"Uncle? What uncle? We never met anyone there." Mei-Ai was confused.

"A-bu, do you mean Uncle Huang?"

"Yes."

"Sis, who is Uncle Huang? Why do you know him and I don't?"

"Remember I went to the camp, the Cross-Island Highway Hiking Team? A-bu worried if it was safe to go hiking in those mountains when I asked her permission to go. Accidently, A-bu mentioned that Uncle Huang died in there. Now, A-bu says she was visiting her uncle, so I take a guess and bingo!"

"A-bu, who is Uncle Huang? He must be very important to you, so you take us to visit him every year."

"Mei-Ai, you are right. Uncle Huang was the person whom I loved the most when I was little. He was like my a-ba. I talked to him more than I talked to my a-ba. He was a smart

271

and knowledgeable man. He taught me and my sisters, Ciou-Jyu and Ciou-Lian, so many things. He saw us as his daughters. He was very poor but willing to give us everything that he had because he loved us very much." Ciou-Tao's eyes were full of tears.

"A-bu, last time you told me that Uncle Huang was your neighbor. Was he your old father's neighbor or new father's?" Since Mei-Ling and Mei-Ai were little, they had known that Ciou-Tao was given away when she was seven years old. They liked the terms, "new father" and "old father," that Ciou-Tao had invented when she was little, so they borrowed them from their a-bu.

"I met Uncle Huang when I was four years old. He wasn't a real neighbor because he lived twenty minutes away from our home on foot. He passed by our home every day to sell steamed buns in the town. One day, Uncle Huang was very tired from the heat on the way home, so he rested by a tree and saw me. That was how we met."

"Remember the song 'Two Tigers'?"

"Of course. Mei-Ai and I loved it when you taught us."

"Uncle Huang was the one who taught me."

"Really? Wow, right now I feel that I am connected to Uncle Huang too."

"Mei-Ling, Uncle Huang also felt connected to me that day, so he gave me the last steamed bun that was supposed to be his lunch and dinner."

"A-bu, how did you know that bun was his lunch and dinner?" Mei-Ai was curious.

"Of course, I didn't know it that day. Later, I heard my parents talking about it, so I knew. Moreover—"

"A-bu, sorry for the interruption. A steamed bun for two meals? Uncle Huang must be very poor."

"Yes, Mei-Ling, Uncle Huang was very poor. However, after the second time we met, Uncle Huang started to give us two steamed buns every day."

"A poor man gave you two buns every day! Oh God, he

must like you guys very much."

"No, it wasn't 'like'; it was love. He loved us very much. In the beginning, I thought that he gave us two streamed buns every day because I told him we loved his buns, but later, when I got older, I knew the real reason was that he loved us, everyone in our family. We also loved him dearly. My parents invited him to have dinner with us every day, which made Ciou-Jyu, Ciou-Lian, and me feel thrilled. Then dinner time became our favorite time of day. Uncle Huang was happy too. Finally, he no longer ate dinner alone. He had a pleasant dinner time like the old days. We talked, ate, and laughed at the dining table. He felt like he was home again."

"A-bu, why was Uncle Huang alone? Where was his family?"

"Mei-Ai, Uncle Huang had a family, a wife, two daughters, and parents, but they didn't come to Taiwan with him. He came to Taiwan with the Chinese Nationalist troops by order in 1948. He thought that he would be back to his family two or three years later, but the Chiang Kai-shek regime fled to Taiwan in exile. Then he never saw his family again before he died."

"A-bu, you mean Uncle Huang was a Chinese veteran?" Mei-Ling was incredibly shocked.

"Sis, Uncle Huang made and sold steamed buns! That is a northern Chinese food!"

How many times had their a-bu told them not to have any contact with the Chinese veterans since they were little? "Don't talk to them! Don't take their candies and cookies! Run away or scream if they try to touch you!"

"Uncle Huang was A-bu's favorite person in the world when she was young, and A-bu goes to visit him in Taroko and Tienhsiang every Lunar New Year. She must have some good feelings for those Chinese veterans because of Uncle Huang. However, she always tells us to stay away from the Chinese veterans or be careful if we are around them. Why?" The two sisters fell into silence.

"I know you two probably are wondering how come I love Uncle Huang deeply but seem to dislike the Chinese veterans very much. There are reasons, and I'll tell you later."

The two sisters nodded in agreement because they wanted to know more about Uncle Huang first.

"A-bu, why did Uncle Huang die in the mountains?"

"A-bu, was he the road builder in the Central Cross-Island Highway construction?" Mei-Ling had learned the history of the Central Cross-Island Highway on the hiking team.

"Yes, he was. He got hit by a rock and fell into the gorge."

"Oh my God, that's terrible!" Picturing that, Mei-Ai felt pain.

"A-bu, that was a dangerous job, so why did he want to join the project?"

"Mei-Ling, he joined the project because he was heartbroken."

"Because he couldn't go back to China and reunite with his family?"

"Mei-Ai, besides that reason, I believe there was a last straw that broke the camel's back. I don't think Uncle Huang had ever thought that he could have a new family in Taiwan and be happy again. I believe that the happiness of having us took away some of his pain and bitterness. Although Uncle Huang loved all the members of my family, he had a stronger emotional connection with Ciou-Jyu, Ciou-Lian, and me. That was why it impacted him a great deal when my parents decided to give us away. He probably felt that he lost his family again. However, he hung in there for us and gave us guidance. He knew that we must feel upset and abandoned, so he talked to us and tried to relieve our anxiety and anger. Moreover, he assisted my father in performing my father's duty to take us to each adoptive family. On the way to our new families, he helped us to know that we were resilient and capable of surviving in any conditions."

"A-bu, he was your a-ba."

"Mei-Ling, in my heart, he was my a-ba, and my sisters

and I were his daughters in his heart. That's why he was sick for more than two weeks after he took us to the new families, and I was down in the dumps when Uncle Huang died, which gave a Chinese veteran a chance to take advantage of me. He pretended to be nice and comforted me, and I trusted him. Immediately, he tried to rape me."

"What?"

"What a bastard!"

"But that's not the only reason that I told you not to have any contact with the Chinese veterans."

"More?"

"Yes."

"More Chinese veterans tried to rape you?"

"Not me. They raped your auntie Ciou-Jyu." Ciou-Tao burst into tears.

Mei-Ai gave her handkerchief to Ciou-Tao.

"In a way, I was glad that Uncle Huang died before Ciou-Jyu. If he were alive and knew what happened to her, he would not only have his heart broken but might kill those people."

"I would kill those bastards too!" Mei-Ling was very angry.

"Me too."

"Ciou-Jyu's husband was the worst man on the earth."

"Was he Chinese?"

"No, he was Taiwanese. He raped your auntie and made her be a prostitute."

"Fucking animal!"

"Mei-Ling, watch your language."

"Sorry, A-bu. But he was an animal."

"I agree with you, Sis."

"He liked to gamble, so he met and knew a lot of Chinese veterans."

"Like our a-ba." Mei-Ling said it with disgust.

"He kidnapped your auntie, tied her up, and locked her in a storehouse. Then he made money from letting those Chinese veterans rape your auntie. Eventually, your auntie's stepson found out and asked for help. In the mess, your auntie's husband killed Uncle Wen-Hua's elder brother, Wen-Zhi, which drove her insane and led her to suicide."

"I feel like killing people right now!"

"Sis, calm down."

"I can't! Why didn't they go home and do their wives?"

"Sis, many Chinese veterans were single, remember?"

"So find someone and get married!"

"Mei-Ling, many of them were like Uncle Huang. They had wives and children in China."

"Then, that's a betrayal."

"To be honest, it's hard to find someone as decent as Uncle Huang, but not all the Chinese veterans are bad. I met some of Uncle Huang's comrades, and they were good people, friendly and kind. Even though they had one another's company, they were very lonely. When I was little, I couldn't comprehend how lonesome they could be. Now, I can understand how painful to be forbidden to go back to their home and families. It is barbaric."

"But it didn't give them the right to buy sex from those women who were forced to be prostitutes."

"I agree with Sis. A-bu, do you feel bad about telling us not to have any contact with the Chinese veterans? Don't. Little girls can't judge who is good or bad. Moreover, you had scary and painful experiences. It's better to be safe than sorry. A-bu, thank you for protecting us, and I am very sorry for your sister. I wish I could meet her."

"I'm sure you both would love her very much if you could meet her. She was a sweet chrysanthemum, a thoughtful person."

"Then her adoptive mother must be a horrible person because she arranged for Auntie to marry a scumbag?"

"Mei-Ling, even a great person would be disliked by some people."

"That's true. But A-bu, I am going to marry whom I love. No one can arrange my marriage."

"Me too."

"Wait, girls. Do I look like an a-bu who would control her daughters' lives?"

Mei-Ling laughed embarrassedly. "Sorry, A-bu. Of course Mei-Ai and I know that you won't do such a thing. What I want to say is that no one can deprive anyone's right to the pursuit of happiness."

"Bravo! Sis, well said!"

"Mei-Ling, I know what you mean. I agree with you completely. Honestly, we are making progress; the situation in your generation is so much better than mine. In my generation, most people were poor and had a lot of children. Furthermore, most people had gender bias. Girls were seen as less worthy than boys. Thus, it was quite common that we, girls, were sent away to be shim-bu-a."

"It's so not fair."

"A-bu, I think A-hue's situation is worse than being shim-bu-a. She is a prisoner and a sex slave." Mei-Ai cried for a long time after she saw A-hue in the restaurant that day. She couldn't accept the fact that A-hue's parents sold her to a te-tiam-a.

"Well, even though we are making progress, many people's minds are still very far away from being civilized. For instance, many men still see women as objects that can be treated without respect, or many parents deem their children as their property."

"A-bu, something bothers me even more. Many mothers look down on or abuse their daughters as bad as the men in their families. In fact, worse than men in many cases, as I know."

"A-bu, Mei-Ai is right. It's hard to believe that those women don't stick together to fight sexism but act against their gender. I try to guess how their minds work. Do they think that they have to do those things to feel that they are not the poor and powerless women anymore? In other words, they are no longer in the victim's group. Or they need a way to ease their anger and heal their wounds. Often, people would do the same thing, how they were treated, to the people who remind them of their past. In this case, those are their daughters or other young girls. Of course, it might be only an act of human nature. Human beings enjoy having power and love the feeling that they can decide others' destiny."

"Mei-Ling, that's deep thinking. They could be all true."

"Sis, I like your opinions very much, but I feel it is an act of revenge."

"But if it is an act of revenge, don't they take it on the wrong people? Shouldn't they punish the people who treated them awfully?"

"Sis, I can't give you a good explanation, but I do believe one of the reasons is an act of revenge. We all know that most people like revenge, and many of them will take it if they have a chance."

"Mei-Ling, Mei-Ai, all your theories are impressive, but I hope you two are more focused on those women who tried hard to survive or fight to change their fates. Their spirits were extraordinary, and we should follow their path to keep fighting. Hopefully, one day we will have a gender-equal society."

"A-bu, don't worry about us. We're always focused on that. Don't you feel the admiration from Mei-Ai and me?"

"Bad girl! Making fun of your a-bu."

"No, A-bu. Sis speaks from her heart. You're our heroine."

"Thank God you're our a-bu. Imagine if Auntie Ciou-Jyu's adoptive mother were our a-bu, and with A-ba, we would have no future for sure."

"Sis, worse—we might be forced to be prostitutes."

"Girls, that's too mean and harsh. Your a-ba is not that bad."

"A-bu, we have seen you crying pretty often since we were little."

"Mei-Ling, I cried for different reasons and things."

"What reasons and things?"

"I'll tell you another time."

"Oh no. Not today, again?"

"Mei-Ling, be patient."

"A-bu, I think that on the day I finally learned all your stories, I would be one hundred ten years old."

"I would be one hundred eight. Too old."

"Dope, it's not too old. It's too dead. I don't even think that we can live over eighty. A-bu will have to tell us her stories in heaven."

Ciou-Tao laughed loudly. "Girls, I won't let you wait that long. I promise to tell you all my stories before I die. I am too tired to tell more stories today. Don't you feel that you need time to digest what we talked about today?"

"OK. Another day, then. But what I need right now is to have real food to digest."

"Me too. A-bu, I have an idea. Can we go to Old Shandong [老山東] to eat steamed buns and drink soy milk?" Mei-Ai proposed.

"Good idea. It's a perfect way to celebrate that we get to know Uncle Huang at last. But I need more food, like sesame flatbreads and meat buns."

"Girls, stop talking. Let's go!"

"A-bu, one more question. Uncle Huang's steamed buns are better or Old Shandong's?"

"Jesus! You're a super-duper dope. Of course it's Uncle Huang's buns!"

15

Taiwanese Hearts

The four-week winter vacation had gone. Some parts of the mother and daughters had gone, too, but something new had filled their hearts.

For Ciou-Tao, she was vastly happy that Mei-Ling and Mei-Ai finally knew Uncle Huang, a person whom she loved and admired the most in the world. She could talk about Uncle Huang freely at last. Furthermore, she didn't need to remind Mei-Ling and Mei-Ai to be careful around the Chinese veterans anymore. They certainly had a full understanding of the danger from learning Ciou-Jyu's tragedy and her experience. It was painful that she had to tell Mei-Ling and Mei-Ai to stay away from the Chinese veterans. It was like betraying Uncle Huang in a way. Besides, Ciou-Tao never knew that telling the truth was such a great feeling, like being released from prison. Moreover, she felt that the connection between Mei-Ling, Mei-Ai, and her was stronger and closer.

Mei-Ling also felt closer to her a-bu. She always liked to listen to her a-bu's stories. She was impressed that her a-bu had been so poor and suffered from many bitter situations but never stopped keeping going. She asked herself if she would have the same spirit if she were in the same circumstance. She had a doubt first, but immediately, she thought that she might be able to because she was her a-bu's daughter. Comparing to the women's lives in her a-bu's generation, Mei-Ling felt that she and Mei-Ai were a lucky generation. However, there were still some young girls, like A-hue, in critical condition. They needed help. Therefore, Mei-Ling considered applying for a transfer, changing her major from history to social work, a profession to help change society to be better and more equal. Besides, Mei-Ling decided to be friendlier to the Chinese veterans. After all, not all of them were bad. There were many good ones, like Uncle Huang and the bei-bei in Old Shandong. She shouldn't be so harsh on them.

Mei-Ai decided to study history at university. She was moved and shocked by many people's life stories. In her heart, the stories of Lan Tian's great-grandfather, Wu Chuo-Liu, Lei Chen, Auntie Ciou-Jyu, Uncle Huang, or her a-bu all needed to be written down and told, and the people in Taiwan should know about them. Mei-Ai believed that change began from knowing. If the Taiwanese people wanted to find their identity back, they had to learn the Taiwanese history, knowing who they are.

"Oh my! You want to study history. Mei-Ai, you build my confidence up indeed. Maybe I should be a teacher so I can change my students' minds, to realize that they are Taiwanese, not Chinese, to love the land where they are living, not the dreamland, China."

"Why not? You did convince me."

"But I want to be a historian and a writer."

"They suit you too."

"Mei-Ai, you are not helping me here. You're very encouraging. Maybe you should be the one to be a teacher."

"Lan Tian, I have a good idea. We can be history teachers."

"That sounds good, but we might lose our jobs very soon. Perhaps be imprisoned too."

"I might lose my job, but you would be imprisoned for sure."

"Hey!"

"You're very outspoken and easy to get excited. Remember the day we met? You said, 'It's bullshit!' right behind me, and right away you told me that not everybody would be happily celebrating Taiwan's Retrocession Day. What if I reported you? You would be dead!"

"Not dead. I would be imprisoned."

"See that. Still joking. Sometimes I worry about you."

"Mei-Ai, don't worry. I only joke like this in front of the people whom I trust. I have been warned to be careful since I was little, after my a-bu told me my great-grandfather's story."

"Now, you remind me. My sister and I also learned a brutal family story from my a-bu two weeks ago."

"Really? Can I know?"

"Sure. My sister and I couldn't believe that my a-bu could keep that story in her heart for all these years. My a-bu's elder sister, Ciou-Jyu, was abused by her husband. He locked her up in a warehouse and let the Chinese veterans rape her to make money. Then her former adoptive brothers went to rescue her, and her husband killed one of them. My auntie couldn't bear the death of her adoptive brother and went mad. In the end, she killed herself."

"Those sons of bitches!"

"They were. That's why we were told to stay away from the Chinese veterans since we were little. That's not the only reason, though. Once my a-bu was almost raped by a Chinese veteran. Thus, those horrible events told my a-bu what she should do to protect us. Even though at the time she only told us not to have any contact with the Chinese veterans, my sister and I naturally disliked them."

"I don't like them either."

"We always thought that my a-bu disliked the Chinese veterans, but you won't believe this: her favorite person in the world was a Chinese veteran, Uncle Huang."

"Holy moly! It's unbelievable!"

"Better believe it. According to my a-bu, Uncle Huang

was a super good man. He loved my a-bu and her sisters with his whole heart."

"Your a-bu must feel relieved after she told you those stories. Perhaps happy too."

"I guess so. Hmm…"

"What?"

"Although I enjoy learning Taiwanese history and my a-bu's life stories, I find that I am not as happy as before. There's always an awful truth behind a story, and it's heavy. I don't mean that I regret knowing them or something. It's the frustration that I have. We talk about being history teachers, for instance, but how much could we do in reality while we are not freemen?"

"I hear you. How about only thinking of the important thing you need to do right now? Do that first. Then listen to your heart; it will tell you what to do later. That works for me all the time."

"Lan Tian, you're very much like my sister, very rational and practical. She calls me a worry worm, always worrying too much."

"Worry worm? Ha!"

"What?"

"My a-bu calls me a lazy worm."

"That's it. I quit worrying. I'm not going to be your worm friend."

"Mei-Ai, have you ever heard that once you are a worm, you'll always be one? Welcome to the worm world! Ha, ha, ha!"

"You're disgusting!"

Mei-Ai did worry too much. Once the schoolwork piled up and exams came one after another, she had no time to think about other things.

Actually, the one who had a headache was Mei-Ling. The

second semester was the time to apply for switching majors. Her mentor suggested that she should apply for double majors. Since she was doing well, why not study two subjects. It sounded excellent to Mei-Ling, but if she did so, she would have to study five years to get all the credits that she needed to graduate. One more year at university meant one more year tuition to pay. Hence, she hesitated. There was a spring break in April, so Mei-Ling went home and discussed the problem with her parents.

"I think you should transfer. Moreover, you should study something like accounting so you'll get a better job to make money in the future," Ming-Hao said.

"But I don't like accounting."

"You mean you don't like money?"

"A-ba, I didn't say that. I'm never good at numbers, so I'm not interested in accounting."

"Ming-Hao, she should study what she likes." Ciou-Tao wasn't happy to hear what Ming-Hao said.

"She worries about the tuition, but she doesn't want to study something that can make more money after she graduates. Yeah, that makes sense!"

"They are two different things, Ming-Hao. How can you judge knowledge with money?"

"Some knowledge is just more valuable than others. Which social worker can make more money than an accountant or a lawyer?"

"They do make more money, but many of them help rich criminals to escape from their crimes. I don't want my daughters to make immoral money."

"Well, then she'll have to earn the fifth-year tuition herself. She is old enough to get a job to pay for her living."

"No problem. I'll do so, A-ba." Anger helped Mei-Ling make a decision. Mei-Ling hadn't liked her a-ba since she was little, but now, she despised him.

Ciou-Tao knew that Ming-Hao had hurt Mei-Ling's feelings badly, so she went to check on Mei-Ling to see if she was OK. Mei-Ling and Mei-Ai shared a room. Because they didn't close the door, Ciou-Tao could see Mei-Ling was crying, and Mei-Ai didn't look too good either. She knocked softly on the door and walked into the room.

Ciou-Tao tried to cheer them up. "Mei-Ling, you are going back to school tomorrow. We won't see you for another two months, so we should have some fun today. How about going to Old Shandong to have brunch?"

Suddenly, Mei-Ling cried even harder.

"What's the matter, Sis?"

"A-bu, can we go someplace else? I don't feel like going to Old Shandong."

"Why?" Ciou-Tao was very surprised. Old Shandong had been Mei-Ling and Mei-Ai's favorite restaurant since they were little. There were usually a lot of customers on Saturday and Sunday, so sometimes they couldn't get a table and had to wait for thirty minutes or so. Ciou-Tao often suggested going to another place, but the two sisters insisted on waiting.

"I don't feel like seeing any Chinese veterans right now." The owners of the Old Shandong were three Chinese veterans who were never on the two sisters' not-to-contact list. In fact, they loved the three old men, and so did Ciou-Tao.

"Why, Sis?"

"I was sexually harassed by two different Chinese veterans in Taipei."

"What?" Mei-Ai couldn't believe what she heard.

"How and where?" Ciou-Tao was very nervous, but she tried to be calm.

"You know Ximending [西門町], right?" Ciou-Tao and Mei-Ai both nodded.

"My friends and I love Ximending, so we go there on Friday evening or Saturday afternoon sometimes to eat or shop. I'm always careful because there are so many people on the streets or alleys, which is a good environment for thieves to steal. Besides, I was also warned by senior female friends at school before, 'Be careful with those Chinese veterans, because they would take a chance to touch women in the crowd.' I was careful with that too. In fact, more careful than my friends. A-bu, you know, you have warned Mei-Ai and I since we were little, so I was very cautious. However, after I learned Uncle Huang's story, I decided not to be so mean to the Chinese veterans. After all, not all of them are bad. That was why I let my guard down and got attacked. You won't believe what they did. They walked in the crowd and looked for some girls or women who didn't pay attention. Then, they bent their arms and used their elbows to hit their breasts. After they did it, they ran and disappeared in the crowd like a ghost. You couldn't do anything but got mad."

"Fucking lowlifes!" Mei-Ai didn't care that her a-bu disliked the use of the f-word. She had to curse out loud!

Ciou-Tao held Mei-Ling tightly, and the anger rose in her heart.

"We shouldn't blame ourselves a bit in this kind of ugly situation. Trying to be kind or friendly is goodwill. People who take advantage of people's kindness and friendliness are sick and low. Mei-Ling, you're one hundred percent correct; not all the Chinese veterans are evil."

"I no longer care if some of them are good. I am blocking them out of my life." Mei-Ai was extremely mad.

"Same here. That's why I am not going to Old Shandong."

"Forever?" Ciou-Tao couldn't believe it.

"Just right now. After all, their sesame flatbread, meat buns, and soy milk are really yummy."

Ciou-Tao laughed, and so did Mei-Ai.

"Sis, do you know that we might not be able to eat there about ten years from now?"

"I know. Wang bei-bei, Lin bei-bei, and Cao bei-bei are getting old."

"As a matter of fact, they might close their restaurant soon."

"Why? A-bu, did you hear rumors?"

"Mei-Ling, I didn't hear any rumors. Remember the big news? Two years ago, November 2, 1987, three months before Chiang Ching-kuo died, he decided to allow the Chinese people who have relatives within the third degree of kinship in China to go back to visit their families. After more than thirty-eight years, the Chinese people who came to Taiwan after 1945 are finally permitted to go home and see their families. Although right now they can only go to visit their families once a year and for three months maximum each time, I believe that the regulation would be modified eventually. Think of it: if more and more businesspeople are allowed to go to China to do business and invest, why can't those Chinese people in Taiwan go back to China and stay? Mei-Ling, Mei-Ai, how many times have we heard those owners of Old Shandong talking about homesickness and how much they miss their families? If they were allowed, don't you think those bei-bei would want to go back to their homes and stay?"

"I do remember. I always feel they're very poor. I would stay if I am allowed."

"I would too."

"That's why I presume that those old guys might close their restaurant soon."

"Sis, so maybe we should go to Old Shandong today. You won't come home for another two months. Things might change."

"Just like that, my agony doesn't matter anymore?"

"Of course it matters, Sis. But you might regret it very much if they closed the restaurant next month."

"How about my dignity? In exchange for the sesame flatbreads and meat buns?"

"Mei-Ling, you still have your dignity despite going to Old Shandong, because they are not the ones who sexually harassed you. In addition, remember what you just said: not all the Chinese veterans are bad. The Chinese veterans in Old Shandong are good men, aren't they? Remember how great they have always treated you and Mei-Ai? Besides giving you those broken meat buns or last cups of cold soy milk, they also gave us the sesame flatbreads and meat buns that just came out of the oven, because once you told them that you loved the hot ones, that they tasted extra good. They laughed and said that this young lady knows what the best is! Mei-Ling, don't you think that they're like your dear granduncles?"

"Sis, I agree with A-bu. They're nice bei-bei, even though I have difficulty understanding them. They're surely not the lowlifes who attack women in Ximending. In fact, to compare them with those sick bastards is insulting them."

"Oh my goodness! After all these years, you still can't understand them?"

"Sis, their accent is too strong, and A-bu didn't bring us there often enough. I didn't have enough chance to learn."

"Bad girl! Look at your sister; she understands them. Instead of blaming your incompetence, you accused your a-bu." Mei-Ai stuck her tongue out and laughed.

"A-bu, to be honest, I don't fully understand them, though. Often, I would take the key words to have a guess. I understand them better than Mei-Ai because I used to stand by the oven waiting for the sesame flatbreads and meat buns. While I was waiting, Wang bei-bei was making flatbreads or buns and talking to me. When I was little, I had no fear and didn't know it was impolite to ask him again if I didn't understand what he said. He laughed every time and said, 'Bei-bei's accent is too heavy for you.'"

"Uncle Huang had an accent too. But not too heavy." Mei-Ling's story reminded Ciou-Tao of the happy time that she and her sisters had had with Uncle Huang.

"Wait! Can we go to Old Shandong now? I am getting hungry from listening to flatbreads this and buns that."

"This time, you go to stand by the oven to wait for the sesame flatbreads and meat buns. Your language ears will improve."

"No, Sis, you go. Wang bei-bei likes you more. He will give you broken ones."

"OK, girls. Quit arguing. Let's go before they sell out all the food."

"Oh, that's right. Speed up!" The wind blew; all the emotional stress was gone. Mei-Ling's heart was light as a fluffy cloud.

Two years ago, 1987, the Chinese Nationalist government had permitted the Chinese people to go back to China to visit their families, and Mei-Ling and Mei-Ai remembered it well for one important reason. Significant government policy change was always an essential question on the university entrance examination. Teachers would remind their students to remember those events when they helped students to review for the exam.

Ciou-Tao remembered it well because it was vastly meaningful to her. That meant her dear Uncle Huang could go home at last. One might think it was silly thinking because this government's permission was meaningless for the dead men like Uncle Huang. Besides, Uncle Huang's spirit probably had gone home after he died, since he was free. It was the justice matter that Ciou-Tao cared about. A good government wouldn't deprive civilians' right of being with their families. Even though Ciou-Tao was little at the time, she could tell how much Uncle Huang missed his family. Back then, she was too young to understand his bitterness and sorrow fully, but as she grew up, she comprehended thoroughly. Sometimes, Ciou-Tao wondered if it was better for Uncle Huang to die early so he didn't need to suffer more than thirty-eight years like his comrades and other Chinese people. Thirty-eight years was about a half of a human being's life. How could the Chiang dynasty and its party be heartless to this degree?

The same year, 1987, four months earlier, before the lifting of the ban on the Chinese people's family visit (開放探

親), martial law was lifted (解除戒嚴), which was much more important to Lan Tian. It meant the rights of assembly and association and the freedom of speech and press would be back to people's hands gradually. One day, he would be free to read any books without fear. He knew that he and the people on the island needed to thank those brave people who risked their lives to fight for that freedom. Moreover, the reason that the Chinese people could finally go back to China to visit their families was that martial law was lifted. In other words, all the evil crimes were from the practice of martial law.

After the spring break, something huge happened. Cheng Nan-Jung (鄭南榕, 1947–1989), a prodemocracy activist and a founder of the magazine *Freedom Era Weekly* (自由時代週刊), had an act of self-immolation to defend freedom of speech when the law enforcement agents were going to arrest him under the accusation of rebellion.

When Cheng Nan-Jung was a student of the Department of Philosophy at Taiwan University, he had believed that Taiwan should declare independence. He didn't get his diploma due to his refusal to study the required course, Three People's Principles (三民主義), Dr. Sun Yat-Sen's political philosophy. In 1984, he founded the magazine *Freedom Era Weekly* to fight for freedom of speech.

The magazine criticized Chiang Kai-shek's family, the intelligence agency, the Chinese National Armed Forces, and others. Those were the topics that most media feared to discuss. Thus, the Chinese Nationalist government saw him as a dangerous person and forbade the magazine to publish. However, Cheng Nan-Jung had prepared. He had applied for eighteen licenses before founding the magazine, so he brought the magazine back again and again after the government banned it each time. As a result, under the threat of the government,

Freedom Era Weekly had five years and eight months of glory.

That was an era that people had a great fear of the government, but Cheng Nan-Jung was active in social movements. He organized protests to ask for the lifting of martial law. In the end, he was arrested and sentenced to prison for eight months. In January 1987, he was released from prison. That year was also the fortieth anniversary of the 228 Incident. He and other human rights activists asked the Chinese Nationalist government to admit their crime and tell the truth of the 228 Incident and redress the injustice for the victims of the 228 Incident and their families. Furthermore, Cheng Nan-Jung and other human rights activists held a public memorial ceremony on February 28, which was the first time in forty years.

In 1988, the magazine published the draft of the Constitution of the Republic of Taiwan on the Human Rights Day. The magazine was banned immediately, and Cheng Nan-Jung was accused of rebellion by the government. On April 7, 1989, Cheng Nan-Jung defended the freedom of speech with his own life. He said, "The Chinese Nationalist Party can't arrest me alive; they only can get my dead body."

Lan Tian cried for the brave man. He cried again when he told Cheng Nan-Jung's story to Mei-Ai.

"Lan Tian, in the news, they said that he was a violent, crazy man. They mentioned very little work that he had done or words that he had said. Thank you for telling me the information that I couldn't get from the newspaper and TV news. There is no doubt that self-immolation was a violent act, but he did it for an unselfish reason, to pursue Taiwanese independence and to fight for human rights. He is, indeed, a courageous man. I respect him sincerely. Look at me, just secretly reading a banned book and several articles in magazines, and I have been very nervous already."

"No doubt, he had guts. He is my hero."

"One thing surprised me very much, though. He preferred not to have a diploma rather than study the course,

Dr. Sun Yat-Sen's political philosophy. To most of us, that's a trivial thing. Just hang in there for a year, and we will get the credit. Why so fussy about it? But he had his own principles and stuck to them. How strong his mind was!"

"That was why he did those things that most of us have no courage to do."

"But I think you're brave too."

"Mei-Ai, I may give you this impression, but the truth is that I only talk a lot in private. My mind is full of opinions and angry feelings, but if I were invited to join some student protests or write an article to criticize the government right now, I would hesitate."

"Really?"

"Really. I am just an ordinary person like everybody else. Terrorism, an act of violence committed by the state, is scary. It gets through people's skins and into the bones to shatter their souls. My great-grandfather and his friends didn't know the character of the Chinese Nationalist government, so they probably couldn't believe what happened to them until the second before they died, but my a-bu and I grew up with fear from the moment we learned the story. Many Taiwanese people are like my a-bu and me, not directly being abused by the Chinese Nationalist government, but we fear them from knowing and seeing others' tragedies. I have tried to fight with my fear but improved very little. After all, they are a supreme big government, and I am a powerless little person."

"Oh, Lan Tian. In my heart, you're a brave person. People like Lei Zhen and Cheng Nan-Jung were extraordinary warriors, and we usually don't get many of them in history. Thank God we have them to lead, so we know what the right path is. Lan Tian, you have made great effort to read many banned books and magazines to brighten your mind. You have fear because you know what happened on our land, and most of us are happy and have no fear in mind because we know nothing about the truths but lies. I don't think you want to have this kind of happiness."

"No, I don't."

"Thus, in my opinion, reading banned books and magazines is brave too. It's an essential first step. It's where hope begins to grow. Of course, before hope grows, fear appears first because the truth makes people angry and terrified. However, this fear is a seed, and it will grow to be a fearless tree. I am glad that I have become a person who has fear in mind, not the ignorant girl who I was."

"Mei-Ai, you're a good thinker. I have never thought about what you said. Maybe I am guilty. I took away your pure happiness, which your a-bu tried to give you."

"Hey, you're not that guilty. After all, I am my own master. I decided to read banned books and magazines myself. However, I don't think that I can read more of them from now on, and I hope you stop reading them too. The university entrance examination is coming in a year. We have to study hard."

"My a-bu tells me the same thing quite often recently."

"So we shouldn't let our parents worry."

"Okeydokey!"

Although Mei-Ai told Lan Tian that she wanted to study history at university after reading *The Fig Tree*, that desire was getting weak while she was studying hard for the university entrance examination. It was a passion that arose after learning some truths of Taiwanese history, but before that, Mei-Ai had always wanted to study arts at university. She loved to paint and was good at it. Obviously, a sudden passion couldn't replace the old love easily when Mei-Ai honestly faced the true feelings in her heart. However, Mei-Ai was a careful person. She wanted to gather more information to make a decision, and luckily, she had Mei-Ling, who could provide the information. Mei-Ai asked Mei-Ling's opinion of studying history at university. Mei-Ling told her that it wasn't as interesting as she had expected. From the second year, it might be a bit better, because students could finally begin to study some real history, American history or Russian modern history, for example. However, most subjects were related to Chinese history—for instance, Chinese Song dynasty history, Chinese art history, or Chinese economic history. Shockingly, there was *only one* course that taught Taiwanese history.

"One? Just one?"

"Yes, and yes."

"Sis, is it possible that the history departments at other universities are different from your school, they have more courses that teach different subjects of Taiwanese history?"

"I don't know the situation at each university, but those that I know are the same as my school."

"Gosh! I can't believe it!"

"I was astonished as you are."

"How is the class?"

"I don't know. That's an elective course for the third-year students. The senior students said it is excellent."

"Oh my good Lord. It seems there is only one course worth studying in the history department. Then I can just have a major in fine arts and later go to take that course in Taiwanese history."

"Mei-Ai, that is a good idea. Honestly, I don't understand why you want to study history just because you learned some horrible truths about Taiwanese history. How can you even think about giving up studying fine arts, your true love?"

"Sis, I feel like doing something for Taiwan after having a lot of conversations with Lan Tian and reading a banned book and a few articles in magazines. It is like if we don't take responsibility to do something for our land, we're guilty too. The Chinese Nationalist government doesn't want us to know our history, which is evil, surely, but if we don't try to do something to let more people know our history, even just one more person, it is like we hand our rights to the government voluntarily."

"But studying history at university can't be helpful, though."

"I suspected that, so I asked you about your learning and opinion."

"It's good that you think and ask. Otherwise, you will regret."

"Then why didn't you apply for a transfer, since it sounds like no fun to study history?"

"Even though it is not as good as what I wish it to be, I still learn something. My classmates and I are, indeed, lucky. In the first year, we had a professor who is very different from other professors. She is great. Well, you may say she is very modern. She opened our minds to think what history is, what materials can be used for writing history, who can write history, what the qualifications are for a historian, and so forth. Besides, I always like history, so I think it's worthwhile to stay and apply for another major. And you, you definitely shouldn't give up your dream, studying fine arts. I believe that pursuing one's dream is one kind of human rights."

"Right! Human rights! I can't believe what I just heard!"

"You'd better believe it."

"You and Lan Tian are like twins—you really can talk."

"So you're very lucky."

"Yeah, right!"

A year later, Mei-Ai and Lan Tian both got into the university. Mei-Ai got to study fine arts, as was her wish. Lan Tian wanted to study law, but his score wasn't high enough. Hence, he followed his hero's steps to study philosophy. They both were very excited and happy.

Mei-Ling was also very excited, because that year, 1991, she could take the course in Taiwanese history. Besides, she could take another course, American history, too. She had wanted to take that course a year before, but a compulsory course that she needed to study in her second major, social work, was scheduled at the same time on Tuesday morning, so she had to give up taking American history.

Mei-Ling didn't expect that she would be hugely impacted by learning American history. The early American history exploded her mind a great deal. She crazily admired the American founding fathers and sincerely respected their spirit and determination for founding a free and democratic country. Well, her mind also was blown up in Taiwanese history class. Right from the first class, she started to learn the things that she didn't know at all but should've known as a Taiwanese person. Mei-Ling felt excited and sad that learning the history of her homeland was brand new to her. Besides, Mei-Ling felt lucky that she had a chance to read the book *The Fig Tree* a year and a half ago. The history of Japanese ruling time would be taught in the second semester, but because she had learned that period of Taiwanese history from the book, she could immediately compare the two nations' feelings about living under colonial rule: what they thought about their identities and the reaction to the state violence. Later, after she learned that part of Taiwanese history from the professor in the second semester, Mei-Ling was exceedingly amazed how much essential information *The Fig Tree* provided to readers.

All Taiwanese students learned the Japanese government's brutality in history class, but they didn't learn many details. In the book *The Fig Tree*, the author talked about his personal experiences, which helped Mei-Ling not only understand how disgusting and arrogant the Japanese government and many average Japanese people had been but also learn how depressed and frustrated most Taiwanese people had been. For instance, the author and other Taiwanese teachers were arranged to live in temples or rental houses that were very shabby, while their colleagues, the Japanese teachers, all had nice places to stay. Moreover, their salaries were only 60 percent of their Japanese colleagues', but they needed to do a lot more work at school. The Japanese government talked about integrating the Japanese people and the Taiwanese people, but in reality, their attitudes and behaviors revealed their thinking that the Japanese people were superior to the Taiwanese people. Furthermore, any Taiwanese people who criticized the problems in the society would be watched, followed, or interrogated by the Japanese police, which happened to the author. In fact, the Japanese police would discipline or assault the Taiwanese people physically in public. Under the unfair treatment, the Taiwanese people wished they could be free one day. Therefore, the Taiwanese people were thrilled when the Empire of Japan surrendered in World War II and gave up the ownership of Taiwan. Later, the Taiwanese people were even happier that they were going to be ruled by China due to the thinking that China was their fatherland. They believed that they were going to have a better life, being free and having dignity. According to the author, that was how the tragedy of the 228 Incident happened. The Taiwanese people had the expectations, but the Chinese Nationalist government was a lot worse than the Japanese government.

Were they wrong to have such expectations: to be free and to be treated fairly? No. No one would deny that that desire was reasonable. Actually, that was the same wish that the people in the Thirteen Colonies had felt in their hearts. However, even though the two nations had the same expectations, they were in different circumstances. Thus, the endings were vastly different.

The people in the Thirteen Colonies had realized the impossibility of being treated justly by the British government, so they decided to fight for their rights of life, liberty, and the pursuit of happiness. However, the Taiwanese people thought that they were already free since they no longer lived in the Japanese colonial rule. Moreover, they believed that the Chinese Nationalist government, the Chiang Kai-shek regime, would practice Dr. Sun Yat-Sen's political philosophy and build Taiwan to be the most beautiful model province of China. The Taiwanese people didn't know how corrupt the Chiang Kai-shek regime was in China, so they got very disappointed and angry when they saw the Chinese Nationalist government officials were as arrogant as the Japanese government officials. They found there was no difference between the two authorities. As a matter of fact, the situation was worse than in the Japanese ruling time. The Chinese Nationalist government officials were arrogant, incompetent, and corrupt, and most Chinese soldiers had no discipline. Furthermore, there was no regulation at all under the Chinese Nationalist government's ruling. The Taiwanese people couldn't believe that the Chinese Nationalist government and some crafty Chinese people actually encroached and robbed civilians' properties. The society was no longer safe, because the government was the biggest criminal. The anger built up and led to an uprising, the 228 Incident. The Chinese Nationalist government took the chance to kill most Taiwanese elites during the 228 Incident to scare the Taiwanese people and silence them. Two years later, in 1949, they announced the imposition of martial law to control Taiwan fully.

Mei-Ling wished that there had been people who knew the truth of the Chinese Nationalist government and warned the Taiwanese people not to trust them, telling them that they didn't need the Chinese people or any other nations to rule Taiwan. They could govern themselves without a master. The Taiwanese people were as intelligent as people of any other nation. However, something was inherited; it was hard to change. In the old times, Taiwanese people especially cared about their family history, where their ancestors came from, where they settled first and later, how many generations of their families had been in Taiwan, something that could tell a person's root. Since China was the root for most Taiwanese people, they naturally felt that they were Chinese even though a lot of them were born in Taiwan and had never been to China. The author of *The Fig Tree* said that the thinking and feeling grew stronger in many Taiwanese people's hearts when they were being ruled by the Empire of Japan. Therefore, they imagined their fatherland with a lot of positive images. They worshipped China. However, fifty years ago, when the fatherland, China, signed the Treaty of Shimonoseki to cede the full sovereignty of Taiwan to Japan in 1895, the Taiwanese people were extremely upset, feeling that they were betrayed and abandoned. People in different ethnic groups— Hokkien, Hakka, and aborigines—organized resistance teams to fight with the Japanese Army. It was a bloody history that people remembered well and repeatedly told their children and grandchildren.

"How could they forget that they were betrayed and abandoned by China? Why didn't they suspect that the Chinese government might betray them again?" Mei-Ling couldn't understand.

"Perhaps fifty years' misery made people forget things and want to put their hopes in some fantasy love," Mei-Ling presumed.

16

Who Are We?

At university, some students would skip class, but in Taiwanese History, there was almost no one absent. As a matter of fact, some students who were from other departments would ask the professors' permission to attend the class without credits.

Professors?

Yes. One professor taught early Taiwanese history, from fifty thousand years ago to the time before Japanese rule, in the first semester. Another professor carried on the rest in the second semester. However, there were so many things to talk about; therefore, the first professor stressed the history of Plains indigenous people (平埔族) and some aborigines and Zhang-Quan armed confrontation (漳泉械鬥) during Qing Dynasty, and the second professor focused on the Japanese ruling time, the Taiwanese Communists' movement, the 228 Incident, and the White Terror.

"It's not fair that there is only one Taiwanese history class. We never learn our history, and there is so much to learn. There should be more courses, five at least, so we can learn the whole Taiwanese history."

"I agree with you, Mei-Ling. But I don't think it's going to happen in ten years."

"You crazy? Ten years? At least twenty years!"

It was OK. Even in just one course, they had learned many things that they must know as Taiwanese. For instance, Mei-Ling found that she and many Taiwanese people might not be pure Chinese as the schools taught them. She might have Plains indigenous people's blood.

The aborigines in Taiwan were divided into two kinds in the Qing dynasty (清朝, 1644–1912), civilized barbarians and uncivilized barbarians. This label was decided by whether or not a person was Sinicized and paid taxes. Plains indigenous peoples were recognized as civilized barbarians by the government. Unlike other groups of aborigines, who lived in the mountains, Plains indigenous peoples lived in the flatlands with the Chinese immigrants, Han people, so they got a lot of influence from them. Of course, the Chinese people learned some customs from the Plains indigenous peoples too. Because of the close interaction, Plains indigenous peoples had the same haircut and dressed like Han people. Despite the similarity of appearance, people still could tell who Plains indigenous peoples were due to some cultural difference. For example, Plains indigenous women did not have foot binding like Han women. However, when the Japanese authority banned foot binding during the 1930s, there were few cultural characteristics left to recognize Plains indigenous women. As time went by, it got harder to distinguish who Plains indigenous people were, since Sinicization had been strongly encouraged, but there was still a way to tell.

In 1905, the Japanese government did a first-time household survey because the Japanese National Diet believed that a modern country should do the Basic National Census and Survey. The survey was conducted every five or ten years in Taiwan. Therefore, there were seven research results accumulated during the Japanese ruling time. Ethnicity was one of the topics in the survey, and the criteria were blood, culture, and where the person was from. About the blood, according to the rule, a person's ethnicity followed the male line. Hence, the survey couldn't show some people's real ethnic backgrounds, since intermarriage happened between Han people and Plains indigenous people. Besides, although the criterion was patrilineality, people still could decide their identities while they were doing the survey. In short, the Japanese government did a thorough survey and kept a good record, but there was a hidden truth behind the data.

After the Japanese government left, the Chinese Nationalist government came to Taiwan. It took over the data of households that the Japanese government had collected and nicely organized. However, many Chinese people fled to Taiwan after the Chinese Nationalist Party lost the Civil War to the Chinese Communist Party in 1949. The need for a household survey was obvious. In the Chinese Nationalist government's viewpoint, the aborigines were those who lived in the mountain. Thus, Plains indigenous people were like Han people, Hokkien and Hakka, the general Taiwanese people. Of course, arguments occurred. Then, during the 1950s, the government announced Plains indigenous people could register as aborigines who lived in the plain. It wasn't mandatory. Plains indigenous people could decide whether or not they wanted to change their identities. According to the research, most of them didn't go to reregister before the expiration date, which was another hidden truth behind the household data.

"Well, despite the fact that the household record can't tell the whole truth, if you are interested in how your great-grandfather identified himself, you can go to the Household Registration Office in the town where your great-grandfather lived and tell the office clerk your great-grandfather's name to ask for the information of household registration in the time of Japanese rule. Then, pay the fee [about USD 1], and you'll get the answer." For the first time, Mei-Ling found that the household survey was vastly important to a family and a country, especially a multicultural country.

Fifteen years later, Mei-Ling learned that the internationally renowned Taiwanese hematologist Marie Lin (林媽利, 1938–) used molecular technology to analyze human DNA and genetic markers and proved that most Taiwanese people have mixed blood types of Plains indigenous peoples and highland aborigines. Mei-Ling laughed and said, "Well, nothing can beat it! DNA is the best record of any kind."

Since Mei-Ling had a double major, she was too busy to go home during the semester. Thus, she had so many things that she wanted to share with her a-bu and Mei-Ai, and she told them all during the winter break.

"A-bu, Mei-Ai, do you know that we might be aborigines?"

"Sis, what are you talking about?"

"Have you ever heard of Plains indigenous people?"

Ciou-Tao and Mei-Ai shook their heads.

"About four hundred years ago, the aborigines were divided into civilized barbarians and uncivilized barbarians..."

"Wait! Sis, 'barbarian' means uncivilized people. What does that mean, 'civilized barbarians' and 'uncivilized barbarians'? It doesn't make any sense at all."

"I know. Actually, the Qing dynasty used the words 'raw' and 'mature' to divide them into two levels, which were judged by whether they were Sinicized and paid taxes or not."

"I understand the standard, Sinicization, but paying taxes is something else to me. So, Sis, you and I are uncivilized right now. Only A-bu and A-ba are civilized, because they pay taxes. Ha!"

"Yeah, we're still pretty raw!" Mei-Ling and Mei-Ai couldn't stop laughing. "Well, I have to say that discussing these things with you is more interesting than with my classmates. Mei-Ai, you're a quick thinker!"

"I agree. And I am more mature than you two." Ciou-Tao also laughed happily.

"A-bu, do you know that the custom that you worship the Master of House Foundation [地基主] on every important holiday was from Plains indigenous people? And also, the

Master of House Foundation was very tiny, only about one hundred to one hundred twenty centimeters high."

"Oh my God, that's why I have to use the little foldable table that you used to do homework to pray. I only learned what food I should prepare and how to pray from my neighbor aunts. They didn't tell me that the Master is a short god."

"Sis, this is interesting. So most families have a little foldable square table at home, which isn't exactly for their little kids playing games or doing homework. It's for our tiny important patron saint."

"Mei-Ai, believe it or not. The first year at university, one of my roommates asked our permission to let her worship the Master of House Foundation in our room."

"She crazy?"

"That was what we thought. Thank goodness. The dormitory manager usually would worship the Master of House Foundation, so she went to pray with her and didn't do it in our room."

"Mei-Ling, I respect her sincerity, but it seemed she didn't know how to worship the Master of House Foundation. People have to place the praying table in the kitchen and face the direction of the living room by the kitchen door to pray. Moreover, usually, we need to prepare two bowls of rice and Three Sacrifices, pork, chicken, and fish. If it's not available, we just prepare three simple dishes, a bowl of soup, and two bowls of rice. Therefore, how could your roommate pray in your room? Not to mention that the worship needs to lit incense sticks and burn Joss paper [金紙]. How could she do it in the dormitory?"

"Sis, she could've burned the whole dormitory. Do you know that?"

"I know. But A-bu, she was very creative, though. When we questioned how she could prepare Three Sacrifices, she said there's no need to be complicated. Just buy two meal boxes; one has a chicken leg, and another has fish."

"Sis, two meal boxes, she also got the two bowls of rice

too."

"Anyway, that was the first time I met a young person who was passionate about worshipping Gods like elders."

"A-bu, why two bowls of rice?"

"Dope! It doesn't occur to you that the Master of House Foundation might get very hungry? But three bowls are too much, and two bowls are just right!"

"Sis, that's your personal opinion, right?"

"Of course. But don't you think it's very reasonable?"

"I want a correct answer."

"Once I heard my neighbor aunts saying that two bowls of rice are for the Master and his wife."

"My oh my, how can I not consider that the Master might have a wife?"

"Sis, don't you think that people are full of imagination and very thoughtful?"

"Certainly, they are."

"Sis, do we have any other customs from Plains indigenous people's culture?"

"Yes. In Ghost Month [鬼月, July in the lunar calendar], when people pray, they put a bowl of water under the praying table and take a brand-new towel to cover the top of the bowl, which is from Plains indigenous people's culture, worshipping water. Originally, they took a coconut shell to keep some water for their ancestors to wash. But, later, they were influenced by the Han people, using a clay pot to hold water, and the pot was a symbol of a house, and the water signified the ancestors. Like I said before, the two sides of people influenced each other. In the Ghost Month, Han people would offer food to the spirits, who had no family to worship them. They took the original Plains indigenous people's culture, giving a bowl of water to the ghosts to wash when they prayed."

"Then why do we put a new towel on top of the bowl right now?"

"Mei-Ai, that's for us. After the rite of praying, people soak the towel in the water and use it to clean themselves.

After all, those are ghosts, not gods, so people need to protect themselves from getting bad luck. Therefore, cleaning themselves means sweeping away the evil spirits."

"Wait! I have a question. People give those ghosts food, which is kindness, but we have to clean ourselves after praying because they might bring us bad luck. That's totally not right. Where is their appreciation?"

"Mei-Ai, my neighbor aunts said that some ghosts are not good. They not only have no gratitude but would harm people. They don't want to leave after having a good meal, and having a ghost around you would make you sick."

"A-bu, then what can we do to make them leave after they eat?"

"My neighbor aunts told me to be sincere but not too friendly when praying."

"Mei-Ai, I don't think that those ghosts would leave if you were the one to pray. You're too friendly to people."

"Sis, I'm friendly but only to the people, not to the ghosts."

"Are you sure? Maybe you might forget they are ghosts while you are praying."

"Sis, stop it. You know I am afraid of ghosts. You're not helping here."

Mei-Ling laughed so hard she choked.

"Sis, I think you just got yours."

Mei-Ling couldn't stop coughing but laughing at the same time.

"But, A-bu, another question. How come we never use the water and towel to clean ourselves after praying?"

"Mei-Ai, I didn't know we need to do that until now. All my neighbor aunts didn't do it either. I guess, when time goes by, people change the custom a little bit."

"Think of it. In the beginning, they didn't even have a towel on top of the bowl. Change. People change, and culture changes." Mei-Ling finally could talk.

"Mei-Ai, your sister is right. In the beginning, people

prayed and offered food to the ghosts because of sympathy. They didn't want those ghosts, who had no family, to suffer and be hungry, but nowadays, people have different thinking. Some don't want ghosts to bother them and give them trouble, so they believe that they need to offer a lot of food to make ghosts feel content. Some hope the ghosts can help them to make a fortune, so they prepare a ridiculous feast."

"A-bu, that's the same situation with the Whole Pig Sacrifice. Nowadays, people do it like a game, brutally feeding the pigs to become enormous for the competition. People who won would be very proud that they have the number one pig on their praying table. By the way, the Whole Pig Sacrifice is another tradition that Han people learned from Plains indigenous people."

"Sis, suddenly, I feel guilty. I always love the Ghost Month Festival. I enjoy seeing people put out a lot of food to pray, what food they put out, and the Whole Pig Competition. I wasn't aware of the ugly parts of thinking behind many people's behaviors."

"Don't be. You only like to enjoy the atmosphere of people's high spirits. Besides, not everyone has the intention to show off or wants to get rewards from ghosts."

"A-bu, yes, that's how I feel. I enjoy seeing that all the neighbors in our alley put tables out and set the tables to be ready for the praying. One might say to another, 'I see you have a fish.' Or, 'I fried some taro today; I'll give you some later.' It's warm and happy. It's like we are having a huge block party."

"No, it's a whole country party."

"Sis, that's right. It's a whole country party. I love it."

"I loved it very much when I was little, because that was the day we could eat better."

"A-bu, I can't believe it. Your adoptive family was like those ghosts, having nothing. You still prayed."

"Sis, so they could have a chance to eat better. It's a good thing."

"True."

"Mei-Ling, I can see you've learned a lot in this course. I love your sharing very much."

"A-bu, I am mighty happy that I finally got to know Taiwanese history, so I am very upset that our government doesn't teach us our history. Without learning our history, how can we know who we are? I didn't even know the existence of Plains indigenous people, but their custom is everywhere in our society."

"Sis, because they are Chinese and want us to believe we are Chinese."

"But, Mei-Ai, there are many ethnic groups in China. Didn't the Chinese Nationalist government tell their people all the culture and history of each ethnic group when they were still the authority in China?"

"Sis, look at what they are doing in Taiwan. I don't think they did. If they did, some ethnic groups might declare independence because they're not Chinese after all."

"Well, you talk about something interesting. As you know, I took the course American History this year, and the early American history has exceedingly inspired me and makes me think a lot."

"Is it another course that I should take in the future?"

"Yes, you definitely should. You just said that those ethnic groups might declare independence because they're not Chinese at all after they learn their history. Yes, many people might think this way. But the early immigrants in North America—well, we should say Thirteen Colonies—were mostly British. If I am correct, about ninety-five percent of them were British. They still declared independence from Britain to found their own country. And, later, many people who were from different countries desired to become Americans. It was because the unchallengeable values that people in the Thirteen Colonies fought for attracted people and caught people's hearts. In other words, ethnicity wasn't the factor that the United States was founded and built upon."

"'We hold these truths to be self-evident, that all men

are created equal, that they are endowed by their Creator with certain unalienable Rights, that among these are Life, Liberty and the pursuit of Happiness.'"

"Mei-Ai, you astonish me."

"Sis, do you remember that you mentioned the US Declaration of Independence to me last time we talked on the phone? I went to library to find it out. I liked it and memorized it."

"That's a beautiful saying. I heard it once."

"A-bu, someone told you?"

"Uncle Wen-Hua told me, and I was sixteen years old."

"Wow, A-bu, you have a super memory!"

"Mei-Ai, it's the sentence 'All men are created equal' that impressed me a great deal. My sisters and I were born in the time that men and women weren't equal. As a matter of fact, women were like worthless objects. Many of us didn't know what the taste of happiness was at all."

"But, A-bu, the women in the United States weren't equal to men then, and there is more to change still."

"Well, Mei-Ling, put this way, I just simply liked the idea and wished it would happen one day in our society. Imagine a poor young girl like me hearing an idea like that. How much would I love it with all my heart? Of course, I got very emotional, too, because I thought about the misery that my sister Ciou-Jyu suffered. Her unalienable rights were deprived. She was like a slave."

"A-bu, I am thinking of A-hue. If Sis and I were born in another family, our unalienable rights might be deprived like A-hue. Thank you. You're a super a-bu who gives us a great life."

"Well said, Mei-Ai. Bravo!"

"Well, kids, I only try to be a normal person. Those people are abnormal."

"Wow, A-bu, your simple words are right on the point and deep. We should call you Socrates."

"Sis, can't. Socrates was sentenced to death by bunches of crazy nuts."

"Do you mean people like our government?"

"Ha, what a coincidence. They're identical."

"OK. Girls, I just want to be myself." Ciou-Tao couldn't stop laughing. She always enjoyed her daughters' intelligent conversations and sense of humor.

"A-bu, you don't want to be Socrates? How about being Plato?"

"Mei-Ling, Socrates and Plato are great, but I just want to be myself." Ciou-Tao believed that if she didn't stop her two daughters, she would be Aristotle soon.

"Yes, A-bu. One can indeed be oneself is very important. Learning Taiwanese history and American history at the same time makes me think about who we really are. Before this year, I always believed that I was Chinese. I didn't have any doubt about it because everything that I learned at schools and from the government made me believe that we were Chinese. Yes, we speak Mandarin and learn Chinese literature, history, geography, and philosophy, and most of our ancestors were from China. We are so Chinese, so impossible not Chinese. However, the moment I started to learn Taiwanese history, there was a feeling appearing in my heart. That feeling was an excitement, like a person who was going to travel and knew that she or he was going to have a great adventure. I don't remember how many times I said, 'Oh, wow,' in my heart. It was like I couldn't believe that there was a history on our island. I know it sounds ridiculous, but that was exactly how I felt at the beginning of the semester."

"Sis, you describe it so well. I felt the same way when I first learned some events that happened in Taiwan. It was like learning another country's history, surreal but amazing. Later, the more I learned from Lan Tian, the more I felt this is us. Suddenly, everything that I had learned about China became a ship and sailed away, but I didn't care much at all. Once, I thought that maybe Taiwanese history was new to me, so I was interested in it. However, it isn't as simple as I thought. That Chinese me is an idea that was instilled in my mind, and the Taiwanese me is a truth that was put to sleep. Once the truth woke up, there was no way that the idea could beat the truth. Therefore, I am willing to let the truth lead my heart to the unknown journey, scary but jolly good. Sis, you'll learn the scary parts next semester. Be prepared."

"Wow, Mei-Ai, you make your sister proud. What you just said is incredible. I love to learn, and I don't mind learning Chinese literature, history, geography, and philosophy. But don't try to erase the fact that I am Taiwanese and take away my right of learning Taiwanese history. I want to be able to be myself freely. Not to mention that governments are instituted to secure these human rights, life, liberty, and the pursuit of happiness."

"And our government has taken away many people's lives illegally and our freedom of speech," Mei-Ai said with rage.

"Oh..." Ciou-Tao burst into tears.

"A-bu, what's the matter?" Mei-Ling was shocked.

Mei-Ai handed her a-bu a tissue. Ciou-Tao just couldn't stop crying.

Mei-Ling and Mei-Ai had no idea why their a-bu was sad like this. "What did we say wrong and upset her?" they wondered in their minds.

A few minutes later, Ciou-Tao calmed down and spoke.

"Girls, I am sorry. Don't worry about me. I just thought about Uncle Huang and his comrades. The Chinese Nationalist government deprived their right of the pursuit of happiness with a great excuse: 'We don't contact and negotiate with the evil thieves, the Chinese Communists.'"

"A-bu, don't be sad. Indeed, it was inhuman and an outrage that a government forbade its people to have any contact with their families over thirty-eight years, but they can go back to China to visit their families now."

"Mei-Ai, we should let A-bu rest. We talked too much today. Reminding A-bu of Auntie Ciou-Jyu and Uncle Huang is too much excitement for her."

"Sis, you're right. A-bu, how about Sis and I go out to get you a cup of coffee?"

"OK. No sugar."

"We know!"

"Mei-Ai, don't you think there was more in A-bu's crying?"

"What does that mean?"

"Oh, no wonder I call you dope! A-bu never cried like that before. Wait! Wait! Correction. This is not the first time that she cried like this. Last time was when Uncle Wen-Hua died."

"Sis, you're right. But why did A-bu not want to tell us the real reason for her crying?"

"Probably it is something that is related to the government, so she doesn't want to tell."

"Perhaps it is. But it's OK. She'll tell us one day. I can wait."

17

Hsieh Hsueh-Hung

Mei-Ling and Mei-Ai enjoyed the winter break very much, so they whined a little before going back to school. Ciou-Tao also enjoyed their company; in fact, she felt very lonely when Mei-Ling and Mei-Ai were not around. However, she also loved to get their phone calls and listen to them talking about their lives on campus and what they learned in different classes, which was very interesting and brought her back to the beautiful memory that she and Wen-Hua wrote to each other while he was studying at Cheng Kung University in Tainan. Therefore, instead of being sad about their leaving, Ciou-Tao told Mei-Ling and Mei-Ai that she couldn't wait to learn more stories and knowledge from them. The two sisters seemed to be cheered up and said, "A-bu, wait for us. We won't disappoint you!"

Well, immediately, in Taiwanese history class, Mei-Ling learned something that she couldn't wait to tell her a-bu, so she called home during lunchtime.

"A-bu, do you know that we had Communists once upon a time?"

"We did? When?"

"The Taiwan Communist Party [台灣共產黨] was founded in 1928 and ended in 1931."

"That was in my a-ba's time."

"A-bu, next time when you go to visit *a-gong* [阿公, *grandfather*, in Taiwanese], you should ask him. He might know about it."

"I'll try, but I don't know if he likes to talk about these sorts of things."

"Anyway, one more thing is very impressive. One of the founders and leaders of the Taiwanese Communist Party was a woman."

"Really? What was her name?"

"Hsieh Hsueh-Hung [謝雪紅, 1901–1970]. *Hsueh* is *snow. Hung* is *red.*"

"What a beautiful name!"

"But it wasn't her original name. Her parents gave her a horrible name, A-Nu (阿女, *a girl*). What name is that? Awful. That was her official name in Household Registration, but at home, her parents called her Jia-nu (假女, *fake girl*)."

"What? Why?"

"Because her parents wanted to have a boy."

"I see. Parents gave their daughters terrible names was very common at the time. Wang-Shi, Wang-Yao, and Zhao-Di were three popular ones, but I have never heard of A-Nu and Jia-nu. This nickname name, Jia-nu, is particularly mean, denying her gender wholly."

"A-bu, listen carefully now. Later, her parents got a baby boy, and they gave him this name, Zhen-Nan (真南, *real boy*)."

"I hate it! I absolutely hate it!"

"Thank God your old father and old mother didn't give you and your sisters those kinds of names."

"What a poor girl! I feel sorry for her."

"A-bu, her parents were illiterate."

"That shouldn't be an excuse. My a-ba and a-bu were barely able to read too. It was about how they thought about things."

"I agree."

"I'm sorry. Please continue her story."

"It's OK. This is how we are, chat chat this and chat chat that."

"True."

"Her family was dirt poor. She had five brothers and two

sisters. She started to sell bananas in the street at the age of six. By the time she was twelve, both her parents died. Because of the costs of funerals, her family had huge debts. Thus, her brother sold her to a family to be a shim-bu-a, and her adoptive mother abused her badly."

"Poor, poor girl!"

"Perhaps the harsh treatment made her want to run away, so she was deceived by a man and became his concubine. She was only thirteen. When she was sixteen years old, she ran away and worked in a sugar factory and met a very wealthy guy. This time it was two people in love, and the guy paid a sum of money to buy her freedom from the marriage. Then they married. However, the man was a liar who hid the fact that he had a wife."

"Oh no."

"The next year, 1917, she went to Japan with her husband, who had a business in Kobe [神戶]. Therefore, she got an opportunity to witness the Taisho democracy period [大正民主, 1912–1926] and the aftermath of the rice riots; the poor rose up against the wealthy, which was her first mind-opening experience. Furthermore, she began to learn Japanese and Chinese. Later, Hsieh Hsueh-Hung and her husband had a trip to Qingdao [青島] in China, which was more than likely before they went back to Taiwan. She was inspired by the May Fourth Movement [五四運動], a student-led protest against the government. Some people said that she changed her name to be Hsueh-Hung because she learned about Russian's October Revolution [俄國的十月革命] in May Fourth Movement. She saw pictures of the October Revolution, blood on the snow, and realized that the price of revolution was blood. We may say this was the turning point; her life changed from here."

"She might be a poor girl who had an awful childhood, but her nature was brilliant and tough."

"Yes, she was. A-bu, I'm sorry. I have a class to go to. I made this quick call because I am surprised and happy to know a special Taiwanese woman in the class and know that you would love to know her. We haven't finished learning her story yet, so I'll tell you more about her next time. I have to say that I admire her a lot even though I despise Communism."

"Mei-Ling, thank you for telling me such a marvelous story. I'm looking forward to knowing the rest of her life story. Take care."

"Bye, A-bu."

"Lan Tian, do you know Hsieh Hsueh-Hung?"

"Yes, I do."

"What? How come you never told me about her?"

"Mei-Ai, I didn't tell you many things that happened in Taiwan."

"But she was an outstanding woman in Taiwanese history."

"I don't like commies."

"Me either. But my sister told me that Hsieh Hsueh-Hung loved Taiwan with her whole heart. She wanted democratic autonomy so Taiwanese people could govern themselves, not be ruled by the Japanese or the Chinese Nationalist government."

"But she believed the wrong political theory. Communism would never work in our world. The Communists are horrible. Think of the Cultural Revolution; they utilized the evil nature in people to abuse people, to destroy those good qualities in people. The worst is that they're very good at drawing a picture of illusion, utopia, an ideal world, to make people follow them. It's bullshit. All lies."

"Lan Tian, somehow I believe her passion for Taiwan."

"Mei-Ai, all Communists say that they have a great deal of passion for their people and country, but the truth is that they love the power and privilege more. There is no doubt that I would love to have a fair society and help poor people to have a better life, but I wouldn't try to find a solution from Communism."

"I think I fully understand your thinking. You know, the Chinese Nationalist government should recruit you. You're their model citizen who is against the Communists a hundred percent."

"Ugh! That would be a shame, not an honor. They despise the Chinese Communist Party because they lost the Civil War and got kicked out of China. It's not because they love people, freedom, justice, and democracy. In fact, there is very little difference between these two Chinese brothers!"

"You're right about them, my Taiwanese brother!"

"Wrong, I am your Taiwanese sweetheart."

One month ago, Lan Tian had asked Mei-Ai to be his girlfriend, and she had happily agreed.

"A-bu, you know Mei-Ai has a boyfriend, right?"

"I know. It's Lan Tian."

"What's the matter? It seems you're not too happy about it."

"Well, a mother always worries about this kind of thing."

"A-bu, don't worry. We've known Lan Tian for years. He is an honest young man who has a good heart. He is not a liar like Hsieh Hsueh-Hung's husband."

"Hsieh Hsueh-Hung, the lady you told me about last time, right?"

"Yes, A-bu."

"Did she find out the fact that her husband had a wife?"

"Yes, she did. She disliked it. Besides, they weren't a happy couple."

"Sigh."

"A-bu, I never understand why many couples were so

happy together but weren't anymore after they were married."

"Mei-Ling, when people are in love, they are in a dreamland. When they are married, they are in reality. Two people might have different ideas and various ways to do things. Thus, disputes occur."

"I thought that love could conquer any problems. I guess some things are powerful. They can consume love and harm a marriage."

"Mei-Ling, marriage is not easy. Moreover, she was living in an era that men completely dominated the world, so women were like objects and their property. Women did not have the right to speak from their minds. Even if a few of them did, they probably would get punished. Therefore, most of them obeyed the demands."

"I guess Hsieh Hsueh-Hung tried to find a way out from the unhappy marriage. When she and her husband came back to Taiwan in 1921, she joined Chiang Wei-Shui's [蔣渭水, 1888–1931] Taiwan Cultural Association [台灣文化協會], which aimed to passively counter Japanese rule by fostering an awareness of Taiwanese nationalism, and she began to care about women's rights. Furthermore, there was a club in the association teaching people to read, and she went. Because of learning, she longed for an independent life. She got a job to teach people how to use sewing machines. The following year, twenty-one-year-old Hsieh Hsueh-Hung used her savings to open a clothing shop. At this point, she had become an independent woman who started to get involved in the political movement."

"How extraordinary! Who would imagine that she was an illiterate poor shim-bu-a?"

"A-bu, she even got into university."

"What?"

"Perhaps she had the idea of leaving her husband for a while. She left her husband when she and her husband moved to China in 1924, and her life began to change. The founders of Taiwan Cultural Association were intellectuals, and their goal was political reform. Although Hsieh Hsueh-Hung was enlightened by the association, she didn't entirely approve of the idea of reform. Therefore, when she was in the Chinese Communists' important base, Shanghai [上海], she had a chance to get to know socialism and loved it right away. Furthermore, she participated in the May Thirtieth Movement [五卅運動], a labor and anti-imperialist protest, and she caught the Chinese Communist leader's eyes. The same year, 1925, she got herself enrolled at Shanghai University and studied sociology, which was her first formal education."

"That's phenomenal! By the way, Mei-Ling, next time you need to tell me who Chiang Wei-Shui was and his Taiwan Cultural Association."

"No problem. Back to the story. At the time, practically, Shanghai University was the Chinese Communists' school. Therefore, although she only studied at Shanghai University for four months, she got an opportunity to get acquainted with the important future members of the Taiwanese Communist Party and study in the Communist University of the Toilers of the East in Moscow later the same year. In 1927, she got an order to form Taiwanese Communist Party from the Communist Party International, so she and her companion went back to Shanghai."

"Wow, even went to Russia! Her world became extremely big."

"A-bu, you see, she had another relationship. I find that she was an avant-garde woman and probably didn't care about people's opinion of her love life. I can almost picture that people looked at her with mean eyes. It's not fair that men could have a wife and several concubines but asked women's purity and loyalty. Moreover, if a wife couldn't give birth to a son, the husband or the parents-in-law could end the marriage. God! It must be very hard to live in that kind of society."

"Mei-Ling, that's why it's so great to see her being so free and independent. Don't you think?"

"Agree! However, she wasn't free anymore ten days later after she and the other eight people who formed the Taiwanese Communist Party in Shanghai. The Japanese police from the Japan concessions in Shanghai arrested them. Besides the fact that the Japanese government hated Communism exceedingly, there was another essential reason that the Japanese police suppressed the Taiwanese Communist Party severely: the party called for Taiwan's independence and Taiwanese self-determination. The Japanese police asked Hsieh Hsueh-Hung to confess, but she denied that she knew Communism at all. Then, they tortured her, using a needle to prick her nipples. However, the Japanese police couldn't get anything from her, so they sent her back to Taiwan in the end."

"That's brutal. That wasn't only a form of torture, but it was also a sexual humiliation and abuse."

"But she didn't give up. After the Japanese police released her, she found her way to develop the party, even though she was the only one of the founding members back to Taiwan. No one could help her, so she used the two legal organizations, Taiwan Cultural Association and Taiwanese Peasants' Union [台灣農民組合], which were against the Japanese government, as her shield. Moreover, she influenced the two organizations to lean to left wing, bit by bit. She made friends with the leader of Taiwanese Peasants' Union, Jian Ji [簡吉, 1903–1951], and got him to become a member of Taiwanese Communist Party."

"She was beyond amazing. That was not only about bravery, but it was more about ability."

"But A-bu, it seemed her ability wasn't good enough for those men in the Taiwanese Communist Party."

"What does that mean?"

"Later, other members of the Taiwanese Communist Party came back to Taiwan. Disputes happened. The party divided into two groups. One was close to the Japanese Communist Party, and another was close to the Chinese Communist Party. Moreover, they not only had different political ideas, but they, men, didn't like to be led by a woman. In 1931, they fired Hsieh Hsueh-Hung, kicked her out of the party."

"Shameless! Outrageous!"

"A-bu, believe it or not, even about twenty years later, in the 1950s—you were about five years old—in the United States, there were still some states that wouldn't allow women to be jurors. As a matter of fact, while men could be jurors just like that, some places asked women to take a jury class to learn how to be jurors or would review if the women were qualified to be jurors. They just thought that women couldn't think correctly and have good opinions like men."

"Sigh. All I can say is that not all the men are like that. I was quite lucky. Both Uncle Huang and Wen-Hua ge valued my opinion. In fact, they inspired me to think too."

"Well, A-bu, those Taiwanese Communist men had a lot of time to think after they fired Hsieh Hsueh-Hung. The Japanese police had never stopped watching them and began to act in 1931. They arrested one hundred seven Taiwanese Communists, including influential leaders and Hsieh Hsueh-Hung. In the court, all men kept their heads down. Only Hsieh Hsueh-Hung defended herself to argue with the judge."

"What a heroine!"

"But our heroine and her comrades were sentenced to at least ten years in prison. However, she was only imprisoned for eight years and released in 1939 because she got tuberculosis. When all of them were out of the prison, they couldn't reorganize the party, because the Japanese police watched them like a hawk."

"Maybe that was better for her. She needed to rest for that illness."

"In 1945, the Second World War ended. Hsieh Hsueh-Hung rebuilt the Taiwan Communist Party again, as she had in 1928, by forming the Taiwanese People Association to push social movements."

"She was a natural-born leader for sure."

"A-bu, I don't think anyone would deny that. OK. After

World War II, the Taiwanese people were happy to be free from Japanese colonial rule and wanted to make a better society, but unfortunately, the excitement didn't last long. When the Chinese Nationalist government came, very soon, Hsieh Hsueh-Hung and most Taiwanese people learned how corrupt and incompetent the Chinese Nationalist government was. In 1947, Hsieh Hsueh-Hung organized the 27 Brigade [二七部隊], which was a guerrilla force formed in Taichung [台中], shortly after the outbreak of the February 28 Incident. The 27 Brigade did have a moment of glory, but it was like a shooting star. The 27 Brigade was disbanded when more Chinese Nationalist troops arrived in Taiwan. Later, Hsieh Hsueh-Hung and her companion were exiled to China, and she never came back to Taiwan again."

"No doubt, she would be killed if she came back."

"But, A-bu, the Chinese Communist Party didn't treat her nice, though. The reason was simple. She insisted on the idea that Taiwan should be granted full autonomy after unification, and they didn't like it very much. We all know how the Communists are. If you have a different opinion from them or they see you as a threat, they will punish you with any ridiculous reasons. Hsieh Hsueh-Hung was defamed as a 'right-winger' and a 'class enemy' during the Cultural Revolution [文化大革命, 1966–1976]. She was subjected to public crucifixion several times in four years. She died in the hallway of a hospital in Beijing with lung cancer in 1970."

"Right-winger? She was more *left* than anyone else!"

"A-bu, they're Communists!"

"So let her die in the hallway of a hospital?"

"A-bu, another thing would upset you even more. In 1968, the Red Guards [紅衛兵] took a picture of Hsieh Hsueh-Hung after they put a sign, 'Big right-wing Hsieh Hsueh-Hung,' on her neck and forced her to bow down and open two arms up like wings. That was one of six famous Red Guards' tortures, 'taking a jet [坐飛機],' during the Cultural Revolution. Those Red Guards who tortured Hsieh Hsueh-Hung were so proud and said, 'Finally, Hsieh Hsueh-Hung, who never puts her head down, bows down!'"

"Oh, how could they? To deprive a person's dignity in such a low way."

"A-bu, they're Communists!"

18

A-bu, Don't Cry

The history that they learned after the stories of Hsieh Hsueh-Hung and the Taiwanese Communist Party was the heavier stuff, the 228 Incident and the White Terror, which pressed all students' hearts and minds exceedingly. Mei-Ling felt so exhausted from learning those miseries. She felt like having a break. As a matter of fact, she was going to have a long summer break because the semester would end in one and a half months. However, Mei-Ling didn't feel happy about it. There were still a lot of things that she didn't know and wanted to learn.

Mei-Ling looked at Professor Jhang (張) and smiled. The first time she saw professor Jhang, she had a familiar feeling, like she had seen him before. In the second class, she realized that Professor Jhang looked like a Buddha. He had a kind face and a beautiful smile. Mei-Ling didn't know that he was a well-respected famous Taiwanese history scholar until a classmate told her later, but even so, she could tell that Professor Jhang had a great passion and a sense of responsibility for his work. Sometimes, Mei-Ling wondered why Professor Jhang didn't get excited or have a mad face when he talked about those horrible stories.

"Perhaps he is a Buddha," Mei-Ling said to a classmate.

"How do you know he isn't a Christian saint?" Well, the classmate was a Christian.

Actually, whether he was a Buddha or a Christian saint wasn't that important. It was his work, researching and teaching Taiwanese history, that made Mei-Ling respect Professor

Jhang a great deal. "He is a man who tells people the truth and leads us to think who we are," Mei-Ling said to her a-bu on the phone. "That's great." Ciou-Tao prayed for the great man secretly in her heart. She hoped he wouldn't get into trouble.

"In the 228 Incident, many Taiwanese elites were brutally killed."

Lin Mosei (林茂生, 1887–1947) was the first Taiwanese to receive a bachelor of arts from Tokyo Imperial University (now University of Tokyo) under Japanese rule (1895–1945). In 1929, he received a doctor of philosophy from the Teacher College, Columbia University. He was a student of John Dewey and Paul Monroe. The two professors tried to persuade him to stay and teach at Columbia University after his graduation, but it was in vain. Lin Mosei cared for education in Taiwan greatly, so he went back to Taiwan. In 1945, he became the dean of the College of Liberal Arts at Taiwan University and founded a newspaper, *People News*, to criticize and give advice to the Chinese Nationalist government. One day, the governor-general of Taiwan, Chen Yi, sent two people to take Lin Mosei to the office to have a chat, and Lin Mosei never came back. His family was never able to find his body and bring him home.

Shih Jiang-Nan (施江南, 1902–1947) graduated from Kyoto Imperial University (now Kyoto University), the second Taiwanese to receive a doctor of medicine under the Japanese rule. He was well respected in Taiwanese society, so people recommended him to be a member of the 228 Incident Settlement Committee (二二八事件處理委員會). However, because Shih Jiang-Nan had malaria at the time, he didn't involve the committee affair much. One day, a person knocked on and broke the door of the clinic. The man took Shih Jiang-Nan away, and his family never saw him again, not even his dead body.

Wang Yu-Lin (王育霖, 1919–1947) graduated from the Department of Law at Tokyo Imperial University and passed the examination of National Judges and Prosecutors in Japan. He worked in Kyoto District Court and also was the first Taiwanese who worked in Japan as a prosecutor. After the Second World War ended, he and his family moved back to Taiwan, and he was hired to be a prosecutor in Hsinchu (新竹) District Court. He was a righteous man who wasn't afraid of or in favor of the people who had power and money, which got him into trouble. He revealed the corruption of the mayor and the commissioner of the police department. The mayor took revenge during the 228 Incident, arresting Wang Yu-Lin and torturing him brutally for days in the prison. At the end of March, they executed him and dumped his body into Tamsui River (淡水河). His family never found his body.

"The Chinese Nationalist government did it intentionally. They wanted to control Taiwan completely, so the last thing that they needed was to have well-respected Taiwanese intellectuals and social elites to tell them what they should do or not do for making a democratic free country. They would be bad influences for the Taiwanese people, and then there would be no peace for the Chiang Kai-shek regime. Therefore, although the Chinese Nationalist government announced the imposition of martial law in 1949, people had started to live in fear since 1947, when the 228 Incident happened. Furthermore, the Chiang Kai-shek regime saw those people who were in favor of Communism or Taiwanese independence as threats and so purged them in the name of espionage and treason. The whole island was in the White Terror. All the people on the island were victimized. Even today, all the victims in the 228 Incident and the White Terror still haven't obtained their justice. The Chinese Nationalist government not only denies their responsibility for their crime but also refuses to hand out the files to reveal the truth. In White Terror, Dr. Chen Wen-Hua was a famous case..."

"Dr. Chen Wen-Hua?"

"He got a PhD degree in statistics from Columbia University..."

"Uncle Wen-Hua!"

"Mei-Ai, we have to go home right now."

"Why? Sis, you scare me by showing up like this."

"I know how Uncle Wen-Hua died."

"What?"

"I just learned it in my Taiwanese history class today."

"In Taiwanese history class?"

"Today, the professor talked about a famous case in the White Terror, and it happened to be Dr. Chen Wen-Hua."

"Are you sure that Chen Wen-Hua was our uncle Wen-Hua?"

"One hundred percent. I even went to talk to the professor to confirm after the class."

"Oh my God!"

"I cried in front of the professor, and he patted my shoulder."

"Sis, we really need to go home and support A-bu. All these years she kept it to herself."

"Remember A-ba said, 'We don't want to get into trouble' when the murder happened? He is really a heartless man!"

"Perhaps A-ba was scared."

"Yeah, right!"

"Lan Tian's family was scared, even after four generations."

"I still think that A-ba is a heartless man. He didn't comfort A-bu at all when A-bu was heartbroken. They are husband and wife, who promise to love and support each other in any circumstance of their lives. He could be scared but still console his wife."

"Sis, I agree with you. You and I have seen so many situations that we don't like in our family since we were little, but I don't have the guts to tell how I feel and what I think because I am afraid that I would say out loud, 'I hate A-ba.'"

"It's him who doesn't like us first. You know how much he wishes we were boys. I hate to tell you this. Accidently, I discovered that A-ba has had an affair."

"Get out! It can't be true!"

"Mei-Ai, we have a little brother."

"No way!"

"Yes way! I heard the boy call him A-ba. I followed A-ba several times and learned that he had another family."

"That's why he is not at home all the time."

"Yeah. Going gambling or being with his real family."

"Sis, do you think A-bu knows?"

"I think she might."

"Why didn't she get divorced if she knew?"

"I think that she stays for us. Her generation sees a divorced woman as a shame. Remember how our neighbors gossiped about a single mother and her children? Nasty!"

"Sis, sorry for changing the subject. I think we have to get to the train station to catch the 15:05 train."

"Oh my God! We have to run now!"

The two sisters arrived in time to catch the train. They found their seats and sat down.

"Sis, we got the oceanside seats."

"I like mountainside better."

"Since when?"

"I don't know. Maybe since A-bu told us about Uncle Huang."

"Sis, we actually should call him Granduncle Huang."

"I know, but 'Uncle Huang' is like a name to me."

"I feel the same way. How come A-bu didn't tell us his name?"

"Maybe she doesn't know."

"Get out of town! How can she not know? He was A-bu's favorite person in the world."

"So we ask her later."

"Sis, I don't know how to start when we arrive home. First of all, A-bu might drop dead to see us both come home together without telling her and before final exams. Then should we bring up that A-ba has an affair after we talk about Uncle Wen-Hua and Uncle Huang?"

"We can only talk about Uncle Wen-Hua and Uncle Huang."

"But we never lie to A-bu."

"It's not a lie. It's just we don't want to talk about it."

"Maybe it's better we talk about it so that A-bu won't feel so alone."

"Mei-Ai, you're probably right. Maybe A-bu would realize that she doesn't have to stay in that marriage for us anymore."

"Sis, why is it so hard to be a woman? The monthly period, father doesn't like you, sexual harassment, threats for being raped, can't get equal pay, and this and that."

"Sigh. I have no answer. But I believe that you don't have to worry about Lan Tian. He is a civilized person who has self-respect and respects people."

"Indeed, he is a great person. He hates to judge things by gender. And, Sis, you'll be very surprised. Lan Tian would buy me a bowl of sweet red bean soup when my period comes. One time, we went out, and my period came. I forgot to put some menstrual pads in my bag. Lan Tian ran to a convenience store to buy a pack of menstrual pads for me right away."

"That's great! He is so caring and doesn't think like old-fashioned men, believing menstrual blood is filthy."

"Sis, do you remember that I was forbidden to go into the temple to pray because I had my period?"

"Yes, I do. I argued with A-ba, and then other people heard and said that I was evil. They said that a woman is very filthy when she has her period, so she can't go into a holy place to pray. It is offensive to gods."

"Lan Tian hates that idea very much. He said that the menstrual blood would become holy if men had it, not women."

"Ha, ha, ha! That's a good one! You must laugh a lot when you are with Lan Tian."

"Yes, I do."

Then the two sisters quieted down and fell asleep gradually. They needed it. How much excitement could a person hold in the heart for an afternoon?

"Hey, you two, come home like this to surprise me!" Ciou-Tao was so happy to see her two daughters.

"It's almost the end of the semester. You should stay at school, not waste money to come home!" There was not a bit of pleasure on Ming-Hao's face.

"Girls, did you have your dinner yet?" Ciou-Tao tried to change the subject.

"No, not yet."

"What do you want to eat? I can cook for you right now."

"I guess I can go home right now since you have two helpers." Ming-Hao left the restaurant.

"Without an excuse, you still leave whenever you want."

"Mei-Ling, stop."

"A-bu, am I wrong?"

"You're not wrong, but he is your a-ba."

"I wish he weren't." Mei-Ling said it in her heart loudly.

While Mei-Ling and Mei-Ai were eating, Ciou-Tao sat with them. After dinnertime, the business usually was very slow.

"Why do you come home today? Something happened?"

"Just miss you."

"I miss you too."

"A-bu, do you miss Uncle Huang and Uncle Wen-Hua?"

"I do, but why do you ask?"

"Nothing. Just like usual, chat chat." Mei-Ling didn't know how to start.

"By the way, what's Uncle Huang's name?" Mei-Ai tried to change the subject. "On the way home, we saw the mountains and thought about Uncle Huang. We realized that we don't know his name, and then Sis said you might not know Uncle Huang's name."

"I know his name. I asked him to write down his name on a piece of paper before he went to work in the mountains."

"Really? Why before he went to work in the mountains?"

"Because I was afraid that he wouldn't come back. Thus, I needed his name so I could go to find him. How strange that I never wanted to know his name until he was leaving. I still have that piece of paper."

"Wow! I want to see it."

"I'll show it to you tomorrow."

"A-bu, what's his name?"

"Huang Da-Shan [黃大山, *big mountain*]."

"Oh my God! And he died in the mountains."

"That's why I blamed his parents for giving him the name when I learned of Uncle Huang's death. Of course, that was a silly thought. I was devastated, so I blamed everything for his death. Actually, Uncle Huang was devastated, so he needed comfort from nature. He loved mountains, perhaps because of his name."

"A-bu, now, when I see those mountains, I will think of Uncle Huang and wish I could meet him. Sis even likes the mountainside seat on the train right now."

"He would love you and be so proud of you. Furthermore, he would enjoy talking to you a great deal because he loved learning and thinking, just like you two. Believe it or not, although he was Chinese, he said that the Chinese Nationalist government should apologize for the 228 Incident, and the Chinese people should reach out their hands first to make peace."

"Wow, he was a righteous man."

"So he surely would be angry to know that the Chinese Nationalist government murdered Uncle Wen-Hua."

"Mei-Ling...what did you just say?"

"A-bu, today, I learned how those bastards killed Dr. Chen Wen-Hua in Taiwanese history class."

"Oh..."

"Ciou-Tao, I want to have two bowls of wonton soup to go."

"Coming." Ciou-Tao got up and went to cook for her neighbor friend.

"I see your daughters are back. They're beautiful young ladies now."

"Yes, they are."

"Ciou-Tao, here is the money. I'll be back to pick up the soups later. My son loves his sugarcane juice."

"Sure. See you later."

What a wrong time to have a customer! However, that was exactly what Ciou-Tao's life was. There was always something coming to hit her and challenge her by surprise. She could only be brave and accept it. Thus, she cooked another bowl of wonton soup and tried to be careful, not letting her tears drop into the soup.

After the neighbor friend came to get her soups, Ciou-Tao closed the restaurant.

"So your professor told the whole class how Uncle Wen-Hua died?"

"Yes, he did."

"I didn't know..." Ciou-Tao was drowned by her tears,

but she fought to talk.

"Shh...A-bu." Mei-Ai held her a-bu.

"A-bu, I cried in the classroom. Twice. When I heard the professor say, 'Dr. Chen Wen-Hua,' I was stunned for seconds. The name sounded so familiar to me. Then the name of the town where he was born, mathematics, National Cheng Kung University, Columbia University, and statistics showed that he was our uncle Wen-Hua. Immediately, I had heart pain and cried because we were learning the White Terror. People were imprisoned or killed barbarically."

"Oh, Sis, I feel so sorry for you."

"A-bu, I hate to bring this up, but do you know the result of the autopsy?"

Ciou-Tao nodded with tears.

"Sis, I want to know."

"Mei-Ai, it's bloody brutal. Uncle Wen-Hua had nine rib fractures on one side and three on the other side and intra-abdominal hemorrhage. The whole lung was damaged. One kidney was ruptured, and another one was swollen. His stomach and intestine had no food. The pubis was broken, and ten fingers were curly and turned black. There was a more than ten-centimeter-long elbow-splitting wound and four lines of blood marks on Uncle Wen-Hua's back. And our *great* government said that Uncle Wen-Hua committed suicide. Yeah, right! After they took him to interrogate."

"Bullshit! They are big fat liars! Like Lan Tian always says."

"But soon, I felt so proud. Uncle Wen-Hua was a brave man. Many of his Taiwanese friends in the United States had warned him not to come back to Taiwan. The student spies must have reported what he had done to the secret police, so it was too dangerous to go home."

"Sis, what did he do to be seen so guilty?"

"Writing articles, talking about his love for Taiwan and the desire for democratization, a free Taiwan." Ciou-Tao's voice was trembling.

"A-bu, you know?"

"Of course. We were like brother and sister since I was thirteen. We always talked, and when we couldn't talk face-to-face, we wrote to each other all the time."

"Oh my God! A-bu, do you realize that the Chinese Nationalist government probably read the letters that Uncle Wen-Hua sent to you from the United States?"

"Mei-Ai, don't worry. It has been ten years since Uncle Wen-Hua was murdered. If there were a problem and the government suspected me, I wouldn't be here right now. I would be long gone."

"Mei-Ai, A-bu is right."

"But I got very scared later. In the beginning, I was weeping for the loss of Uncle Wen-Hua with a great deal of anger. He was like my blood brother. I know that my sister Ciou-Jyu asked him to look after me, but he did it with all his heart, not like he was performing a duty only. He really saw me as his own little sister. Thus, which sister wouldn't be sad about her brother's death and hate the government's brutality? However, weeks later, I could think better with a clear mind, and then I began to be afraid. I was terrified that the Chinese Nationalist government might hurt my family and me, so I knew that I shouldn't tell anyone about Uncle Wen-Hua's death and that we were related. A while later, I was ashamed of myself. I felt like I had betrayed my Wen-Hua ge."

"A-bu, being afraid or not talking about Uncle Wen-Hua wasn't betrayal."

"Perhaps I wish I could tell the world that the government murdered my brother. No, it's I 'should' tell the world, but I was cowardly unable to do it."

"But, A-bu, most people—especially family, friends, and neighbors—would prefer that you did nothing. As quiet as a mouse is better for everyone. After all, people are also afraid of the government's brutality."

"Mei-Ling, you're right. I have learned that fact for years."

"That's why my professor told me to be understanding and give you support."

"He did?"

"He also said that it's necessary to understand humanity if we want to study history."

"Sis, that's a great concept. History is about human beings' lives. How can we not learn human nature?"

"That's why I cried again in front of the professor."

"What does that mean?"

"Your sister was comforted and touched by a gentle idea; being thoughtful, put yourself in one's shoes."

"There're more. To understand humanity means to get to know how people would deal with problems and challenges. I thought about how brave A-bu has been with all those problems in life and how you never gives up believing in the power of goodness."

"A-bu is always a heroine in my mind." Mei-Ai said it with her chin up and a big proud smile.

Ciou-Tao smiled with tears in her eyes.

"A-bu, before you said, 'I didn't know,' and then you cried. What did you want to say?"

"I have been thinking of telling you about Uncle Wen-Hua for quite some time, but I didn't know how to start. It is a horrible murder, not some sort of happy stuff. Thus, there is always no good time to tell."

"A-bu, sorry for the interruption. Last time we talked about how our government deprived our freedom of speech and murdered many people, you cried awfully. It was because you thought about Uncle Wen-Hua's death, right?"

"Mei-Ling, you're very sensitive. I am sorry that I didn't tell the truth, but as I just said, I didn't know how to tell the whole story. Furthermore, I didn't want to scare you and Mei-Ai."

"A-bu, Sis and I are grown-ups now. Moreover, we have been learning the brutal Taiwanese history, so our hearts are stronger than you think. Don't worry about us."

"Mei-Ai, I know. But learning other people's miseries is always easier. Even though you and your sister never met Uncle Wen-Hua, I believe that you feel very close to him in your hearts."

"Yes, we do."

"Therefore, it would be a massive shock for you to learn of his murder."

"Yes, A-bu. You're right. This semester, I have been in hell. There has been so much tribulation that happened on our island. I can't have a moment of peaceful mind in the class, and heart pain has become my learning companion. However, today, when I learned of Uncle Wen-Hua's murder, I found another kind of pain that is deeper and stronger, that only belongs to victims' families. This pain won't easily go away after class. It stays. I don't know whether I would be the same me if you had told us of Uncle Wen-Hua's murder when we were little."

"Sis, I understand what you mean. The truth of a crime is powerful, but there is no truth of any crime that can compare with our truth."

"Mei-Ai, what you said is exactly what I wanted to say. In my heart, Uncle Wen-Hua's murder is the biggest crime in the world. However, I didn't know that it was taught at university. In fact, I thought that no one would remember this murder at all. That was why I was extremely shocked when I heard that your sister learned of Uncle Wen-Hua's murder in the Taiwanese history class. Although Uncle Wen-Hua was an outstanding scholar, I didn't think that his death would be remembered in the history. The history that we have always learned is all about the emperors and generals and their remarkable achievements. Little people like us are anonymous, are not worthy to be remembered."

"According to my professor, not anymore. History is not only kings and men's history. We all take part in it."

"Sis, like Hsieh Hsueh-Hung, such an extraordinary Taiwanese woman, but ninety-nine percent of people in Taiwan have never heard of her. Of course, it's hard for the Chinese Nationalist Party to talk about commies, but they can talk about her other outstanding achievements. Don't you think?"

"You crazy? Talking about her other achievements? She wanted Taiwan to be independent. She hated dictators. Not to mention, if her 27 Brigade had enough manpower and ammunition, Chiang Kai-shek and his party would have been stuck in China or vanished in Taiwan."

"OK! OK! So she is not allowed to be in the history textbooks!"

At last, Ciou-Tao laughed. Her heart was puffy like a cloud. It wasn't only because her daughters were too funny, but she didn't need to hide her Wen-Hua ge's murder anymore. Moreover, people knew and remembered Dr. Chen Wen-Hua. That was one small step toward justice for her Wen-Hua ge. She was happy and wanted to celebrate.

"Girls, want to eat pan-fried cabbage pork buns?"

Mei-Ling and Mei-Ai looked at their watches.

"Oh my God! It's twelve thirty in the morning already?"

"Great, it's like old times now. Mei-Ai, you stay here to help A-bu to clean and close the restaurant. I'll go to buy pan-fried cabbage pork buns and cold soy milk. How many buns do you want?"

"I want four."

"Mei-Ling, I want four too. But I want two cabbage pork and two chives pork."

"Okeydokey!"

"Be careful, Mei-Ling."

"A-bu, I'll be fine. It's just around the corner."

"Sis, don't forget to get some chili sauce."

"Won't forget!"

19

Chinese Bei-Bei

Before Mei-Ling and Mei-Ai went to junior high school, they had slept in the restaurant at night. Every night, after Ming-Hao and Ciou-Tao finished closing the restaurant, Ciou-Tao would wake up Mei-Ling and Mei-Ai and take them home. Once in a while, they would have a midnight family party. Before they went home, Ming-Hao or Ciou-Tao would go to buy some pan-fried cabbage pork buns and soy milk. Even though the two little girls were very sleepy, they liked that the whole family sat down together, eating and talking.

"A-bu, do you remember that years ago there was a dog-meat restaurant on the other side of the ditch?"

"I certainly do."

"Every time I heard those dogs' howling, I was so scared."

"I was scared too. It was like they despaired. They asked for help, but no one helped them. A-bu, do you know that some of the dogs were kidnapped from the streets? Mei-Ai and I despised the two old men who owned the restaurant when we were little."

"Mei-Ling, they weren't old men, though."

"Really? Couldn't be."

"A-bu, are you sure? I also remember that they were old."

"They were about in their fifties."

"A-bu, they looked older than that, like seventies."

"When the Chinese soldiers arrived in Taiwan, most of

338

them were in their twenties. They came to Taiwan from 1945 to 1949. Therefore, in 1980, you were ten years old, and they would be in their fifties."

"Then why did they look so old to me?"

"They had a hard life, the war; they couldn't eat well; they were homesick and poor, which aged people easily."

"A-bu, remember that two years ago I was sexually harassed by the Chinese veterans two times in Ximending?"

"Yes, I do."

"Believe it or not, those Chinese veterans in Ximending looked just like the owners of the dog-meat restaurant, the same old face."

"A-bu, I agree with Sis. For example, the three owners of the Old Shandong have almost never changed a bit at all since the first time we saw them."

"Perhaps their lives stopped and their looks stopped changing too. It isn't like Uncle Huang and Uncle Wen-Hua, lives ended. They had been waiting for their Generalissimo Chiang Kai-shek and his son Chiang Ching-kuo to bring them back to China. They couldn't continue their old lives in China, but a lot of them did not build a life in Taiwan, either, while they were waiting. When they realized that there was little chance to go back to China, twenty or thirty years had gone by. Don't you think the situation was like life stopped or ended?"

"I never thought this way before, but I think you're right, A-bu."

"Mei-Ai, it's not that we didn't think about their situation. It's that we didn't care about them at all. Since we were little, we had been afraid of them and kept ourselves away from them. As a matter of fact, we didn't like them at all. Of course, not all of them, but most of them. Who would care about the people whom they don't like?"

"Sis, this is a complicated situation that involves almost everybody in Taiwan, if you think of it. Start from A-bu. When A-bu was little, she didn't know the 228 Incident. Thus, she didn't have the negative feelings for the Chinese veterans.

Before she learned some bad things about them, she met Uncle Huang, a good man. However, later, A-bu was almost raped by a Chinese veteran, and Auntie Ciou-Jyu was raped by a bunch of Chinese veterans, which made A-bu dislike them. About us, we always trust A-bu and keep her words in our minds, so we were especially careful around the Chinese veterans. In other words, they were practically excluded from our lives. Well, who would care about the people who were excluded from their lives? Besides, people like Lan Tian, whose families were killed in the 228 Incident, certainly wouldn't like the Chinese veterans. Since they don't know which Chinese veterans brutally tortured and killed their fathers, grandfathers, or great-grandfathers, they just hate them all. The last, the people, who witnessed and knew the 228 Incident, and their families surely wouldn't like those Chinese veterans. Therefore, even if those Chinese veterans wanted to build a life in Taiwan, it would be hard, because they were not welcomed or accepted by many Taiwanese people."

"Excellent point, Mei-Ai. However, besides the fact that they are not accepted by many Taiwanese people, I believe that many Chinese veterans don't want to integrate themselves into Taiwanese society. Some feel that they are superior to the Taiwanese people. Never want to learn Taiwanese languages, try Taiwanese food, listen to Taiwanese folk music and opera, or learn Taiwanese customs. Some are afraid of the Taiwanese people and so isolate themselves. Some only want to live in their own community, little China, speaking their own dialects, cooking their own food, talking about their lives in China. Believe it or not, according to Professor Jhang, these are the situations that the Chinese Nationalist government wishes to see."

"Sis, you mean that the Chinese Nationalist government wants the Chinese veterans to think that they are the ruling class?"

"Yes and no. In the Chinese Nationalist government's eyes, only Chinese elites and high-ranking officers are superior. Those low-ranking Chinese veterans are uneducated, vulgar people. However, they need this big group of loyal people to support them forever. Therefore, it's better that they don't interact with the Taiwanese people too much."

"So, Sis, that's why the government built so many Chinese communities?"

"Again, yes and no. The Chinese people need the comfort and company from their own people too."

"No matter what reasons, some of them made their lives stop in a way. If people didn't try to bond to the land where they live, they wouldn't have a sense of belonging to the land. Uncle Huang felt that Taiwan was his second home. He missed his home and family in China, but he also loved it here. Have I told you that Uncle Huang could speak Taiwanese? He taught us Mandarin and learned Taiwanese from us, and because he was an intelligent man and loved to learn, he spoke Taiwanese well. One time, I went to sell the steamed buns with him, and a middle-aged woman said to me, 'Is he your father? He looks like Chinese but speaks excellent Taiwanese. Is he Chinese or Taiwanese?' I answered her, 'He is Chinese and also Taiwanese. He is my godfather. His buns are really good!' Both Uncle Huang and the woman laughed, and the woman said, 'Then I want to buy five buns if they are this good.' Do you know what Uncle Huang said? 'For a new friend, I give you one more for free!' The woman laughed and said, 'Then I'll tell my neighbors to come!' See, when you are friendly, reach out to people, people will warmly do the same. I believe that it made Uncle Huang, a lonely and homesick man, cheer up and forget the sorrow for a moment."

"A-bu, I love listening to you talking about Uncle Huang. Every time I learn a little something about him, and I like him more and more."

"Me too. Some people are willing to make efforts. Therefore, they live better, and their lives don't stop but expand. I think that Uncle Huang and the owners of Old Shandong are the same type of people."

"Mei-Ling, you're right. That's the reason I went to Old Shandong and took your a-ba and you to eat there later. I can see some of my uncle Huang in them."

"How about going to Old Shandong tomorrow? And it's on me. I just got my first paycheck in my life."

"Sis, you did? Did you get that tutoring job?"

"Yes, I did. And the boy whom I am tutoring is very well behaved."

"Mei-Ling, I told you not to worry about the tuition. I have savings. There is no problem even if you and Mei-Ai go to graduate school. Two majors and a part-time job are too much for you."

"A-bu, it's OK. Really! It's only three times a week."

"Once you find it's too much for you, don't hesitate to quit, OK?"

"Yes, A-bu."

"Girls, it's late. We should go home."

"Good morning, Wang bei-bei [伯伯, *old uncle*]!"

"Mei-Ling, Mei-Ai, good morning!"

When anyone went to Old Shandong, the first owner of the restaurant they saw was Wang bei-bei, who was baking sesame flatbreads and pork buns outside of the restaurant. In winter, it wasn't too bad by the oven, but it was like hell during the summertime, even with a huge fan bellowing.

Since Mei-Ling was little, she loved to stand by the fan to watch Wang bei-bei working, and Wang bei-bei always told her to be careful.

"Mei-Ling, don't get too close to the fan. Your beautiful long hair might get sucked into the fan. We don't want our little princess to get hurt."

Then Mei-Ling would laugh. No one in the world but Wang bei-bei, Lin bei-bei, and Cao bei-bei called her and Mei-

Ai princess. Later, when she and Mei-Ai went to high school, they began to call them little ladies. Mei-Ling believed that if these three bei-bei had their own daughters, they would love and adore them very much.

"Wang bei-bei, do you have any children?"

"No."

"How come?"

"Because I don't have a wife. Ha, ha, ha…"

"How about Lin bei-bei and Cao bei-bei?"

"The same."

"Oh…"

Mei-Ling didn't ask the further question, "Why don't you get married?" She was twelve years old, old enough to know that it's not polite to pry.

The three bei-bei had different personalities.

Wang bei-bei would make bread and buns and sing or talk to people. People could hear his laughter all the time. Mei-Ling and Mei-Ai often would look back to see what made Wang bei-bei so happy while they were eating.

Lin bei-bei was the one who took orders, brought food to the customers, and collected the money from customers. He always had a smile on his face but didn't talk much. Mei-Ling and Mei-Ai were amazed about his memory. Not only could he remember each group of customers' orders, but he also remembered what the regular customers liked to order. Once in a while, Lin bei-bei would surprise Mei-Ling and Mei-Ai.

"Congratulations, Mei-Ai! Best student of the year."

"Mei-Ling, good luck with the speech contest."

It seemed that Lin bei-bei had magic to know people's lives. The truth was that people liked to talk, and he listened.

How about Cao bei-bei?

In Mei-Ai's opinion, Cao bei-bei was like an octopus. While waiting for the food, Mei-Ai usually liked to see Cao bei-bei working. She found that Cao bei-bei could do everything in a few seconds, pouring hot soy milk into a bowl, putting a fired breadstick into sesame flatbread, or taking out a steamed bun from the streamer, like having eight hands. Therefore, he talked to almost no one but Lin bei-bei. However, Mei-Ling argued with Mei-Ai. She thought that Cao bei-bei was more like a bear than an octopus.

"Listen to Cao bei-bei talking. His voice is low but powerful. When he calls, 'Old Lin,' don't you think it sounds like a bear's roar? And look at his body, strong and big, a bear, no doubt!"

"But a bear can't move nimbly like an octopus."

However, Cao bei-bei was neither a bear nor an octopus. He was a gentle lamb, who liked to read. Several times, Mei-Ling and Mei-Ai saw Cao bei-bei sitting outside the restaurant reading with a cup of oolong tea after the restaurant closed in the afternoon.

"Hi, Cao bei-bei!"

"Hello! Mei-Ling and Mei-Ai. How are you?"

"Fine, thank you."

"Where are you going?"

"The library."

"Good! The best place in the whole world."

"Cao bei-bei also goes to the library?"

"Every week. See, this book is borrowed from the library. Great book!"

"What's the name of the book?"

"*Pride and Prejudice*, by…"

"Jane Austen!"

"Mei-Ling, you know? It's interestingly romantic, isn't it?"

"Yes, it is. Cao bei-bei, do you know that the name of the novel was *First Impressions*, originally?"

"Really? It fits the story, but *Pride and Prejudice* is better, in my opinion. Have you both read the book?"

"Only my sister has."

"Mei-Ai, you have to read it when you have a chance."

"I certainly will. My sister keeps telling me how good it is."

"Your sister has a taste of literature. Trust her!"

"A taste of literature." The two girls couldn't believe that those words came from the mouth of Cao bei-bei. Moreover, which bear or octopus would read *Pride and Prejudice*? From that day on, Mei-Ling and Mei-Ai called Cao bei-bei the gentle lamb.

After saying good morning to Wang bei-bei, Mei-Ai and Ciou-Tao went inside the restaurant to find a seat, and Mei-Ling stayed outside to talk to Wang bei-bei as usual.

"Wang bei-bei, my mom told me that you and Lin bei-bei and Cao bei-bei closed the restaurant for a month to visit the families in China. Did you have a good time?"

"No."

"What? How come? You and your family didn't see each other for nearly forty years. It should be nice to reunite."

"My parents both died during the Cultural Revolution. They were tortured because of me, a sergeant of the Republic of China Army."

"Oh no."

"My two brothers were mad at me. They said that I owed them. They wanted me to build a house and buy a television and a washing machine for them since people in Taiwan are rich. I went to my parents' graves to say goodbye and gave my brothers all the money I had; then I left. I don't have a home there anymore. Taiwan is my home."

"I am so sorry to hear this, Wang bei-bei."

"Don't be. War hurt people and changed people. Moreover, the relationship between brothers is different from parents and children. But you can be happy for Lin bei-bei and Cao bei-bei. They are much luckier than me."

"Are their parents alive?"

"Mei-Ling, your mom and Mei-Ai are waiting for you. Go to eat. Our stories are not that important."

"OK. I am going to eat. Mei-Ai and I have a train to catch. Wang bei-bei, I believe that everyone's life story is meaningful."

"Mei-Ling, you and Mei-Ai are sweet little ladies. You always make bei-bei very happy. Take these broken pork buns to the trip."

"Aren't they your lunch? What're you going to eat later?"

"You remember?"

"Of course. Once you said, 'These broken ones are my lunch.'"

"Yes! Yes! My punishment! Doing bad work. Ha, ha, ha!"

"No, they're yummy, broken or not!"

"That's why you should bring them with you. Go! Go! Eat your food."

"Thank you, Wang bei-bei."

In the train station waiting room, Mei-Ling told Ciou-Tao and Mei-Ai the story Wang bei-bei had told her.

"That's horrible! How could his brothers blame him for everything? Why didn't they blame their Chairman Mao? He created the Cultural Revolution."

"Because Wang bei-bei was Generalissimo Chiang's Nationalist soldier, their parents got more torture than others."

"Lan Tian is right. There is little difference between the Chinese Communist Party and the Chinese Nationalist Party. After all, they're brothers."

"Ha! Right on! Lan Tian is great. Smart and thoughtful. A-bu, do you know that Lan Tian would buy red bean soup for Mei-Ai when her period comes?"

"Yes, I do. Mei-Ai told me. He is a gentleman."

"I feel very sorry for Wang bei-bei, though. He had missed his family for decades, but now, he feels that he doesn't have a home in China anymore."

"Mei-Ling, Wang bei-bei isn't the only one who has great disappointment. I have heard some similar sad stories. Some of the Chinese veterans couldn't find their homes because their villages or towns changed a great deal. Some of them eventually found their families, but their families' situations upset them. For example, both parents had died, their wives had remarried, or the son had grown up to be an uneducated rascal. Some of the veterans also felt very hurt that it seemed their families just wanted money but didn't care about them. Of course, some veterans had a wonderful reunion, but most of them felt disappointed and sad. In fact, like Wang bei-bei said, he doesn't have a home in China anymore. Many Chinese veterans feel the same and don't want to go back to China to visit again."

"A-bu, forty years is a long time. They had not been in each other's lives for a long time. All they have are the memories that they were together before the separation and the forty-year bitterness. It's hard to have a happy ending as a fairy tale."

"Sis, we've got to go now; the train will arrive in ten minutes."

"Girls, call me when you get back to your dormitories."

"OK, A-bu. Bye."

20

Hometown in Dusk

Calling me, calling me
Hometown in dusk calls me from time to time.
Calling me, a suffering body,
a wanderer, a homeless migratory bird.
Came to a foreign country alone,
I miss my hometown often
Today, I have heard it again
Oh—the calling

Calling me, calling me
Hometown in dusk calls me from time to time.
I miss the scenery of the hometown,
the valley that was under the moonlight,
the mountains, and the rivers
always embrace our dreams.
Tonight, I have dreamed of it again
Oh—it's like the hometown is waiting for me

Calling me, calling me
Hometown in dusk calls me from time to time.
With sorrow and tears,
calling me to go home endlessly.
The cloud, if you are going to my hometown,
please bring my thoughts to my mother.
Oh, please don't forget to tell her.

The name of this song is "Hometown in Dusk" (黃昏的故

鄉). A Taiwanese singer, Wen Xia (文夏), took the melody from a Japanese song that was published in 1958 and wrote the lyrics. It was Wen-De's favorite song. As a matter of fact, many Taiwanese who were forbidden to go back to Taiwan by the Chinese Nationalist government loved to sing this song when they got together. It would be better if they listened to the song together, or one would be drowned by her or his tears. It would be better they sang the song together, so they didn't have to be brave for a moment.

Wen-De, a familiar name. Yes, he was Wen-Zhi and Wen-Hua's elder brother. In 1962, his last year at university, Wen-De got the lawyer license and also passed the entrance examination of the Graduate School of Law in Taiwan University. However, because the deaths of Wen-Zhi and Ciou-Jyu had impacted him tremendously, he didn't go to graduate school. He went to fulfill the three-year compulsory military service instead. Sadly, although three years wasn't a short time, it wasn't long enough to mend Wen-De's broken heart. He knew that he needed to change the scenery and be away from home, so he applied for and got into Yale Law School and went to the United States in 1965 after finishing the compulsory military service—of course, with the government's permission.

The new scenery did change Wen-De vastly. In a new environment, there were many things that he needed to learn, and the people and the culture interested him very much. Moreover, being able to access all different kinds of books, newspapers, and magazines thrilled him very much. As a matter of fact, he could read the magazines that were banned in Taiwan. "free! I am in a free country!" he shouted. Breathing the free air made Wen-De begin to think about human rights, and his pain and sadness gradually became an energy concerned with any kind of human violence.

In September 1964, something significant happened. The professor of Taiwan University, Peng Ming-Min (彭明敏, 1923–), and his students Hsieh Tsung-Min (謝聰敏, 1934–2019) and Wei Ting-Chao (魏廷朝, 1935–1999) published "Declaration of Formosan Self-Salvation" (台灣自救運動宣言).

First, they pointed out the truth that it was impossible to reconquer China. However, the Chiang Kai-shek regime used it, the reconquest of China, as an excuse to declare martial law to control Taiwanese people and a method to gain loyalty from the Chinese soldiers, veterans, and civilians, who fled to Taiwan with the Chiang Kai-shek regime.

Second, they talked about the fact that the Chiang Kai-shek regime didn't represent anyone. The Chinese Nationalist government, the Chiang Kai-shek regime, claimed that they were the only legitimate government of China, but the truth was that the people in China had chosen another government, the Chinese Communist government. Besides the fact that the Chiang Kai-shek regime didn't represent the people in China, they couldn't represent the Taiwanese people either. Of the three thousand representatives of the National Assembly, fewer than twenty were Taiwanese, and there had been only six Taiwanese out of 473 seats in Legislative Yuan. Moreover, their terms of office had ended twelve and fifteen years ago. Besides, the Chiang Kai-shek regime couldn't represent the Chinese Nationalist Party either. Although they had always had the politic idea of "party-state," the Chinese Nationalist Party is authoritarian, not democratic. Most of the party members had no right to express themselves. They could only listen to the teachings of their leader, Chiang Kai-shek, clap, and bow.

Third, they said that the Chiang Kai-shek regime tried very hard to sabotage the relationship between the Taiwanese people and the Chinese people to prevent them from cooperating to pursue democracy.

Hence, they stated, "One China and one Taiwan has been

a solid truth, and it is time for people in Taiwan to form a democratic free country."

Rebels!
Lock them up!

The same year, 1964, before they distributed the fly sheets to people and social groups, the three men were arrested. Peng Ming-Min and Wei Ting-Chao were sentenced to eight years in prison, and Hsieh Tsung-Min received ten years. Peng Ming-Min was pardoned in 1965 because of the concern from Amnesty International and the pressure from the government of the United States. With friends' help, in January 1970, Peng Ming-Min successfully escaped to Sweden and arrived in the United States later the same year.

Their work wasn't in vain. In 1965, the World United Formosans in Japan for Independence[6] published the "Declaration of Formosan Self-Salvation" in their monthly magazine, *Taiwan Youth*. Many Taiwanese people who lived abroad were inspired and enthusiastically passed it on to their friends. In 1966, the "Declaration of Formosan Self-Salvation" was translated into English. Moreover, the Taiwanese people who studied in the United States raised funds to get a half page to advertise the "Declaration of Formosan Self-Salvation" in the *New York Times*. At the same time, the members of the United Formosans in America for Independence divided into two groups for two routes, the West and East Coast, and drove to the cities and campuses to share the information with the Taiwanese people. The trip enlarged the United Formosans in America for Independence; more Taiwanese people joined to be members, and the mailing list of their magazine grew from four hundred people to four thousand. In short, many Taiwanese people in the United States were inspired and united by the "Declaration of Formosan Self-Salvation."

Wen-De arrived in the United States in 1965, so he

caught up with the movement of Taiwanese independence. He sincerely admired Professor Peng Ming-Min and his students Hsieh Tsung-Min and Wei Ting-Chao. He thought that they were brilliant men who courageously pointed out the important truths.

As a law school student, Wen-De always found that the political situation in Taiwan was so ridiculous.

"According to the Constitution of the Republic of China, the mainland of China and Outer Mongolia are the territories of the Republic of China. In 1949, the Chiang Kai-shek regime was replaced by the Chinese Communist Party, which means the legitimate government of China is the Chinese Communist government, so the Chinese Communist government owns the mainland, not the Chinese Nationalist government. It also means that the Chinese Nationalist government had died in a way. Not to mention that Outer Mongolia is recognized as an independent country internationally."

Some friends asked him, "Why doesn't the Chinese Nationalist government amend the Constitution of the Republic of China so it can reborn to become a new country in Taiwan?"

"Well, besides the fact that they have no desire, there are some legal issues. The drafting of the Constitution of the Republic of China began in 1936, and there was not a single Taiwanese participant, because Taiwan was Japan's colony at the time. The ratification process for the constitution ended in 1947, and Taiwan was still Japan's colony because the Treaty of San Francisco (舊金山和約) was signed in 1951 and the Treaty of Taipei (台北和約) was signed in 1952. Moreover, in both treaties, Japan signed for renunciation on Taiwan, not handing over the sovereignty of Taiwan to the Republic of China, the Chiang Kai-shek regime. This explains why the government of the Republic of China has never exercised Article Four of the Constitution of the Republic of China, 'The territory of the Republic of China according to its existing national boundaries shall not be altered except by resolution of the National Assembly.' In conclusion, firstly, the government of the Republic of China has trusteeship, not ownership, of Taiwan. In other words, the government of the Republic of China illegally occupies Taiwan. Secondly, the Constitution of the Republic of China can't be amended by the Taiwanese people. Lastly, according to the international law, the Republic of China is a zombie, a dead authority that was replaced by the People's Republic of China and is clinging to Taiwan to live. Hence, the Taiwanese people need to draw up their own constitution and found their own country."

Learning these truths was a great shock to Wen-De's friends, because they had always been told by their history teachers, textbooks, and media that Taiwan was restored to China according to the Cairo Declaration. What they believed was actually a big fat lie. Outrageous!

When Wen-De gathered all the information to study and had a clear conclusion of the Taiwanese future, he felt terrified for a moment. He knew anyone who embraced those truths and facts was a rebel in the Chiang Kai-shek regime's eyes. Of course, if he didn't talk about them in public or tell his family and friends, just kept them to himself, he wouldn't get into trouble. However, could he not talk and tell Taiwanese people about those truths and facts as a Taiwanese person himself? "If we don't stand up to fight, we will lose freedom and also the Taiwanese identity. It's time to stop being ruled and to be masters of ourselves." This conclusion hit Wen-De's heart and pained him.

Some people had never been their masters of themselves. They were shim-bu-a.

"Shim-bu-a, what an ugly custom! Treating young girls like a piece of meat. This ugly custom is so inhuman, denying the fact that a person has feelings and can think." No matter how much time had passed, whenever Wen-De thought about

Ciou-Jyu, his heart hurt.

The day Ciou-Jyu came to his family, Wen-De liked her right away. Love came gradually between them, but Ciou-Jyu was arranged to be Wen-Zhi's future wife. Wen-De despaired.

"Why isn't she arranged to be my future wife?"

However, hope came suddenly. Wen-Zhi wanted to cancel the engagement because he knew Ciou-Jyu and him were in love and wanted Ciou-Jyu to be happy.

The hope brought courage. Suddenly, Wen-De believed in miracles. However, they were fighting with the unshakable custom and a stubborn mother.

"Love is affection between two people. It's beautiful. Ciou-Jyu and I love each other. Why should we be forbidden to be together just because she was arranged to marry Wen-Zhi? As a matter of fact, by law, she is not Wen-Zhi's wife." Wen-De tried to persuade his mother but to no avail.

Perhaps Wen-De's mother felt that she was challenged and didn't like it; she married Ciou-Jyu to a man who had a very bad reputation, a scumbag, in the town.

"Mother is mad. Ciou-Jyu called her A-bu for five years. How could she be so cruel? How come parents can have such absolute power to decide children's fate? Are we parents' property? Are parents unchallengeable even if they are wrong?"

"I should've been brave and acted." During the three years in compulsory military service, Wen-De tortured himself with that thought. "Because I didn't act, Ciou-Jyu not only was in hell but was abused to death." Wen-De felt that he killed Ciou-Jyu and Wen-Zhi. If he didn't worry how people would think or criticize him and took Ciou-Jyu to Taipei with him after his mother denied his request, both Ciou-Jyu and Wen-Zhi wouldn't have died. While he hesitated, his mother married Ciou-Jyu away.

Well, Wen-De's worry wasn't only about others' criticism. He was born into a wealthy family, so he had never had a hard life. Furthermore, he was the best student all the way to university. He didn't know what failure and hardship were. Taking Ciou-Jyu to Taipei with him would be a big scandal, elopement, in the town. He also would have to be financially independent. "Am I capable of being independent?" Wen-De had doubts and fears. The reality was ruthless. Before Wen-De found the courage to take the challenge, Ciou-Jyu had married to a monster. Later, with remorse and shame, Wen-De comprehended that the pursuit of freedom and happiness needed courage and only brave people could find their freedom and happiness. Thus, joining the movement of Taiwanese independence was like Wen-De's atonement.

Article 100 of the Criminal Code of the Republic of China (Offences Against the Internal Security of the State, 內亂罪):

"A person who commits an overt act with **intent** to destroy the organization of the State, seize State territory, by illegal means change the Constitution, or overthrow the Government shall be punished with imprisonment for not less than seven years; a ringleader shall be punished with imprisonment for life. A person who prepares or conspires to commit an offence specified in the preceding paragraph shall be punished with imprisonment for not less than six months and not more than five years."

According to Article 100 of the Criminal Code of the Republic of China, Wen-De and many other Taiwanese people—who declared to pursue Taiwanese independence, believed in socialism, or joined the Taiwanese Association, not the Chinese Association, while they were studying or working abroad —were criminals. In fact, the Chinese Nationalist government took advantage of the word *intent* to abuse human rights. Any ideas or acts that the Chiang Kai-shek regime disliked or saw as threats would be defined as offenses against the internal security of the state. In other words, under the Chinese Nationalist government's rule, people in Taiwan were not allowed to think whatever they wanted to think. Their brains must be full of love and passion for the Republic of China and the leader Chiang Kai-shek but nothing else.

The criminals with thought crime who lived in Taiwan were very easy to take care of, but it wasn't that difficult to deal with those who were in foreign countries either.

Because of student agents' good work, the Chinese Nationalist government had a blacklist. Therefore, the government revoked those thought criminals' passports, or the Republic of China Oversea Mission would refuse to renew their passports to make them become stateless people. Besides, if the thought criminals had citizenship of another country, the government would refuse to give them a visa.

However, the Chinese Nationalist government couldn't entirely stop some fighters from going back to Taiwan. Besides taking an airplane, some took a boat to sneak into Taiwan. Some were immediately deported; some got arrested; some successfully sneaked in and played hide and run all the time. There were more, like Professor Peng Ming-Min and Wen-De, staying where they were to fight overseas.

In a way, Wen-De was luckier than many Taiwanese people who were forbidden to go back to Taiwan. He had family in the United States.

Wen-Hua had severe myopia, so he was exempted from the compulsory military service. As a result, a year after he graduated from the university, four years after Wen-De had been in the United States, he arrived in New York. One year later, Wen-De got a teaching job at New York University School of Law. The two brothers lived together like old times at last.

Wen-De was six years older than Wen-Hua; therefore, when they were little, there had been a gap between them. Moreover, when Wen-Hua entered junior high school, Wen-De left home for college in Taipei. Since then, they had barely had chances to hang out and talk. A decade later, they finally united. In no time, they were as close as any brothers could be.

There was another thing, the love for Taiwan, brought them closer. They got to know Taiwanese history in different ways, but they met in the end and had the same conclusion on Taiwan's future. However, the experience of being scolded and warned by the military education instructor because of reading banned books had imprinted as a reminder, so Wen-Hua wasn't as active as Wen-De in the Taiwan independence movement. Sadly, he underestimated the Chinese Nationalist government's brutality and the excellent work they had done to spy on them. Thus, he still went back to Taiwan despite the warning and worries from friends and Wen-De.

It was 1981 when Wen-Hua went back to Taiwan. He had left home for twelve years. He missed home, and so did Wen-De. When they first arrived in the United States, they were busy with settling down. Later, schoolwork, the Taiwan independence movement, jobs, and getting married and having their own families, fully occupied their minds, which made time fly. One day, in a quiet moment, a strong desire arose like a flood and nearly drowned Wen-Hua: "I want to go home." Then he went home, with his wife and daughter and a little impatience.

Wen-De had the same longing from time to time, but he knew that he would be arrested at once when he showed up at the airport in Taiwan. He wasn't a coward, but he loved his freedom. Furthermore, he believed that it would be more helpful to stay free. He could do more work for the Taiwan independence movement. He told Wen-Hua the thinking, but he really couldn't stop a man with extreme homesickness. He prayed hard for Wen-Hua's safety. That was why Wen-De was so relieved when he got a phone call from Wen-Hua and told him that he arrived home safely. However, a week later, Wen-De got a phone call from his father and learned of the death of Wen-Hua.

"Dead?" Wen-De was shocked. His brain went blank. "Dead? Wen-Hua is dead?"

Soon, the anger dominated him. "Suicide? Wen-Hua was happy and had a wonderful life, and he committed suicide? Totally bullshit!" Wen-De couldn't calm down. He wanted to have a loud shout, but he couldn't. His daughter and son would be frightened to see their gentle father go mad. He wanted to go back to Taiwan right away, but he couldn't. He might be murdered like Wen-Hua. His parents only had one son left. He had to be alive for them. If he could, he would kill Chiang Ching-kuo and all his thugs. However, Wen-De really couldn't do anything, like a lion in a cage.

Wen-De fell into deep sadness after the anger retreated.

"Taiwan is a beautiful island blooming by the law of nature, but we are ruled by the nation who has no natural law in their lives. Hence, people's natural rights are deprived, and Wen-Hua and many others had to die." Wen-De felt so helpless and useless. After two or three generations' effort on Taiwan's liberation, he still couldn't see the light of hope at the end of the tunnel. He wished his children didn't need to continue their work. They could be free as people in the United States, France, Sweden, or Britain.

About ten years ago, Wen-De was profoundly touched and inspired by the letter that the second president of the United States, John Adams, wrote to his wife, Abigail, in May 1780: "I must study politics and war that my sons may have liberty to study mathematics and philosophy. My sons ought to study mathematics and philosophy, geography, natural history, naval architecture, navigation, commerce, and agriculture, in order to give their children a right to study painting, poetry, music, architecture, statuary, tapestry, and porcelain."

"Oh...liberty is indeed the best gift from a father's greatest love." Wen-De wanted to be a father like John Adams.

"What a great politician with a vision!" Wen-De praised. "We don't have great politicians. We only have dictators and evil monsters who work for the dictators!"

Wen-De couldn't believe what his father told him. Wen-

Hua had nine rib fractures on one side and three on the other side and intra-abdominal hemorrhage. The whole lung was damaged. One kidney was ruptured, and another one was swollen. His stomach and intestine had no food. The pubis was broken, and ten fingers were curly and turned black. There was a more than ten-centimeter-long elbow-splitting wound and four lines of blood marks on Wen-Hua's back.

"What kind of animals are they? How could they torture and kill people like that? How much pain had Wen-Hua suffered? He must have been terrified. How frightening it would be to know you are on the road to death. I should've tried harder to stop him from going back to Taiwan. Why didn't I?" Wen-De eventually cried. He blamed himself that he wasn't a good brother.

Who was to blame? Anyone who had a conscience knew. However, what was the use of blame? Two brothers had separated forever. Unbearably, Wen-De couldn't even go to the funeral to say goodbye. In fact, people who were on the Chinese Nationalist government's blacklist all couldn't go to their family members' funerals. That was why they sang "Hometown in Dusk" in their gathering, whether they lived in Boston, New York, Houston, San Francisco, or Tokyo. Furthermore, almost no one wouldn't cry when they sang the song. Years ago, Wen-De and Wen-Hua cried for homesickness. After Wen-Hua died, Wen-De would cry with unbearable heart pain and feel very lonely when singing "Hometown in Dusk."

Two years later, Wen-De's mother passed away. She couldn't bear the fact that Wen-Hua was murdered by the government and knew that it was impossible to get justice for Wen-Hua, so the sadness and anger attacked her aggressively. She cried nearly every day. Furthermore, she hadn't seen Wen-De for two decades. She missed him a great deal and wished he could come home. However, she knew the reality very well: the government wouldn't allow her to leave Taiwan, and Wen-De was on the government's blacklist and might be murdered as well if he came back to Taiwan, which meant she wouldn't be able to see him for the rest of her life. She despaired of losing all three sons. One afternoon, she died in her sleep because of a heart attack.

Five years after Mother's death, Wen-De's father died. Wen-De learned from several friends about how his father had defended and fought for Wen-Hua. Wen-De was surprised and got very emotional. His father had always been a quiet man who didn't show much emotion, so he couldn't imagine that his father would fight with the government. He should have been the one to do the fighting, not his father. He felt that he was a useless son who let the old father carry the duty. Wen-De believed that his father was sad and angry like his mother; however, it was easier for a quiet man to hide his grief and indignation, so he looked and sounded fine to people. "He definitely wasn't fine. Who could recover from state violence without having justice?" A few years later, Wen-De found a letter in his father's study. It was for him. His father said that he was so proud of him and Wen-Hua. He knew that Wen-Zhi would do the same to fight for Taiwanese independence if he were alive. "Keep fighting. Never give up until the day comes." Wen-De was surprised to know that his father approved of their work on the Taiwanese independence. He believed that his father knew nothing about it until Wen-Hua died. He must make a lot of effort to learn what Wen-Hua and he were doing. He certainly couldn't bear that the Chinese Nationalist government defamed his son, so he exhausted himself to find out the truth that his son was a brave and righteous man who fought against the dictator and the entire criminal system. "Perhaps Father found his own peace after knowing the truth," Wen-De presumed.

Wait!
Finding a letter in his father's study?
Wen-De came back to Taiwan?

That was an era for change.

In 1987, martial law was lifted, and the Chinese veterans and civilians were finally allowed to go back to China to visit their families.

In 1988, Chiang Ching-kuo died, and Vice President Lee Teng-Hui (李登輝, 1923—) succeeded as president.

In 1991, President Lee Teng-Hui declared the end of Temporary Provisions against the Communist Rebellion (動員戡亂時期臨時條款) and abolished the Act for the Control and Punishment of Rebellion (懲治叛亂條例).

In 1992, Article 100 of the Criminal Code was amended.

Because of many people's effort, those evil laws were abolished or amended, and a new president had different thinking from the Chiang regime. Finally, on July 7, 1992, the blacklist was lifted; Wen-De, who had left home for twenty-seven years, and many others could come home at last.

Oh, it must be a dream.
It's too good to be true.
Is it a trap?

Wen-De couldn't believe that his dream was finally not a dream. He actually asked around to confirm the news. His friends all laughed happily and told him to believe it. Wen-De was not used to trusting the Chinese Nationalist government. Although the new president, Lee Teng-Hui, was Taiwanese, he, after all, was the chairman of the evil party, the Chinese Nationalist Party. "Can he be trusted?" Wen-De worried.

Surprisingly, President Lee Teng-Hui was dubbed "Mr. Democracy" by *Newsweek* in 1996, four years after the blacklist was lifted. Well, who could foresee the future? Better to be safe than sorry. However, homesickness beat everything. Two weeks later, Wen-De brought his wife and children home. Because of him, his wife hadn't seen her family for twenty years after they married. Wen-De felt guilty about it. However, she said, "This is my choice with free will. When I made my choice, I knew who you were and what you were doing, and I chose to marry you."

21

I Am Home

On the other side of the world, Taiwan, many people happily welcomed the people who were on the blacklist to come back home. They were friends at schools, comrades in the Taiwan independence movement, acquaintances from old times, and families, of course.

That was Friday afternoon. Someone called Mei-Ling, and she turned back to see who was calling her.

Ah, it was Professor Jhang!

"Good afternoon, Professor."

"It's summer break. Why are you still at school?"

"I got a summer job in the library."

"I see."

"How are you, Professor?"

"Happy."

"That's great."

"Happy to see my friends come back to Taiwan. They were forbidden to come home for decades."

"I heard that on the news. They deserve a medal."

"Yes, they do. By the way, Mei-Ling, do you know that Dr. Chen Wen-Hua's elder brother came back to Taiwan?"

"He is one of them?"

"Yes, he is. He couldn't come home for twenty-seven years."

"Twenty-seven years? My God! Professor, honestly, I know almost nothing about him. My mother only mentioned him two or three times. I don't even know his name."

"His name is Chen Wen-De. He is a professor of New York

University School of Law. Do you want to meet him?"

"Yes, I do. If it is appropriate."

"I think he would be very happy to meet you."

"He probably would be even more happy to meet my a-bu."

"I am sure he would. Mei-Ling, as a matter of fact, I am going to a gathering of friends right now, and Wen-De will be there too. Are you available?"

"Yes, I am. Oh my. I am going to meet Uncle Wen-De right now. I am so nervous."

"Don't be. He is an easygoing guy."

"My friend, you're finally home." Professor Jhang hugged Wen-De emotionally.

"Yes, I am home. It's so good to be home."

"Wen-De, I want you to meet someone."

"Who? The young lady you came in with?"

"So you saw her."

"Yes, I did. She looks very much like someone whom I knew in the past."

"So she grabbed your attention."

"Yes."

"Well, let her tell you who she is." Then Professor Jhang and Wen-De walked to Mei-Ling, who was observing people in the room.

"Mei-Ling, this is Dr. Chen Wen-De."

"Pleased to meet you, and welcome home. My name is Chen Mei-Ling, and my mother is Lin Ciou-Tao." Mei-Ling smiled.

"Ciou-Tao! I know that name! She is Ciou-Jyu's little sister." Wen-De's heart was trembling. "My goodness! No wonder she looks so familiar. She is Ciou-Jyu's niece, and she looks just like Ciou-Jyu!" Wen-De became very emotional.

"Oh, Ciou-Tao's little girl. Can uncle give you a hug?"

Mei-Ling hugged Wen-De. The tears raced down his cheeks.

"How is your a-bu?" Wen-De wiped off tears.

"She is fine."

"Can I see her?"

"Of course, but she is not in Taipei."

"So she is still living in the town."

"Yes."

"I guess you are a college student."

"One of my best students," Professor Jhang said proudly.

"Of course she is. Little Jhang, that runs in the family. Her a-bu is smart, and her aunties were smart too."

"I am not that smart. I can't compare myself to my younger sister at all. She is really intelligent."

"She studies in Taipei too?"

"Yes, she does. Her name is Mei-Ai. She studies fine art. Her work got selected in the National Art Exhibition this year."

"What an accomplished girl!" Wen-De found himself feeling proud.

"This young lady is too humble. She has a double major. As accomplished as her sister."

"Mei-Ling, since you're one of the best students of Professor Jhang, I assume that one of your majors is history."

"Yes, uncle. And another major is social work."

"Wonderful! You must care about people very much."

"Wen-De, Mei-Ling told me that she wants to study the White Terror victims' trauma. Combine the knowledge of two fields in her study. How great is that!"

"I am not surprised but proud. You know, her aunt was my adoptive sister. Practically, in a way, Mei-Ling is my niece..."

"Wait! Wait! Wait! You can only be proud, but you can't take any credit!"

"Mei-Ling, you see, that's the problem when you have a

good friend who knows you so well. He can see through your intention!"

Mei-Ling couldn't stop laughing. Wen-De made a face and then looked into her eyes. She, at once, comprehended how much Uncle Wen-De loved her auntie Ciou-Jyu.

After the laugh, Professor Jhang left them alone.

"Mei-Ling, it's summertime. Why are you still in Taipei?"

"Uncle, I have a summer job in the school library."

"You're very independent. That's great."

"I can't give my a-bu too much burden."

Immediately, an image of a little girl trying to find something out of the trash can rose before Wen-De's eyes.

"Mei-Ling, I don't mean to pry. Do you have financial difficulties? If you do, uncle wants to help."

"Thank you, Uncle. We're OK. My parents have a small restaurant. The business is fine. We're not doing very good, but we're not in poverty. My sister and I don't have student loan debt at all, so you see, we're fine."

"This might sound odd to you since we just met. In my heart, your a-bu and sister and you are my family. If you have any trouble and need help in the future, please come to me."

"Uncle, I don't feel strange because I know that we are sharing the love that you have for Auntie Ciou-Jyu. We are lucky, and I am very grateful."

"How could she talk so much like Ciou-Jyu? Proper, polite, and appreciative. However, there is one big difference. Mei-Ling is loved and cherished. Her talent is allowed to develop. She is confident and accomplished. That little Ciou-Tao has made a massive change for Ciou-Jyu and herself. Bravo!" Wen-De was touched. He saw John Adams's spirit in Ciou-Tao.

"Mei-Ling, I am lucky too. You know that I lost my two brothers. Then, several years ago, my parents both passed away. I was very sad because I lost everyone whom I loved in my young life. But now, I've found my little sister and her daughters, which I couldn't ever expect. So Uncle intends to live positively and cheerfully from now on."

"Uncle, I don't think anyone can be more positive and cheerful than the people who were on the blacklist, but you sound like you weren't."

"Mei-Ling, we are human beings, not supermen. We have a big dream for Taiwan, and we also have human frailty."

"True. Any brave people also have low points and moments of feeling down. My a-bu cried badly when she learned of Uncle Wen-Hua's death, which shocked my sister and me very much. That was our first time to see our cheerful a-bu sadly crying like that. We were scared and helpless because she is our sunshine and northern star. Perhaps, in our minds, we want our hero and heroine always to be brave and cheerful."

"Well said. Mei-Ling, you should write. Write people's stories. I enjoy listening to you telling stories and feelings very much."

"Uncle, you think so? I have been told that I talk too much since I was little. My third-grade teacher said, 'Mei-Ling, you love to talk, so I believe that you'll do very well on speech contest.' Then she signed me up for the contest. My a-ba told me that girls shouldn't talk too much. It's not a virtue. My a-bu said that's nonsense and sexism."

"She is a great mother. A modernized and civilized person."

"She is. Uncle, you'll like her."

"I already liked her very much when she was little."

"You have met before? I didn't know that. Mei-Ai and I feel that my a-bu's life is full of secrets and surprises, so we like to dig around. But we failed all the time when we were little. We didn't know about Uncle Huang until I was in high school, and we learned of Uncle Wen-Hua's murder only one year ago. So you see how good she is at keeping secrets."

"I believe that she has her own reasons for keeping secrets. By the way, I think that I have a picture of Uncle Huang at home."

"Holy mackerel! Please, Uncle, you have to find it and make a copy for my a-bu. The only thing that she has that is related to Uncle Huang is a piece of paper. It's sad. The day that Uncle Huang went to see my a-bu and told her that he was leaving the town to work in the mountains, my a-bu asked him to write down his name. She said to him that she wanted to know his name, but the truth was that she was afraid of losing him. She wanted to have his name so that she could go to find him in the mountains if he didn't come back."

"And he really didn't come back. Your Auntie Ciou-Jyu was mournful when she learned the news of Uncle Huang's death. She wanted to go to the funeral, but my mother didn't allow her to go."

"Why?"

"Because Uncle Huang wasn't Ciou-Jyu's family or relative; it's inappropriate to go to a strange man's funeral, according to my mother."

"A strange man? He was like their father, according to my a-bu!"

"I know. That's why I was extremely mad. However, back then, I wasn't a courageous person, so I didn't try to find a way to take your Auntie Ciou-Jyu to the funeral."

"Uncle, I have to say that you made a huge jump, from not wanting to disobey your mother to fighting against the crazy evil government."

"Already making fun of your uncle!" Wen-De laughed and was amazed at Mei-Ling's thinking ability.

"Oh no. Uncle, I meant to say that I admire the spirit; people challenge their personalities."

"Relax, Mei-Ling. I am joking. As you said, I did challenge myself. I promised Uncle Huang to take good care of your auntie Ciou-Jyu, but I failed to keep my words. I regretted a great deal that I wasn't brave, so I tried to conquer that problem later."

"Uncle, my a-bu does not think it's you or your brothers'

fault. She said that monsters are out there all the time and innocent people get beaten up sometimes."

"Your a-bu is very kind and positive. But if good people don't do anything to help the people who are abused or bullied, they can't be called innocent at all."

"Uncle, I agree with you completely. I think that my a-bu has to think that way so she won't feel so despaired and angry. She had been through so much misery in her young life, so my sister and I like to make her happy when we can. Uncle, I am still thinking about the picture. If my a-bu could have that picture, she would fly to the sky and scream happily. By the way, Uncle, I am very curious why you have a picture of Uncle Huang."

"Before Uncle Huang left for the job in the mountains, he went to school to say goodbye to your auntie Ciou-Jyu and walked her and Wen-Hua home. At the time, I was playing with my first camera, learning to use it. You can imagine that I immediately wanted to take a picture of him and Ciou-Jyu together. I thought that it would be a comfort for your auntie if she had a picture of Uncle Huang. The picture was successfully printed out, and I gave it to your auntie. She was so happy and asked if I could print two more copies. She wanted Ciou-Lian and Ciou-Tao to have the picture too. I said yes, but I forgot to do it. And she never asked me again. I guess she didn't want to bother me because I was busy on the university entrance examination. So that's me, an unthoughtful person."

"Uncle, people forget sometimes. You made her very happy to have a picture of Uncle Huang and her. She might have felt that she was talking to Uncle Huang in person when she held the picture and talked."

"She did do that. I saw it one time."

"Really? My a-bu would surely love to hear these stories."

"And I want to see your a-bu very much."

"Believe it or not, I was on the way to the train station when Professor Jhang called me. If Uncle is available, we can go home together later or tomorrow."

"Let's go right now!"

On Friday, some people liked to have a party to celebrate the end of the week. Some just wanted to go back to their places to relax their bodies and comfort their souls. Some who came to the city to work would go back home in the south.

That Friday evening, Mei-Ling and Wen-De were going home. The two hearts were excited.

I am going home.
A-bu, I am coming home with someone.
I am going to see my little sister. Will she remember me?
A-bu, he is Uncle Wen-Hua's elder brother.
Will she see me as family?
A-bu, don't cry.

The uncle and niece arrived in the town!

"This is the air I dreamed of!" Wen-De threw back his head and had a deep breath.

"Uncle, the air is different from Taipei, right?"

"Different from any place in the world! Sweeter."

Mei-Ling looked at her uncle and wished no one in this world would be banned from going home.

"A-bu, Mei-Ai, I am home!"

"Mei-Ling...he is...you are..." Ciou-Tao couldn't talk, and gradually, tears welled up in her eyes.

"Ciou-Tao, I am..."

"You're Wen-Hua ge's elder brother, Wen-De ge." Ciou-Tao wiped off her tears.

"Ciou-Tao, you remember me?"

"I don't forget anyone who is important and nice to me."

Then Ciou-Tao hugged Wen-De.

Mei-Ling and Mei-Ai quietly closed the restaurant. It was not a good time to have any interruption. Last time, when they brought up the murder of Uncle Wen-Hua, a customer came. They remembered how awful it was.

"Wen-De ge and Mei-Ling, did you eat?"

"We ate on the train, but I am hungry."

"How about Wen-De ge?"

"I am hungry too."

"I can make something for you. What do you want? Oh, I think I should cook everything—the noodles, wontons, and rice dumplings—so you can taste them all."

"Ciou-Tao, don't get too busy."

"Uncle, let her be. A-bu is very excited right now. Cooking will do her good."

"Mei-Ling, you're a bad girl!"

"You must be one of the artists in the National Art Exhibition, Mei-Ai."

"Sis, you told Uncle? You're really bad like A-bu said!"

"I also told Professor Jhang." Mei-Ling stuck her tongue out.

"Mei-Ai, Uncle is proud of you. I will bring my wife and children to see the exhibition next week. If you two can be our company, that would be wonderful. No, your a-bu needs to come too. Or we all should meet here first to spend some time together. Then we'll go to Taipei together..."

"Uncle, I think you're excited as my a-bu now." Mei-Ling laughed.

"Bad girl, I am going to see your a-bu cooking."

Both Mei-Ling and Mei-Ai were chuckling.

"Ciou-Tao, you're sweating and crying."

"I am too happy."

Wen-De gave her his handkerchief.

"You know, Wen-Hua talked about you all the time

when we lived together in New York."

"And he talked about you often in the letters that he wrote to me."

"We only met a few times when you were little, but because of Wen-Hua, it's like I have known you forever."

"I feel the same way. Now, let's sit down and eat together for the first time."

"Yes, ma'am."

Oh, that "Yes, ma'am."
Ciou-Tao missed it crazily.
She was poor but felt happy.
She looked forward to seeing her Wen-Hua ge all the time.

It wasn't because she needed the chicken legs, hard boiled eggs, tangerines, or guavas that he brought for her.

It was his company that she needed.
Yes, ma'am.

The next day, they had lunch together.

"Did you sleep well last night, Uncle?"

"Like a teenager."

"Uncle, do you mean like a baby?"

"Mei-Ai, you're very quick and right. Even though my parents passed away, I asked those loyal old servants to stay. In fact, they didn't want to leave either. Moreover, where could they go? Our home is their home too. Anyway, they keep the house very well. Everyone's room looks exactly the same as old times. Can you believe that I actually wore the pajamas that I wore in high school last night? For a moment, I felt like a teenager again. All the memories came to me, so I couldn't fall asleep for a while. However, I was too exhausted and fell asleep eventually, and slept well, like a..."

"Teenager!" Mei-Ling and Mei-Ai said it together.

Wen-De laughed and took out an envelope.

"Here, this is for you, Ciou-Tao."

Mei-Ling's and Mei-Ai's hearts were beating very fast.

"What is it?"

"Just open it. You will like it."

Ciou-Tao was speechless. Soon, she cried. Then, she laughed.

"Did you take this picture for them?"

"Yes, I did."

"You did a good job."

"Thank God, I did. At the time, I just got my first camera and learned to use it."

"A-bu, sorry to interrupt, but can we see it? We really want to see Auntie Ciou-Jyu and Uncle Huang."

"You both know about this picture?"

"Sis told me last night."

"Uncle told me yesterday afternoon."

"Mei-Ling reminded me that I have the picture when she talked about Uncle Huang."

It was like a confession. Ciou-Tao chuckled.

"Sis, Auntie looked like you!"

"You dope, it's I who look like Auntie."

"Forget who looks like whom; you two really look alike."

"You think so? A-bu, what do you think?"

"Yes, you look very much like my sister."

"Then how come you never told me?"

After a few seconds of silence, Ciou-Tao said, "I don't know."

Ciou-Tao actually knew why. How Ciou-Jyu died was a tremendous pain to Ciou-Tao. When she was young, she had extreme anger about that crime. After she became a mother, she started to worry that her beautiful daughters might get hurt like her sister. Thus, she tried to tell herself that they weren't Ciou-Jyu. They would grow up fine and well.

"Your a-bu wants you to be you, not anyone else. You're the only one and special one in the world."

Ciou-Tao looked at Wen-De with gratitude.

Mei-Ling sensed a little awkwardness in the air, so she said, "Look at Auntie Ciou-Jyu. She was a lady, but I am a tomboy. It's hard for A-bu to think we're alike."

Mei-Ai went along with it. "Sis, I think you're right. Look at how Auntie stood. You would never stand like that. Not to mention that you always tie your hair up into a ponytail and never use ribbon to tie your hair. Too girly for you."

"Mei-Ai, I'll kill you!"

"Ciou-Tao, I think you have great fun to have two daughters."

"Your daughter and son don't fight?"

"They do, but very different from your girls' fighting. I like girls."

"Once my a-ba asked Uncle Huang why he and his wife didn't try to get a boy, and he answered, 'Why should we? We already have two beautiful girls. I am happy and content.' Then he said to my a-ba, 'Don't you find girls are just as good as boys? But they are sweeter than boys.' I was too little to understand many things, but I had already learned the culture that boys were more important to a family. So I was very surprised to hear what Uncle Huang said. Honestly, when my parents gave us away, I hated them. I wished my a-ba were Uncle Huang, because he wouldn't give us away."

"Ciou-Tao, you weren't wrong to get mad and hate your parents. I would feel the same if my parents gave me away."

"I would too."

"I crazily love Uncle Huang now and also wish that he were my a-ba."

"Me too." Ciou-Tao was surprised because she could tell that Mei-Ai was angry. Ciou-Tao always knew that Mei-Ling and Mei-Ai didn't like their a-ba, but angry? Why?

"I love Uncle Huang too. One time I saw him in the market. He was selling steamed buns. He seemed to know everyone in the town. He said hi to this one and said hello to another one, and many people would stop and talk to him. When I got close to him, I heard him talking to a middle-aged woman in Taiwanese. I almost dropped dead, because Uncle Huang spoke Taiwanese fluently. Oh, well, with a little accent, but who cares? I liked it anyway."

"He told us that he wanted to learn Taiwanese very much after he arrived in Taiwan but couldn't. At the time, he was still in uniform. Besides having a duty to his job, which Taiwanese people would want to talk to or teach a Chinese soldier to speak Taiwanese? Thus, he started to learn Taiwanese in the simple old way, listening and observing. He learned more and faster after he sold steamed buns in the market. Believe it or not, because Uncle Huang could speak a little Taiwanese, people found it interesting and let down their guard against him as Chinese. Once they talked to him, they found Uncle Huang was a nice person and liked him. His Taiwanese improved a lot after he became our family. He asked Ciou-Jyu, Ciou-Lian, and I to teach him Taiwanese. He really wanted to learn."

"That's very different from many Chinese people who came to Taiwan with the Chiang Kai-shek regime. Many of them think that they are better than the Taiwanese people and Taiwanese language is vulgar."

"Uncle, Mei-Ai and I always can feel that kind of attitude at school from some people, even right now at university."

"That's why I like and admire him. Uncle Huang lived. He didn't keep himself away from Taiwanese society. He shared his food culture to the Taiwanese people, and he walked into Taiwanese people's lives to learn their customs. These prevented him from being blinded by the Chinese Nationalist government. That day we walked home together. On the way home, he said that most Chinese people trusted the Chiang Kai-shek regime. As a matter of fact, many of his comrades saw Chiang Kai-shek as their father. They were expecting and waiting for Chiang Kai-shek to bring them back to China. The Chinese Nationalist government told them to be careful with the Taiwanese people. The Taiwanese people were violent and disliked the Chinese people. If they got the power, they would push the Chinese people out of Taiwan and hand over all the Chinese people to the Chinese Communist Party."

"That was rubbish! They brainwashed people."

"Uncle Huang said that he began to be suspicious of what the Chinese Nationalist government told them after he observed the Taiwanese people. Furthermore, he also was tired of hearing how evil the Chinese Communist Party was and being ready to fight with them. It didn't mean he didn't think that the Chinese Communist Party wasn't evil or he wanted to quit fighting with it. He just wanted to live a little bit. He wanted to see Taiwan and get to know the people and their culture on the island. Moreover, the government kept telling them to hang in there, but the government was unable to bring them home and did not want them to settle down, either, which was torture. Therefore, he decided to live and trust what he saw and heard."

"Wow, how important to have independent thinking. It actually can help a person to see through the government's lies and fight against its violence."

"True. Well said, Mei-Ai. But at the time, I wasn't capable of thinking as deep as you. I only felt that Uncle Huang was an honest man who had courage and wisdom. I respected him."

"Wen-De ge, I envy you. You had a chance to have a decent conversation with Uncle Huang. I was too little."

"Unfortunately, I only had one chance."

"Uncle, but it was a wonderful one chance."

"True. Uncle Huang's words enlightened my mind."

"In my memory, Uncle Huang was a person who loved. He knew how to love, and he loved us very much."

"What a remarkable man who lived and loved," Wen-De praised.

"Uncle and A-bu, how about going to visit Uncle Huang after lunch?"

"Visiting Uncle Huang?" Wen-De looked puzzled.

"Uncle, Sis meant going to Taroko and Tianxiang, where he died."

"Wen-De ge, after I grew up and got a job, I went to Taroko and Tianxiang alone every Lunar New Year. I began taking the girls there when they were little, but they didn't know the reason for going to Taroko and Tianxiang until they were in high school. I choose one day during the Lunar New Year to see him, because it's the most important holiday for family members to get together. I can't let my dearest uncle be alone in the gorge."

"We used to think that A-bu loved the beautiful place very much and so wanted to visit it every year."

"Oh, Ciou-Tao. You're also a person who loves. Why wait? Let's go. I also want to talk to the man who I respect."

Two weeks before summer vacation ended, Wen-De and his family went back to New York. Two years later, after both their children went to university, they moved back to Taiwan. Before moving back, they visited Taiwan every three or four months. After all, the blacklist was history.

Mei-Ling and Mei-Ai felt a little bit sad when they said goodbye to Uncle Wen-De and his family. It was like Mei-Ling had said to Wen-De when they first met: in the beginning, they shared the love that Uncle Wen-De had for their auntie, Ciou-Jyu. However, they bonded quickly, so they spent a lot of time hanging out and traveling together. Mei-Ling and Mei-Ai took them to eat all the different famous Taiwanese foods that only locals knew. Wen-De and his wife took Mei-Ling and Mei-Ai and their daughter and son to those places, such as coffee shops, small restaurants, parks, hiking trails, that they had visited when they were young. Ciou-Tao closed the restaurant to join them sometimes, which made everyone feel the happiness was completed. The best time that everyone had was at the seacoast. The young, old, and new met the past and happily looked forward to the future. In brief, Mei-Ling and Mei-Ai had the most unique and marvelous summertime ever. They learned many different things from Uncle Wen-De, his wife, and their daughter and son, which impacted them a lot and made them think. However, autumn tiger (the Taiwanese way to say "Indian summer") roared, time to go back to school. Once school started, they didn't have time to think anymore. In fact, the busy life made a lot of feelings go dormant gradually. After all, they were young and ambitious. There were dreams in their minds to chase. They were also eager to enjoy their beautiful young lives.

The young should be young. Ciou-Tao wanted her daughters to be like that. She did want them to know who they were—Taiwanese not Chinese—and she wanted them never to trust the Chinese Nationalist government. However, she didn't want them to get involved in politics like their uncles, Wen-Hua and Wen-De. It was selfish thinking but a mother's love.

"Politics is too dangerous," Ciou-Tao said to Wen-De. "Even if one doesn't get killed, one can't get out of it easily once he or she has gotten in. It's like marriage."

"Comparing marriage to politics?" Wen-De was surprised but worried right away.

Ciou-Tao was very honest with Wen-De when he asked her about her marriage. Wen-De was very upset to know that his little sister was suffering, and he encouraged Ciou-Tao to walk out of that awful situation. She told him that she would stay at least until Mei-Ling and Mei-Ai were married. She didn't want them to have difficulty on the road to their marriage. Many parents were still very traditional. They believed that people who were from single-parent families couldn't grow up being normal, like they were bad seeds, so they wouldn't allow their children to marry them.

"When will we move on from this damn ugly culture?"

"Wen-De ge, from us and our children."

22

The Truth That the Little Frog Learned

Ten Years Later

"Mei-Ai, have you watched any political talk shows this week?"

"No. I have been busy."

"That's right. How can I forget the upcoming exhibition next month?"

"It's OK, Sis."

"I have to say it again. The theme of the exhibition, *The Faces of Liberty*, is absolutely brilliant."

"I hope people will like it and be inspired."

"I'm sure that they will."

"Sis, thanks. What did they talk about?"

"Oh, right, the political talk shows. They have been talking about Chinese veterans' bitter lives."

"Don't most people on the island know about it? What else can they talk about?"

"Mei-Ai, that's why I am calling you right now. I heard something that you won't believe. Chiang Kai-shek regime forbade the low-ranking Chinese soldiers to get married in 1952."

"What? Sis, are you sure about that? A government can have the power to forbid soldiers to get married?"

"Mei-Ai, I was shocked and didn't believe it like you. But I also saw Professor Jhang and another respected journalist talk about this topic on channel twenty-eight. They not only said the same but also told a lot more details of it."

"So it's true then!"

"Mei-Ai, listen to this. According to the regulation, only officers who were over twenty-eight years old could marry. All the sergeants, privates, and soldiers, no matter how old or how young they were, were not allowed to marry."

"Oh my God, Wang bei-bei, Lin bei-bei, and Cao bei-bei were banned from getting married."

"You know, once I asked Wang bei-bei why he didn't get married. I am an idiot."

"Sis, you didn't know."

"I still touched his pain."

"What were the reasons for making that regulation?"

"Well, for one big reason, the government wanted them to be ready for fighting with the Chinese Communist Party."

"Get out! Getting married and having a wife and children would make them not want to fight with the Chinese Communist Party?"

"The Chinese Nationalist government believed that the marriage and family would take away their full attention on war. The country, the Republic of China, wouldn't be the top priority in their life anymore."

"So Chiang Kai-shek, whom they saw as their father, didn't want them to live and love."

"Perhaps once the soldiers had their own families, they would want to settle and see Taiwan as a second home. The desire of fighting against the Chinese Communist Party might be weakened or gone."

"But it doesn't mean that the government had a right to deprive their right to the pursuit of happiness."

"Mei-Ai, I agree with you. At the time, most Chinese soldiers were about twenty to thirty years old. They needed love and companionship very much. Not to mention that most of them came to Taiwan *alone*."

"I can tell that regulation would cause problems just from my imagination. The government couldn't?"

"With this government, you can't think in a normal way. They don't care about people. They only love money and power. Mei-Ai, listen to this, the president of United States, Harry Truman, said, 'They're thieves, every damn one of them. They stole seventy hundred fifty million dollars out of the billions that we sent to Chiang. They stole it, and it's invested in real estate down in São Paulo and some right here in New York.' And our textbooks praise Chiang Kai-shek to the sky."

"Truth really has to be known."

"Back to the Chinese veterans. There were quite a number of officers who were under twenty-eight years old, and low-ranking soldiers got married secretly. Furthermore, more than eighty percent of them married to Taiwanese women."

"Why?"

"More Chinese men than women came to Taiwan."

"Oh, that's right."

"And most Chinese women who came to Taiwan after 1945 were married. They came with their husbands. Besides, some of the officers and soldiers actually liked to marry Taiwanese women because their salaries were low and the Taiwanese women were more capable of making a living than the Chinese women at the time."

"Sis, do you realize that most people in Taiwan are not *pure* Chinese like the Chinese Nationalist government has been telling us? Intermarriage happened. Since hundreds of years ago, Han people and Plains indigenous people have married to each other, and it is still happening. During the Dutch colonial rule, from 1624 to 1662, some Dutch and Taiwanese people got married, and the same situation happened during the time of Japanese rule, 1895–1945. After the Second World War, the new Chinese immigrants who came to Taiwan after 1945 married to the Taiwanese people. Yeah, we *all* are pure Chinese!"

"Hey, they have to say that. Everyone, including Taiwanese, on the island has to unite together to fight with the Chinese Communist Party. So we All are Chinese."

"Sis, we used to say, 'We Chinese, blah, blah, blah', because the school taught us that, and I believed it. Now, I no longer believe it. I know I am Taiwanese, but I slipped out, 'We Chinese...' sometimes. God, they did a great job to brainwash us!"

"I have the same problem! I hate it. But I believe we'll conquer it eventually, like dictators all die eventually."

"Ha! Good one!"

"That dictator, Chiang Kai-shek, later compromised, though. The regulation didn't have punishment to come with. Hence, they couldn't control all the soldiers as they wished."

"Surely they didn't have the nerve to punish those soldiers who got married secretly. The Chinese Nationalist government needed their loyalty and devotion very much."

"Believe it or not, the government had a study. It found that those Chinese soldiers had great homesickness. Furthermore, Taiwan is in the subtropical zone, which made those young men have stronger sexual desires."

"That needed a study? Oh boy. That government loved money and power, and they were dumb!"

"In the beginning, the government legalized many te-tiam-a to satisfy those soldiers' needs, but it didn't work out good. In fact, it created problems. Besides not having enough prostitutes, many girls were minors who had been kidnapped or deceived to become prostitutes."

"Sis, what is the difference between those young girls and Comfort Women in the World War II?"

"There is not much difference to me! They were all sex slaves. But the Chinese Nationalist government was smarter, though. First, they gave licenses to make the prostitution legal; therefore, in a way, they could think that they didn't commit crime. Later, if the legal te-tiam-a illegally took in girls, it would be their fault, not the government."

"Yeah, smarter! Sneaky snakes. Sis, our friend, A-hue, was a minor. I wonder where she is right now."

"I meant to tell you but kept forgetting. A while ago, I learned that she is the concubine of the owner of the te-tiam-

a. The owner of the te-tiam-a is the biggest gangster and the speaker of the council in our county."

"Well, perfect! Sex, lies, and the evil government. We have it all."

"Mei-Ai, I was very upset when I learned that A-hue became a criminal's concubine. What kind of life can she have? There is no future."

"Sis, maybe this is a life that A-hue chose for herself, to stop being a prostitute."

"Sigh, maybe. Mei-Ai, do you remember that once we thought that the gangster was A-hue's father?"

"Hard to forget. At the time, you and I kept thinking how a gangster could have a sweet daughter. It happens in reality, but we were too young to understand it. And now, he took her to be his concubine. How disgusting is that?"

"Very disgusting and depressing. By the way, those legal te-tiam-a that provided services to the military were graded into two levels, grade A and grade B."

"Wait! Don't tell me that grade A was for generals and officers and the grade B was for low-ranking and general soldiers."

"You got that right!"

"This government truly embraces hierarchy, don't they?"

"Yes, indeedy. They are an authoritarian regime who doesn't know the meaning of respect, humanity, and equality. What do we expect?"

"Hateful!"

"Mei-Ai, we thought that all Chinese people came to Taiwan with Chiang Kai-shek regime were prohibited from writing to their families in China, but it wasn't true."

"What does that mean?"

"The Chinese Nationalist government officials who were in high position could write to their families in China, and the Party would send the letters for them. People whose financial situation was better or who had a good social connection would covertly find a way to send letters to their families in China. Those like Uncle Huang, Wang bei-bei, Lin bei-bei, and Cao bei-bei, who were poor or had no connection, were forced to obey the damn rule."

"I can't believe this! That was cheating, lying, and bullying. That government utterly took advantage of the poorest people."

"Mei-Ai, about the military dependents' villages..."

"The same, right? Generals have better houses than officers, and officers have nicer houses than soldiers, right? It fully explains why decades ago only officers could get married in the interdict."

"However, because the interdict created so many social problems, and there were more and more soldiers who got married secretly, the hateful dictator, Chiang Kai-shek, in 1955, gave an indication, soldiers could be rewarded to get married when they got three or more major merits from their meritorious deeds."

"To me, that wasn't any better. It sounds like you couldn't get married because you were not good enough. Therefore, it was your own fault, not we forbade you."

"Well, according to the government, they had to have a limit on the number of soldiers who were permitted to get married every year due to financial difficulty. The more soldiers got married, they needed to pay more family allowances, which was one of the military benefits."

"Financial difficulty? Did the US government send billions to them? Oh, I forgot. They stole $750 million."

"Ha! Mei-Ai, the Chinese Nationalist government hates you very much now."

"And I don't give a damn."

"The real important reason that the government softened the regulation was because soldiers, especial low-ranking soldiers, got very upset. Like we said before, the Chiang Kai-shek regime needed those soldiers to be healthy and confident so that they could win the war. Thus, to know how their

Chinese soldiers felt was needed. They found that those soldiers not only had severe homesickness but also were upset about not being able to have a son to carry their family names, which might lead to the loss of their loyalty and spirit on fighting the war with the Chinese Communist Party."

"Again, this government was very evil and super-duper stupid. They acted like they didn't know the thousand-year-old ugly culture, not having a male heir is the greatest sin."

"However, those officers and soldiers who got married secretly and had children didn't feel good either."

"Really? Why?"

"Many of them felt guilty from breaking the regulation. Furthermore, because their marriages were considered illegal, they couldn't go to register. It means that their children were bastards. Unless those children took their mothers' family names and were registered as unwedded women's children, which was very difficult at the time though, the children wouldn't be able to go to school later. In brief, their lives entirely became illegal. Who could bear that? Some of them applied for retirement as a solution, but many of them couldn't support their families at all after they retired. Some couldn't take the pressure and killed themselves. Some committed crimes. Finally, in 1959, Chiang Kai-shek gave an indication again. This time was to abandon the regulation."

"Sis, that's eight years. Most of them weren't young anymore. Wasn't it harder for them to find someone to get married?"

"Yes, it was harder. Firstly, they were dirt poor. They had very low income and didn't have any property since they fled to Taiwan in exile. Many Taiwanese parents didn't want to marry their daughters to someone who was in poverty and Chinese. Secondly, many of them were illiterate or had little education, so they felt inferior. Thirdly, they weren't young anymore. As a result, a lot of soldiers married to the women who were physically or intellectually disabled, who were widows with several children, or stayed single for the rest of their lives."

"Oh, Sis, they just longed to have a family, a sense of belonging. Before they came to Taiwan with the Chiang Kai-shek regime, most of them had been in war for years. They probably didn't see their families for four or five years, or more. Then, they fled to Taiwan, couldn't go home, and were forbidden to contact their families who were in China. In fact, they might be imprisoned or killed if the Chinese Nationalist government found out that they wrote to their families. The worse came to worst, they were banned from getting married. Like Uncle Huang said to Uncle Wen-De, they hung in there, couldn't live and love, for the greatest leader, Chiang Kai-shek."

"Mei-Ai, I forgot to tell you that many Chinese soldiers were kidnapped by the Chinese Nationalist Army and forced to join the troop."

"Get out! No way!"

"A lot of them were teenagers. Some were even only eleven or twelve years old when they were kidnapped, and they were forced to work as laborers in the troop."

"How could they?"

"Mei-Ai, I learned a sad story, and it broke my heart and made me cry badly. At the time, he was a teenager. One day, his mother sent him to buy soy sauce. On the street, he was kidnapped to join the Chinese Nationalist Army. He never went home again. Decades later, in 1987, the government ultimately allowed them to go back to China to visit their family. The sixty-year-old man went home. Unfortunately, his parents had passed away. He went to his parents' graves and said, 'Mom, I am back. These are the two bottles of soy sauce you wanted.'"

"Oh, Sis, my heart hurts."

23

Our Stories, Our Truths

"Why is this beautiful island full of sadness?"

After talking to Mei-Ai, Mei-Ling felt low. She decided to have a walk. It was Saturday afternoon, sunny and windy. Perhaps the wind blew the sad mood away. Mei-Ling felt better after a long walk—and hungry too. Thus, she walked into her favorite fast food restaurant.

After she got her food and coffee, she found a seat to sit down. A person at the next table gave Mei-Ling a friendly nod and smile. He and his three friends at the table were Chinese veterans. No need to ask why Mei-Ling could tell they were Chinese veterans. She knew; most people on the island just knew. The look, the jacket, the pants, and the accent told it all.

A few hours ago, Mei-Ling had just had a long conversation with Mei-Ai, talking about Chinese veterans' miseries. Now, she bumped into several of them, so she couldn't help observing them quietly.

Two bei-bei looked clean and dressed nicely. One of them was the one who nodded to her. The other two looked a little scruffy, and one of them just came back from outside. He bought a bowl of congee. After he put down the congee, he went to the counter to buy a bowl of corn chowder soup. Finally, he sat down and ate. He had several spoons of congee first and put some corn chowder soup into the congee. Mei-Ling was surprised that the workers in the fast food restaurant didn't come to warn him not to bring outside food in, and it seemed all the bei-bei at the table didn't worry about that.

When Mei-Ling walked out of the restaurant, she

laughed. She found herself being very silly. Although she knew that the bei-bei was wrong to bring outside food, she didn't want him to get kicked out either. Therefore, she worried about him the whole time she was eating.

A few days later, Mei-Ling passed by the same fast food restaurant, and she saw the same four bei-bei. Two were sitting at the same table, and another two were at the next table. Mei-Ling looked at her watch. It was 4:00 p.m. She wondered if those bei-bei got together every afternoon in this restaurant. Suddenly, someone waved to her.

Ah, it was the bei-bei who nodded to her last time!

Mei-Ling remembered them, and he recognized her.

Mei-Ling waved back and smiled.

The next time, when Mei-Ling passed by, two bei-bei waved to her, and the other two bei-bei looked at her with smiling faces.

"They know me?"

"All of them?"

Mei-Ling kind of liked it.

A week later, Mei-Ling decided to walk in and say hi when she was getting close to that fast food restaurant. After she walked into the restaurant, she found that only three bei-bei were sitting at the table. The bei-bei who was the first to interact with her wasn't there.

He had died three days ago, they said.

Mei-Ling couldn't hear anything else that they said.

He looked healthy. It was impossible.

He looked much healthier than his friends. It couldn't have happened.

With tears on her face and hand, Mei-Ling walked out of the restaurant.

Life slipped away in the blink of an eye, just like that.

"I don't even know his name."

All of a sudden, some feelings and ideas that were dormant woke up. Mei-Ling recalled how she believed that history doesn't belong to big men only. Ordinary people shouldn't be forgotten in history. More importantly, history is not history if it is a dictator's story.

"Mei-Ai, I decide to write."
　"That's great! It's about time."

[1] "Of the Origin and Design of Government in General, with Concise Remarks on the English Constitution," UShistory.org, assessed January 8, 2020, https://www.ushistory.org/paine/commonsense/sense2.htm

[2] Some background of Wen-Hua is borrowed from White Terror victim Dr. Chen Wen-Chen (陳文成, 1950–81). The reasons why Wen-Hua was taken away for the inquiry, how he was killed, and the wounds that he had were all Dr. Chen Wen-Chen's real sufferings.

[3] The story of Lan Tian's great-grandfather is borrowed from a famous Taiwanese painter, a victim of the 228 Incident, Tan Ting-Pho (陳澄波, 1895–1947). In 2002, Tan Ting-Pho's work, *Chiayi Park*, was sold for HKD 5,794,100 (about USD 739,211) at Hong Kong auction. In 2015, Google Doodle commemorated his 120th birthday.

[4] "The Cairo Declaration," November 26, 1943, History and Public Policy Program Digital Archive, Foreign Relations of the United States, Diplomatic Papers, The Conferences at Cairo and Tehran, 1943 (Washington, DC: United States Government Printing Office, 1961), 448–449. https://digitalarchive.wilsoncenter.org/document/122101

[5] "Of the Origin and Design of Government in General, with Concise Remarks on the English Constitution," UShistory.org, assessed January 8, 2020, https://www.ushistory.org/paine/commonsense/sense2.htm

[6] In 1970, the Taiwan Independence movement organizations in Canada, the United States, Japan, Europe, and Taiwan united and established World United Formosans for independence to advocate Taiwan's independence.

About The Author

Tsai Chia-Ling (蔡嘉凌)

She is from a beautiful town in eastern Taiwan. She studied history and social work at university. Now, she lives in Brooklyn, New York, and has a column in Taiwan People News. Since 2020, she has written about U.S. current affairs for Radio Taiwan International (RTI).

Made in the USA
Middletown, DE
25 June 2020